PRAISE FOR

OF FIRE AND ASH

"Wow. If you're looking for the epic fantasy of your dreams, this. is. it. Simply put, *Of Fire and Ash* is a masterpiece, and Gillian wields the skill of both fearless Outrider and writing queen in her delivery of it."

— NADINE BRANDES, award-winning author of *Romanov, Fawkes,* and the Out of Time Series

"Gillian Bronte Adams continues to amaze! In this first book of The Fireborn Epic, her storytelling burns smoking hot. Rich worldbuilding, beautiful language, awe-inspiring creatures, a cast of imperfect and utterly compelling characters, *Of Fire and Ash* has everything I want in a fantasy. It is a triumph in every way, and I can't wait for book two."

— SHANNON DITTEMORE, author of *Winter, White and Wicked*

"Full of hope, magical horses, courageous outcasts, and traitorous enemies, *Of Fire and Ash* grabs your attention from the first page, and leaves you eager for the sequel! Highly recommended."

— MATT MIKALATOS, author of *The Crescent Stone*

# of FIRE and ASH

Books by Gillian Bronte Adams

The Songkeeper Chronicles
Orphan's Song
Songkeeper
Song of Leira

The Fireborn Epic
Of Fire and Ash

Out of Darkness Rising

THE FIREBORN EPIC
BOOK ONE

GILLIAN BRONTE ADAMS

Of Fire and Ash

Published by Enclave Publishing, an imprint of Third Day Books, LLC

Phoenix, Arizona, USA.
www.enclavepublishing.com

ISBN: 978-1-62184-203-3 (hardback)
ISBN: 978-1-62184-205-7 (printed softcover)
ISBN: 978-1-62184-204-0 (ebook)

Cover design by Darco Tomic and Jamie Foley
Typesetting by Jamie Foley

Printed in the United States of America.

To Mom and Dad

You raised me on stories and encouraged my wildest dreams.

This book would not exist without you.

RHIAKKOR
CRAIGNORM
MABASSI
HARNOTH
CRATER OF KOLTAR
GIMLEAL
GAUROTH RANGE
HURRON
SORAS FORD
RYSINGER
BAY OF SYLNA
TEL RENAAIR
IDOLAS
LOCHRANN
RUIADH
N
CENYON
RIVER TAIN
ARDON
TO THE EMPIRE OF NADAAR
SOLDONIA
AND ITS CHIEFDOMS

PROLOGUE: FIREBORN

The scream of the fireborn stallion shivered against her spine. Heat blasted behind, and sparks stung the backs of her legs. Ceridwen staggered upward toward the rim of the crater, resisting the call to battle that surged through her blood. There would come a moment for vengeance, a day for retribution. But now . . . now there was no time.

Bair had no time.

He hung limp across her shoulders, and she held him tight, left arm hooked over his leg and clenching his wrist. Tight, lest her gloved hands lose purchase on his blood-slicked arm. Tight, lest his body fail and his spirit flee and her grip alone might save him. *Stay with me!* Bent beneath his weight, she rammed her boots into the fire-bitten earth, fighting to reach the rim.

The stallion screamed again.

Rock shook at the sound, stirring ash that drifted away before her.

Muscles trembling, Ceridwen lunged over a rough patch. Bair's chin thudded against her shoulder, and a ragged moan escaped his lips. She fought to hold him steady as his bruised and broken limbs hung limp. Blood coated his chest. It plastered her long red braid to her neck and dampened her singed leathers. So much blood. *Too much.*

She thrust the burst of panic from her mind. Steeled fear and hope from her heart as well as she lurched upright. No hooves yet drummed at their heels. The stallion did not pursue them. It lurked below, concealed in that dense cloud of smoke stirred by the frenzy of the herd.

So, she staggered onward. Upward. For Bair. For her brother.

Her head throbbed with each jarring step. Pain danced a blistering trail across her skin and lodged in the seared flesh of her left forearm. Before the stallion's focused blast, her treated leather vambrace had crinkled like dried leaves and disintegrated, leaving a raw, weeping wound behind. But Bair had borne the brunt of the attack, caught off guard when her catch-rope failed, freeing the stallion to whirl upon him and unleash the wrath of a firestorm.

"Hold on, Bair," she rasped. "Hold on."

Atop the rim, her legs gave out. Her knees struck, and she eased Bair down. He slipped from her hands and landed with a sickening thud. But he made no sound. Her heart caught. Gasping, she pulled his shoulders into her lap. *Merciful Aodh.* Here, above the smoke that had smothered the crater in the wake of the struggle, his injuries were clear. The sight of shattered bones and burned flesh set her gut heaving, though her stomach had long since emptied in a rush that had left her dizzied as the fireborn stallion trampled him, pounding hooves descending again and again, grinding his body into the ash. And it was her fault.

Her pride had driven the challenge. The ritual claiming of a solborn from the wild, the Sol-Donair, was an ancient tradition little honored of late in the kingdom of Soldonia. Wildborn steeds were volatile, and the war-chiefs had turned to breeding instead, maintaining rich bloodlines of pasture-raised steeds. But she had goaded Bair, daring him to race on the eve of their seventeenth year to claim a fireborn to prove their worthiness to the blood of Lochrann.

Now he was dying.

Or perhaps already dead.

Bile rose in her throat, and she forced it down, blinking the sting of smoke from her eyes. It swirled in the wind that constantly gusted through this rugged country, whispering of death as it curled around shattered rocks and rattled dry scrub. Steeling herself, she lowered her ear to Bair's mouth and held her breath. Listening.

Air rasped faintly in his throat. He lived. He *lived*!

Training resumed control. She tore open her satchel and dug for bandages. Thank Aodh and the warrior spirits too that it had survived the struggle. Her fingers left scarlet stains on the cloth as she bound the worst of Bair's injuries, applying pressure to halt blood loss, support for shattered bones, and a covering for burns.

The bandaging soaked through before she was done, so she added more. And more. Tying. Pressing. Bandaging. Until her stock ran out and her hands dripped red.

Her chest constricted. "Hold on, Bair."

She lurched to her feet, head pounding, searching the surrounding crags for something–anything–that could help. Loose rock crunched beneath her boots. On foot, they had traveled, without even common horses–tolf–to speed the journey. It was a requirement of the Sol-Donair: rider alone striving for mastery over a wildborn steed. The hunt had drawn them miles from aid, deep into the fire-blasted wilderness of the Gauroth range on the farthest edge of the chiefdom of Lochrann. Few lived here, save the herds that roamed the craters, the scavengers that haunted the clefts, and the falcons that nested on the plateaus.

Still, she scoured the horizon. To the east, the Gauroth range bowed before the mountains of the chiefdom of Gimleal where miners wrestled metals from the ribs of the earth and delivered them to the sheltered fortress of Lord Craddock. A day's walk. Or two, considering her burden. To the west, the rugged march of hills dwindled, dark firerock melting into the flaming brilliance of the sunset. There, bathed in light, sprawled the sweeping plains at the heart of Lochrann. There lay home. Five days' march.

Gimleal then.

A groan drew her to Bair's side. His eyes flickered open, so dark they seemed coals in his bloodless face. His lips moved, but only a ragged, breathless sound issued, and she knew that it was too late to strike out for Gimleal. Too late for anything. He was almost gone.

"Shh, Bair, it's . . ."

All right? But it wasn't all right.

He was dying, and she was to blame. *She* had issued the challenge. With a lesser steed—a stormer or a riveren—Bair would have been content. But she would have nothing less than a fireborn. A creature with fire and ash beneath its skin. Like her.

"Oh, Bair, it's all my fault."

But there was no reproach in his eyes. Shuddering, he tried to speak again and failed. Words mangled by a groan. By the blood that stained his lips. Yet she had ever been able to read the unspoken in her twin's gaze.

"Home." Her voice broke at the realization. "You want to go home."

His eyes drifted shut, and tears scorched her cheeks.

"It's all right . . . all right . . . I promise, Bair, I will get you home."

Once more, she bent beneath his form and staggered upright. Face to the west, she began her solemn march, pressing on through pain, weariness, and the fever of exhaustion. She felt the moment when the breath left his body and his spirit fled its tent, for it felt as though hers flew with it. Grief shattered through her and left a gaping emptiness behind. In darkness, she walked, even in the light of day. Swaying with weariness. Aware of little more than the will required to place one foot before the next.

On the evening of the sixth day, blaring horns heralded her approach to the great house of Rysinger, Lochrann's chief fortress. Her boots thudded hollowly across the drawbridge before the inner wall. She lifted bleary eyes. Torchlight cast a lurid glare over the horrified expressions of the mounted warriors guarding the entrance. None hindered her passage. They parted, shuffling back on their steeds, dreamlike figures in the shadows.

"Tell the king . . ." Her voice broke. "Tell him his son has returned."

Then her limbs gave way, and she fell upon the bridge.

The shrouded form at the king's feet held her gaze. Ceridwen would not let herself look away, even as the king's voice rang out in judgment against her. Bound in embroidered linens and laid upon a bier of evergreen limbs with his hands resting upon the sword on his chest, Bair would be sent to rest as a warrior, as he deserved. As the smoke rose from his pyre, his kin would sing the litany of his deeds so that his spirit might ride with the warriors of yore.

Her voice would not be allowed among them.

She did not cry. She could not. The last of her tears had come and gone in the days she had walked, staggering beneath Bair's weight, all the way from the Gauroth range. Now her eyes felt as dry and burnt as the crater she had left.

Rough hands seized her by the shoulders, forcing her to the massive hearth in the center of the Fire Hall. Sizzling embers filled the hollow of the stone ring, and in her peripheral vision, gloved hands wielded rods to stoke them into blue-tinged flames. Sweat prickled her brow and ran into her eyes. She sucked in a deep breath. Swallowed.

The scorched air only heightened the ashen taste on her swollen tongue. Dimly, she became aware of those pressing around her. Witnesses. Only breaths had passed since the judgment, but already they gathered. Out of the corner of her eye, she saw a man to her right bearing the verdant green banner of Ardon, with its white-gold sun and dawnling rising in gold relief, rearing, forelegs flying in the traditional *noon-strike* battle form. On her left, a woman held Cenyon's banner of sea blue, curled like a breaking wave with a shimmering seablood leaping from the spray in *surge* form, forelegs tucked and head flung high. One witness would rise for each of the seven chiefdoms of Soldonia sworn to the king's will. She could not see the others, but their voices formed a muted roar beneath the throbbing in her ears, exuding a vague sense of emotions that clashed with her own.

Anger. Shock. Shame.

The hands on her shoulders bore down, though she did not struggle. She would not. She clung to that vow, let it plate her spine in steel. Pride was all she had. Heat seared her throat. Cold stone was a shock beneath her knees. The contrast dizzied her. She clenched her fists at her sides, and the burn on her left forearm throbbed. Broken strands of mane clung to her blistered fingers. Each breath made her singed leathers creak. They hung stiff from her shoulders, crusted with sweat and blood and ash from the crater of Koltar.

Metal scraped as a gloved hand drew a brand from the hearth. It glowed like molten lava. Like the eyes of the fireborn stallion she had sought to claim, before the world turned to fire and hope vanished like smoke into a wintry sky. Shaped like an *X* that formed a diamond at the top, it was the *kasar.* The mark of the blood debt. It rippled before her eyes, distorted by the haze of heat. The wielder took a step toward her—in her narrowed vision, she saw only his armor—and then the brand dipped before her eyes. Consuming all else.

She caught her breath, and a tremor seized her bones.

Blazes, she would *not* struggle.

The wielder paused and twisted to the side. "My lord, you are resolved?" In the gravel that roughened his aged voice, she recognized the man. Lord Glyndwr, war-chief of Harnoth, one of the seven chiefdoms. The king's closest adviser. Bair's mentor. For a moment, through the tempest inside, she felt the world shift into place. Of course. It was fitting that it should be he.

"I am resolved."

Words of stone from the king. No hint of pity. No tremor of regret. Only frost-bitten rage that leeched the heat from her bones.

Oh, Bair . . .

She steeled herself for the brand.

Still Glyndwr hesitated. "My lord, I beg you to reconsider."

In that instant, she despised the war-chief. More than the plague that had stolen her mother, the fate that had denied her the love of her father, or the fireborn stallion that had claimed her brother's life. The judgment had been passed. Those words, spoken before witnesses and sealed with the crash of the king's rod upon stone, rang still in her ears. The blood atoning of the *kasar* had been demanded, and she would answer it. She *must* answer it for Bair.

She did not beg, and neither should he.

Let it be done before her courage broke and she shamed herself further.

"Claiming a wild solborn in the Sol-Donair is our oldest tradition," Glyndwr said. "The challenge is not a crime. Lives have been lost before and never has a blood atoning been required. Bair's death is a tragedy we all mourn, but my lord, it should not claim the life of–"

Someone thrust Glyndwr aside, and familiar, broad shoulders filled her gaze. Grief twisted harsh lines across the king's face, but it was not meant for her. Barehanded, he seized the brand. His fingers clenched around the metal, and the burnished gold of his signet ring seemed a band of flame.

A step, like the turning of the earth, and he towered over her. His eyes confirmed the judgment. Bair te Desmond, son of the king, had died. His blood rested upon her head. Henceforth, she was outcast, unnamed, branded with guilt. Until the *kasar* was atoned for, Ceridwen tal Desmond, daughter of the king, was no more.

The brand hovered before her eyes and then plunged against her forehead.

ONE: CERIDWEN

Fireborn vary in color from rust-sorrel to burnt-brown to coal-black and are renowned for being swift, hot-blooded, and fierce.

The stench of death lingered on the forest air. Ceridwen sensed it first in the subtle changes in her fireborn steed, Mindar. The way his muscles quivered, the twist of his head, the flame flickering across his mane. She eased back on the reins and slid a gloved hand down his neck, smothering the fire before it blossomed fully. Heat radiated through her gloves but could not penetrate the treated leather. Well-tended gear often parted life and death for any solborn rider, but for fireriders most of all.

"Can you smell it?" Finnian te Donal reined to a stop and rose in his stirrups, scanning while his wolfhound ranged ahead. Unlike Mindar, his steed–a shadower–stood still, as if rooted to the ground. It seemed as much a thing of this forest as the mossy trees. "Fresh blood."

"Aye." Her hand strayed to the sabre belted at her side.

Finnian tracked the action, and his skeptical glance mirrored her own. "Such luck?"

It hardly seemed likely. Scarcely a day in the saddle and already upon the trail they sought? As Outriders, they were tasked with patrolling the wildlands of Soldonia, ensuring the safety of the seven chiefdoms from brigands, thieves, and foreign threat. Often, they chased a trail doggedly through wind and heat and sleepless nights for weeks before claiming their quarry.

Yet only that morning, with a twitch of his one bright blue eye and a wolfish grin as he downed his ale, Markham te Hoard, Apex over all the Outriders, had warned their assignment was dangerous. Worthy of the two riders in his *ayed* with "necks stiffer than an earthhewn's." High praise coming from Markham, followed by an offhand introduction. "Finnian te Donal, meet Ceridwen tor Nimid. Te Donal, tor Nimid. Shadower and fireborn. You'll be riding together." He swigged ale and swept his hand across his mouth. "Try not to kill one another."

Thus far, they had abstained.

Ceridwen studied Finnian out of the corner of her eye. He sat loose-limbed astride his steed, a quiver of arrows at his hip. Dark hair shadowed his eyes, but she caught their glint within like the gleam of moonlight on a blade. The tightness of his shoulders, hard edge of his jaw, and the way his hand strayed to the bow sheath belted to his saddle betrayed his unease.

It echoed her own. Striking the trail so soon might be chance, but coincidence did not rest well with her, not riding upon the heels of a warning from the Apex. Not to mention their unusual pairing. Among the thousand riders that formed an *ayed,* Outriders were broken into units of a hundred, patrols of ten, and paired solborn steeds of the same breed. It made sense. A fireborn's volatile nature often clashed with amphibious steeds like seabloods or riveren, while the massive earthhewn were prone to trampling any smaller than themselves.

Save for one ill-fated pairing early on, Markham had allowed Ceridwen to ride assignments on her own. If fireborn could be volatile, how much more could she? The disinherited daughter of a king, outcast, banned from her father's fortress under penalty of death. Three years had not lessened the shame of the brand she bore or the ache of Bair's loss. Far better to keep others at a distance while she sought atonement in a life dedicated to protecting her people. Alone.

Releasing her reins for an instant, she bound the crimson scarf she wore over her forehead more firmly in place, tucking strands of red hair that had escaped her braid beneath its covering. "I do not hold with luck."

Finnian nodded grimly. "That is one thing we have in common."

At his whistle, the wolfhound trotted onward, scarred nose lifted to the wind. Mindar pranced after him, snorting black smoke and tossing his head. Sparks rained from his mane and were trampled beneath his hooves. When he was not flaming, his coat gleamed bright copper in the sunlight, and his mane and tail shimmered with strands of red, gold, and deep umber. But when he ignited, he was an inferno incarnate. Fire coiled from his mane and tail, his eyes turned bright as embers, and then his jaws spewed flame. Tamed fireborn flamed only on command. But her wildborn, painfully won and trained, had not yet mastered such control.

Finnian and his steed glided alongside, vanishing and reappearing every other stride. The shadower's mottled brown coat melted into the layered treescape, and Finnian's dark clothes were subtly patterned to do the same. Even his soft gray cloak seemed to float effortlessly upon the wind. Shadowers were renowned for their ability to move in silence and disappear in shadow. *Ghosting*, it was called. Ideal for stealth attacks and scouting missions. But seeing it—or rather, *not* seeing it—so close unnerved Ceridwen. Perhaps it was only habit that led Finnian to ghost with his steed now, but it left her feeling vulnerable and exposed beside this rider she hardly knew, and her fingers ached for the cold and steady comfort of her sabre hilt.

"Hold," Finnian whispered from her left, three horse lengths ahead. The shadower's outline became clear as it halted before a break in the trees and then faded again.

Flies buzzed in the hazy stillness. The scent of blood was sharper now. It had Mindar on edge. His nostrils flared and heat radiated from his ribcage. Soon, he must calm or release the flame. Ceridwen looped her leather half mask over her nose and chin and tugged the hood of her long-sleeved jerkin down over her forehead. Like the rest of her gear, both had been treated to shield against fire. Then she urged Mindar beside the shadower and scanned the tree break.

Broken soil. Trampled foliage. Dead solborn.

Gut bloated, hide flayed, raw flesh exposed—she did not see their quarry, but this was clearly his work.

"Hold here while I—"

She silenced Finnian with a tap on the arm. Nodding toward the tree break, she gestured to herself, then pointed at him and swept her wrist in a circular motion. His eyes narrowed, but she did not wait for his objection.

Shift of the seat. Touch of the spurs.

Mindar sprang like an arrow from a bow.

Across the tree line, she slid her spurs back across his sides, and flames roared from his throat. Shrilling the cry of the Outriders, she charged the dead solborn. Another shift, another touch, another twitch of the reins, and Mindar dropped into a spin, a firestorm unleashed. His flames coiled around her, but within the ring, shielded by treated leathers and the bond forged between rider and steed, she was safe.

Finnian emerged on the opposite side of the clearing, shaking his head. *Nothing*. They were too late.

Ceridwen halted Mindar, threw her leg over the saddle, and dropped with a jangle of spurs into ash. Scorched earth now formed a ring around the dead solborn. Sparks winked out beneath her boots, drawing her gaze to a frayed rope, half-buried. She bent to investigate. It stretched from the dead solborn across the clearing.

"What were you thinking?" Finnian demanded beside her.

"*Blazes*." Too late, she tried to conceal her surprise at his sudden appearance. The shadower had crossed the clearing so noiselessly and swiftly, like a gust of wind. It was unnatural. "Do you want to get yourself flamed?"

He dismounted silently—the wonders of the sol-breath upon a shadowrider. "Do *you* want to get yourself killed?"

Rolling her eyes, she followed the rope, but Mindar shied from the dead solborn, jerking against her grip and snorting dingy smoke. "Easy, boy. Easy." The half mask muffled her voice, so she yanked it down to her neck. He stilled under her gloved hand, still blowing hard.

"Markham failed to mention your steed was raw."

"Raw?" Ceridwen shot Finnian a glare. "He is wildborn. That is all." Three years under saddle, and he was still wild in some ways. Indomitable in the blaze of battle, shying from a fallen cloak the next. But it was often so with fireborn, pastured or wild. They were true to passion in all things. Even fear. Still, owing to her mother's half-Rhiakki heritage, Ceridwen had spent half her time in the Outriders on the northeastern border, skirmishing with Rhiakkor. Mindar could handle the stresses of battle, and she could handle him. She *could.*

"You should have waited. We needed a plan." Tension radiated from Finnian's lean frame like the heat from Mindar's skin. "What if the poacher had been here? What would have happened then?"

She shrugged. "Battle." Offered a smile. "*Glorious* battle."

He offered no smile in return.

This was why she preferred to ride alone. When she tried to work with others, her efforts flamed in her hands. She was weary of wading through the ashes of scorched relationships. Why had Markham insisted on this pairing? Sighing, she steeled herself against the familiar sinking feeling in her stomach. "And we did have a plan. I handled the distraction while you maneuvered to the rear. It was a sound action. Even Apex Markham would agree."

His eyes narrowed. "Markham said you were reckless."

"Odd. He told me *you* were stubborn."

He snorted at that, but she caught the faint smile on his lips before he turned away, shadower trailing him to the dead solborn. Crouching, he fingered a tuft of blue-gray hair. "It was a stormer. The heart's missing, mane shorn, wings plucked, hooves ground down." Disgust flooded his voice. "Even its teeth are missing. Solborn poachers. *Shades.*"

Ceridwen nodded. "Flames take them all."

On this, they could agree. Solborn poachers deserved every curse in every tongue under the sun. Common horses—or tolf, as they were called—could be found nearly anywhere, but wild solborn inhabited only the seven chiefdoms of Soldonia. Fireborn, shadowers, stormers, and more–all faster, fiercer, and more powerful than tolf. The mysteries of their taming and the bond, known as the sol-breath, that tempered riders to their steeds' abilities were kept secret.

It was small wonder other nations desired them. Or that some attributed magical properties to their bones. Poachers frequently attempted to breach the borders to harvest steeds. The Outriders were tasked with capturing them as much as shielding the seven chiefdoms from threats. This one had left a gruesome trail of rotting corpses, both solborn and human, including the last Outrider pair Markham had dispatched to bring him in.

Finnian whistled softly. "Eyes too. Must be worth a fortune in Canthor, in the right market." In that island empire, the scholarly elite were known for dissecting and reducing all living things to facts and numbers, while the masses clung to superstitions and myths. "Hold on." He reached to lift the steed's head. "There is something underneath–"

"Stop!" Even as the warning left her lips, Ceridwen knew it was too late. The rope she had been trailing ran taut, springing up in a shower of leaves.

Something *twanged* beyond the tree line.

She snapped her rein hand, summoning Mindar's flame. Roaring filled her ears. When it dwindled, three charred crossbow bolts fell to the ground.

Finnian's widening eyes met hers. Those bolts had been aimed at him.

He whistled sharply, dispatching the wolfhound. She swung into the saddle and urged Mindar from the clearing before her feet had even fallen into the stirrups. Branches scraped her head. She caught a glimpse of Finnian mounted and angling to meet the wolfhound, hastily fitting arrow to bowstring before he vanished. Pressing deeper, she swept wide around the clearing, searching for signs of the archer.

Still nothing. How could he have fled so fast?

"Trip wire," Finnian said on her return, lifting a crossbow

as explanation, his own bow stowed in the sheath on his saddle. He did not seem shaken by the attack. But Ceridwen's heart still pounded like a galloping steed in her chest.

Had Mindar flamed a breath slower, Finnian would have died. Like Bair. Like the Outrider from her first disastrous pairing.

Death rode ever at her heels.

Finnian's words reverberated strangely in her ears, as though she were underwater. "Our poacher wasn't fooling. He had three crossbows rigged to release with pressure on that rope. Probably why we found the trail so soon. It was a trap, and . . . are you all right?"

"Fine. I'm fine." She blinked away a vivid image of him lying dead with three bolts in his chest and dismounted to retrieve them for him.

He sniffed the shafts, inspected the barbed heads, and ran a finger across what remained of the fletching. "That wood's not Soldonian, and the tips were coated in something. It's mostly burned, but there's some residue left."

Residue as in . . . "Poison?"

Shrugging, he stowed the bolts in his saddlebags. "Not uncommon in Canthor, and I would wager a guess that's where our hunter is from. Or at least where he's going." He ran a hand through his hair in a gesture that reminded her of Markham, leaving a ridge standing on end. "Fortunate you spotted the rope–" He ground to a halt, gaze locked on her forehead.

She reached for her scarf and found only the brand burned by her father's hand.

The treacherous cloth dangled from a leafy bough across the clearing, no doubt torn from her head as she forged into the woods. Skin flaming, she stared Finnian in the eye. She had never attempted to conceal her identity from the Outriders. It would have been useless, even had her pride and her shame not forbidden it. Yet it was one thing to know what had denied her the use of her rights, title, and father's name, and another to see it cast in waxy lines.

The *kasar.* Marking her a blood traitor, kinslayer, and outcast.

Beyond the clearing, the wolfhound bayed. Finnian seemed to shake himself. "Cù has found the trail. Are you ready to ride?"

Only then did she realize she had been holding her breath, awaiting his judgment. She exhaled and then took in a whiff of smoke-charged air. A step to grasp the saddlebow, and she swung astride Mindar. Finnian held his tongue as she retrieved her scarf. Her eyes dared him to speak as she deftly worked the knot. But his were guarded now, and his face was cast like marble. Whatever his thoughts, he kept them safely locked away.

"Onward?"

She gave a nod. "Onward."

TWO: RAFI

Come sun. Come storm. All tides shift soon enough.
– Alonque saying

Screaming sea-demons jarred him from sleep. Not the rudest awakening Rafi had experienced, but then it had stiff competition–like the time he'd woken up inside a python's jaws or the night he was hauled from bed to the news that his chambers had been permanently relocated to the dungeons. Still, the eerie shrieks shivering across the rain-soaked beach to penetrate the palm-thatched walls of the fisherman's hut chilled his spine. Made him wonder if he really *had* awakened, or if he was trapped in the nightmare that awaited him every time he closed his eyes.

Sea-demons haunted him there too. Always they called him to remember.

Always he tried to forget.

Rafi tried to sit up, and the world flipped. He smashed into the floor with a pain that was all too real and rolled over onto his back, wheezing until his lungs remembered they had mastered that critical skill known as breathing and he was able to inhale again.

He didn't bother rising. Just lay there, legs tangled in a sweat-soaked sheet, shivering as a damp breeze seeped through the thatch and set his hammock swinging jauntily above him, as if the ornery thing enjoyed dropping him on his head. He could hear Torva snoring from the second hammock. Rafi consciously aligned his breathing with the old fisherman's and coaxed his mind back from the nightmare's grip. He had been falling there too, wind whistling in his ears as he hurtled into an endless drop. That had not been the worst of it though. It never was.

Exhaustion prickled his spine, but now that he was awake, sleep would not return. It always slipped away from him like sand through his fingers. He had been lucky enough to snatch a few hours before the monsters started screaming. Outside, the shrieks reached a piercing note that crawled beneath his skin and made his skull feel like it was going to split.

Well, he could lie here while the hours dripped like melted wax. Or he could get to work.

His legs protested as he hauled himself upright and picked his way across the cluttered floor in search of the rock oven to heat a cup of seaweed tea. He stoked coals to life beneath the copper water pot and swept a space clear of woven baskets, conch shells, and half-braided ropes so he could sit, then dragged a torn net into his lap and began splicing the broken strands together. Narrowly missed slicing his left hand on a broken harpoon embedded in its bulk and had to spend the next five minutes working to extract it.

"Really, Torva?" he mumbled beneath his breath. "Place is a death trap."

Probably, the old fisherman had dumped both net and harpoon months ago, intending to fix them eventually. But abandoned things pooled here like the refuse forever thrown ashore by the sea. In a way, Rafi was just one more thing Torva had collected. All those castoffs were weighted with memory, grounding the hut even as the wind shook it on its stilts. Maybe that was why Rafi could never sleep. His life depended on forgetting.

He *would* forget.

"I am Nahiki." Speaking it, even in a whisper, helped root the identity. It let him ignore his headache and his uneasiness at the thought of the night hours stretching haunted and wakeful before him. No matter how much he might be Nahiki during the day, at night, when the sea-demons screamed, he was only ever Rafi.

And at nineteen, Rafi was supposed to be long dead.

"Nahiki. Half-Alonque. Guest of the fisher tribe of Zorrad.

Diver. Tamer of wild hammocks." He tested his splice. It held. "And mender of nets. *Nahiki.*"

"Ain't no need to tell me, boy."

Rafi jerked at the rasping voice and dropped the net. Torva was awake, sitting up in his hammock with his calloused feet dangling above the floor. His dark skin was seamed and wrinkled like the hide of a shelled turtle. He looked like he had lived more lifetimes than all the other inhabitants of the village of Zorrad put together.

"Can't sleep again?"

"Sleep?" Rafi shrugged. "Sleep is for mortals. I have given it up."

Torva grunted and shuffled to the oven to start the tea steeping. Not a moment too soon. The ache had lodged behind Rafi's eyes, blurring his vision. He dug his fingertips into his scalp. He must have drifted a bit then, swept up by pain and an exhaustion that snatches of sleep could never quite banish, because it seemed only an instant before the fisherman handed him a tiny steaming cup. Hot liquid burned his tongue, but the scent—salty and fresh—began to sweep the fog from his head. He mumbled his thanks.

"Not them sea-demons, is it? Ain't no need to fear those screamers."

Rafi choked on a sip. "Others say differently, Torva." Sea-demons didn't even belong so close to shore here on the Alon coast in the empire of Nadaar. They were monsters of Soldonia, that warlike nation across the sea where barbarians rode to battle on steeds of fire, rock, and water. Still, there were stories. Mostly vague superstitions of curses and impending doom, so he'd never given them much thought.

But then, he didn't fear the sea-demons. Only what they made him recall.

"Eh, who says this? Cetmurers?" Torva thought little of city dwellers and even less of those who inhabited Nadaar's capital, Cetmur. "What do they know? I've heard them all my life, and I'm still breathing. If you ask me, scadtha are more worrisome."

True enough. Those massive amphibious creatures that hunted along the Alon coast were considered sacred in the Murlochian worship that dominated Nadaar. But with their segmented, many-legged bodies and venomous pincers, "horrifying" struck Rafi as a better word. Harming one, even by accident, was a sure path to a painful execution, though odds stood you'd be dead long before you could face judgment.

Shaking his head, Torva limped to his hammock, and Rafi tried not to begrudge him sleep. He hadn't meant to wake him. Eyes closed, he breathed in steam from his tea and did not look up when footsteps shuffled toward him again.

"Look, Nahiki, I don't rightly know what you run from–"

"I'm not running from anything."

It was a lie, and they both knew it, but in two years, Torva had never demanded truth.

"But maybe . . . it's time to stop."

Rafi's throat clogged. He should have known this was coming. The old fisherman wanted him to move on just as he had left countless other temporary refuges over the past five years. But this place–even with its weight of memories and the sea-demons who would not let him forget–had felt different somehow. More like a home.

"Take it."

His eyes snapped open to a cord knotted with beads of varying hues of blue and yellow, and that thickness in his throat solidified into a lump. It was Alonque custom to track ancestral lines in beads. Torva wore his cord tied behind his ear. His son would have worn this same pattern, but the boy had been claimed by the sea years before Rafi's parents had been born.

"Take it," Torva repeated, firmly setting the cord in Rafi's left hand and folding his fingers around it. His eyes were misty, his voice hoarse. "Aodh alone knows who you were. But I know who you are now. Be free, Nahiki, and let this be your home."

The beads dug into his palm, pressed against the puckered scar that cut across the base of his thumb. Torva was offering far more than a roof. He was offering a place in the tribe, a welcome as his own son.

Rafi swallowed. "Torva, are you–"

"Tired? Aye. Some of us are still mortal. Try to sleep?" The old fisherman looked like he had aged another lifetime as he fell back into his hammock with a groan. His snores started up again, competing with the shrieks of the sea-demons.

Rafi gripped the beads and sipped his cooling tea as the coals burned low, watching as his reflection slowly faded from the copper pot: sharp cheekbones, wry lips, and the thin mark like a teardrop below his right eye, carved by a knife almost six years and a lifetime ago.

"I am Nahiki of the Alonque," he whispered to the dark. "Rafi *is* dead."

Beads rattling in his jaw-length black hair, Nahiki of the Alonque jogged with a swing in his stride down the jungle path toward the beach in the humid hour before dawn. Huts on stilts were clustered in twos and threes among the palm trees behind him, already alight with the glow of cooking fires, steaming with the scent of rice cakes, and rattling with the chatter of graybeard monkeys scrambling from canopy to rooftop. He was almost late. Normally, he was the first to the boats, bleary-eyed with exhaustion after another restless night. But somehow, he had slept and awakened this morning sprawled on the torn net with a sheet thrown over him and Torva gone.

He slowed when his heels struck sand and wove through the Alonque clustered around the beached fishing boats. Tongues flew and hands flew faster as they prepared to shove off into the sea to let down their nets before sunrise and catch the fish rising toward the warmth. Meeting Torva's raised eyebrow with a sheepish grin–"*Welcome back to the mortals, sleeper,*" that eyebrow seemed to say–he took up his position alongside Torva's fishing boat across from Sev.

The young fisherman grinned, flinging his shoulder-length black hair from his face and setting the eight beads on his cord clacking. He stood shorter by a head but was sturdy as a boulder, whereas Nahiki had the lean strength of a neefwa tree. "You missed a storm, Nahiki. Gordu's in a temper!"

Nahiki laughed. "Gordu's always in a temper." His voice rang across a sudden hush, and he hastily ducked a scowl from the burly, bald village elder. He'd tasted the man's wrath before, even caught a few knocks from his hammerlike fists, and had no desire to repeat the experience.

"Not like today," Sev whispered. "Seems his boat split a seam, and he's convinced someone knocked a leak in it on purpose." He winked conspiratorially, ever the rebel in word if not in deed, then regarded Nahiki. "You look alive today."

"I *feel* alive today."

"So, I take it your talk with Yeena went well yesterday?" Sev jutted his chin toward the girl scampering past with an armload of baskets. She looked up, meeting Nahiki's eyes, and lowered her head shyly behind a waterfall of dark hair that couldn't quite conceal the smile on her berry-red lips. "Not like you to be late to the boats . . ."

"We didn't talk much."

"Oh?" Sev's eyebrows rose.

Nahiki felt his face warm. "No, I didn't mean–"

Before he could explain that Yeena had started blushing before he even got her name out, and that had been the end of it, someone tackled him from behind, elbow crooking his neck, bony knees clinging like a limpet. He went down on one knee and rolled his back, throwing his attacker into the waves. A wiry boy crawled out and sprawled on the sand, laughing, revealing a broken front tooth in a grin that otherwise mirrored Sev's.

"Oh, get up, Iakki." Sev flicked a hand at his brother. "Can't you see we are working?"

"Working? You were talking about Yeena! You going to wed her, Cousin Nahiki?" Iakki was only nine, but that mischievous gleam in his eyes made him look far older.

Nahiki's mind went blank. "Uh . . ."

Iakki burst out laughing, rolling on his back in the sand until Sev toed him into the shallows in time to take an incoming wave to the face. Rolling his eyes as Iakki sputtered, Sev turned back toward Nahiki. He smiled broadly as he jabbed a finger toward the bead strand tied behind his left ear. "So, old Torva did it then?"

Nahiki's fingers rose to brush the cord. "Last night."

"High time, I say." Sev clapped his shoulder. "What did Yeena say about it? Should we start scouting a location for your hut? Maybe the clearing next to mine?"

Nahiki flailed for an answer. There was a terrifying permanence to such talk. But this was what he wanted, wasn't it? No more ghosts, no more fear, no more anything from Rafi's past.

"Ain't you coming diving later, Nahiki?"

Once again, Iakki saved him. He reached down to where the boy lounged in the damp sand and hauled him to his feet. "Sure, cousin."

"Hoy!" Torva limped up, cracking his knuckles, as the other boats began moving out. "Ain't you boys ready yet? We got us a catch to make!" His arrival sent all three of them scrambling to grip the boat's sides. Throwing their weight forward, they ran, slinging sand and spray until the sea caught the boat, and they splashed aboard and took to their oars, rowing toward the first glint of dawn.

Nahiki basked in freedom as he immersed himself in the familiar work. Sweat dripped down his back as he threw out the nets, sorted the catch, juggled fuzzy yellow simba fruit for Iakki's amusement during occasional lulls, and ignored the drift of hours until their baskets were full and they could race the others ashore. Zorrad's market served several deep-jungle Mahque tribes, but Elder Gordu claimed the first four catches each day to haul on his water buffalo cart to a larger inland town for a share in the steeper profit. Today, they were the second boat in, which meant they would have coin for rice, spices, *and* Nadaar's high war-tribute the soldiers would soon come to collect.

"Ches-Shu smiles on us, cousin!" Sev threw an arm over

Nahiki's shoulders as Gordu's overloaded cart wobbled away and they trooped back to the beach to wash their nets. Although the empire demanded its territories bow to Murlochian Dominion, among the Que tribes, worship of the Three Sisters lingered: Ches-Shu, goddess of the sea, was honored most by the Alonque, while the Hanonque favored Cael of the sky, and the Mahque praised Cihana of the earth. Torva, oddly, stood apart in his devotion to the one called Aodh, Bearer of the Eternal Scars.

"Kaya would have you eat with us tonight." Sev hooked his elbow around Nahiki's neck and hauled him closer. "She did not wish me to say, but Yeena comes too."

"Kaya would have me netted and wed," Nahiki said.

"And that is a bad thing?"

With a year of marriage as the wind in their sails, Sev and his wife delighted in throwing matches Nahiki's way, including Kaya's sister, Yeena. Was it a bad thing? As Torva's adopted son, he was a member of the tribe now. He could build a hut and a life of his own here as Nahiki.

Rafi is dead . . . isn't he?

"You'll come then?" Sev asked.

He found himself backing away. "Promised Iakki I'd go diving. Another time." Maybe.

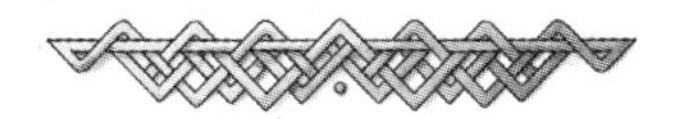

"Last one in is a turtle's egg!" Iakki shrieked and plunged in head first.

Two more splashes rocked the boat as his twin cousins followed, leaving Nahiki to stow the oars on his own. Guess that made him a . . . turtle's egg? Casting off his shirt, he dove over the side, clutching the rock anchor and letting its weight carry him down into a world as vibrant and lively as the Mah jungle lurking beyond the village of Zorrad. Colorful fish split around him and darted behind delicate sea fans, only to scatter again as the boys zipped over the sea floor, knocking oysters loose and stowing them in weighted nets dangling from the boat.

Most of the oysters here had long since yielded their pearls, but that didn't stop Alonque youths from looking. One pearl meant a water buffalo. A boat. A fresh start. Nahiki found himself thinking increasingly in those terms as the sixth anniversary of Rafi's "death" neared. Surely, at long last, he deserved to begin life anew.

Sand swirled as the rock anchor settled and he pushed off to search for oysters. He only snagged one before he had to surface. He'd never been able to dive as long as the fisher tribe, even the young ones like Iakki and his friends. The sea itself pulsed in their blue Alonque veins but it was diminished by Nadaarian scarlet in his. Though the Que territories had been absorbed by the empire a hundred years ago, the tribes–Alonque, Mahque, and Hanonque–all clung to their identity with a ferocity that reinforced Nahiki's outsider status and kept the Nadaari bristling at rumors of revolt. So long as Nahiki was left in peace, he didn't mind.

Diving again, he pried at a second oyster, only to lose it when Iakki shot past and snatched it first. He caught Iakki's foot and dragged him back to wrestle it free. Sharp edges nicked his left palm, and blood tinged the water. He shoved the smirking boy away, snagged a strand of seaweed and wrapped the stinging cut, fumbling to tie it with his less adept right hand. Blood was dangerous. It attracted predators, like sharks and other . . . nastier . . . things.

Wriggling for the surface, Iakki stuck out his tongue. Then his look changed into one of horror. Something stirred behind Nahiki. He spun and caught a flash of silver scales on powerfully churning legs, of a rippling mane and tail, of hooves that gleamed like abalone. He blinked into eyes of a blue so bright it stung like sunlight reflecting off glassy water.

Those were the eyes of a sea-demon.

THREE: CERIDWEN

Shadowers often have coats of dull gray, brindled brown, or muted roan that serve as camouflage and blend into their surroundings.

"Onward." Blinking away weariness, Ceridwen whispered the word as day melted into night and still Mindar's hooves drummed on. Force of will alone bound her to the saddle as the wolfhound led the way and showed no signs of slowing. Once on the scent, a wolfhound would run until halted, even if the pads of its paws wore away, leaving bloodstained prints behind.

Finnian did not halt the wolfhound.

She caught only brief glimpses as his steed drifted from shadow to shadow, but in the tension of his shoulders, she sensed the same limb-numbing, bone-aching weariness that threatened her, and in the flint of his gaze when he looked back, she saw her own determination: *onward*. It was a strange word. Both fate and battle cry. Fate, for there was no altering the past and no sense in denying it. Battle cry, for one must forge relentlessly ahead. When the past lay in ashes, onward was all that remained.

"Tor Nimid?"

His voice startled her. They had barely spoken since leaving the westernmost border of Lochrann at noon where he had caught her glancing to the east, toward the distant fortress of Rysinger where her father ruled over the other six chiefdoms of Soldonia as both a war-chief and king. Since then, the golden plain had begun a gradual descent toward the salt grasses and windswept dunes of Cenyon, the coastal chiefdom that bordered the sea.

"You hold your mother's name now?"

An ache shot through her, followed by a spike of anger. Unwarranted perhaps, but he might as well have asked her about the *kasar* since it was the reason her father's name had been denied her, and all of Soldonia knew it. Daughters of kings could not be cast out without the tidings spreading like a blast wave around them.

"Te Donal." Her response cut the silence. It was not an answer, and in that regard as good an answer as any. "And you, your father's?"

Oddly enough, that silenced him.

She logged it away. Fathers, evidently, made for painful conversation.

Night deepened over Cenyon. A wan moon daubed the land with light and shadow beneath Mindar's coal-black hooves. Solborn were hardy stock, capable of greater endurance than any common tolf. But even so, when cold, gray ash flecked Mindar's coat and his smoke turned a sickly white, Ceridwen called the halt. The instant her head sank against the saddle she had removed to serve as a pillow, welcome darkness settled over her.

She awoke at the first touch of dawn upon the horizon. The wolfhound's head jerked up from Finnian's chest as she hefted saddle and bedroll over her shoulders. His contorted upper lip, misshapen skull, and fur that grew in tri-colored patches around old scars made him one of the strangest hounds she had seen. She wanted to beg his tale from Finnian, but insulting his dog seemed a poor start to conversation when they already danced tenderhoof around one another.

Jaws gaping in a yawn that exposed his snaggleteeth, the wolfhound shook his head, ears flapping, then swept his tongue over Finnian's face.

"What in–" Finnian bolted upright, spluttering. "*Shades*, Cù. Come here!" He wrestled the shaggy beast to the ground, where, growling and grappling, they rolled toward the picket line where the two solborn grazed.

Mindar shied back, flames glowing in his throat.

Ceridwen's voice caught, but she leaped forward, hands raised, and the fireborn swung toward her instead. He heaved a deep, snorting breath, and his flames died. *Blazes*. He had startled so easily, come so close to flaming without command.

"Reckless beasts, fireborn," Markham had observed, sole eye twitching beneath his weathered brow, as she had dismounted, bloodied, bruised, and flushed with victory at earning her place among the Outriders. "No hope in taming them. Not truly. Fireriders must strive for mastery and mastery alone." And in the cadence of his words and the slow upward drag of his eyelid, she had read his doubt.

Doubt about her, her steed, and her skill.

A trickle of that doubt always wormed through her veins. She buried it deep and stroked Mindar's nose until his fires cooled, then inspected her tack while saddling. Aside from minor pitting on cinch and saddlebow, it was in fair condition. Frequent skivva oil treatments kept gear resistant to flame, but it was extracted from plants that grew only in the burning craters of Gauroth and so was costly enough that only fireriders made the investment. Once, she would not have considered that cost. Now, she winced at how close the pot of oil in her saddlebags was to running out and felt twice for weaknesses in Mindar's hackamore before sliding it over his ears.

Snorting pale, gray smoke, he dipped his head so she could scratch the thin white stripe between his eyes. "Aye, you reckless, inflammable, *glorious* beast," she whispered. "You are mine." And he was. Just as she was somehow his.

Tolf-riders could not comprehend the connection the sol-breath created between riders and steeds. Her leathers shielded her, but the sol-breath made her less susceptible to heat, less vulnerable to flame. Focused blasts could harm her. But not since bonding Mindar had she been burned like that day—that worst of days—in the crater of Koltar. She instinctively gripped her arm against the memory of blistering heat that had consumed leathers and flesh and left only raging pain. Pain that was nothing compared to the agony of seeing Bair—

No. She could not think on that now.

Finnian rolled past her, wolfhound in a headlock, teeth bared in a matching snarl.

"Are you coming?"

His head jerked up.

Blazes. That had sounded harsher than she intended. Memories of Bair always stripped the softness from her voice as though her throat was still raw from screaming and choked with ash.

Finnian broke from Cù and rose to his feet. Deliberately cracked his neck and shoulders, then snatched his cloak and bedroll and stalked away without a word. She almost chased after him. But an explanation felt weak, and an apology knotted her tongue, so she left him to saddle while she braided her hair and rummaged out dried meat and an apple from her saddlebags. Mindar nuzzled at the apple, so she dropped the core when she finished, whistled a cue, and he crisped it in a spurt of flame before gathering it up into his mouth.

He had just crunched down when the shadower slid into their path, halting while the wolfhound trotted ahead. Finnian had saddled swiftly. A point in his favor. She could grant him that without the admission causing too much pain, which was an improvement.

She mounted her dancing steed and smiled at his eagerness to run. "Let us be off."

The shadower did not move.

There was a gleam of challenge in Finnian's eyes as he crossed his vambrace clad arms over his jerkin. Atop his lanky steed, he sat two hands taller than she did. "Tame yourself, tor Nimid. We need to speak. You may not fear flaming out, but I intend to rise far before I do. You put that at risk."

His gaze flicked to her forehead. It lingered only an instant, but his meaning was clear. She bore the *kasar.* Any failure earned at her side could forever mar an Outrider's name. All this she read in that dart of his eyes, but if he wished to speak, then she would force him to acknowledge his fear. "I put it at risk?"

"You are too reckless."

"And *you* are stubborn."

He gave an offhand shrug. "Apex Markham wants us to work together."

Why *had* Markham paired them?

"And?" she demanded.

"If we must be paired then we should function as a pair, don't you think?" He met her gaze levelly and made no attempt to disguise the doubt lurking within. She could respect that. Riding as a pair meant trusting him, and her trust was not easily won.

But neither, it seemed, was his.

Risky, her heart screamed, for ash fell in her wake. But the sooner they completed this mission, the sooner she could convince Markham to let her ride alone before Finnian could be caught up in her firestorm to his ruin. In the meantime, it was not so bad . . . to not be alone.

She nodded. "So be it."

He seemed surprised by her assent, but as he backed out of the way and rose in his stirrups to whistle for Cù, she couldn't resist. A twitch of the reins sent Mindar spinning past, leaving the shadower to vanish in his dust. And in that glorious burst of energy and speed, Ceridwen whispered the word once more. "*Onward.*"

Fate. Battle cry. And occasionally, a prayer.

"Markham would be proud, I think," Finnian said, a grin apparent in his voice. With no trees to offer shade on the bare dunes, he and his shadower were visible, and he had swept his unruly hair back from his forehead, baring his face to the morning.

Free in a way Ceridwen longed for. Exposed in a way she feared.

"How is that?" she asked, turning to scan for their quarry. Markham's pride was not easily earned and failing this mission because they lost focus would not prompt any favors.

"Come on. Three days' pursuit without killing one another? I count that a victory."

"Four days, and you must admit, it came close."

"No, three. The first doesn't count. I wanted to be rid of you then–"

"Oh?" She glanced at him. "Likewise."

"Really. I had no idea. Careful, tor Nimid, or I might change my mind back!"

Ceridwen snorted at the thick drawl of sarcasm coating his voice in imitation of Markham, and Mindar let out a puff of black smoke. Finnian smiled then, really smiled, and the light of it spread over his whole face, crinkling his eyes and smoothing any hint of concern. It was brilliant, that smile. She had to look away. She fingered the horse-head pommel of her sabre, drawing comfort from its familiarity and its battle-tested strength.

Side by side, they crested the dune, trailing Cù as he tracked the poacher through salt grasses stirred by a breeze that bore the tang of the sea. Soon, they would reach the coast. They must catch the poacher before then, before he could barter passage and sail beyond their reach.

"*Shades.*" Finnian halted abruptly. "It's him."

Ceridwen rose in her stirrups to see past him. Across the valley between dunes, a man stood adjusting the cinch of a shaggy horse while two massive pack horses grazed beyond. All three were clearly tolf, not solborn, and even at a distance, she could see the dark stains pooling in the corners of the sacks. She blinked away the image of the dead stormer and only half heard Finnian urging her to pull back, to follow the plan.

They had worked it out while riding the second day. Rehashed it twice on the third. Evidently, Finnian disliked leaving aught to chance.

But it was already too late.

"He's seen us."

The poacher's posture gave him away–limbs coiled, body

unnaturally still, head raised as if to sniff the wind. He bore all the signs of a quarry poised to flee.

She nodded at Finnian's bow. "Within range?"

"Too far."

"Then we close in." Before the poacher ran. Ceridwen raised her half mask, yanked down her hood, and spurred Mindar down the slope. The shadower made no sound, but she heard Finnian cursing and knew he and his wolfhound followed.

"What are we doing, tor Nimid?"

"Improvising."

It was the soul of battle. When plans failed, the ability to change leads was life or death.

Below, the poacher seized his pack steeds, mounted, and hammered his heels into the horse's ribcage. He meant to run for it? Ceridwen's mouth twitched as Mindar surged into his stride, devouring the ground. For all the man's supposed cunning, anyone who attempted to outrun solborn on a tolf trailing two pack horses was a fire-blasted fool.

So, let him run. Let him see the fury of the solborn raging hard at his heels.

A whip cracked in the poacher's hand, forcing a frenzied, plunging spring into his horse's stride as they swept into the next valley. It nearly unseated him. He rode loose and untethered, limbs flapping wildly. He had no skill in the saddle that could win this race.

Already sparks stung his horse's tail, and with her arms outstretched, reins slack, Ceridwen urged Mindar to more speed, more heat, more flame. She was so close now, she could see the Canthorian ink markings on the poacher's arms and noted his high cheekbones and shaved skull when he twisted to look at her. So close, she could not miss the savage grin that flashed across his face in the instant before water dashed up beneath the tolf's hooves and showered Mindar's chest. He had run them into a salt marsh.

Mindar plunged to a halt on the edge and danced back, hooves steaming. Ahead, the three tolf charged through the shallow water and raced away, trampling knee-high reeds. Flames take him! Ceridwen cursed the poacher's cunning and her foolishness, and her ill-tamed wildborn and his fear of water too. Snorting ghostly smoke, Mindar tried to sidestep, but she boxed him in with her heels and summoned a halfhearted leap that landed him in the middle of the marsh with no way out but onward. He wallowed through, mud splattering his belly.

Out of the corner of her eye, she glimpsed the shadower running alongside. Silent still. Undeterred by uncertain footing. Finnian flashed a teeth-bared grin that resembled Cù, as neck and neck they cleared the marsh and tore uphill.

Ceridwen's sabre rang from its scabbard. It burned with firelight in her hand. She relished the hunt, the race, the blaze.

The glory.

"Look out!" Finnian shot past her.

Atop the dune, the poacher twisted in his stirrups, bringing a crossbow to bear upon her.

Riding was seat and legs and heart and hands all working in harmony. It was communication in a tongue all its own. It was that breathless, unconscious moment when steed and rider simply moved as one. So as Mindar slowed and whipped around, and Ceridwen summoned flame to halt the bolt midflight, she did not think. She moved.

But only a dribble of white smoke answered. The salt marsh had quenched his flames, and the slope slowed his turn. And for a moment, she stalled before the thought of a bolt ripping through Mindar's throat. Of blood gushing from his veins. Of his fire extinguished forever. Mindar pitched to a halt, and death grinned at her behind that crossbow.

She heard the impact but felt no pain.

The poacher swayed.

Then fell.

Reins hanging slack, Finnian nocked another arrow and set thumb ring to string, slowing the shadower with seat and legs to avoid trampling the body. Only then did Ceridwen see the copper-fletched arrow in the poacher's throat. Fired uphill at a run? *Blazes*, such a shot.

"Markham would be proud, I think," she said, breathlessly riding up. "I owe you now–" She broke off as he stiffened and bent his head, grimacing. "You all right?"

"Fine . . . just . . . do you hear it?"

Suddenly, beyond Mindar's ragged breathing and her own pounding heart, she *did* hear it, carried over the dunes on the salt-tinged breeze: voices shouting, spears rattling, hooves pounding sand. There, the keening screams of seabloods. There, the clash of steel. And there, a war horn shrilling the rallying cry of Soldonia's coastal chiefdom.

"Aye, I hear it." She met his dark eyes and swallowed. "Cenyon is under attack."

FOUR: JAKIM

Aodh is true.

Salt spray tinged the air with the scent of purpose. Perched in the branches of a mango tree, Jakim breathed it in and held it until his lungs burned and his fingers began tingling. Dawn warmed his cheekbones, and a dying breeze rippled through the loose weave of his tunic and trousers, chilled his newly shaved scalp, and eased the burn of the freshly inked seal on the top of his head and the scripts on his forearms, symbols of his vows as a Scroll of Aodh. He let the breath out in a whoosh and slowly filled his lungs again.

There, in the lull between, he heard it: waves breaking against the shore.

Located just off the coast of the island empire of Canthor, Kerrikar was a small spot of jungle exploding with plant and animal life. No matter where you stood, the sea was near. Yet the sea and all that lay across it had never been closer than it would be after today. His gut churned in anticipation. Or was that hunger?

He broke an overripe mango off a drooping branch, tore away a strip of skin with his teeth, and sucked at the sweet fruit, ignoring the tiny, gold-breasted hummingbird that thrummed repeatedly past his ears. It must have a nest nearby. Behind him, the Sanctuary began to awaken. Chickens and pigs cackled and grunted within the cacti fence. Bees buzzed around their hives. His fellow Scrolls emerged from rattan huts, calling greetings in a dozen different tongues on their way to the meeting place. It was almost time to begin. Finally. He swung down a branch, mango between his teeth, and readied to jump.

Something slithered in the grass below.

He jolted and almost slipped from his perch. The churning sensation shot into his throat. Hugging the branch, he peered down and caught a flash of the sinuous red and gold form of a Canthorian spine snake—as long as his leg and wide as a stone-eye tiger's tail—and in front of it, a tiny splash of color. A fledgling, fallen from its nest.

Aodh have mercy. He *hated* snakes.

The half-eaten mango left his hand, hurled at the snake's head. He lunged for another, but wind chimes rang out from the Sanctuary, startling him. This time, he did slip. Barked his chin, raked his shins, and landed in a pained heap on the ground. He bolted upright, ready to run if the snake struck. But he saw only its tail vanishing through the grass. Well, there was one reason to be thankful for his clumsiness. He'd scared it off.

Gently, he cradled the fledgling in his hands. Its heartbeat fluttered against his palm, and downy gray-green fluff stuck to his brown fingers. He found himself smiling, awed by its beady eyes and the iridescent sheen just visible beneath the fluff and—

He was going to be late.

Within the Sanctuary, the Scrolls were about to commission Enok for his journey to Broken-Eliam, the lost homeland of Jakim's exiled people. He had to be there. But he couldn't abandon the fledgling. Clutching the creature to his chest, he climbed the mango tree one-handed, pushing up through thick, glossy leaves until he found the cuplike nest, tucked the fledgling inside, took in one last salt-and-purpose-tinged breath, and dropped to the ground. He raced back to the Sanctuary, mud squelching beneath his bare toes. Down here, he could smell only the richness of earth, rain-drenched then sun-warmed and hungry for tending. But he would not forget the tang of the sea and the promise those distant waves repeated in his ears.

"Soon, Siba, soon," he panted.

Jasmine bloomed on vines surrounding the entrance to the meeting hut. Jakim skidded to a halt beneath the dangling strands, catching the murmur of Scrollmaster Gedron already speaking inside, then ducked through, praying he wasn't too late. He was . . . and he wasn't. Scroll Enok stood beside Gedron beneath the hand-carved wind chimes at the front. The four dozen other Scrolls who lived in the Sanctuary were seated in even rows on the floor before them. So, the meeting had begun, but Enok's team had not yet been chosen.

His relieved sigh broke across a hush. Enok's face had been marked by years of smiling, Gedron's by scowling, so the expressions that greeted him as he crouched at the back and made his way through the others, muttering apologies, were no surprise.

Gedron cleared his throat. "Won't you be seated, Scroll Jakim?"

Scroll Jakim. He grinned. Four days since his vows, and still just hearing it gave him a thrill. He slouched deeper out of respect but couldn't bring himself to fully sit. On his left wrist, he fiddled with the woven cord Siba had given him—a necklace for the boy he had been, pressed tearfully into his hands before he was dragged away. Threads of red, orange, green, and yellow had faded to dullness from years of wear. It was his last piece of home.

Soon, though, soon . . .

Gedron was speaking again, outlining the mission, but Enok had already told Jakim, so he fidgeted, wiping the mango juice from his hands onto his trousers. Every decade, a mission was sent into the heart of Eliam to recover unrecorded sections of the holy writ from the walls of their ancestral city where it had been carved centuries ago, before the land's breaking and claiming by the empire of Nadaar. Few Scrolls actually shared Jakim's Eliamite blood, but their order had been built by exiles, and in service to Aodh, Bearer of the Eternal Scars, they embraced that heritage. Since so much had been lost in the breaking, those exiles had adopted the Canthorian custom of inking their skin, preserving the script on their bodies as well as on parchment, so that as long as their order remained, the writ would survive.

Over the years, the Kerrikar Sanctuary had established a number of refuges around the world, but only once a decade did they return to the rubble of Eliam. Funding such a journey–by outrigger canoe from Kerrikar to Canthor, trading ship from Canthor to Nadaar, then lengthy travel on foot across lands inhabited by the Que tribes but dominated by the empire, before finally reaching the most dangerous stretch of all, Broken-Eliam itself–was no easy matter.

This was Jakim's one chance.

"Who among you wishes to join Scroll Enok on–"

Jakim bolted up before the Scrollmaster finished speaking. Around the room, a handful of others stood more slowly and offered their palms, revealing the truths scribed across their forearms. Gedron wove through their ranks, selecting one, two, three Scrolls before halting so close to Jakim that he could smell the honeyed jasmine tea on the master's breath as the man studied his face. Was there . . . something on his chin?

He swiped at it and found smeared blood and tree sap.

Gedron turned abruptly away. "Scrolls Huldah, Asaiah, and Myrnah will accompany Enok, and may Aodh's Eternal Scars shield them all."

Murmuring the prayer, the others sat again.

But Jakim's knees had locked. Was that it? It couldn't be. "Scrollmaster–"

"Your vows are newly sworn, Scroll Jakim," Gedron replied without turning. "The ink is barely set in your skin. Your zeal is laudable, but it would be wiser for you to stay to select your course of study and complete your training."

"But I can translate." Languages came easily to him, and he'd picked up half a dozen in the past seven years away from home. "And . . . I have family among the exiles." He studied his toes, avoiding Enok's gaze. Only Enok knew his full story. Only he might suspect that something more than this mission drew him seaward. "They could help us reach Broken-Eliam."

"You understand the purpose of our mission, Jakim?"

Of course, avoiding Enok did no good when the man limped

up in front of him. Scars like the one that twisted his leg were the only sign he had once been a soldier, and even so, Jakim struggled to imagine the gentle, smiling Scroll carrying a weapon, much less wielding one. That smile of his could be deceptive, though. It concealed a gaze as inescapable and penetrating as a stone-eye's.

"Of course."

"You also understand that no other purpose can distract us?"

"I . . . yes . . ." And he did, but he also could not deny that tugging sensation within that drew him to claim this mission along with his own. "This is my purpose. I feel it."

If Aodh willed it, why could he not accomplish both?

Gedron eyed him narrowly, then squeezed his shoulder. Jakim flinched. Old reflexes. "Aodh's purposes are not always apparent. Nor does his hand always guide where we expect. This calls for wisdom and patience. Next time, perhaps, you may go."

But as Gedron moved on and began leading the Scrolls in a recitation from the holy writ, Jakim felt sick. He couldn't wait a decade for the next mission, and attempting to buy passage on his own with what he could earn as a freed slave and a foreigner, well, that would take years too.

"Aodh's hand is upon you."

Siba had promised him that, and he'd almost dared believe it. But now? He would sooner face down the chilling stare of a Canthorian spine snake again than the knowledge that Enok and the others would leave without him.

"I have been there!"

All eyes swung toward him.

Gedron faltered, midway through the three paradoxes.

"The City. I have seen it." He ignored the pinch in his stomach at the lie and was unsure what to do with his arms. He finally crossed them over his chest. Enok had told him that the last mission had ended without the return of a single Scroll and none here had ever attempted it. Lie or not, if anything could change Gedron's mind, this was it.

Still, was it his imagination, or was Enok's smile somehow thinner than before?

"Seven years since you left as a boy of ten," Gedron said at last. "Yet you would guide the mission?"

Within the hut, he could no longer hear the waves brushing the shore, and yet somehow the sea still throbbed in his ears, echoing Siba's words: *"You, Jakim, will save our people."* That he could not do from Kerrikar. He had to go home.

Deep breath. "Yes."

Scroll Enok grasped his shoulder, and this time, he did not cringe. "Then may Aodh the One and His Eternal Scars shield us all."

FIVE: CERIDWEN

Seabloods are colored a dark bluish-black at birth and grow lighter and more dappled with age. Glistening scales cover their legs, speckle their throats, and form patches around their eyes.

Side by side, Ceridwen and Finnian rounded the dune into battle. Cenyon warriors wheeled in pairs across the strip of sand before the sea. Garbed for war in steel breastplates, greaves, and plumed helmets, they rode upon seabloods–solborn with blue-gray hides slicked with foam and shimmering scales on their legs. The fight ranged around a longboat run aground on the beach, surrounded by soldiers in scarlets, oranges, and golds. Those were the colors of Nadaar, the conquest-hungry empire across the sea.

"*Shades.*" Finnian's voice was hoarse. "What are the Nadaari doing here?"

Here, in Cenyon. Here, on Soldonia's coast.

As Outriders, they were sworn to defend the borders of the chiefdoms from threats. An attack took precedence over all else. Ceridwen drew a sharp breath and twitched her reins at Mindar's stamping. The battle frenzy stirred his blood to ignite. That was good. It did not matter why the Nadaari were here. Not now. All that mattered was that they were stopped.

"I must fight," she said.

Finnian slumped in the saddle. "Aye . . . *shades* . . . we must."

The shadower glided forward, and Ceridwen urged Mindar alongside. "So, you will agree, just like that? Don't you want to settle on a plan? Or three?"

His expression darkened at her jab. "We ride. We fight. Aodh grant we survive."

Two more longboats slammed into the beach as they neared, propelled by the surf kicked up by the swarm of seabloods in the water. Soldiers disembarked beneath the cover of a rain of arrows. Behind them, a single Nadaarian ship swayed at anchor, just visible around the curve of the headland. Long spears flashed in the newcomers' hands.

Scattered riders gathered in the shallows behind a tall warrior on a dappled blue steed. The seablood reared, spray flying from his hooves, and screamed a call that passed from steed to steed until it rang across sand and sea and the sky itself echoed the noise. For an instant, the Nadaari quailed. In the cry of the seabloods was all the raging fury and haunting loneliness of the deeps. It was a cry to shake a man, to leech his strength and weaken his resolve.

To Mindar, it was a call to arms.

He tore into the battle. Head high, smoke roiling from his nostrils, hooves shredding sand. Ceridwen loosed the Outrider yell and lightly rolled her spurs across his flanks. Flames roared from his throat, engulfing the Nadaari spearmen. They staggered back, screaming. She sprang among them, blade swinging high to low, broad sweeping strokes that cleaved wood and bone.

She wheeled away from a collapsing steed, jamming her knee against the dappled blue seablood. The tall warrior turned toward her, offering only a glimpse of pale skin and bright blue eyes beneath the helmet's gated visor before the press of battle swept them both away.

Hands seized her knee. A spear scored the leathers guarding her ribs. The soldier fell beneath Mindar's hooves, and a spout of fire cleared her retreat. Blood slicked the grip of her sabre. The bones in her forearm and shoulder rang with each blow of sabre on spear, on shield, on armor. Mindar coiled and spun and wheeled around, a firestorm consuming all in its path.

Until the Nadaari broke and the solborn onslaught drove them toward the sea.

"'Ware the boats," Finnian cried behind her.

The outgoing tide, no longer stirred by the seabloods, had left the longboats beached. A handful of Nadaari vaulted aboard and caught up the sweeps while others dragged the longboats across the white sand. A hail of javelins barraged the longboats, dropping corpses until the frothing water ran red. One boat came free and soldiers lunged aboard. With a shout, the tall warrior plunged into the sea after them, followed by a dozen seabloods. A moment later, the second longboat launched.

Blazes. They were all going to escape.

Ceridwen leaned low over Mindar's neck and sped across the beach. Spears and arrows bit into the sand around her, but she did not slacken pace. Straight for the sea, she drove him, then slid to a flying stop between the remaining longboat and the waves. Fire poured from his throat, vaporizing arrows and snapping the longboat into flames.

Howling soldiers fell away from the inferno, diving into the shallows where javelins and hooves and the flashing teeth of seabloods awaited them.

Something crashed against Ceridwen's skull, and pain shot down her spine. The blow snapped her forward against Mindar's neck. Vision swimming, she caught flashes of a spear driving toward her chest. She struggled to raise her sabre.

Just before the strike, Finnian appeared. Ghosting from the low-hanging smoke, the shadower slid noiselessly behind the Nadaarian, and Finnian bent and planted a long knife in the gap between his breastplate and helm. The soldier dropped and Finnian lurched in the saddle, strangely off balance. Or was that only her blurred vision? Ceridwen forced herself upright, teeth gritted against the dizziness.

Feet slapped sand.

A soldier bolted away across the beach. He made it only a dozen strides before a trident struck him in the back and pinned him to the ground. A sleek, silvery seablood pranced to his side, and the rider leaped down to ram the trident in again. She swept it free and grounded it, then removed her helmet, revealing a flood of wavy black hair surrounding a young face that struck Ceridwen as familiar, with its skin like sand and eyes like ocean spray.

The dappled blue seablood loped ashore in a shower of water and came to a dancing halt before Mindar. Ceridwen unstrapped her half mask on one side and let it hang, then slid her hood back as the two solborn snorted at one another. A quivering flame darted between Mindar's teeth, and the seablood tossed his head.

"Settle your steed, tal Desmond." The tall warrior lifted her helmet to reveal the pale skin, arched brows, and forever taut expression of Cenyon's war-chief, Lady Telweg tal Anor. Water slicked her silvered black hair to her skull and tangled the braid tumbling down her back. In her steely gaze, Ceridwen read the same assumption of guilt she had seen after she crossed the threshold of Rysinger with Bair in her arms.

"Lady Telweg." She held her head high, refusing to bend. "I am *tor Nimid* now." She eyed the pinned soldier. "Why kill him? He could have given us information."

A single Nadaarian ship and three boatloads of soldiers were only enough to be slaughtered on the beaches of Cenyon. They could not conquer the white stone fortress of Tel Renaair where Lady Telweg and her seabloods ruled the coast, nor could they hope to advance into the other six chiefdoms of Soldonia as past invasions had sought.

"He is dead because I willed it," Telweg said. "Astra"–to the younger dark-haired woman–"see to the wounded and summon another unit of seariders. I will have that ship."

Astra nodded. "It will be done, Mother."

Ceridwen blinked as Astra gracefully leaped into the saddle, caught up her trident, and wheeled away. That was Telweg's daughter? She never would have recognized the timid girl she had once known in the warrior she saw now, despite her resemblance to her mother.

"Come, tal Desmond," Telweg said. "You must ride for Rysinger at once."

"Rysinger?" Ceridwen's breath caught. The *kasar* forbade her return to her father's fortress, and Telweg knew it. As she knew that breaking the ban was punishable by death. "Why?"

"Come and see." Telweg spun her seablood up a jutting arm of land that overlooked Tel Renaair, and Ceridwen followed. Below, foam-crested waves flashed across the Bay of Sylna. The great house of Tel Renaair, a long, open building with tall columns and green courtyards, ran down to the water's edge where ships lined the white stone quay. At the far end of the bay, the land curved to create a narrow inlet across which the great chain of Cenyon had been raised between the two towers stationed on the points, and everywhere Ceridwen looked she saw battle.

Soldiers dove from a lone Nadaarian ship sinking in the bay and were swarmed by seabloods and Cenyon vessels. A second ship veered away from the chain in the open water beyond, close-hauled and listing dangerously to one side.

Behind, a dense cloud of ships bore down upon the coast. The chain held them at bay, but already longboats were launching and winging inland beneath mighty strokes of their sweeps, while flaming bolts fired from ship-mounted ballistae splintered against the towers.

"Cenyon is under attack," Telweg said, and somehow her voice was calm in the face of the danger threatening her chiefdom. "An invasion fleet and the might of Nadaar has come. All of Soldonia is imperiled. You must ride to warn the king and muster the war-hosts to arms."

"This is it then?" Finnian halted his shadower and dismounted. He stumbled forward, shoulders hunched. "War has come and with no warning."

Ceridwen could not respond. She stared at the conflict raging below and knew she should weep for the sorrows of her people. This invasion had been brewing for centuries. Since consuming its own continent, the empire of Nadaar had attempted eastward expansion before and had been repelled. Still for it to come here . . . now . . . it should shock her to the core of her being, to the part that still clung to the knowledge that she might have been their queen. *Once.*

But Telweg's expression demanded an answer.

"I cannot go to Rysinger." Ceridwen spoke through gritted teeth and still felt a coward as disdain shot across the war-chief's face. "It is forbidden."

"I will go," Finnian offered quietly.

But as he gripped his saddle and set foot to stirrup, his legs buckled, and he sagged against his steed, head rolling back, face ashen and glistening with sweat.

"Finnian?" Swiftly dismounting, Ceridwen reached his side as his grip gave out and managed to ease his fall to the ground. Her hand snagged on the broken stub of a bolt in his left shoulder, and he groaned. The thick shaft looked like the ones the poacher had rigged to fire from the tripwire beneath the slaughtered solborn.

Blazes, when had he been shot?

Her mind ground to a halt.

She could see herself bandaging wounds in vain, blood spilling fast, too fast. In a breath, Bair—no, *Finnian*—would be gone and—

Telweg brushed her aside, stooping over Finnian to set one long-fingered hand against his forehead. She tipped his chin back to inspect his eyes and monitor his shallow breathing. "The wound itself is not grave. Likely the bolt was poisoned. My medics shall see to him."

But when had he been struck? That mattered didn't it, how long the poison had been coursing through his system? Stubborn, stubborn man. Ceridwen shakily wiped the sweat from her face. One assignment. One. And already the firestorm that followed her had caught him up and spat him out in ashes. "What of the poison?"

"I cannot say." Telweg eyed her, considering. "But word must be delivered to Rysinger without a moment's delay. All my warriors are needed here. No searider can be spared if Cenyon is to stand until aid arrives. But a firerider is useless to us." The war-chief straightened with the fluid grace of a seablood and arched one dark brow at her. "What say you, tal Desmond? Are you not an Outrider sworn to protect Soldonia? Will you forswear your oath, or will you go? And perhaps"–her voice fell–"find atonement in the sacrifice?"

Finnian lay nearly lifeless in the sand, and *blazes*, leaving him felt wrong. If no messenger could be spared to ride to Rysinger, then none could bear word to Apex Markham of what had befallen them. But Markham would learn soon enough. All of Soldonia would.

Her throat was a desert. Dry and ashen as the crater of Koltar. She must go. But she would not let Telweg hear the reedy wind of fear in her voice.

When words failed, action must speak.

Sheathing her sabre, she mounted and let Mindar rise into a rear. Telweg's seablood skittered back, but the war-chief stood firm. Sparks shot from Mindar's hooves as he alighted, and smoke coiled from his nostrils. Ceridwen rolled her spurs, releasing a burst of flame as she urged him into a sand-raising gallop and tore down the slope.

Sixty leagues and more lay before her. Sixty leagues that must be crossed at a speed that her steed could maintain, lest she risk injuring him and failing her mission. Sixty leagues without an Outrider border posting where steed or rider could be exchanged. This task would fall to her and her alone. There was no escaping that.

So, for now, she would run.

Seabloods darted out of the way. Warriors fell aside. Across the beach, Mindar sped, then over the dunes of Cenyon toward Lochrann, toward the fortress of Rysinger, toward home.

SIX: RAFI

Love like the sea. Forgive like the sand.
– Alonque saying

Rafi jolted to his feet, gasping for air as the wailing of sea-demons tore him from sleep. For one teeth-shattering moment, the wail blended with the trailing scream from his dream–from his past–and he couldn't breathe. Couldn't move. Couldn't see. He blinked into pitch darkness, convinced of the drop only inches beyond his feet.

One step. One. And he would fall.

He would join Delmar.

His foot hovered over nothingness.

Rafi clenched his fist, arm shaking, and felt a stab of pain. The scream dissolved before its rush, and the darkness vanished in a crash of thunder. Pale lightning washed over him, revealing the blood trickling down the side of his hand, spattering his bare feet and the cluttered floor beneath with dark spots. Slowly, his mind caught up.

The floor–he was in Torva's hut.

The blood–he was gripping his harpoon by the blade, metal biting into his palm.

The scream, the nothingness, the sense that he was about to fall–only another memory dredged up by the sea-demons' shrieks and that close call on his dive only days before. He still didn't know how he'd survived. By the time he'd clawed his way to the surface, the sea-demon had been gone. Only a hissing, fizzing string of current left in its wake.

Yanking stiff fingers apart, he released the harpoon. It clattered to the floor. He shook his head, drawing in sharp, gasping breaths. Six years ago, tonight, his life as Rafi had ended.

I am a ghost, he thought wryly. *Haunting only myself.*

But even that was not true. He was not the ghost he feared.

With the storm raging outside only an echo of the one in his head, the hut was suffocating. He needed to get out. Snagging his harpoon, he staggered to the door and twisted the latch awkwardly with his injured left hand. The wind swept it away and rain pelted his face. Half-blinded, he reached back to snatch his oilskin coat from its peg on the wall and then wrestled the door shut.

He ran through lashing rain, wet sand flying beneath his feet. Running. Running. Running. He had raced this same track across the beach so many sleepless nights, it wouldn't have surprised him to find his footprints permanently scored in the sand. But sand was not cursed with memory. Nor did the sea recall.

He staggered to a halt, hands on his knees. White-tipped waves broke to his left and retreated, leaving broken shells and jagged coral behind. The sea moved, ever changing, never fixed. But to his right loomed the dense Mah jungle, the rainforest that sprawled across most of central Nadaar and reached northward to carpet the steep slopes of the Hanon mountains. There was a place rooted in memory.

Rafi was the rainforest, but Nahiki must become the sea. Forgetting and forgotten. Free.

Something thudded behind him. It was such an unexpected sound on that empty, storm-lashed beach that he spun, clutching his harpoon to scan the line of fishing boats. He blinked away rain and saw the sea-demon. It lurked beside the boats, a shadow melting into the haze of the rain-washed night, visible only because of the soft blue luminescence of its eyes. He knew at once it was the same creature that had interrupted his dive days before, snatching the seaweed from his hand and then disappearing into the depths, all in the second it had taken for the air to burst from his lungs and send him kicking in a panic for the surface, desperate to escape its familiar blue eyes, so like . . .

So like Delmar's.

His sodden coat flapped against his legs. Rainwater stung the cut on his hand. He shifted involuntarily, muscles tensing. A sea-demon's scream was unnerving, but its silence was worse. Should he run? Bad idea. Fight? Suicide. Sev praised his aim, but he didn't trust himself to take down a charging sea-demon with one throw. Raising the harpoon defensively, he backed away.

The creature plunged forward and the boat shifted with it. Rafi almost broke and ran. But the sea-demon jerked to a halt and pawed the ground–trapped. Somehow, it had gotten a hoof wrapped in a net dangling from the boat.

He was safe. It could no more run him down than he could fly.

Curious, he inched closer for a better look. Scales climbed its legs, speckled the bridge of its nose, and circled its eyes. The creature tossed its head, short mane flapping limply in the rain. Flanks heaving, muscles bulging, it thrashed, and silvery blood oozed from deep cuts on its legs where cords had sliced deep. A strand of seaweed dangled from its mouth, forgotten in the struggle.

Rafi glanced to the clumps of seaweed wedged in the net–this was old Hanu's boat, and his failure to care for his gear drove Gordu near to distraction–and suddenly understood. "You were eating, weren't you? Came ashore for an easy meal?"

The creature blew out a sharp blast, muscles trembling beneath its dark blue coat. For a legendary monster, it looked surprisingly sheepish. Young too. Only a colt.

"No shame." Rafi found himself saying, murmuring the words soft and low like the song of the sea. His outstretched hand hovered inches from the colt's shivering hide. But what was he going to do, cut it loose so it could attack him? "My gut's gotten me in its fair share of trouble over the years, if you'd–"

The colt screamed, and Rafi jumped back, pulse surging.

But its ears were pricked toward the sea, and even as Rafi's back struck Hanu's boat, knocking him to his knees, he heard it: a hissing, chittering sound that spiked every hair and made his gut churn with dread. Lightning flashed as a monster boiled out of the ocean. Massive, sinuous, many-legged. Fifteen feet long with horns that swooped back from its head and a pair of red-tipped pincer claws below its mouth oozing venom. Rafi ducked behind the boat and clutched his harpoon to his chest, gaping, mesmerized as dozens of rippling leg-pairs propelled the beast through the surf and across the sand.

"*Oh, Ches-Shu,*" he breathed.

First a sea-demon. Now a scadtha. It was a night of horrors.

SEVEN: CERIDWEN & RAFI

Fireborn are volatile steeds, capable of breathing forth streams of fire and prone to catching their manes and tails–not to mention their environment–ablaze. Beware rousing them.

Ceridwen descended upon Rysinger like a bolt of lightning from a tempest. Storm clouds shrouded the fortress, deepening the night despite the struggling torches. Wind beat against the wooden battlements and the metal breastplates of the warriors stationed at the outer gate. Ceridwen pulled her hood tight, shielding her ears from the wailing wind and her forehead from the guards. But at the sight of the Outrider badge on her shoulder–twin gold horse heads crossed over a field of black–the guards waved her onward, and onward Mindar ran.

Thunder rumbled in the distance, but the true storm was still to come.

Crossed lances barred the way into the inner fortress. Six horned earthhewns lined the drawbridge, and all six riders turned to face her as Mindar clopped toward them. The last time she had entered the fortress, it had been with her brother's body over her shoulders. There, she had fallen. And there, she had been cast out again, branded with the *kasar.*

She reined Mindar to a stop. He shivered beneath her, and she shivered with him. Over the long run, his fire had dwindled to embers. White ash flaked from his mane, and his heaving nostrils emitted little smoke.

"Speak, Outrider," the nearest earthrider demanded. "Declare your purpose."

Beneath her hood, Ceridwen found her voice. "I bear urgent tidings from Lady Telweg of Cenyon for the war-chiefs and his majesty, the king. Let me pass."

"Not thus cowled." He flicked his lance toward her hood. "Reveal yourself first."

In those unflinching tones, she heard echoed the judgment that had forced the brand to her flesh. Mindar shifted uneasily. He jerked against the reins and snorted, and to her surprise, the smoke curling from his nostrils was black once more.

Perhaps she had time to wait. Perhaps she could explain and let another deliver her tidings. Perhaps she need not break the ban of the *kasar* outright.

Telweg's whisper filled her ears. *"Atonement."*

But at the sight of the fortress, the moment of her branding burned afresh in her mind, and all the rage that had thrashed in her chest then surged to the surface, demanding to be unleashed. Sixty leagues and more she had run over the past five days. She would not be halted now. Strategy and tactics rammed her thoughts. Drawn shoulder to shoulder, earthhewns could form an impenetrable line. But these six had not yet closed ranks. They formed a gauntlet, eyes fixed upon her. In a charge, earthhewns were an unstoppable force, but in close quarters, in the sparse maneuverability of the bridge, there the speed and fury of a fireborn could win.

She did not hesitate.

At her asking, Mindar shot forward. Thought blurred into breath and movement. Twisting past the first earthrider before his lance could shift into their path. Unleashing flames toward the second and third and then diving *into* the blaze as they dodged away. Feeling the heat blossom across her skin before Mindar broke out into the wind again. Lunging around the fourth earthhewn. Skidding to a halt before slamming into the fifth. Spinning away again in fire as the dull pain of a lance raked across her back. Racing beyond the sixth earthhewn and barreling through the gate and across the greensward, the grassy courtyard that sprawled between the inner wall and Rysinger's great house.

Warriors reached for weapons. Solborn shied from their path.

Like a firestorm from the heart of Koltar, Ceridwen tore up the shallow steps into the great house, clattered down tapestry-lined hallways, torches gusting in her wake, and skidded to a halt before the door to the great hall. Three spears high the door stood, crafted from ebony and carved with images of solborn and riders from centuries past. In the center, wreathed in the flames of his fireborn, Uthold the Bold rode in wrath from the fiery craters of the east.

Ceridwen called upon Mindar to rise in the *noon-strike* form, and his pounding hooves struck the door. Sparks ricocheted across the wood. Thrice, he struck. And thrice the door shook with the weight of his fury. At the fourth strike, the hinges yielded, and the slap of wood on stone echoed like the crack of thunder. All eyes fell upon the opening as she entered the hall in smoke and flame.

Rafi did not consider himself overly superstitious. But when a man contemplates the anniversary of his own supposed death in the company of a sea-demon *and* a scadtha, crouched behind a boat, cradling a flimsy harpoon for comfort, only inches and one misstep away from being eaten, he can't help wondering if someone somewhere has it out for him.

Then the colt's wail snapped him back to reality, and he knew that the monster had come ashore for the same reason as the sea-demon: netted prey and an easy meal.

Go, the voice of a ghost whispered in his head. *Run for it, brother.*

Just as the living voice had whispered six years ago. He could do it. Break across the beach. Not get involved. Survive. His muscles screamed to run as the scadtha lunged. Washed in the blue of the colt's eyes, the monster twisted impossibly fast to evade its kicks. Only one connected, crunching chitin, before the scadtha crashed into the sea-demon. It coiled up over its back and neck, pinning the colt against Hanu's boat. Clawed legs pierced the colt's hide. Pincers opened, ready to flood the colt's throat with venom.

White-rimmed eyes rolled to meet Rafi's, terrified but filled with proud, desperate defiance. He knew that look. He had seen it in Delmar. All the colt needed was a fighting chance. But life was cruel. It pitted the weak against the strong and never even blinked when the weak were crushed.

Rafi groaned and shot up from behind the boat. He rammed his harpoon up, ripping away the scadtha's left pincer. It thudded to the sand. Hissing and clicking like a swarm of crabs, the monster swung toward him. That loosened its grip on the colt. One moment, the sea-demon stood, trembling. The next, it transformed into a wild, thrashing hurricane that knocked the scadtha down and snapped half a dozen legs. Shivering at the sound, Rafi dove onto the net and sheared through the cords—so fast, the harpoon slipped and nicked the colt's leg. Flat teeth sank into his forearm. He shoved its head away, barely registering the pain.

The colt realized it was free and reared, shrieking, as lightning flashed behind. The storm had slackened, clouds rolling back, splashing moonlight over the beach. Sand sprayed as the colt wheeled toward the sea, and Rafi drew in a relieved breath of salt air.

Then hissing scalded his ears.

It sounded like boiled-over water sizzling against a hot stone oven. Rafi hit the sand as the scadtha crashed into Hanu's boat, legs scrabbling to pin him. Fisting the net, he hauled his body clear. But somehow, the monster curled in over itself and came at him again. It defied natural laws, twisting in impossible ways.

Rafi rolled aside, knocking his head against the next boat. The old familiar ache began behind his eyes. Vision blurring, he blinked at the dark strip between boat and sand before registering the vessel's position—hull up for repairs with a gap beneath. He dove in. The monster slammed into the hull, legs skittering over the wood. Rafi fumbled his harpoon, cursed, and caught it up again, his breathing echoing harshly inside the hollow space.

He'd survived enough sticky situations to know this couldn't end well. Had he actually expected the scadtha to chase the colt when there was a tasty human to eat instead?

The boat groaned and shifted and was whipped away, exposing Rafi like a shelled crab. Seawater spattered his face as the scadtha reared back, boat pinned in its legs. He bolted. Moments blurred into a lifetime. He heard the boat crash. Saw the scadtha sprint, legs rippling like the surface of the sea. Felt it closing in and spun to the side.

It caught him, and dozens of claws pierced his flesh. They did not tear. Not yet. Scadtha feasted on paralyzed but living prey. Being eaten alive–not how he'd envisioned dying. He jabbed his harpoon up, but rows and rows of legs snapped shut, caging him against its slimy segmented underside. Then it began to squirm. Plates and legs shifted, pushing him inexorably upward, rough chitin tearing clothes and scraping skin, toward its mouth. Toward that red-tipped venomous pincer. Toward those wicked mandibles that would rip the flesh from his bones while he–

Rafi?

That was the ghost's voice again, somehow sounding more distinct, more real, more . . . disappointed . . . than ever before. Mere inches separated him from death now, and still he could not live up to Delmar.

He would never have given up. *He* had always been a fighter.

Brother, I–

The voice trailed off in a fading scream.

Something snapped inside Rafi, ripping a yell from his throat. He wedged the harpoon under the next plate so the monster's own push forced the blade deep into the flesh beneath. The scadtha spasmed, spilling him onto the sand, inches from the severed red-tipped pincer claw.

Rafi didn't hesitate. He seized the claw in both hands and rammed it into the wound beside his harpoon.

Roaring filled his ears. Flailing legs sliced his chest. He tripped over the wreckage of the boat, and his head slammed against the ground. Pain flared like lightning. He looked blearily up at the sky and saw the ocean rise in a massive tidal wave, lashed by the hooves of a sea-demon with luminous blue eyes. The wave crashed into the scadtha, pounded Rafi's battered frame, then yanked him up and sent him spinning, bleeding, away.

Sand. Water. Sky.

All passed in a blur.

Then there was nothing.

Bristling spears awaited her. Warriors of all the chiefdoms of Soldonia had abandoned their feast tables and drawn up in battle array before the splintered door. Nearly half the room had risen—weapons drawn, bench seats overturned, flasks discarded and soaking the fragrant rushes underfoot while dogs scrambled to snatch the abandoned food. Once, Ceridwen might have found their reaction amusing, but now pulsing fury drove all thought of humor from her mind.

Only one thing in all the hall could hold her focus. Or rather, one person.

She sought him at the center of the raised trestle table across the hall where the war-chiefs sat beneath banners embroidered with metallic threads depicting the solborn breed historically connected to their lands, displayed in one of the classic forms used to train steeds for war. Once, each chiefdom had boasted war-hosts of a single breed—the one most commonly found wild on their lands—but as the tradition of the Sol-Donair waned and access to pasture-bred steeds offered variety, many war-chiefs diversified their forces, until it was as common to find an earthhewn in Lochrann as a fireborn.

There—the king.

It was the torchlight glinting off his crown that captured her gaze, and once caught, she could not look away. Not even as warriors formed a ring of spears and closed around her. Mindar snorted and pawed at the rushes, igniting a flame beneath his hooves, and Ceridwen came back to herself. Slowly, steadily, she released the reins and raised her hands. She shed mask and hood and let the crimson scarf flutter to the ground, baring the *kasar.* Someone gasped, and her name rippled through the crowd.

They would speak of her defiance. They would speak of the brazenness of her ride into the great hall upon the wildborn steed whose quest had ended her brother's life. They would speak of the breaking of the *kasar.* And of the penalty.

Ceridwen stifled her dread. Let them whisper. She would speak soon enough.

Behind, shouting neared and pursuers flooded the broken doorway. She urged Mindar onward, and the warriors yielded step by step as he advanced, hemmed in by spears and yet strutting. Head high, neck arched, sparks dripping from his mane, a fireborn in all his glory.

She halted before the high table and all fell silent. Even Mindar seemed to sense the gravity and for once stood still beneath a loose rein. One by one she met the eyes of the war-chiefs. Only four were present beside the king, representing the chiefdoms of Harnoth, Craignorm, Ruiadh, and Ardon. Glyndwr looked shocked, Eagan intrigued, Ormond frightened, and Rhodri looked ready to cut her down.

Lastly, she turned to him, to the man who had been her father.

Desmond te Darar, King of Soldonia, sat slumped beneath a heavy blue cloak. Eyes lowered, he gripped a bronze stein in one hand and a knife in the other. His white-knuckled grip was the only sign that errant fireriders did not commonly blast into his hall without warning–not to mention exiled daughters. In the grief-stricken void that lurked behind his hooded eyes, a sense of floodwaters dammed tempered her tongue and quelled her anger.

She bent her head, suddenly feeling a fool. "My lord." Why had she flamed in here? Must she turn all to ash? "I, Ceridwen tor Nimid of the Outriders, beg permission to speak."

A muscle ticked in his jaw, but he did not respond.

He did not even look at her.

"Beg?" Glyndwr rasped. Over his head, the banner of Harnoth, his chiefdom in the north, bore a winged stormer upon a field of black streaked with gold thread, performing the most challenging battle form, the *thunderbolt*, a vertical leap with a hindward kick once all four hooves had left the earth. Stormers typically required a lengthy run at full speed to take flight, but those who mastered the *thunderbolt* could harness its momentum to become airborne. "Indeed, you must beg, child. Beg mercy for trespassing within these walls bearing the *kasar* unanswered. Beg mercy for riding into the king's presence geared for war. Beg mercy for–"

"It is not mercy I seek."

"Nor should you get it, Ceridwen." Rhodri's soft voice always simmered with an intensity that drew listeners as moths to flame. She glanced at him and wished she had not. His expression wavered between disdain and pity as he sat at the king's right hand, in the place that should have been hers. Or Bair's. And the one thing she could never accept from Rhodri te Oengus was pity. She had been seven and he fourteen when his father's death brought him to Rysinger. Even then, Desmond had treated him as a son–for the memory of his father, he had claimed–taking him beneath his wing, commanding his training in sword and fireborn, and readying him to bear his father's mantle as war-chief of Ardon, Soldonia's southern chiefdom rich with vineyards, olive groves, and pastured herds. Had Rhodri ever guessed why she had set her mind on completing the Sol-Donair? Why she'd chosen the crater of Koltar? The truth rattled against her teeth, and she wanted to spit it out

Glyndwr cleared his throat.

She forced her gaze back to the king, but however earnestly she searched his face, she found only a stranger. "My lord, I bear dire news. Invasion has come. A Nadaarian fleet amasses on the coast. Cenyon is under attack."

An uproar broke out across the hall, but the king did not react.

He rotated his stein slowly, one way then the other, gaze plumbing its amber depths.

"My lord? We must prepare for war."

Wine splashed across the table as Ormond upset his goblet. He jumped to evade the spill too late and scowled as he swiped at the stains on his soft leather doublet. It had been dyed a muted aquamarine to match Ruiadh's banner, which featured a slender riveren performing the *water-dance*, neck arched, limbs prancing. A subtle reminder of his new rank? Only recently had he filled his mother's vacant seat among the war-chiefs. She'd been a formidable woman, capable of matching wits with Telweg. He, with his wispy mustache and sparse goatee, his untamed thatch of brown hair and soft features, seemed a foal in comparison. "War? Invasion? Those are . . . weighty words. Should we not, perhaps, send word to our envoy in Nadaar to seek audience with Emperor Lykier for explanation?"

Eagan snorted, and the twin scars that carved down his bronze cheeks flared in the torchlight. His eyes looked green against the olive of his surcoat, but the copper threading gave them a golden tint whenever he turned his head. Behind him, Craignorm's brown banner portrayed a shadower in a swift, sliding halt, silhouetted against a pale moon. "A fleet attacking our coast needs no explanation. Only blood."

"I thought only perhaps they are renegades, acting alone—"

"Hardly renegades," Ceridwen interrupted. "The might of Nadaar is upon us." As it had come upon them three times and more in centuries past. The timing was unexpected, not the event. Conquest was the Nadaari way. Their god Murloch demanded it. "We must muster the war-hosts to withstand them."

"Must we?" Rhodri leaned back in his chair, stroking his close-trimmed beard. It was several shades darker than the wheat-colored hair he kept bound at his neck. The beard aged him more than the past three years should have, lending him an air of gravity and authority, and his moving fingers flashed a hammered bronze ring.

Ceridwen gaped at it. That was the battlemaster's ring,

traditionally bestowed upon the king's most trusted adviser. Not only did Rhodri sit at the king's right hand, but he had been given ultimate authority over the war-hosts of all the seven chiefdoms.

Her eyes shot up and met his.

Rhodri quirked an eyebrow in challenge, but his voice remained calm and measured. "This is a matter for the war-chiefs alone. I suggest we withdraw to the Hall of Fire."

Glyndwr sighed and leaned in toward the king. "What say you, my lord?"

Only then did the king stir. He rose slowly, unfolding from his chair like a beast emerging from its den, cloak sweeping like shadows around him. He stood before Lochrann's crimson banner with its fireborn emblazoned mid-*firestorm*—stretched low in a spin, breathing stylized flames that curled into a decorative edging—and Ceridwen, seated upon her fireborn, awaited his words.

He turned away.

Over sixty leagues she had ridden, through wind and heat and sleepless nights, and every step of the way she had feared this moment. His wrath. Or worse, his kindness. But it had been three years, and he would not even acknowledge her presence?

Ceridwen tightened her reins and Mindar tensed, snorting sparks across the high table. The crowd gasped. Boots shuffled and weapons clanked as the spear wall closed in.

The king halted.

"What of the *kasar*?" Eagan asked.

"Will you rescind the ban?" Glyndwr sounded hopeful. "Or does it stand?"

Shoulders rigid beneath his cloak, the king met her gaze. It was as if she stared into the void of a moonless, starless night. Fury she could withstand, for it could not overpower her own. Guilt she had worn as a shroud upon her heart since the moment Bair fell, stricken at her feet. Shame had become her banner since the *kasar* seared her flesh. But there, drowning in the nothingness that filled his eyes, it seemed that she had ceased to exist.

His jaw clenched. "It stands."

EIGHT: JAKIM

Aodh is just.

"Tell me, Scroll Jakim, what was it like?"

Enok's wind-whipped words barely registered in Jakim's ears. Gripping the rigging, he flung his head back, drinking in the rush of movement as the Soldonian merchant ship carved through the foggy morning. Clinging spider-like above him, a sailor boy with a graybeard monkey scampering across his shoulders flashed a grin. Jakim grinned back. Coils of mist washed over him, and beads of moisture formed on his skin. He would be soaked through soon, but he did not care. Ten days at sea, and still he could not escape the wonder that it was *happening.* At last, at long last, he was going home.

He took a breath. "It is . . . glorious!" Below, he saw Enok standing alone, squinting up through the fog. The other three Scrolls were probably still seasick from the night's tossing. It had been rough, but nothing compared to the filth-ridden, body-packed hold of the slave ship that had carried him to Canthor years ago. "But come up, Scroll Enok! It is clearer up here."

Already the mists were thinning. Soon, the sun would burn it all away.

"I haven't your head for heights." A wry chuckle filled Enok's voice. "And I was talking about the City, Jakim, in Broken-Eliam. Not your climb. But you weren't listening, were you? Forever with your head in the clouds."

Oh. Right.

Jakim's forearms itched, and his grip on the rigging prevented scratching. After two weeks, the markings were supposed to have healed. It was *supposed* to be comforting, having the holy writ with him always. Instead, the words had begun to irritate him as much as the markings. His eyes constantly snagged on the first line, inked so neatly below his wrist: *Aodh is true.*

But he, Jakim Ha'Nor, was not.

The lie he had told Scrollmaster Gedron still made his skin crawl.

"We will reach port in Nadaar soon," Enok continued. "Since you have seen the City, it would help to know what to expect. Broken-Eliam has gained an ill reputation of late." Enok was an Eliamite too, and they spoke Eliami now as was common in the Sanctuary–though, Jakim's Soldonian had come in handy for bartering passage. But Enok had been born in southern Nadaar and had never lived among the exiles who wandered the wastes of their lost homeland. He trusted Jakim to know the way.

Better to reveal the truth to Scroll Enok now before they landed on hostile soil and he was expected to guide them. Jakim sighed and moved to swing down from the rigging, but something caught his eye.

A dark shape loomed in the mist.

The sailor yelled a warning, and his monkey chattered in alarm. Shouts broke across the deck, bare feet thumped, and weapons rattled. But the air already hummed with the noise of a thousand bees. Jakim gulped, immobilized with one foot swinging free. No. Not bees. Flaming bolts, some as big as spears. They rained from the sky amidst a hail of whistling stones. Something struck the yard supporting his section of rigging, and it shuddered.

Wood cracked. Sailors screamed.

The mist parted, revealing the hulking form of an enormous ship springing into the light like a tiger from its den, flying the streamered scarlet-and-orange flag of the empire of Nadaar. Jakim gaped. Then the rigging went slack, and the ship dipped, and his stomach flew into his throat as he hurtled toward the sea.

"You, Jakim, will save our people."

Even as he plunged into the water and the deeps sang to him their eerie, angry song of death, those words had power over him. Seven years and a lifetime later, still they breathed in his chest. Rooted in his bones. Strengthened his limbs as he clawed to the surface to gasp for air.

Water slapped his face. He coughed, eyes stinging. Something solid bumped up alongside, and he clutched at it, blinking until his vision cleared.

Scroll Enok's lifeless eyes stared back at him.

Jakim jerked back, kicking to keep his head up as he stared at Enok's shocked face, at the bolts piercing his chest. Dead. Just like that. Gone before Jakim could tell him the truth.

Oh, Aodh, have mercy!

It was as much a plea for help as a cry of denial. His throat tightened as waves lapped at his ears. His loose tunic bogged down his arms, and the hungry sea tugged at his ankles. He wrestled the tunic free and twisted in search of rescue.

Ropes lashed the two ships together, hulls splintering as they collided and rocked apart, jostling him in their wake. Luckily–or rather, by Aodh's mercy–he had fallen toward the merchant ship's tail and avoided being smashed between the two. Swimming closer might get him crushed. Or shot. But staying away would get him drowned. Eliamites were a people of the earth, keepers of herds, crops, and works of the hands. Few mastered the art of swimming, and neither Canthorian slaves nor the Scrolls of Kerrikar spent much time in the water.

Something trailed across his hands, and he yanked them back, imagining snakes slithering underwater. Foolish, really. There was no such thing as sea snakes . . . was there? In any case, this was a rope, not a snake. Part of the rigging he'd been clinging to when the yard snapped–

His eyes widened. The other end still draped the ship's side like a ladder. He lunged for the rope, accidentally gulped water and choked as he hauled himself up. His arms and legs quivered by the time he reached the rail and tried to drag himself aboard. Too weak. He slipped and caught himself, thumping against the hull.

Throat raw, he summoned a shout. But what language should he use? Eliami was known to few outside his homeland or the Sanctuary, but without knowing who had won the battle above—or even if it was still raging—choosing either Soldonian or Nadaarian was a risk. Canthorian then. Safest choice.

Before he could call out, rough hands seized him from above, hauled him aboard, and flung him back against the rail. He froze as a blade stung his bare chest. Two soldiers in blood-sprayed Nadaarian armor sneered at him.

"See? It is as I said," the shorter soldier said, gesturing at Jakim's shaved skull and the lines of holy writ inked into his skin. "He is a holy man. See the markings? I've seen those before. Scrolls, they call themselves. We shall be blessed for rescuing him from the sea."

The other's voice was like a tiger's growl. "What care we for holy men who are not of Murloch?" He twisted the blade into Jakim's skin, forcing him to stand up straight.

His heel struck something soft, and his stomach twisted. It was the hand of a dead sailor, fingers curled, nails digging into wood. Not just any sailor—the boy he'd spied climbing with his monkey in the rigging. Ten days at sea, and Jakim hadn't even learned his name. Sickened, he realized the deck was littered with slain. Shredded sails and broken blocks of tackle creaked and swayed overhead. Fire licked at dangling lines. Atop the mast, streamers snapping in the wind, the orange-and-scarlet banner of Nadaar flew.

He licked his cracked lips. Enok, gone. The merchant ship, seized.

But what of the other Scrolls—Huldah, Asaiah, and Myrnah? Were they *all* dead?

"No blessing for us, holy man? Has the sea stolen your tongue?"

The other seized Jakim's chin and yanked it up to reveal the waxy scar circling his neck where he could still feel the slave collar choking him whenever he took a deep breath. The soldier barked a laugh. "Not a priest or a holy man. Only a slave. Throw him back in the sea. Or toss him in the hold. He is as good as dead either way."

In the stifling hold, Jakim huddled with his knees to his bare chest, listening as the surviving sailors nursed their wounds and bemoaned their fate. Some cursed various gods. Others called on them for rescue. Few could answer his questions. The captain and most of the crew were dead. The Scrolls too. No one understood why a Nadaarian warship would attack a Soldonian merchant in neutral waters. No one had heard rumors of war before leaving Canthor. No one knew what fate awaited them now.

Jakim's spine prickled, and he tightened his arms around his knees. It was not the first time he had endured this. He could endure again.

He would survive.

He would return home.

He would complete his mission.

But how . . .

Sweat trickled down his neck, stinging the cut on his chest. It sliced across the large triple diamond symbol inked into his skin in imperial gold. That was the oldest of his markings and the hardest won–his mark of freedom, bestowed by noble decree and meant to shield him from being enslaved again. In Canthor, at least. But it had barely been a year since the collar was struck from his neck, and he was already a captive again. What if he was not meant to be anything more?

"You will save our people."

For years, those whispered words had been his lifeline. When Siba first uttered them, he'd been an injured child, too young and too distracted by fever and pain to understand their weight. But he had never forgotten the look in her hazel eyes as she bound his wound with a poultice, held him until his shivering eased, and then tapped his forehead with a sap-stained finger.

"The hand of Aodh is upon you, Jakim. You will save us."

Her expression had dared him to challenge her conviction. So of course, he had scoffed just to annoy her. Then he had not understood what it meant to have the tribe's Wise Woman for his sister. Then he had not believed. Still, Siba's words had defined his life even so: forging in him a faith and brewing in his brothers a jealousy. On the trek with the slave trader's caravan from the tents of his tribe to the sea and across it to Canthor, those words had strengthened him. Days ago, in the mango tree with his plans unfolding before him, they had whispered to him of purpose, and even the salt spray on his tongue had tasted like hope.

But with Scroll Enok dead, their mission unfulfilled, and his future uncertain, how could he see Aodh's hand in this?

NINE: CERIDWEN

Stormers are equipped with thick feathered coats colored in various hues and patterns of dappled gray with wings that range from dazzling white to midnight black.

Clang. The door slammed shut. Keys rattled. Bolts rammed into place. Her guards' heavy footsteps clanked away, leaving Ceridwen blinking in the weak glow of the torch outside her cell. But she was not alone. She could sense him there, lurking in the shadowed hallway. "What do you want?" She shoved down exhaustion and clung to anger. It was he who had escorted her here. He who had commanded warriors to corral her steed. He who rose ever higher in her father's esteem while she fell farther still.

He who was worthy when she was not.

"Did you stay to gloat?"

Sighing, Rhodri stepped up to the bars and leaned against them, shaking his head. "Do you think I wanted this?" He actually sounded pained at the idea. Once . . . they had been friends, hadn't they? So long ago. "Why do you persist in tormenting him? He is your father."

"He is not yours." She barred all emotion from her voice, offering it as simple fact.

His fists clenched around the bars.

Only rarely had he spoken of his departed father, but she knew how long such wounds could remain fresh. Maybe it was cruel to cast it in his teeth, but she had no other weapons. They had taken them. And no shield against despair but her anger.

"He is king." Still, Rhodri did not raise his voice. He never did. "And you are not worthy of him." Spinning on his heels, he left, and she could hear the jingle of his spurs and the thud of his boots until the door far down the hall closed behind him, and she was alone.

She sagged with weariness and surveyed her surroundings. Rushes littered the floor of a space so small it made her skin crawl, with its solid stone walls and barred door. On the way in, marched within a phalanx of warriors, she had snatched glimpses of other cells, mostly empty. She was buried deep beneath Rysinger, and yet, this was a mercy. With the *kasar* unatoned, the king could have demanded her life. Perhaps he yet would.

Down the hall, a voice rang out, followed by a rumble of laughter from the stationed guards. Ceridwen's leathers hung heavy from her shoulders. Fingers clumsy with weariness, she undid the ties and stripped down to her tunic and breeches, leathers sliding into a pile on the rushes. She toed the discarded bundle, noting how brittle the leather had become, stiff from exposure to Mindar's heat. She needed to oil it again. If she ever got out of here.

"What madness possessed you, child?"

Ceridwen swung around, reaching instinctively for sabre and steed.

"Or are you simply bent upon destruction?" Glyndwr strode toward her cell, torchlight catching on his sharp cheekbones, revealing the hollows beneath. A heavy cloak tented his narrow frame over a quilted gambeson and boiled leather stormrider harness that had no doubt better fit him in his strength. He tracked her hand, and his frown deepened. "I come as a friend."

Truly? He had pleaded at her branding. Was he here to deliver the king's will again?

"Would you have food or drink first? I can send for them."

"No." She pressed a hand to her burning forehead. "Just speak."

"Very well." He clasped his weathered hands behind his back. "I have come at the behest of the king and his war-chiefs to hear your report on the threat to Cenyon."

"Let me stand before them and–"

"Impossible." A spark ignited in his eyes. So, he was not merely the concerned friend he portrayed. "You challenged the warriors at the gate, broke into the great hall, and rode a fireborn into the presence of the king. Had you declared yourself and awaited judgment regarding the ban upon you, perhaps then you could have delivered your message in peace. Perhaps even to the gratitude of the war-chiefs and your father–"

"The king," she snapped.

"Aye, and you would do well to remember it."

His voice echoed harshly off the walls, making her cell seem even smaller than before. Ceridwen swallowed. "What became of my steed?" When the warriors had closed around her, only her grip on Mindar's mane had restrained his flames. She had dismounted and allowed herself to be taken away as he was herded in the opposite direction.

"The stablemasters have taken it in hand. It is a vicious beast. I marvel you are yet alive." Glyndwr fell silent, expression morose, and the specter of words unspoken swirled between them. Perhaps it was Bair's specter, for in reflecting upon her survival, he must recall Bair's death beneath the hooves of a fireborn like her own.

She tasted ash on her tongue. Felt heat on her cheeks.

If she looked down, she would see Bair broken at her feet–*No.*

She drew herself upright. She was an Outrider, nothing more, here to give her report. Swiftly, she explained the attack she had witnessed, prompting Glyndwr's brow to furrow.

"Then you think Nadaar will gain a landing? The Cenyon are unparalleled upon the sea."

"But the Nadaari had many ships and machines of war. They will win their landing. I sent word from every village I passed to the Outrider patrols on the borders. With aid, Cenyon may hold out until the war-hosts muster but . . ." She shrugged at the weak hope that offered.

Glyndwr urged for details on the soldiers–weapons, numbers–and the ships–troop transports or ships of war? He pressed for word of Cenyon's defenses–vessels in the harbor, active seariders, the condition of the great chain, and more. She was humbled to find that some answers evaded her. With each response, Glyndwr seemed to shrink, bowed beneath the weight, until finally, he started away with a sigh.

"All of Soldonia is at stake," Ceridwen called after him, voice ringing with the conviction that had spurred her grueling ride from the coast. "For this reason alone, I returned."

He paused, back toward her. "Then tell me, why break the *kasar* so brazenly, if defiance was not your intent?"

"I could not do otherwise." Only in speaking the words did she understand their truth. "I could not appear before him humbled and in chains. It is not in my blood."

"No . . . it is not." Shaking his head, Glyndwr returned to her cell, voice gaining in strength. "You had to appear on your own terms, defiant and foolhardy and hopelessly reckless. In Harnoth, tales are told of a fireball that raged across the sky in the dead of winter many years ago. It was a blaze of flame and glory that halted men in their tracks, awestruck. But for a breath, child, only a breath, before it was gone. So are you. A spark raging for an instant before the void. Behold the results of your terms. Could you have been any more humbled than now?"

He drew something from his cloak and passed his closed fist between the bars. "Deny it all you want, child, you two are more alike than you know." Wrinkled cloth slipped from his fingers, and he was gone. Leaving only the scarf she had abandoned in the hall.

TEN: RAFI

One weak thread can ruin a whole net.
– Alonque saying

"Oh, Nahiki." Torva's quiet, raspy voice drifted to his ears, muted as if by water, and reeled him in from a whirlwind of pain, cold, and sickening fear. He tried to push up, to just lift his head, but his body refused to obey. "What have you done to yourself, boy?"

Calloused fingers prodded his skull. He flinched and jerked back.

And realized he could not see.

Panic burst in his mind like a thunderclap, a dozen horrifying scenarios unraveling before him: He was blind. This was death. The world itself had ended.

"Torva," he gasped, reaching for the old man. "Torva, I can't see. I can't–"

"Hold still, boy." Rough cloth rubbed at his face. "Aye, that's a nasty slice on your head, but see, it's naught but blood and sand sealing your eyelids. Better?"

Sure enough, he managed to peel his eyes open and blink against the sting until Torva's wrinkled face came into focus, lit from below by an oil lamp. Night still blanketed the beach, but the lamp's lurid glow reached the monstrous form sprawled across the wreckage of Hanu's boat. He scrambled back on his haunches. His fingers brushed the scarred shaft of his harpoon, and he seized hold.

"It's dead, boy."

Nahiki stilled at Torva's quiet assurance and only then saw

the scadtha's vacant eyes, curled legs, cracked plates, and gaping wounds. Dead, yes, and *he* had done it. Struck the fatal blow even before the sea-demon crashed in on the wave and–

The sea-demon.

He lurched upright to scan the beach but saw no trace of luminous blue eyes. Heard no hint of the ghostly whisper that had demanded he fight and so saved his life. There was only the old fisherman standing limp before him, shoulders bowed and face haggard and drawn. Only the ruin of the boats. Only the slain scadtha.

"Oh, Nahiki, do you know what you have done?"

Nahiki shivered, insides twisting, head pounding with the rumble of the colt's hooves. What had he done? Saved a sea-demon and killed a scadtha and . . . condemned himself in the process. That realization was a dash of salt water against his wounds. Once Elder Gordu saw the harpoon marks, it would be over. He would send runners to summon priests from the nearest temple, and they would demand a sacrifice to appease Murloch's wrath.

The sand seemed to shift beneath his feet, and he sank toward it until Torva's thin shoulder caught under his arm and held him up, and the resulting flare of pain everywhere burst the haze clouding his vision.

"Easy, boy, easy."

"We have to . . . get rid of it."

Could they hitch it to Torva's boat and tow it out to sea? One glance at the mass smothered that idea. They could never drag it that far, not even with Sev's help, and it wasn't fair to involve him in this. Bad enough Torva was here.

"No time." Shaking his head curtly, the old fisherman wheeled him toward the jungle with a wiry, storm-hardened strength. "Those are nasty cuts you have, like as not to sour. You need shelter and tending. Dawn is coming."

And with it, the fisher tribe.

He could not hide what he had done, but they needn't find

him standing over the carcass when they emerged to launch boats into the sea.

His headache intensified with each step, disrupting his vision. His legs wobbled and went limp, and he slid from Torva's grasp. Not so much falling as sinking inevitably into the sand. It cushioned his head, tilting his face toward the sea. And there, silhouetted against white-capped waves, stood the colt. Tangled strands concealed its eyes, but he felt its gaze like a knife in his gut as it nickered and pawed at the water hissing around its hooves. A chill slithered down his neck. Had it . . . come back for him?

"Go," he whispered. "Leave me be."

Torva snorted and hauled him upright. "Ain't no one leaving you, boy."

As they rounded the first curve of the path, Nahiki strained his neck back, but the colt was gone. Vanished into the sea without a trace. *Good riddance,* the part of him that was Nahiki whispered, for so long as he had to listen to sea-demons scream, he would never be able to truly forget or be free. The part of him that was Rafi held his tongue.

"Oh, there you are."

Nahiki pried his eyes open, catching a brief glimpse of a face with thick, dark eyebrows, unruly hair, and a broken front tooth, then quickly shut them again as afternoon sunlight made his head throb. He swallowed, his throat rough and edged like fish scales. "Iakki?" he croaked. "What are you doing here?"

"Looking for you. What are you doing here?"

"Sleeping."

"In the jungle?"

Nahiki forced his eyes open again, blearily aware of his surroundings: hammock swaying underneath, palm leaves crisscrossed overhead, insects humming in the brush, and the pervasive warm, earthy scent of the Mah forest. He'd been in a feverish haze when Torva dragged him out here to lay low until trouble blew over. But how long ago had that been? It all blurred into a fog of days and nights spent alternately shivering and burning with fever, broken by clearer moments of choking down steaming fish broth or groaning as Torva cleaned his wounds by moonlight. Stained bandages swathed his bare chest and long arms, and his trousers were rumpled and soaked with sweat, but his mind felt clearer now and–

"Iakki!" He jolted up on one elbow, and the treacherous hammock threatened to tip him out. "How did you . . . what are you doing here?"

Iakki scowled. "Told you. I came looking. You promised we'd go diving again, but you didn't show. Not yesterday. Not today. Torva said you'd gone trading inland, but his nose twitches when he's lying. So, I followed him. He left you food." Iakki lifted an empty bowl and shrugged. "I ate it."

Nahiki rubbed at his aching head. "Iakki–"

"What? You were sleeping forever. I got hungry."

"You can't tell anyone you found me. I'm . . ." He stumbled to a stop. Rafi had died. Nahiki could too. It was only an identity after all. One he could easily set adrift. He fingered the beads knotted into his hair. If he had been thinking straight, he would have capsized one of the boats offshore following the fight to make it look like he had fled and drowned.

Iakki crossed his arms. "You kill that monster?"

"I . . . uh . . ."

"Thought so." The boy managed to sound remarkably unimpressed. He thrummed his fingers on the hammock ropes, producing a *twang* that Nahiki felt along every inflamed nerve. "Want to go diving? Kaya says you should find a pearl if you want to net Yeena."

"What? No, I don't–"

"I knew it!" Iakki jabbed him in the ribs. "She is too boring for you, cousin. She doesn't dive. Or laugh. Or kill scadtha."

Cold sweat prickled his chest. "Look, Iakki, you have to promise not to tell–"

"Don't worry, cousin. Yeena won't hear it from me." Iakki tossed the empty bowl into Nahiki's lap then whirled into the jungle, neatly evading his grasp. "But Sev will!"

"Iakki, no! Come back!" The hammock lurched and Nahiki fell back with a groan.

"Back? I only just arrived." Torva's wrinkled face appeared over the edge of the hammock as the old fisherman limped up and deposited a bundle on the ground. "Forgot the salve and went back to fetch it. I see you found the food I left and your appetite is back too. Reckon that means you're mending, thank Aodh."

The old fisherman's hands were calloused, his fingers knotted with arthritis, and yet he managed to gently peel back the bandages on Nahiki's chest and wipe away congealed blood and pus with a damp cloth before applying the salve. It was orange and smelled sharply of onion, and it stung as Torva smeared it into an inflamed cut across his ribs.

"Iakki was here." Nahiki eyed the fisherman, who simply pursed his lips and dug for a clean bandage. "That doesn't worry you?"

"When your boat is sinking, why bother mending your net?"

"That bad, is it?"

Torva met his eyes. "You killed a sacred beast, boy. The whole village is in uproar. Elder Gordu is out for blood–doesn't much care whose it is. With rumors of revolution stirring among the tribes, it ain't the time to bait Nadaar's soldiers. Or Murloch's priests."

Nahiki shuddered. From fever, no doubt, not fear. And it certainly wasn't fear that netted his tongue as Torva tended the rest of his cuts. Only . . . well . . . he of all people knew the dangers of enraging the empire of Nadaar.

"Nahiki!" Sev slapped aside a palm branch and burst into the clearing like a crashing wave. Nahiki struggled to sit only to be slammed into a painful hug. "You have Ches-Shu's own luck. Look at you! Killed a scadtha and came away barely scratched." He broke off with a curse as Iakki scaled him like a monkey and clung grinning to his broad shoulders. "Get down!"

Torva raised an eyebrow. "Barely a scratch, eh?"

"I am insulted by your dismissal of my great and terrible injuries," Nahiki said with a laugh. "Do not diminish my pain!"

"Fine then." Sev peeled Iakki away and casually tossed him aside. "Your fortitude astounds me, and you will doubtlessly be scarred for life. But you should be dead." He didn't know how true that was. "Seriously, a *scadtha*, Nahiki. How?"

"Would you believe it was an accident?"

"Own it, man! I would."

"*I* am not a rebel."

"You should be." Pride varnished Sev's grin. He'd always harbored a rebellious streak, but Nahiki had never before realized how deeply it ran. "Gordu has summoned Murloch's priests, can you believe it? What right have they to pass judgment on us? We claimed this coast long before any Nadaari set foot on it. It is time they remember–"

Torva rapped Sev's skull with his knuckles. "Net your tongue! Would you see your wife killed? Your village burned? Ask the Mahque if you would know what revolution betides."

"Ow." Sev rubbed his head. "Well, I needn't ask the Alonque what submission betides. The priests come and we know what they will demand." He tipped his chin at Nahiki, suddenly serious. "I'll hide a satchel with supplies inside the lightning tree–you know the one?"

Nahiki forced a swallow, throat dry, and nodded.

"Take it, cousin. Leave."

"You said you would own it."

"To the tribes, yes, not to the priests! I don't have a death wish. Run before it is too late." Shaking his head as if biting back more, Sev beckoned Iakki. "Come. Kaya has food waiting."

Iakki flopped to the ground. "Aw, why don't you argue with Torva some more? I want to see you get your head rapped again."

"Now."

The boy made a face and slunk after him, disappearing into the jungle with a rustle of leaves. Nahiki eyed the concern knotting Torva's brow as the old fisherman moved about, collecting soiled bandages.

"Think I should run, Torva?"

Torva scratched his chin. "Eh, there's sense in running. Sense in staying too."

Nahiki rubbed at his eyes. The incessant headache had started up again. "Someone will have to pay for that scadtha."

"Reckon so. It is the way of the world. Someone must bear the scars."

Tension prodded Nahiki to his feet. His legs felt strange, shaky, like they answered to another. Rotting leaves squelched underfoot, making him long for glistening sands forever washed by the sea. *Forgetting. Forgotten. Free.* From here, thick growth concealed the village, but he could just hear its distant chatter. It was only a speck wedged between the sprawling Alon coast and the vast Mah jungle. Over the past six years, he had stumbled into and sneaked out of a dozen such villages, shedding identities each time like a snake its skin. He could run. Snatch Sev's satchel. Disappear. Let Torva denounce him once he was gone.

But the priests would demand blood.

His. Or someone else's.

Rafi had seen a man sacrificed to Murloch. Bound to a stake in the waves, veins slit, left to bleed out. Or drown. Or be eaten by sea-scavengers. The man had fallen screaming to the latter. He fingered his beads. Breathed deep. "Reckon it will have to be me."

The old fisherman was silent a moment before whispering, "Aye, son, reckon so."

ELEVEN: JAKIM

Aodh is powerful.

The sun. The sun. Aodh be praised! Jakim tipped his head back, drinking in the sunshine as he scrambled up out of the hold, heedless of the soldiers waiting on deck to jostle him and his fellow captives against the rail. His eyes teared up at its brightness, but he wouldn't look away. Not after so long in the dark, haunted by the wails of distant battle, with the deeps singing their death song only the width of the bulkhead away.

Voices rang out in Soldonian.

"No, *no*."

"Tel Renaair has fallen!"

Next to him, a sailor cursed. "Skies be blazed and the Nadaari too!"

His vision cleared, and he saw a white city in ruin, choked with flame, smoke, and shattered stone. There were bodies everywhere. Some floated in the bay, bobbing on the waves like fallen leaves. More were stacked in piles on the quay. Not just men and women but horses too. That was enough to tell him where he was, and the stunned expressions of his fellow captives confirmed it.

Jakim caught at the rail. He was in *Soldonia.* It was a kingdom of fierce warriors and demon-steeds, spoken of in awed whispers in Canthor, hated in Nadaar, and as far from his home as Kerrikar.

Suddenly, the sun didn't feel so warm or bright.

Dazed, Jakim stumbled after the others as they were hustled into a line and set to work unloading the ship. Soldiers barked out orders. Slave masters lashed them with whips. Cargo workers loaded them like beasts of burden with barrels, crates, and sacks, and off they staggered down the gangplank onto the bloodstained quay where crushed stone jabbed their feet as they created new stacks, only to be rushed back onto the ship for another load.

Jakim lost count of the trips he took. Chalky dust caked his soles. His legs quivered and his back ached. Step by step, he shuffled along, and step by step felt himself slipping back into the habits that had helped him survive seven years of slavery: *hold your tongue, keep your head down, don't think, don't speak, don't make eye contact.*

A whip cracked, stinging his legs.

He tripped, jostling the captive sailor next to him who was bowed beneath a grain sack. Blood seeped beneath a stained cloth wrapped around his forehead, too narrow to conceal the ugly wound beneath. The man grunted and managed to steady them both until the whip cracked again, driving them apart.

"Strike me one more time," the sailor muttered in Soldonian, "and I'll tear that whip away and shove it down your throat. Better yet, I'll make you eat it slow."

Luckily, the slave master didn't hear him.

Or didn't speak Soldonian.

Or maybe didn't care what slaves said so long as they worked.

Still, Jakim had learned early on that troublemakers were bad news, so he tried to put some distance between them. It worked until a cargo worker dropped one end of a crate into his hands and the bloodied sailor caught the other, but the sailor just grunted and maneuvered to hold it behind his back as he walked down the gangplank.

Some kind of a commotion broke out ahead, stalling the line of carriers. Jakim winced as the sailor came to an abrupt halt beside one of the piles of corpses and tried to get his legs better positioned under him to support the crate's weight.

"You learned in the holy writ?"

Jakim startled at the rasped Soldonian words.

"Yeah, you." The sailor looked over his shoulder, revealing

rough features, a hard jaw, and a sharply slanted mouth. Tangled strands of straw-colored hair reached his chin. He didn't seem to feel the weight of the crate like Jakim did. Maybe because he was built like a water buffalo, all lean muscle and corded limbs with a neck as thick as a palm trunk. "Must know some of it, being a Scroll and all. Tell me, what hope does the holy writ offer here?"

The answer came by rote, words he had memorized, truths inked into his skin. "The hope that Aodh crafts good out of all things. It is in the holy writ sixty times and more." He had counted it when he first came to the Sanctuary, desperate for something to counteract his anger.

"Then the scriptures lie." The sailor's voice was flat. He jerked his chin toward the corpses piled high beside them, and Jakim ducked his head, not wanting to see. But there was a gravity to that mound that drew him to look despite himself and name what he saw.

There, a hoof. There, a hand. There, a face.

Everywhere, death. Bile flooded his throat, and he choked it down.

Leaving Kerrikar had seemed so right, despite Scrollmaster Gedron's warning that Aodh's purposes were not always clear, despite his advice to stay and continue learning, despite the lie that had fallen so readily from Jakim's lips. Maybe if he had listened, he would know what to say now. Maybe none of this would have happened.

Raised voices interrupted his thoughts. Was that Canthorian? The line was inching forward again, and in the gaps between slaves, Jakim caught glimpses of a helmeted Nadaarian officer glaring at an elderly man standing between him and a stoop-shouldered figure leaning on an iron-tipped cane and clad in flowing trousers and a high-collared robe, tapestried in the style favored by wealthy Canthorians. Gold markings swirled across his shaved skull, and the symbol for the number ten was inked on his pale forehead, labeling him a high-ranking scholar of the tenth order. Jakim couldn't remember which discipline that order claimed:

mathematics, alchemy? His final master had been a scholar too, but in the seventh order, philosophy.

As they neared, Jakim overheard the elderly man speaking in Nadaarian. "My master demands an accounting for his missing trunks. He was assured by the tsemarc that his belongings would be treated with the utmost respect and–"

The officer cut him off. "Tell your master this is an invasion fleet and we have no space for luxuries. Something had to stay behind. Better his trunks than supplies for our soldiers. They will be delivered when reinforcements ship out. Until then, he can make do like the rest of us."

The elderly man began to translate the words into Canthorian, but his master spoke sharply over him. "By the thirteen orders, the man is an imbecile! Ask him what Tsemarc Izhar will say when he discovers that my most important manuscripts, the research vital to his success and the whole reason I am here in this savage country, were left behind–"

"Wonder what's the rock in his hoof?" the sailor muttered, snapping Jakim's attention from the conversation.

Rock in his . . . *hoof*? That was a new idiom.

Jakim logged it away, translating by habit as he had for Scroll Enok since leaving Kerrikar. "Some of his belongings were left behind when they sailed. He is displeased." Which was putting it mildly.

"You speak Canthorian?"

He shrugged. "Yes." Not as well as his native Eliami or Nadaarian but better than Soldonian or the three or four other languages he had collected since the slave caravan hauled him kicking and screaming from his home.

"Huh." The sailor picked up the pace to sidestep the heated conversation.

Unfortunately, the Canthorian scholar chose that moment to turn, colliding with the crate. He collected himself, then lashed out with his cane, catching the sailor's arm with a sickening crack as he swept past. The sailor dropped his end of the crate. Jakim stumbled, unable to steady it on his own. It slipped and fell with a crack, and he danced back to keep his toes from being crushed. A shadow fell over him, and he looked up to see the scholar studying him with a strange expression on his face, taking in the markings on his arms, the symbol on his bare chest.

The sailor lunged, fists clenched.

"No!" Jakim caught his arm. And a glare. "No, you'll be killed." His risked glance revealed only the scholar's back as he strolled away, apparently unconcerned. Jakim still dropped his voice. "Keep your head down. Bide your time. Trust me, it's the only way to survive as a slave."

Chest heaving, the sailor yanked his arm away. "I expect you know much about being a slave, *Scroll*. But I was not born to be one."

Me neither. Jakim bit back the words. The sailor's disdain reminded him of Amir, and that rattled him, but he wasn't ready to speak another lie so soon. Siba's prophecy had never seemed farther from fulfillment. Maybe he was destined to be only a slave. What was he to do then, accept his lot? Forget his vows, his family, his mission?

Never. He bent over the crate and flinched as a lash grazed his shoulder.

The sailor cursed, glaring at the slave master. "We're going! What's the rush? Afraid the Cenyon will return to plant your heads on tridents? Now that's a sight I'd die to see."

Slowly, the slave master coiled his whip with a grin that didn't exactly strike Jakim as afraid. When he spoke, it was in startlingly fluent Soldonian. "No, demon-rider, we march inland. The Dominion of Murloch has come for your nation. But do not worry. You will live to see it."

TWELVE: CERIDWEN

Riveren are akin to seabloods but with coats of muted browns and dappled grays that are far better suited to the freshwater rivers, pools, and streams where they dwell.

"Stubborn as a sand-blasted earthhewn, now didn't I say that?" Ceridwen would recognize that rangy drawl anywhere. She rolled up to her feet, muscles aching after exercising to relieve the boredom of her imprisonment, and wiped her face with the back of her hand, only then bothering to look. Cloaked in the grime of travel, Markham te Hoard, Apex of the Outriders, lounged against the bars, a wolfish tint to his scowl. She had not heard him approach, but then he was a shadowrider, and though the sol-breath affected all riders, some showed it more truly than others. None so truly as the Apex.

"Always knew that fire-pit between your ears would be your downfall." He shook his grizzled head, disheveled hair sticking out along the strap of his eyepatch. "Warned te Donal about your stubbornness. He was supposed to keep you from doing some fool thing like, oh I don't know, flaming at the king in his own hall."

"You told him I was reckless."

"Aye, that too." His scowl twisted into a grin. "You look like Koltar spat you out again."

She felt like it too, tunic and breeches stiff with grime and sweat, leathers still rolled in a bundle she had been using as a pillow. She glared at him, dragging her tangled hair over her shoulder and wrestling it into a braid. "It's been three weeks."

Three weeks since she had stormed Rysinger and been doomed to this tomb. Three weeks of inaction that, after three years more often in the saddle than out, had set her bones on edge as the walls seemed to close in, intent on crushing the air from her lungs. Even worse, it had been three weeks of silence from the king. No word on her fate. Or the nation's.

Markham squinted. "That long?"

She knew better than to expect sympathy from him. His had been a gruff and unshrinking tutelage since the moment she'd ridden up on her plunging fireborn and demanded to join the Outriders. "Ride for it," he'd said with his wolfish grin, and she had not understood his meaning until the riders of his patrol formed a gauntlet of flashing hooves and scabbarded sabres. She had been beaten soundly. Still, she'd clung staunchly to her wild steed, fresh from the crater, and Markham had not only accepted her without a second glance at the bandage on her forehead, he had given her a place in his own *ayed*. He had equipped, trained, and armed her for battle. But he had never sheltered her.

If he had come here now . . .

Markham barked a sharp laugh, and she caught the gleam of his one good eye beneath his shaggy gray hair. "Relax, tor Nimid. Not even the threat of your execution could have forced me to set foot within the shadow of these lifeless walls." In all the time she had known him, he had refused even a tent, preferring to sleep with his face to the sky. "*Keeps a man honest,*" he'd told her, "*knowing that the stars are watching.*" Twitching aside his cloak, he drew a flask from his belt and tossed back a swallow. "But war, it rides us all."

"How goes it? War?"

"I'm here, aren't I?" Corking the flask, Markham waved a guard forward with a key. The lock groaned, and the hinges creaked open. "Gear up, tor Nimid. You're free."

Stunned, she simply stood there as he strode away.

The guard rattled the door, and she scrambled to seize her leathers and hurried after Markham. His long, loping stride had already carried him to the end of the passage, but she caught up as he exited the great house, skimmed down the steps, and set off across the greensward. Here, the fortress pulsed with the atmosphere of war. Banners from all seven chiefdoms dotted grass torn by the passage of hooves. Solborn and riders darted past on errands while streams of sack-laden youths marched between storehouses and supply wagons. Soldonian war-hosts traveled at speed, each warrior carrying only three days' worth of supplies. Waiting for the convoy would slow them, so youths served as runners, riding unarmored on shadowers and stormers to restock the main forces.

"This is the second wave preparing to ride," Markham said without slacking pace. "We gather at Idolas on the border of Cenyon. The Nadaari march inland as we speak."

So, it had happened then. The coast had been lost.

Ceridwen's steps stalled. She had trained all her life for war. In the saddle as soon as she could stand. Sword in hand as soon as she could lift it. Countless hours spent studying the tactics of ancient battles. As an Outrider, that training had assumed flesh and bone. She had sworn to defend the land as tor Nimid, even if she could not as tal Desmond. This was her fight, and she had wasted weeks in a cell while the kingdom burned. To *blazes* with her wretched pride.

She shook her head. "How did this happen?"

"Numbers. Sheer mathematics. Neither solborn nor riders are invincible, you know."

"No, how did we not see it coming?" That question had been plaguing her. Commanding the defense of Soldonia's borders required Markham to keep his ears to the ground for whispers of threatening movement. He should have heard rumors of such a massive invasion.

"All reports from our envoy in Nadaar indicated the emperor was focused inward on rebels among the Que tribes, while his troops amassed to march northward to dispel uprisings in Slyrchar," Markham informed her. "Blinded us to the threat. Now, word is that our envoy has been dead for months. Sand-blasted shame. I actually liked the man."

"So the reports were–"

"Faked, aye. Cunning devils."

Ceridwen had never before seen Markham caught off guard. He struck her as a man flexing his arm after his sword has been beaten from his grip.

"Nadaar's envoy, Tormark, disappeared just before the invasion." He snorted. "Not that having him in hand would mean aught for negotiations, but an execution does raise morale."

She raised an eyebrow. "How did you get me released?"

"The king and his war-chiefs have far weightier concerns than your foolish stunt. The Fox himself championed your release."

"Eagan?"

The war-chief of Craignorm was half-Rhiakki like her mother. His relation to the pale-skinned fighting tribes that inhabited the mountains of Rhiakkor beyond Soldonia's embattled northeastern border could be seen in the changing nature of his eyes, from light brown to green to blue to gold, depending on the light. It had shown in her mother's eyes too, but Ceridwen's eyes and skin were bronze like her father's.

She shook her head. "Why would Eagan want *me* released?"

"Not from pity, no fear of that. Some foolery about it being better for the nation if the warrior spirits decided your fate." Markham lifted a forefinger to the center of his brow as they passed the Sanctuary of the Scrolls. She had forgotten he was so devout. Most Soldonians offered only nominal acknowledgment to the deity who bore the wounds of the world. It was the spirits of ancient heroes and their mighty steeds that most sought to honor by earning glory in battle and in strength of arms. Ceridwen found the pursuit of their favor thrilling, if somewhat . . . unfulfilling? How could one know their favor had been earned? Was survival sign enough?

She had pleasant memories of visiting the Sanctuary with her mother years ago. It had been run by a kindly old woman then, but the thatched building was shuttered now, its garden withered, and the carvings of holy writ upon posts and lintel no longer legible. The death of his wife had rattled the king's faith. The death of his son seemed to have shattered it.

"He's right about one thing," Markham continued as they neared the stables lining the inner wall of the fortress. "Every sword will be sore needed. We may all stand before Aodh soon enough. Pray he shows you mercy and Eagan's bloodthirsty spirits have no say–"

"Ceridwen?"

That voice was beautifully, achingly familiar.

She spun around. "Gavin?"

Wiry arms wrapped around her. "It has been too long."

She stood stiff until catching a whiff of ginger clinging to his clothing. That scent released a surge of memories. Her mother's heritage meant she had few relatives in Soldonia, and even at twelve years her senior, her cousin Gavin had always been the closest. A childhood disease of the lungs had left him little stamina for swordplay, but few could match his skill as a riverrider. And when it came to tactics, she had finished many a strategy game baffled as he claimed the victor's crown over her slaughtered pieces. Sometimes, they had played as teams–Gavin and her against Bair and Rhodri. Those had been sweet, simple times then.

Blazes, she hadn't seen him since before the *kasar.*

Markham coughed. She drew back and Gavin released her. "Your steed's at the back." Markham jerked a thumb toward the stable doorway. "Tack up, await my return, and keep that pit-spawned fireborn in check. Maybe if you're set on taming him, you'll be less likely to spark a fire you can't quench." Judging from his stance as he strode away, he didn't hold out much hope.

"You should have come to us, Wen." Gavin brushed a strand of hair the same shade of copper as hers from his eyes. His face was thinner, his eyes more shadowed, and his shoulders stooped as his cough rattled in his chest. He had been named a chieftain of Lochrann since her exile, one of seven sworn to answer her father as war-chief and king, yet he greeted her as though nothing had changed. "Fiona and I would have welcomed you at Soras Ford. You need not have been alone."

She had not sought out any kin after the branding. Shame had forbidden it. Pride too.

"Still, you are home and riding to war as a daughter of Lochrann. All will be well."

He sounded so hopeful, but it had been long since she had considered Rysinger her home. Longer still since she'd considered the king her father. "I ride as tor Nimid of the Outriders, Gav. I am nothing more."

Gavin's eyes narrowed. He, like Bair, had ever chosen his words with care. "You *are* more, Wen. Your father may not admit it, but he needs you. And you need him."

She needed atonement, and if risking her life to deliver tidings of the invasion was not enough, then she would seek it on the battlefield and find it too, in death if need be. She turned to leave and swung abruptly back to face him, a prayer for his safety rising in her throat. But she had not prayed since her screams had echoed back unanswered from the crater walls. "Gav–"

"I know," he said softly. "May Aodh be with you too."

Just as Markham had said, Ceridwen found her "pit-spawned" fireborn in a stall at the back, pacing restlessly before a charred feed-rack. The stables were divided into sections designed to accommodate the needs of each solborn breed. Seabloods inhabited an open space where Cenyon white stone seeped salt into the trickle of water that spilled from aqueducts above. Earthhewns dwelled within solid, mountain-root stone fitted with iron bands to withstand an accidental hoof strike. Shadowers grazed in cool airiness within a wooden hall crowned with an ivy-thatched roof that rustled in every breeze. Here in the fireborn enclosure, the half walls were constructed from the dark, rippled stones of the

Gauroth range, embers flickered in braziers, and firerock from the hearts of craters radiated warmth underfoot.

Solborn were not meant to be caged, so in peace, the stables were reserved for the ill and injured while the greensward served as a practice ground for warriors and free range for their steeds. But in war, every space was needed to house the mustering war-hosts.

Mindar's ears pricked at her footsteps, and he nickered. She slipped into his stall, noting her saddle on a rack outside gleaming beneath a fresh coat of skivva oil, then ran a hand across his neck. She pulled back before any sparks could singe her gloveless fingers. "Missed me?"

He snorted into the empty feed-rack.

"Missed food, more like."

He pawed the ground, and the smooth curve of his hooves caught her attention. Someone had trimmed away the rough edges worn by their journey. One of the horsemasters? Once, she had spent every spare moment pestering them for the secrets of their trade: the art of bonding with all the solborn breeds. Mornings begun before dawn, observing the herds; afternoons drenched in sweat out on the greensward, learning the use of seat, weight, leg, and hand; and evenings dreaming of the Sol-Donair when she would claim a wildborn from the crater of Koltar.

Memories seeped like smoke from every corner of this place: there, she had saddled her first steed and mounted under her father's watchful eye; there, she and Bair had tripped Rhodri into fresh manure, and she had never laughed so hard; and there, she had oiled her catch-rope and leathers after issuing her challenge to Bair.

She had been so confident, so certain of her own invulnerability. And his.

Shivering, Ceridwen dropped her bundled leathers and plunged her arms into a nearby water trough, sweeping a space clear of floating debris. Three weeks in a cell after that sixty-league ride had left grime rooted beneath her skin. She dunked her head, worked her fingers through her tangled hair, and then flung her head back. Water splashed down her neck and shoulders and soaked her tunic. Shaking it away, she spun and rammed shoulder first into a man's chest.

He grunted and stumbled back. "*Shades.*"

Growling, a wolfhound lunged for her legs. She lurched back, reaching for her sabre, and her fingers grasped at nothing. No belt. No scabbard. No blade. No steed to flame–

"Peace, Cù."

The wolfhound sat, still snarling softly.

Ceridwen met the man's eyes and caught her breath. "Finnian." Theirs had been a short, strained pairing, as Outrider pairings went, but seeing him so unexpectedly doused her again in the fear of that moment on the beach when he had fallen with a bolt in his shoulder and poison in his veins. Caught by the firestorm that swirled in her wake.

He bore no sign of that injury now, only a hint of stiffness as he worked his shoulder. But his stained jerkin and torn cloak looked battle-worn, and the scruff of several days' growth darkened his chin. She was suddenly acutely aware of her own damp tunic, the stink of the cell clinging to her clothes, and the wet hair matted against her neck, and something plummeted uncomfortably inside her.

She forced herself to move, sidestepping him to retrieve her leathers. "Not dead yet, I see."

"No, nor you."

"Too stubborn, I suppose."

He cracked a smile at that. "Can't deny it."

Beneath her saddle rack, she found her pot of skivva oil–replenished, no doubt by Markham–and a damp rag. Her sabre hung from the saddlebow. She rubbed her thumb across its worn grip and lowered herself cross-legged onto the warm firerock, spreading out her leather chaps, jerkin, boots, and gloves. Dipping the rag, she began to work the viscous liquid into the cracks. If it was to war she rode, she must be ready for fire. But Markham had been short on details. Perhaps Finnian could fill her in.

"Were you in Cenyon when the coast fell?"

He nodded, leaning with his back to the stall. "It took five days." His words came slowly, thick with memory as he described the fall of the city to a hundred Nadaari ships and the final stand of the Cenyon on the quay, where crushed stone crumbled like chalk beneath the hooves of their steeds and the slain clogged the bay. "Once the city had emptied, we retreated. Left a third of our forces dead. Two days later, the Nadaari marched inland. They outnumbered us ten to one, but still we charged them. Day after day. Might as well have tried stopping a boulder from rolling down a mountain. The impetus behind their march could not be broken."

Only five days. Then Tel Renaair had fallen the same day she'd reached Rysinger.

"No help came?"

"Some trickled in. Lord Rhodri brought seven thousand from the war-chiefs, and Markham's *ayed* joined us, but ten thousand is little enough against thirty."

Ceridwen dropped her rag. "Thirty *thousand*?"

"Aye, and more arrive daily."

This was war on a scale Soldonia had not faced in centuries. The might of Nadaar and all its conquered territories had come and would not stop until their fields were scattered with bleached bones, their strength crushed, their life sucked from the marrow. Sickened, Ceridwen capped the oil and shrugged into her gear as it dried, numbly fastening straps and belting on her sabre.

"So long as they control the coast," Finnian said, "Nadaar can summon reinforcements at will, and Aodh only knows how many kingdoms now supply levies to their banners. Markham is here to meet the king. Brought me along for my report–"

"Blast his earthhewn stubbornness!" Markham te Hoard stormed into the stable with three Outriders at his heels. Their sudden entrance startled a spray of sparks from Mindar that sizzled harmlessly against stone, but Ceridwen leaped to his head to calm him before he released a more dangerous blast. "Thought I told you to tack up, tor Nimid? It's time to ride."

Finnian straightened. "Are we headed back to the fight?"

"Not yet. I don't need you at the fight. I need three thousand more like you." Markham's eye settled on Ceridwen again. "What are you waiting for? Get moving."

Ceridwen rapidly saddled her steed as Finnian's whistle sent the scarred wolfhound bounding away. Cù returned a moment later with Finnian's shadower trailing behind. Now *that* was a handy trick. Meanwhile, her fireborn shifted impatiently as she tightened his cinch, sparks flying from his stamping hooves, unconcerned with how incompetent he made her appear.

"Need a hand?" Finnian asked

Mindar snorted, flooding her with smoke. Blinking through the sting, she shot Finnian an exasperated look. "Depends. Do you want to keep it?"

He raised both hands in mock surrender. "Whoa, just asking."

"If you two are finished . . ." Markham's voice dripped acid as he lounged on the half wall, and, duly sobered, Finnian fell in with the others while Ceridwen bridled. "I'm dispatching the lot of you to the border stations to muster the rest of the Outriders to Idolas. Our king would have us ride at his side."

"His *side*?" Ceridwen jerked back, leaving the throat-latch undone.

Once, the king had been a mighty warrior, an earthrider and expert lancer. But the man she had seen in the great hall had no place on a battlefield. Not any longer. Her fault. Something in him had died with Bair.

"Aye, tor Nimid." Markham sighed. "Recklessness seems a family trait. Now mount up. The king rides to war."

THIRTEEN: CERIDWEN

Stormers are bred for swift aerial attacks and can summon lightning from a storm-charged atmosphere and direct it upon their foes. Beware their powered strike.

Below, the valley of Idolas burned. Ceridwen halted her ash-streaked steed atop the central hill of the four that formed the Soldonian lines, eyes wide at the sight. A thousand flickering tongues of fire rose from a sea of torches, revealing the strength of the Nadaarian army sprawled across the westernmost three of the seven hills ringing the valley—thirty thousand, Finnian had said? *Blazes*, their numbers must have grown.

She urged Mindar onward, following the ridge rearward toward the command tent. After ten days in the saddle, she had feared to find the battle already ended. It seemed she had arrived just in time. The hills were alive with the muffled stamp of hooves, creaking tack, and rattling weapons as the war-hosts drew up in ranks. Mindar's flanks were cool and lathered with ash from their latest run, and pale smoke rose from his nostrils. Still, he lifted his legs high, prancing, and the muscles stood out on his arched neck as he wove through the tide of moving solborn and warriors, blood stirred by the sense of impending battle that permeated the hillside.

Something was about to happen.

Markham slouched on a barrel outside the command tent, reins draped across his knees. Motionless in the shadows, like a shadow himself within the folds of his cloak, save for the glint of moonlight in his single eye and crooked grin. He acknowledged her with a nod. "Tor Nimid." Uncorked his flask and tossed back a swallow.

"Apex." She dismounted, landing with a jolt. She craned her neck and rolled her shoulders, working out the stiffness. Markham offered the flask, and she downed a sip. Ninety leagues and more had been her assigned circuit of the Outrider border stations, while Finnian and the others had ridden in opposite directions to do the same. Each station she'd visited had dispatched riders to carry the summons onward before making their way inward, a hundred tributaries all rushing to the sea. Or in this case, to Idolas and war.

"Have the others returned yet?"

Markham pursed his lips and nodded. "Most. The *ayeds* have been pouring in—not a moment too soon." A jerk of his chin indicated the command tent. Within, voices rose in heated discussion. Rhodri's calm voice soothed the others, answered a moment later by Glyndwr's rasp. Ceridwen caught herself straining to hear one specific voice and cursed herself for a fool. Still, with Gavin's words outside the stable still fresh in her mind, she could not refrain from asking.

"And the king?"

"Aye." Markham took another pull from his flask. "That's all of them in there—save Telweg. She split off to stalk a raiding party, and the Nadaarian advance cut her off from our lines. Last report, her forces had drawn up a mile or so to the rear of the Nadaari—"

Mindar shrilled a whinny, head rising. The keening scream of a seablood answered, and a dappled steed skidded up to the command tent with another half dozen at its heels. Sweat slicked its hide, and mud spattered its scaled legs. Mail clinking, the rider leaped down. Ceridwen recognized her even before she lifted her visor, revealing a face like Cenyon's white stone.

"Lady Telweg." Markham bowed his head in acknowledgment. All the acidity had melted from his tone. It sounded so unlike him that Ceridwen flicked him a sideways glance. "We heard you were cut off."

"Aye, were." Telweg's breastplate was dented and splashed with blood, yet in her tilted chin and flared nostrils, Ceridwen read a steely satisfaction. "These foot-bound Nadaari are no match for bonded riders. I trust your Outriders will shield our lines better?"

Ceridwen stiffened at the woman's dismissive gaze, and the dampened fire in her chest burst aflame again. She had risked life and freedom to carry Cenyon's call for aid to Rysinger. Gratitude was too much to ask for. But what price must she pay for respect?

"My Outriders know their duty," Markham said simply.

Motioning for her warriors to remain, Telweg swept toward the command tent. Four lesser chieftains emerged as she entered and rode off with warriors at their heels, energy surging in their wake. It resonated in the predawn hush, hummed among the Cenyon warriors waiting beside their steeds, and whispered in the silent descent of riders toward the valley. It left Ceridwen with the same sensation she felt when flames pooled in Mindar's gut, heating his ribcage and showering sparks from his mane: it was an unleashing.

She turned back to Markham. As Apex over all five Outrider *ayeds*, Markham held as high a ranking as any war-chief, answerable only to the king and battlemaster. He belonged in the command tent on the eve of battle. If he sat without, matters must have already come to a head. Or his patience had run out. "It's beginning, isn't it?"

"Aye, tor Nimid." Markham released a breath, and for an instant, she saw the man within through the naked gleam of his eye. It was a strange and humbling thing, for though he had seen her broken down a dozen times and more since she'd joined the Outriders with her fireborn untamed and *kasar* brand yet raw, he did not lower his guard lightly. "It is beginning."

Mindar perked his ears, nickering deep in his throat.

"Then I timed my arrival poorly," Finnian called, striding up alongside his shadower. Out of the corner of her eye, Ceridwen watched Markham seal himself like a flask, becoming impregnable again behind his caustic grin. "Hoped you'd ended the war by now, and I'd be free for that leave you've been promising."

"On the contrary," Markham drawled, "the battle hosts have

awaited your arrival. Now that you have seen fit to appear, the horns sound at dawn. You two are stationed in the rearguard. Next hill over. Report to chieftains Kilmark and Ondri. Move fast enough and you may snag an hour or two of sleep before the fight."

Finnian halted with one foot in the stirrup. "We are riding together?"

"Aye, te Donal. You are a pair."

"Well yes, but–"

Ceridwen cut him off. "We are assigned the rearguard?"

Markham rolled his eyes to hers. "Is that a question, tor Nimid? Because–unless my wits fail me–I believe I gave you your orders. King Desmond has named Rhodri his battlemaster, and Rhodri has named the Outriders his eyes and ears. If you ask me, it's a pit-spawned waste of manpower and horseflesh when we've summoned nigh all our defenses from the borders. But I'll thank you not to ask me and simply do as you're told. And if you find that task too painful"–he tapped the flask at his belt–"I'm told hearty application serves as a balm for wounded pride."

But it was not her pride that troubled her as she visited the Outrider's armory tent, where she added a red cuirass and mail skirt to her leathers, and then rode away with Finnian to the rearguard, where she no doubt would be able to snag some sleep. They would have little enough to do in the coming fight. And that was the problem. Her release had been secured so her fate would be decided by the warrior spirits. She had expected a death mission. In truth, she had hoped for it. If only so she could be rid of the *kasar* once and for all.

Dawn had not yet broken when the muffled rumble of hooves stirred Ceridwen from fitful sleep, followed by the throb of heavy wings filling the air. She bolted upright, tightened her cinch, and swung into the saddle to overlook the valley from her assigned position beside Finnian. Behind, the rest of the rearguard, nearly four hundred riders, spread out over the hill. Then all was silent again, save for the sound of those wings.

The stormers had launched.

Ceridwen could barely distinguish the blue-gray shapes gliding overhead, broad wings rising and falling, tails streaming behind. They held tight formations, wingtips nearly touching, covering the sky. What must it be like to ride the winds? Harnessed in a saddle, stroking bowstring and fletching while soaring above friend and foe to rain down death from on high?

"Cloudless," she observed. "No lightning today." Even her whisper sounded loud in that expectant hush.

Finnian tilted his head back, sniffing. "Aye, it does not smell like rain."

In the energy-charged atmosphere of certain clouds, stormers could summon lightning upon their foes. Clear skies meant arrows would open the battle instead. Not nearly so dramatic as a lightning strike but effective enough. It also meant no rain would dampen Mindar's fire or mood–not that he would have opportunity to flame trapped in the rearguard. She fidgeted with her sabre, scanning the surrounding grim faces, taut reins, and anxious steeds. Did they share her restlessness? Four hundred strong, mostly riders bearing the decorative sun emblem of Rhodri's chiefdom, Ardon, with a unit of Outriders scattered among them. Another unit patrolled with whistling signal arrows in case the Nadaari sought to outflank them.

Blazes, she wished she was among them. Moving rather than waiting here.

Hooves thudded as two chieftains swept up to view the valley. She recognized the earthrider, a tall man with long dark hair that nearly concealed the double-blade of the axe strapped to his back: Kilmark te Bruin. She had sparred with him once–she a reckless child, he old enough to know better. It had ended in a draw, but Kilmark's skill had since become renowned. That balding, brutish shadowrider at his side would be Ondri te Velyn, who had five sons said to be as thick-skulled, brash-tongued, and obstinate as he. Both were minor chieftains sworn to Rhodri's banner.

"It's a strange thing," Finnian said, and in the glassy sea of his eyes, breaking light paled the reflection of distant torches. "One moment, it's just another dawn."

Above, a thousand bowstrings sang.

His jaw tightened. "The next, the world burns."

They could not hear the hiss of a thousand arrows descending, but the spreading light revealed the enemy position, sheltered behind an earthen breastwork at the base of the three hills. The stormers fired in waves as they soared overhead, each line wheeling to the rear and advancing again. War horns blared, arrows fell in sheets, and Nadaari screamed and died. But they did not retaliate.

Rumbling shook the earth. Below, two lines of earthhewns advanced into the valley and gradually picked up speed. Fireborn followed in a loose mass, shielded behind the larger steeds with their legs of iron, necks like cedar, and hides like stone. They would be tasked with weakening the breastwork. That was where she should be. Atonement could not be earned in the rearguard. Maybe that was the goal, to deny her the chance to be rid of the *kasar* through glory or death.

"What is this?" Finnian muttered. "Why don't they attack?"

Gongs crashed in the wake of his voice, resounding through the valley. Spear-like bolts launched from the Nadaari and swept a cloud of stormers from the sky. Riderless steeds sheared away and steedless riders flailed as they fell. Whistling filled the air, and stones arced out and dropped, tearing through the fireborn, felling riders, and smashing into the earthhewn who stumbled but staggered on, for stones alone could not halt them.

"*Blazes*!" Ceridwen rose in her stirrups, searching for the barrage's origin. "You were saying?"

"There. On the hills."

Of course, Finnian had spotted it first. His eyes rivaled his wolfhound's for sharpness—though he'd left Cù behind in Rysinger for safekeeping. She tracked his arm and then could see where clustered soldiers had concealed the war machines on the enemy hilltops and flanks: ballistae and mangonels, one like a giant crossbow, the other with a scoop for throwing stones.

"Rhodri should have attacked at once. Not tarried while they built fortifications and war machines." Finnian waved his hand in frustration. "They wield our delay against us."

But such designs were the craft of the island empire of Canthor not Nadaar, and until today, had existed for Ceridwen merely in the manuscripts she had been required to read as a king's daughter training for war. Now she watched, helpless, as riders charged into the onslaught. Hails of arrows glanced off the front ranks of earthhewn. Ballistae bolts hammered them and shattered. Beneath an avalanche of hurtled stones, they advanced until only a hundred strides away, then the earthhewn line melted into smaller columns that pulled back to regroup, while the fireborn dashed through the deadly hail and flooded the breastwork with flames.

"I need a patrol." Abruptly, Kilmark te Bruin wheeled and jogged down the line. "You seven with me, and you, you"—Ceridwen straightened as he skipped past Finnian to her—"and you, at once."

The selected riders fell into a double-file column behind him, and Ceridwen found herself in the center. Dark smoke shot from Mindar's nostrils. After forced inaction, he was ready to run, to burn, to rage against the world, so she stroked his neck until he settled into a rocking gait that matched Kilmark's pace as he led them over the saddle between hills and the battle unfolded before them again. The valley shuddered as earthhewns charged in three massive blocks. As their strides lengthened, the front block sharpened into a *V* formation for maximum impact. Bone crushing, rock shattering, mountain breaking—it was the ramming charge.

Shadowers raced after them, ghosting in and out of the smoke of the fireborn at their heels. Stormers wheeled around the war machines—some attacking from above, others landing and striking from the ground. For all Rhodri as battlemaster might be faulted for delaying the fight, this was a bold stroke, calculated to overwhelm the Nadaari. The hills were emptied of cavalry. All were committed now, save the rearguard and–

Ceridwen's breath caught.

There, in the front beneath the flaming banner of Lochrann, rode the king.

Mounted on a massive black-horned earthhewn whose powerful strides devoured the ground, he sat tall in the saddle, this father of hers, fierce in plate mail, lance couched, sinking deep in the stirrups to brace for impact. For a moment, she saw the warrior king and not the absent, grief-stricken husk he had become.

With collision imminent, a gong crashed, and the Nadaari soldiers lining the breastwork turned and fled. They *fled*! Ceridwen shrilled the Outrider battle cry as the lead earthhewns leaped and pummeled the breastwork. It crumbled beneath hooves that could demolish a stone wall, and the roar of its fall and the shout of a hundred, hundred tongues sent heat swelling through her veins, while the banner of Lochrann soared over the steeds surging past the collapse.

Blazes, it had worked.

Then the earth opened beneath their hooves and swallowed them.

Riders hauled on their reins, but nothing could halt an earthhewn charge at its peak. Those behind rammed into those in front, and the column dissolved into a thrashing mass that poured over the edge of a pit. Screams ripped across the valley and the blood roared in Ceridwen's ears, until all other sounds faded before a single, raw, heart-wrenching wail.

Somewhere in that teeming sea of death, was the king.

Her father.

FOURTEEN: RAFI

Only a fool seeks wisdom in the gaze of a stone-eye.
– Choth adage

Rafi arrived last to the beach on the day he would die.

Gongs had crashed as the sun starting sinking toward the horizon, summoning the villagers down the jungle path to the shore where the temple procession paraded toward the scadtha's sun-bleached corpse. Arriving first would only have weakened his resolve, left him shivering and unmade and incapable of carrying out his plan, so Rafi had dawdled while the others began their silent march, savoring the warmth of the sun on his skin, the taste of cool mint leaf on his tongue, the scent of the sea.

Now he worried that arriving last might make him look afraid.

You are afraid, his own voice whispered in his head.

Yes, but he didn't want everyone to know it. Breath stale in his lungs, he gripped his harpoon as he caught up and plunged into the sea of clenched knuckles, set jaws, and bowed shoulders. The atmosphere seethed with quiet resentment, stifled terror, and anger.

Elder Gordu glared at him as he jostled into place beside Torva. After a week recuperating in the jungle, alternately tormented by stinging flies and Iakki's pranks—sometimes, he wasn't sure which was worse—Rafi had melted back into village life under cover of a lie about hiking inland to establish trade with a distant Mahque tribe. Two weeks later and Gordu was clearly still suspicious, but Rafi had only held to the lie to shield Torva from the consequences of sheltering him. There would be no living with Gordu once he admitted the truth. Then again, Rafi wouldn't *have* to live with him. He would be dead. For real, this time.

Torva set a hand on his shoulder and squeezed.

Tears–no, *sand*, of course, it was sand–stung his eyes.

Gongs crashed again, parting the villagers so the temple procession could flood the ring. Massive stone-eye tigers drew gilded chariots carrying four priests in flowing scarlet robes and ornate gold headpieces. Chains draped from manacles on their wrists and necks, jingling with the rattle of the wheels. Rafi dropped his eyes as the tigers passed, not wanting to be trapped by their gaze. Nadaari soldiers marched behind, five of them, trailed by three devotees in loose orange robes and veils that seemed to float as they danced with blue scarves flying from wrists and elbows, almost like wings or fins or rippling water.

Painful silence suffocated the beach. No noise but the shuffle of feet in the sand; the clank of the priests' chains; and the deep, snuffling breaths of the tigers. It made Rafi want to shout, just to break it, as the seconds crawled and the shadows lengthened, reaching out from the jungle to claim the shore. The priests at last descended from their chariots to circle the scadtha, and, spears in hand, they began to chant. Not loudly at first. Just a muttered string of incomprehensible words that somehow conjured images in Rafi's mind nonetheless. Blood. Dripping. Staining the sacrificial waters. And looming above, the cold eyes of the Silent One, lidded in slumber.

Splashing broke the spell, snapping Rafi's attention to the soldiers wading out into the surf carrying wooden stakes. His stomach tightened. Almost time.

As one, the priests crashed their spears together, and the chanting stopped.

"Judgment rises to claim you, an unholy people," one of the priests, a gaunt man with mountains for cheekbones and caverns for eyes, intoned. Yellow flecks in his irises marked him as being of Choth descent, one of the first tribes conquered by the Nadaari long ago. "You waver in submission to the Dominion of Murloch.

You cling to ancient deities and harbor one who has committed an unthinkable crime–"

"Holy one!" Gordu broke from the crowd and knelt, his muscled bulk straining the beaded vest that proclaimed his status as village elder. Sweat trickled down his blocky face into the gray scruff dusting his chin. "We are not all-seeing like He-Who-Slumbers. The scadtha's slayer is hidden from us, or we would have–"

The priest cut him off, lip curling in disgust. "I am Cortovah, priest of Murloch. It is in his name that I come to see the sacrificial waters rise and blood for blood paid."

This was it then. *Time.*

Rafi tipped his head back to drink in one last salt-tinged breath and locked eyes with Iakki across the ring. Seeing that foreign, fearful expression on the boy's face felt so wrong, Rafi would do anything to change it. He ignored Sev's scowl and the reminder of that hidden satchel and the itch in his own feet to run, *run*, *RUN* before it was too late, and watched as Kaya gripped Sev's arm with one hand, the other wrapped protectively around her stomach, while Yeena–shy, blushing, boring Yeena–glared so fiercely at the priests that for the first time, Rafi thought seriously about kissing her.

Somehow, long before Torva gave him that string of beads, this place had become home, this tribe family, and Nahiki dove open-armed into the net they represented while Rafi knew he had been a fool to let himself be noosed. These were the things that got a man killed.

Rafi released all hope of ever being free and opened his mouth to speak. But the voice he heard was not his own.

"I slew the beast."

It was not the voice of a ghost either.

It was a quiet, raspy, familiar voice, and just the sound of it numbed Rafi's limbs and smothered his own confession unspoken. He gaped as Torva limped forward, hands raised, and the priests closed around him like scadtha legs caging a kill.

"I slew it," Torva repeated. "Take me, and let my blood cleanse the village."

No . . . no.

Rafi tried to speak but no sound came.

Cortovah took a step closer, looming over the old fisherman, then lashed out with a barehanded strike that left a thin line of red marking his forehead. Cut as if by a blade. "*You,*" the priest snarled, "did not slay the beast."

Blinking, Torva raised a gnarled hand to the cut.

"But your blood will be accepted. Take him."

Voices swelled as the soldiers dragged Torva away. Iakki yelled. Sev shouted. Yeena cursed. Gordu sputtered. All of it pounded in Rafi's head, driving a spike of pain between his eyes until it was swallowed up by a roar that shocked him back to his senses as the largest stone-eye tiger strained against its traces.

"Wait." He found his voice. "Wait!" He shoved through the Alonque, dashing aside restraining hands, and tossed his battle-scarred harpoon at Cortovah's feet. "I did it. It was me. I slew the beast with my own hand–harpoon, that is, with my own harpoon and–"

He was babbling.

The priest turned away.

Rafi seized his elbow. "I did it. You must take me–"

Something slammed into his stomach. He doubled over, gasping. Glimpsed the spear pulling back before it hammered into his spine, dropping him to his hands and knees. His lungs screamed. He spat out blood from where he'd bitten his tongue and winced at a stinging pain in his forehead.

The ghost's voice suddenly thundered in his ears, as if he had broken through the surface of the sea to find a storm raging above. "There you are!"

It was a voice he knew and yet it was different too. It was the difference that made him shudder. His fingertips came back bloodied from his forehead as the spear came for his throat, forcing his chin back until he could see the gleam of excitement on

Cortovah's face. There was something strange about the priest's outstretched hand. The index finger was missing and had been replaced by a claw. Was that what had stung his forehead? It looked like it was made from some dark material. Metal, maybe?

He hoped it was metal.

"Yes." Cortovah licked his lips. "You are the one."

Priests clapped Rafi on either shoulder, and the spear at his throat caged him in. But Torva's captors were still dragging him toward the sea. Why hadn't they let him go? He twisted and found a thin-lipped smile on Cortovah's face.

"Oh, this you will want to watch."

"What?"

Cortovah turned away.

"Hey, hey! Watch what?" Rafi lunged after him, but the spearpoint jabbed his throat, and blood trickled down his neck. He shouted himself hoarse instead, as one by one the villagers were herded beneath the sting of Cortovah's claw. Most were released, but a few were escorted after Torva into the sea where not one but seven stakes awaited the incoming tide.

But he had confessed.

Why didn't they just sacrifice *him*?

"No, let me go!"

That was Iakki's scream.

Rafi jerked his head up. He caught a flash of wiry arms and kicking legs as a priest dragged the boy away. Sev shouted and lunged after him, took a soldier's fist to the jaw and went down. He was up again in an instant, skinning knife in hand. In a blink, the soldier fell to one knee, knife buried in his leg. Sev snatched his spear and cracked him across the head.

One of Rafi's captors cursed. "Release the stone-eyes before we have a riot!"

One set of hands left his shoulders, but the spear digging into his throat killed all hope of breaking to Sev's defense as two soldiers rushed to attack. But Sev no longer stood alone. A handful of young

Alonque swarmed the soldiers with fists and knives, and Gordu waded into the fray after them, shouting for peace.

His blood sprayed the sand.

Blade dripping, Gordu's attacker stepped back. Silence snapped across the beach. Rafi felt the change coming like a storm-charge in the air moments before furious shouts broke out. The spear at his throat wavered as his guard twisted to look. Rafi knocked it aside and threw his weight onto the chain dangling from the priest's manacled neck. They both landed sprawling in the sand, Rafi only inches from the harpoon he had tossed at Cortovah's feet. Seizing the haft, he shot up and slammed it across the priest's back, dropping him with a groan.

"Hurts, doesn't it?" Rafi flicked his wrist, rotating the harpoon point down. But what was he going to do? Stab him in the back? Just the thought made him sick.

"Nahiki!"

Rafi spun at Iakki's scream. He knew from experience that wrestling the boy was like trying to fight an octopus barehanded, so it was no surprise the priest had only managed to drag him—kicking, hitting, and digging in his heels—to the shoreline. Rafi took off, caught up as Iakki bit down on the priest's hand, and cut the man's howl short with a swipe that took out his legs and a blow to the head that left him drooling.

Iakki launched into him, arms cinching around his neck. Heart thudding in his chest, Rafi held the boy as he scanned the beach. Waves hissed around Torva and the other captives stumbling from the shallows, forgotten in the confusion. The rest of the villagers were scattered, some fighting, some dead, most fleeing for the jungle.

In the thick of it, Sev jabbed a spear in the air. "Nahiki, here!"

Rafi lurched toward him and met a stone-eye tiger's gaze head-on. A yellow wave engulfed him. His vision snapped into bursts of light. Hearing faded. Limbs stiffened. Screaming made no sound. Iakki yanked his arm, and he willed himself to move, but his body resisted.

Then Iakki was gone. Just . . . gone.

And his ears burned with Cortovah's soft laughter.

Someone shoved him back. He fell into a wave that crashed overhead, breaking the spell. Saltwater burned his nose and stung his eyes, clouding his vision. As if through sheeting rain, he saw the wiry old fisherman standing between him and the tiger.

It pounced.

Claws struck. Jaws snapped shut.

"No!" He sloshed to his feet and felt as though his chest had been split open as the tiger jerked its head, tossing Torva's limp form across the sand. He lunged for the fisherman, knowing in his heart that it was too late. That Torva was dead. That there was nothing he could do. Again.

Cortovah cut him off with Rafi's own harpoon.

Rafi yelled and dove into him, dashing the blade aside. It sliced his right arm as they crashed beneath the waves, but he latched on, wrestling it away before kicking free and surfacing. Cortovah's waterlogged robes slowed his rise, so Rafi knocked him down again and anchored the harpoon against his throat.

Chest heaving, he spoke in gasps. "Hear my terms, priest. Leave this village. Swear never to return. You survive. Refuse? I'll kill you like I killed that scadtha."

"Would you kill the boy too?"

Maybe it was the throbbing pulse in his head or the stab of loss in his chest, but it wasn't until Cortovah's gaze flicked past him that he understood. *Iakki.* Slowly, carefully, he shifted until he could see the hulking soldier standing chest-deep in the surf, pinning the boy so waves slapped against his face.

"What is he to you, I wonder? A brother to replace the one lost years ago?"

Rafi choked, startled back to the priest by the trailing echo of a scream in his ears. Smugness oiled Cortovah's expression and voice, and there was a knowing grin on his face. But . . . he couldn't know, could he?

"Oh, yes." Cortovah nodded. "The Voice has spoken. He knows

your name, Rafi Tetrani of House Korringar, second son of Nement late Emperor of Nadaar. Lost. Presumed dead. But currently breathing unless my eyes deceive me, though"–his voice twisted wryly–"that may soon be remedied."

Before that utterance of name and title, the thin veneer that was Nahiki the Alonque shattered, until only Rafi remained. He swayed as waves crashed against his knees.

"Tell me, Rafi, did you watch your brother die?"

Iakki's cry cut off as the soldier shoved him beneath the waves. His limbs thrashed. One hand punched the surface.

"Let him go!" Rafi sprang for the soldier. "Iakki–"

Searing cold ripped into his left side and brought fiery pain in its wake. He doubled over, gut heaving. Cortovah stood in a rush of water, blood dripping from the blade in his hand, and stepped back with a flourish. "Death, O Prince, comes to all sooner or later."

Soonest to Iakki if Rafi could not save him.

His senses reeled as the soldier waded ashore, leaving Iakki's limp form to float in on the tide. Iakki wasn't . . . wasn't struggling anymore. Rafi's vision darkened and his knees gave out. The salt sting shocked him alert. Shouts rang out but no one halted him as he floundered toward Iakki. Caught him and forced his head above water. Pounded his chest until the boy gasped in a sputtering breath and clung limply to him as he tried to swim.

The boy was Alonque. Practically half-fish. He would be fine.

So long as Rafi could swim them far away from this beach where the priests and their beasts prowled, but his limbs were weak, and Iakki was an anchor dragging him down, down, down, until the sea closed overhead. He sank through a cloud of crimson blossoming from his wound, and the underwater world was not vibrant now. Only cold.

Shadows loomed before him. A whiskery kiss scraped his forehead. Blue eyes, so familiar, gazed into his own.

"*Delmar*?" he breathed. *At last.*

FIFTEEN: CERIDWEN

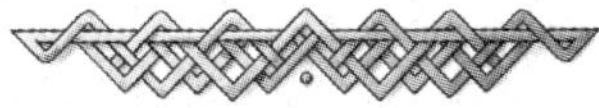

Earthhewns grow largest, become strongest, and endure longest of all solborn. Their hides are armored and colored the dark reds, grays, browns, and blacks of soil. Over time, a single spiraling horn grows from the brow of the mightiest steeds.

Ceridwen gripped her reins with trembling fingers. She closed her eyes, but the collapse was seared across her vision. Screaming warriors, falling steeds, her father. All branded in her mind. Beside her, an Outrider cursed. "Flames take their devilish hides and–"

Something wet struck her face. She jerked her head up to see the arrow in his throat before the Outrider collapsed and Mindar shied away.

His movement saved her.

She felt the blade rush past her face. Glimpsed the wielder on her right–dull gray leathers, shadowrider cloak–as she drew her sabre. Metal flashed on her left. *Blazes,* two attackers? Too late to block, she wheeled Mindar and blasted the swordsman with flame. An arrow splintered against her cuirass. Shards struck her half mask, missing her eyes. She rammed Mindar chest-first into the shadower before it could ghost in the smoke. Flames slammed into the shadowrider's face, and his howl cut off as her blade cleaved into his neck.

Blood splattered the sun emblem on his chest. Ardon's sun.

He twisted as he fell, and her blade slid free of his weight.

Shouts rang behind. Ceridwen spun, sabre raised, as an

Outrider brought her stormer's hooves crashing down on an unhorsed warrior. Kilmark te Bruin lurked beyond. Their eyes met and Ceridwen knew it then, knew it with a cold certainty that knifed through her gut: he meant to kill her.

In the valley, dying screams, shrieking steel, and colliding horseflesh roared. That was where the fight should be—where she should be. While their countrymen bled, these riders of the south dared betray their own?

Gravel shot beneath the stormer's hooves as it fled. Three Ardon warriors veered in pursuit. This low place between hills prevented a launch, so the Outrider would have to run for open ground to gain enough speed for flight. The remaining riders surrounded Ceridwen: two swordsmen, an archer, and Kilmark.

Blazes. She could not battle four and emerge victorious. Could she?

The swordsman to her left fought to calm his plunging riveren. Nostrils flared and suffused with blood, it backed away from Mindar. Close quarters made her flammable steed an advantage—small, perhaps, but she would claim it. How many times had Markham warned her that fireborn were dangerous? Reckless. Ill-tamed. Volatile.

"But bloody fierce . . ."

She counted on it.

Wood creaked as the archer drew. Mindar flamed as he reared, charring bow and arrow. His descent invested Ceridwen's stroke with blinding force. Her blade hewed through the archer's coif and lodged in his collarbone. The impact reverberated up her arm. She spun Mindar, flames spewing from his throat. Summoning too much too fast risked winding him, but she needed to force her attackers back before their numbers overwhelmed—

There, an opening.

Ceridwen dove through with a wild backhand slash that barely missed Kilmark's knee. A sword scored her saddle and carved a glistening red line across Mindar's hindquarters as he plunged past and stretched into a full-out run. Reins loose, urging him onward, she looked back only once more before committing to her race.

Riverrider and earthrider pursued.

The sword-wielding shadowrider had ghosted.

Even if Mindar could not outrun all three, a long pursuit would scatter them, diminishing the advantage of numbers. She just had to hold out. Regroup with the rearguard. Find Finnian. That last goal throbbed in her mind with each beat of Mindar's hooves.

Something snagged her focus as she whipped through a grove of trees in the shadow of the hills: a faint, misplaced shimmer. She flung herself against Mindar's neck. A sword crashed against the pauldrons guarding her shoulders. The missing shadower appeared alongside in a shaft of light that parted the trees, rider overextended from the strike. She rammed her elbow into his ribs, jostling for room to swing her blade. Winced as her elbow struck the metal plates sewn into his quilted gambeson. His pommel rammed her right thigh. Numbness shot down her leg.

She coaxed a burst of speed that thrust Mindar's nose ahead to flame in the shadower's face. The steed reared back, dropped stride, and lost ground. But riding on was not an option. If the shadowrider ghosted again, he could catch her unawares—too great a risk when she might soon be distracted fighting another. She spun Mindar to close in.

Their blades clashed, stroke after stroke as they circled. The shadowrider fought to stay on her flank, shielded from Mindar's flame. She sought to strike head-on but dared not lose sight of him. Even up close, she struggled to fix steed or rider in her vision. Edges blurred. Depths distorted. Visible one moment. Not quite there the next. Like trying to focus on a single blade of grass in a wind-whipped field.

The ground shook.

Ceridwen tore her gaze to the solid black mass hurtling toward her. She heard the clank of plate mail on horse and rider. Felt the ragged puff of the steed's breath. Smelled the tang of blood on hooves and blade and horn.

Then Kilmark's earthhewn rammed broadside into Mindar.

She flew from the saddle and crashed into the earth. Her senses fled. Hearing returned before sight: wheeling hooves, ragged coughing. Somehow, she was already standing when her vision cleared, but her limbs shook and her back–*blazes*, it hurt. Steel in her hand steadied her. Markham would be proud. She had gripped her sabre through the fall.

Kilmark bore down on her again, and daunting as an earthhewn charge was from the saddle, it paled before standing flatfooted on the trembling ground, mouth dry and palms slick, each breath bringing a hitch of pain as that massive armor-plated chest, horned head, and stony hide filled her vision. Iron-shod hooves split the earth, flinging clods of dirt. She envisioned those hooves tearing into her flesh.

Three steps. Two. One.

Ceridwen dove to the side, rolled, and lurched up again as the earthhewn barreled past, gleaming horn piercing the air where she'd stood. Kilmark hauled on the reins, but his steed's blood was up. It plunged heedlessly onward.

She spun, looking for Mindar. Paces away, he staggered upright, blood dripping from flared nostrils and from a gash carved across the crest of his neck. Dark smoke coiled in a wisp from his mouth. That eased her bucking heart. His flames still burned.

She started for him but a whisper of movement behind chilled her spine. *Move.* She rammed her sabre beneath her left arm, back into the shadower's heaving belly. That twisted her upper body to the left an instant before pain blazed through her right thigh. Her leg gave out. She lurched to keep from falling and gritted her teeth shut around a cry, eyes drawn to the blood spilling from a gash in her leathers.

Behind, the shadower collapsed with a thud.

The rider's blade must have been descending before she struck. *Blazes*–ice swept through her gut–it would have killed her if she hadn't moved.

"Yield, tal Desmond." Kilmark's voice rang hollowly inside his helm. It was the voice of a specter, the howl of death. "Sigre's horns call for the blood of Lochrann today. Can you not hear them?"

Not yet.

She clung to the flaring pain, let it shock her out of the seeping cold that would root her to the ground to tamely await her death. The earthhewn stalked forward. The groaning shadowrider rolled free of his thrashing steed and blocked her path to Mindar.

But the blood of Lochrann was not the blood of a coward.

She would not yield. She would not flee. She would fight.

Dropping her sabre into her left hand, she jammed her right tight against the wound. It felt like a red-hot shard tearing through muscle and bone, but she stood, waiting, blade and teeth bared for her enemies.

A copper-fletched arrow hissed past, felling the shadowrider.

Ceridwen stared only an instant before instinct seized the reins, pitching her toward her steed, head ducked against a barrage of arrows that shattered on the earthhewn's hide and glanced off Kilmark's breastplate. One struck with a meaty *thwack*, and Kilmark grunted. It had lodged in his chest, piercing his armor. It brought him up short, gasping.

But pain was a sensation Ceridwen knew well. She dragged herself into Mindar's saddle, and he calmed beneath her hand, snorting blood-tinged spittle. But she did not want calm. She wanted fire and ash. Ramming her sabre into its scabbard, she spun Mindar out of the grove and rolled her spurs across his ribs. Perhaps it was the surge of the fight that made his fire burn hotter. Perhaps he sensed her anger or her wound. Whatever the cause, his breath summoned an inferno as they circled the grove, and the blaze leaped from tree to tree, ringing her foes.

Breathless, she eased back on the reins. "For whom do the horns call now, te Bruin?" Pain returned in a surge, the earth rushed upwards, and she nearly slid from the saddle to meet it, but a firm hand caught her elbow.

"Don't halt."

She blinked, disoriented, and found Finnian riding alongside.

He flicked the hair from his eyes, the strands leaving trails of red across his forehead. "Can you ride?"

Her tongue felt too thick for words, but the mass of downed steeds and riders hung before her eyes, so she struggled to form the question anyway. "The battle?"

"Lost. We must flee. Everyone is fleeing. Or dead."

Dead.

The king.

Ceridwen yanked free and pushed Mindar into a run, ignoring Finnian's shout. Throbbing pulsed through her leg with each stride, but she pressed against the wound and refused to halt until she reached the crest of the hill. There, the reins slipped from her fingers.

Dead warriors and steeds littered the valley, draped with fallen banners like funeral shrouds. Even the stormriders had been driven from the sky. Only a small cloud still harassed the Nadaari soldiers pouring rank by rank from their encampment, trampling the dead. Chariots roamed before them, drawn by enormous tigers. One stormer hovered too close, too long, and claws gouged its barrel while the chariot driver speared its rider. Both fell in a tangle of wings.

Closer, Soldonians rallied in clusters, but their uneven charges broke against rigid spear and shield formations, and everywhere, solborn were pitted against solborn. Fireborn against shadower. Earthhewn against seablood and riveren. Soldonian warriors rode over their own, watering the valley with their blood.

Ripping cloth tore her gaze away. On foot, Finnian pressed a strip from his cloak to her wound. A gasp escaped her and Mindar shied, shuffling his hindquarters around. She groped for the reins, but Finnian reached them first only to yank his hand back, cursing, as a thin trail of smoke rose from Mindar's skin. "*Shades*!"

Ceridwen clung to her steed, steadying him while Finnian bandaged her wound. He held pressure until the blood flow lessened and then bound it tightly. "We should help them, Finnian. We should–"

"Our mounts are spent." His voice was harsh, the truth even more so. "You are wounded. The war-hosts have fled. But they will regroup and we"–he drew in a breath, and his voice softened–"you must gather with them, Ceridwen tal Desmond."

Always that name was a blade to her heart. But never more than today.

Blood seeped from a cut on Finnian's head, washing his face in crimson. Her cheeks were wet too but not with blood, and for once, she felt no shame at the tears. "It is true then."

"What is?"

"All is lost."

SIXTEEN: JAKIM

Aodh is merciful.

"Aodh have mercy," Jakim whispered, picking his way by smoking torchlight through a pit where thousands had died. But mercy had no place here it seemed. Flickering light snagged on broken steeds and twisted riders and glinted red off the sharpened metal stakes protruding from the mass.

It was so quiet.

He could have thought himself the only living thing.

But the slave masters patrolled at intervals above, and the other slaves were here too, wading through blood and viscera, scattered in search for the body of the Soldonian king. His armor would identify him—plate mail with a flaming steed on the breastplate, a gold crown on the helmet. Sorting the dead was dangerous work, of course. One misstep and Jakim might wind up impaled on a stake of his own. Still, the Nadaarian tsemarc wanted proof, and the slave masters would not let them rest until they found it.

So, he searched. Head down. Mouth shut.

Unfortunately, that left him trapped in his own miserable thoughts with nothing to distract him. Before marching inland, the Nadaari had fastened iron collars on all their slaves. It chafed his throat, weighed down his neck. Raw blisters oozed on his palms, and his damp rag of a tunic—pilfered from a dead man—pulled at the weeping lash marks on his back. These past few weeks had been some of the worst of his life. But nothing compared with the horror of the battle today.

Just being down here brought the noise of the collapse roaring back: snapping limbs, screaming men, shrieking and thrashing steeds. Crouched behind the Nadaari lines, he had watched the staged retreat, soldiers cursing as they crossed the platforms covering the pits–pits he and the other slaves had been forced to dig, bristling with stakes they had planted. Those platforms had been engineered just strong enough to support the soldiers and just weak enough to collapse under the Soldonian charge–ingenious and deadly.

Something snagged his ankle.

Jakim jerked back, heart pounding. It was a hand. Fingers twitching. Alive. He traced it to its owner, a man half-buried in the mass of corpses. Mud and blood caked the man's beard and smeared his armor. He had no helm but a mail coif bunched around his neck, and a massive, reddened swelling had spread over half his forehead. Something wild lurked in his gaze as Jakim crouched by his side. He groaned. Were there words in the sound?

Jakim leaned closer. Yes, that was Soldonian.

"Water . . ."

He drew back and raised his empty hands. "I . . . I have none."

The man's eyes closed. Dead? Jakim held his breath. No, he still heard faint breathing. But soon, surely. Scrollmaster Gedron would have known what to do. He was trained in the arts of healing. And even if it was too late, he could have administered the rites of the dying. But Jakim hadn't even learned those yet.

He sank back on his heels, fists to his temples, sick with frustration at his own uselessness. His gaze fell on a waterskin dangling from a saddle to his right. One of the seams had split, spilling water over the dead horse's neck, but the bottom still sagged with liquid. Jakim scanned the pit's rim. No slave masters in sight. But being caught idling would be dangerous. He should resume the search. Instead, he scrambled up and snatched the waterskin from the saddle, cradling it like that fledgling hummingbird back on Kerrikar.

Droplets splashed the wounded man's face as Jakim tipped

the waterskin over his mouth. His eyes flicked open. He choked down a swallow and then coughed, spraying bloody spittle across his breastplate. His gaze darted from Jakim's arms to his head. Self-consciously, Jakim fingered the stubble of new hair covering his seal. "Scroll . . ." The man's voice was deep and rough and punctuated by gurgling in his throat.

"Jakim. Scroll Jakim Ha'Nor."

Strong fingers gripped his wrist, pulling his palm flat against the man's breastplate. He felt the man's lungs rattle as he sucked in a shuddering breath. On his face, streaks of ashen skin marked the path of spilled water droplets through the muck. "I . . . am . . . dying."

Oh. He wanted the rites.

Jakim had witnessed their administration several times but never learned the words. But he couldn't just sit here. He had to say something. Haltingly, he began to recite the truths inscribed on his forearms, translating them into Soldonian. "Aodh is true. Aodh is just. Aodh is compassionate. Aodh is–"

"Merciful." The man's eyes slid shut. "Is it true, Scroll? Is he . . . merciful?"

So the holy writ said. So he must believe.

So he must hope.

"Yes."

"I would be merciful." Resolve strengthened the man's voice so Jakim no longer had to strain to hear. "Take my ring, Scroll Jakim." His eyes opened and flicked down to indicate a thick gold signet ring on his forefinger. "You must give it to her. My daughter. My heir." He broke off coughing. "Swear it in Aodh's name."

Once sworn, such a vow could not be broken, and Siba's voice still called Jakim. Soon, he must find a way to escape and return to his people and to his mission. But a dying request was sacred. It could not be ignored. Jakim gently worked the ring over the man's swollen knuckle and folded it into his own palm. "In Aodh's name, I swear it will be done."

Coughs racked the man's broken body.

The empty waterskin was limp in Jakim's hand. "I will find

more. Wait . . . wait." As if the man could do anything but wait as Jakim hurtled away. His search carried him far across the mound of dead before he found a small flask and hurried back.

Two warriors now stood over the wounded man. One winced as he struggled to square an axe over his head, favoring an injured shoulder. The axe hung suspended, blade already edged in crimson, then fell with a sickening crunch.

The flask slipped from Jakim's fingers.

"Huh, who would have thought it?" The second man seized the severed head and lifted it by the hair. He snorted, and a brutish grin spread across his slab-of-meat face. "See, Kilmark, even kings bleed red."

"Aye." The axeman cradled his wounded arm to his chest. "Long live the king."

Understanding struck Jakim like the crack of a whip. He dropped behind the bloated belly of a dead horse, planting one hand in the muck to hold himself steady. He was shaking. Both men were speaking Soldonian. Both wore armor like the man he had stopped to help, dull steel and earthy leathers, not the gilded mail or scarlets and oranges of Nadaar. They were traitors, and they had just beheaded their own king.

Within his fist, the ring was a cold lump.

He squeezed it tighter and tilted his chin to peer over the horse's ribcage, watching as the axeman–Kilmark–pulled out a sack and the other tossed the king's head in, careless, like a chunk of a rotten fruit and not a skull that had worn a crown.

"Look at his hands, Ondri. It isn't here."

"Maybe not, but his crown is." The second warrior dug through the pile of the slain and held up a dented helmet with a battered gold crown at the top. One side twisted inward. "Looks like he took a nasty kick to the head."

"That's not what we came for. Leave it."

"Fine." Ondri tossed it aside. It landed with a clank beside the headless corpse. "Think he left it behind? Back in the command tent maybe?"

Kilmark swore again. Soot streaked his armor, and a burn reddened one side of his face. Did he ride one of those wild flaming steeds spoken of in legend? "He will not be pleased. The head alone means nothing."

"Eh, then he can do his own blasted work next time."

"Yes, but I've failed once–"

"And have the wounds to prove your loyalty. Come on."

Jakim sank back into the muck as the two traitors slogged away. It soaked through his ragged trousers, but he was beyond caring. He already reeked. He peeled his fingers back from the ring on his palm. Mud concealed its design but not its value. Or its weight. This was worth a kingdom. And he had sworn to deliver it to the king's heir, his daughter, and . . . Aodh help him, he didn't even know her name.

Escape was his only hope. Had been since his capture. But once he was free, his path was supposed to lead toward the coast. Toward home. Not farther into Soldonia. And how was he to find an unknown woman in a foreign country?

Groaning, he let his head rock back, brushing a leather string attached to the dead horse's saddle. Mud squelched under his knees as he crawled up and snapped it free, threaded the ring on, then tied it around his neck to hang inside his tunic.

First, he had to survive.

That meant getting out of this pit.

Back on his feet, he retrieved the flask and scrambled back to the dead king's side. *Don't think. Don't feel.* He placed the crowned helmet beside the man's hand and then upended the flask over his breastplate, scrubbing until the flaming emblem appeared. He took a deep breath. And shouted for the slave masters.

SEVENTEEN: RAFI

Mountains crumble. Trees fall. The sea endures.
– Alonque saying

Death, it turned out, was not what Rafi had expected. It was more damp and less painful, though still uncomfortable enough. Bristling whiskers brushed his forehead. Warm, fishy breath heated his cheeks. Water eddied and pooled around his feet, and the blaze in his side had deepened to a raw, molten thing.

The ghost snorted in his head, once again a thin echo of the voice he had known and not the harsh thunderous voice from the beach. *You're not dead, brother.*

Not dead? He forced his eyes open.

Two bright blue moons stared down at him from a star-spattered sky. It took a moment to clear the grit from his vision and bring the world into focus. Not moons. *Eyes.* He scrambled away and screamed at the tearing pain in his side. Fell back panting on the sand instead. But like the sun, that blaze burned away the fog in his mind until he could think clearly again.

The sea-demon colt stood over him, dark coat and silvery scales glistening in the glow of a full moon that hung low over the black expanse of the sea. He remembered sinking, lungs seizing, limbs slowing, mind drifting into blackness, and there in the final gasp before oblivion, blue eyes. Delmar's eyes, he had thought them and welcomed the reunion even in death.

But death, it seemed, had not welcomed him. Again.

The colt took a snuffling breath, nostrils flaring, then snorted.

Salt water sprayed his face. Rafi blinked as cold droplets trickled down his cheeks. Spat. Lifted a hand–and was shocked at how it trembled–and wiped the mucous from his face before grinding his palm into the sand. Almost as gross as being covered in scadtha slime and–*the scadtha*! He jolted alert, mind reeling to catch up. *Iakki.* Iakki had been with him when the sea-demon came. Where was he?

Rafi lurched upright, startling the colt. It skittered back, snorting. "Iakki?" His voice was a croak, his legs unsteady, his vision swimming as he scanned the beach. It was familiar, located maybe an hour's walk from Zorrad, though he had only ever made the hike twice.

"Nah-Nahiki?"

Next thing Rafi knew, he was flat on his back, side a boiling cauldron of agony, while Iakki clung to him. Was the boy sobbing? Not without reason, given what he had been through, what he had seen. But it still caught Rafi off guard. He was used to an Iakki who wasn't fazed by anything–not diving into the heart of the sea, not swinging from treetops on vines, not even the death of a scadtha. It only made him more furious with the priests–if that was possible, when he already longed to see them ripped to shreds by their own stone-eyes.

"You ain't dead," Iakki choked out. "You ain't dead."

"Not yet, I'm not," Rafi assured him. "Now, let me up. I can't breathe."

Swiping a hand under his nose, Iakki sat back on his heels. "Thought you was dead for sure. All that blood spilling from your innards. You looked like a gutted fish."

"Yeah, thanks, I needed that image in my head."

"It's true."

Rafi put a hand to his side and grimaced at the warm wetness pooling there. This was going to hurt. Nothing for it though. He couldn't lie here and wait for help or death to come. Not when Iakki needed him. Not when he didn't know what had happened to Sev and the rest of the Alonque in Zorrad. Not when all of this was his fault. Teeth clenched, he shrugged out of his shirt and tossed it to Iakki. It hit the boy's chest with a wet splat and fell to the ground.

"Hey! What was that for?"

"I need you to . . . rip it . . . for me." His teeth were chattering, making it difficult to form his tongue around the words he needed to speak.

"Okay, but what for?"

"Strips, Iakki . . . for bandages."

"Oh."

He let his eyes drift shut, clinging to sound instead of sight to anchor him in consciousness. Heard his shirt tearing, Iakki moving, and seaweed crunching between the teeth of the colt as it grazed nearby. Sea-demons were supposed to be dangerous monsters, but this one hadn't harmed him. It had *saved* him. Why?

"Here."

Cloth fluttered against his face. He caught the strips against his chest then forced himself up on one elbow. "I'm . . . going to . . . need your help."

Iakki made a face but didn't complain.

Sucking in sharp, rapid breaths, Rafi shoved strips of cloth into and against the wound and yelled for Iakki to hold it until the bleeding stopped as he collapsed back, sweat beading on his forehead. Water. Sand. Sky. All seemed to spin around him again.

He was falling. Falling. Falling. And the whistling in his ears was only the echo of a trailing scream: *Rafiiiii–*

"Nahiki?"

He jolted back to the present where Iakki crouched wide-eyed over him and a sea-demon colt stood guard. Maybe a side effect of evading death too long was a slow spiral into insanity, because this couldn't be real life. "Still not dead," he rasped, motioning for Iakki to wind a bandage around his ribs to hold the dressing in place. Once done, Rafi felt at the complex knot. It was already damp with blood, but it would hold. It had to.

Back at the village, Torva could–but no, Torva was gone.

He choked on the thought and let his head sink back, a tear leaking from one eye.

"You dying again?" Iakki clutched at his arm in a panic, unintentionally squeezing the harpoon slice, and Rafi gasped.

"No, no, not me."

"You gonna get up then?"

"Thinking about it." Just still not convinced he could stand. Not wanting to worry Iakki, he passed it off as a joke. "It's just that the sand here is so comfortable. Makes a bed fit for an–" He broke off, but Iakki supplied the word.

"Emperor?"

"Yeah." He shifted uncomfortably, remembering the truths Cortovah had spilled on the beach, the names he had conjured up out of the past. *"Rafi Tetrani . . . the Voice has spoken."* How much had Iakki heard over the crash of the waves? Did he know who "Nahiki" truly was? Did it even matter? Torva had been right when he said to look at the Mahque to see the consequences of revolution: swaths of the jungle reduced to ash, villages razed, and bones left to bleach in the sun. The empire of Nadaar did not suffer insurrection. Once word of his presence and Sev's rebellion spread, that wrath would descend upon Zorrad.

He had to get back and warn them. He ignored the chilling whisper of the ghost in his ears urging him to run, ignored his own cynical voice insisting that Sev and the others were surely already dead, and got to his feet. Darkness spotted his vision and his legs shook, but when the dizziness passed, he was still standing.

"We going back?" Iakki asked.

"We're going back."

On the shore, the colt's head shot up, ears perked toward them. It made a soft grumbling noise in its throat and stamped a hoof. Rafi froze at its shivering scream, fear prickling his neck, but its bright blue eyes did not burn with anger, only a strange sort of sadness that mirrored Rafi's own as he relaxed and let Iakki tug him away. Their path lay through a finger of the Mah jungle that curved down to the shore. Navigating in the dark would be challenging, but short of swimming out to sea to round the coast, it was the only way back, and he'd had enough of almost drowning for one night. Looking back through the trees, Rafi saw the colt standing as if carved in relief against the sea. Only its mane and tail moved, rippling like the waters of a stream. He pitied the beast. It was bound to the deeps just as he was bound to his past.

But one day, he would be free.

Rafi clung to that hope as he stumbled after Iakki into the dark of the rainforest. Vines snared his limbs, dead leaves squelched underfoot, and spiked plants clawed at his ankles. He hated walking blindly like this. He kept his hands outstretched to break a fall, at least save his nose from a smashing. He could almost hear the ghost mocking his vanity.

But it *was* a decent nose–like his father's. Smashing it would be a shame.

"You know what I think, cousin?" Iakki asked as they ducked beneath the hanging roots of an enormous banyan tree and wove through the maze of its many trunks–most formed by roots that had twisted into columns to support the sprawling canopy.

"No, what do you think?" Only half listening, Rafi twisted to get his bearings. He recognized this tree. Night concealed the charred streak where lightning had blasted a jagged scar, but he knew the sprawl of its root system. Here, Sev had hidden that satchel of supplies. Just beyond, they would strike the path to Zorrad. So close, Rafi found his steps slowing, his reluctance to arrive growing, while somehow Iakki seemed to have shed both his panic and his grief like ill-fitting clothes, becoming his usual carefree self again.

"I think you should net Yeena," Iakki said.

"Yeena? I thought you said she was boring?"

"Sure, but that was before she kicked a soldier in the tailbone. You ask me, that's what you got to look for in a wife."

"Tail-kicking?"

Iakki nodded sagely. "Better net her before someone else does and then you and Sev and Kaya and Yeena and me can all be family together."

But not Torva, the ghost reminded him.

"What if Yeena ever kicks me in the tailbone? What do I do then, oh wise one?"

"How should I know?" Iakki caught one of the hanging roots and swung with his bare feet churning. "Sev always says–"

Rafi didn't hear the rest of it. Over the creak of the root and the incessant whine of mosquitoes, the rattling of chariot wheels caught his ears. Not coming from the direction of the village, so it wasn't the priests returning to their temple . . .

He acted on instinct. "Get down, Iakki."

"Wha–"

He yanked on the boy's legs. The root snapped, dropping Iakki into his arms. It felt like the knife pierced his side all over again, jagged and red hot. He collapsed against a massive column where the roots had grown together, slid to the ground, and dumped Iakki beside him.

"Ow!"

Rafi clapped his hand over Iakki's mouth and strained to hear, senses so heightened he could tell the boy was glaring, even before the world brightened with the lurid glow of torchlight glinting off the waxy undergrowth, and he actually could see. Not just the deep scowl carved between Iakki's dark eyebrows, but the waterfall of roots descending from the leafy canopy above to shelter them and the muddy stain of blood on the bandage beneath his left hand.

Beyond the rattling wheels, he heard the steady tramp of feet and the distinct jingle of armor and weapons. Someone–no, many someones–approached.

Rafi squeezed Iakki's bony knee, "Don't move," and pushed up to peer through a gap in the twist of roots. His stomach plummeted at the sight. Soldiers in scarlet and orange flooded the path toward Zorrad, following a chariot drawn by two stone-eye tigers. He started counting spear tips but lost track somewhere near thirty, distracted by the lead charioteer. Beneath a gilded breastplate, the man wore a priest's flowing robes but no headpiece shadowed his face.

In Rafi's mind, a ghostly scream trailed off.

Cold sweat broke out across his skin. He knew that face. Knew that curly dark hair, high-bridged nose, and slanted jawline. Knew the ruthless expression that twisted those full lips into a sneer. Knew it as well as the veins that lined his own eyelids or the pattern of thatching in the roof of Torva's hut because he had seen all three over too many haunted, sleepless nights.

"Sahak," he breathed, and saw his cousin stir.

There was no way his voice could have pierced the clamor of the march, but still Sahak straightened in his chariot and scanned both sides of the path. Rafi felt the blood drain from his temples as after six years he looked Delmar's killer in the face.

EIGHTEEN: CERIDWEN

What of the dawnling? It is a rare steed, a dying breed, and a thing of beauty beyond words. Look to the noonday sky. Look to the sun. Look to the radiance of a star come to earth.

Finnian's mouth tightened as he peeled back the last layer of soaked bandaging. Air struck raw flesh, and Ceridwen held her breath behind gritted teeth as he gingerly probed the wound. Flickering firelight glanced off the bones of his face but did not touch the dark shadows beneath his eyes or in the hollows of his cheeks.

She ran her tongue over dry, cracked lips. "Surely it is not so bad."

"Could be worse." He shrugged, scratching at his forehead. Dried blood flaked beneath his fingertips, drawing her eyes to the cut below his hairline and then down to the stains on his leathers and the tattered shreds of his gray cloak. He had seen battle too, before he appeared at her side. "Looks like the blow glanced off your mail skirt, and the leathers absorbed much of the force. Still, it narrowly missed releasing a flood of your blood that would have killed you and"–his eyes flicked up to meet hers briefly–"this will burn."

Amber liquid splashed over the gash, a rain of fire that set her muscles spasming. She groaned. His hand fell on her shoulder, steadying her until her body stopped trembling and she sank back against the saddle he had removed from Mindar's back, drenched in sweat and gasping.

"Isn't that . . . Markham's?"

"Used to be." He corked the flask and tossed it aside. "Empty now."

"Did you steal it from him? Find yourself in need of salve for wounded pride often?"

That earned a grunt she could almost have mistaken for a laugh. "Only when I am around you, tal Desmond." He rose to fetch his saddlebags from the other side of the fire. She could not see the shadower there, but the red glow of embers showed where Mindar grazed in a patch of scorched grass just beyond the ring of light.

After fleeing the valley of Idolas, they had ridden fast and far to evade the pursuit of both chariots and solborn riders. Ridden until their steeds were stumbling and all feeling had vanished from Ceridwen's limbs, save that pulsing drive within her chest: *onward, onward, onward.* Twice, she had almost fallen from the saddle before Finnian called the halt in a hollow sheltered by a gentle rise and the upraised arms of ironwood trees. She watched the flames licking at the small pile of dry wood gouged from the heart of downed branches–dry so there would be little smoke, small so the light would not be seen. Little risk, if they had truly outpaced the pursuit. It was the way of armies. Once the initial rout was completed, the army would rest, regroup, and advance as one.

"Needs stitching." Finnian flipped his saddlebags open, removing a curved needle and thread. "Ready?" Without waiting for a response, he drew the wound closed.

She gripped the hilt of her sabre, but compared to the previous inferno, this didn't hurt so much as make her cringe at the prick of the needle and the slither of thread through her skin. "Your head, how did it happen? Did the Nadaari overwhelm the rearguard?"

His jaw tightened. "Ondri's men turned on us. Slaughtered the Outriders and swept down into the valley to strike our forces from the rear. It was utter chaos. I was able to ghost away once all was lost. Others may have escaped. But not many, I think. There was . . . nothing I could do."

And yet he sounded uncertain, as though he sought to convince himself. But four hundred solborn striking unexpectedly at once would have thrown the column into chaos, and with the front already destroyed, there would have been no chance of survival for those caught between, not once the Nadaari released their stone-eyes and chariots. One look into the eyes of those monstrous tigers and even the hardiest warrior lost the will to fight, to move, to do aught but stand and wait for death.

It was no way for a warrior to die.

Neither was falling to the force of your own charge, swallowed by the earth. She flinched from the image of her father moments before death. "So Ondri te Velyn and Kilmark te Bruin, two chieftains of Ardon, are in league with Nadaar. How could Rhodri, our battlemaster, have been so blind?"

Finnian shrugged, palming his knife to slice the thread, and then dug for a roll of clean bandages. "Treachery makes fools of us all. You cannot blame Rhodri for the deeds of others." He bound off the bandage tightly, the pain knotting her objection behind her lips. "It is done."

And it was.

The king, her father, was dead. The battle was lost. And she was yet an outcast. None of that could be changed. She released her breath and her anger with it, as Finnian tossed her a wedge of cheese and then settled beside the fire with an elbow propped on one knee and a strip of dried meat in hand. He should not bear the brunt of her wrath in any case. He had come for her, saved her, tended her wound. For all her brazen fury, Kilmark's earthhewn would have trampled her, grinding her bones into the dust.

"How did you find me?" she asked.

"I . . . uh . . . smelled the smoke."

"You smelled smoke? In the middle of a battle, *that* caught your attention?"

He tore off a bite of dried meat and answered around his chewing. "Each fireborn's smoke bears a unique scent. I knew it was you and your wildborn."

"And you came?"

"Yes, tal Desmond, I came." A hint of impatience edged his voice. "We are a pair, are we not? Apex Markham made that clear."

"Not by your wish." The blood had risen to her cheeks. She could feel the throb of it and the rising pulse in her chest daring her to act. Holding his gaze, she undid the knot of the scarf concealing her brand. The cloth fluttered to her shoulders. Rid of it, she felt strangely unclothed. And at once, free.

Finnian looked away.

"Does it offend you so?"

"It is the blood debt." A muscle in his jaw twitched. "For traitors."

"Is that what you think me?" She envisioned herself tempered steel, but somehow Finnian's words still sliced deep. "But you came back. Maybe you should have left me."

He gave no answer.

In the fire's embers, shadows raged a mimicry of the battlefield slaughter. Ceridwen closed her eyes, but she could not escape it: the king on his earthhewn, falling, the weight of the charge crashing down on his head. Her father lost in the crush of dying men. Her eyes flew open, and she caught the glint of Finnian's gaze beneath the sweep of his hair.

"No . . ." His voice was soft. "I cannot think you a traitor."

Perhaps it was the gentleness of his voice, reminiscent of a horsemaster approaching a wild steed. Perhaps it was the guilty relief of knowing they had survived the slaughter when so many had not. Perhaps it was the setting itself, for firelight and darkness aid more in the sharing of truths than ale. Whatever the cause, Ceridwen found herself speaking again. "Once he was my father. Now he is dead and I cannot weep, for I feel as if he died years ago."

Silence trailed her words.

The fire crackled. Mindar stamped. The unseen shadower snorted.

And she was ashamed to have spoken.

Finnian stirred at last to stoke the dwindling fire, snapping twigs and sending sparks ascending in a whirlwind. He stared at the livened embers. "The man who raised me was a miner by trade. A hard man, accustomed to the use of his fists. Made harder still when the drink took him. My mother deserved better." His voice took on a brittle edge. "He drank every coin he earned and worked out his anger on her and on me until I grew tall enough to look him in the eye and strong enough to make him rue the fight. Never saw him again. Heard of him, though, after he was strung up for poaching solborn."

He lifted his eyes then, and they were dark as the shadowed hide of his steed. "That is why I must earn my place in the Outriders, why I must make a name for myself and mine if I am ever to build a life unstained by his crimes. Nothing can threaten that. Nothing."

It was a plea not a threat, and yet his words seemed to sap all the heat from the fire, leaving only a chill that penetrated to Ceridwen's bones. There was no denying that death rode at her heels or that her shame tarnished those around her. She shivered in her damp tunic and leathers, felt the fresh prickle of sweat on her forehead as she picked up the scarf and bound it in place again. Finnian swept the cloak from his shoulders and held it toward her.

"No, I can't–"

"Take it, tal Desmond." He dropped it in her lap and threw himself back beside the fire, arms crossed behind his head. "Markham would have my hide if you survived the battle only to die of fever now."

Maybe. But the war-chiefs would undoubtedly be pleased.

With stiff fingers, she tugged the cloak up beneath her chin. Finnian called her *tal Desmond*. He wished to regroup with the war-hosts. He thought the daughter of Lochrann was needed. He was mistaken. If her brand was a threat to him, then surely it was an even greater threat to the kingdom. Tomorrow, she would decide where her steed would take her. But for now, she owed Finnian his freedom. At least that.

She found her sabre beneath the cloak and knotted her fingers around the hilt. A blade oath was a mighty thing. "I will speak with Apex Markham and ask for reassignment. Nothing will threaten your rise in the Outriders, Finnian te Donal. I swear it." She offered it as he had offered his tale and wondered what he would say.

He said nothing, and that was answer enough.

NINETEEN: JAKIM

Aodh is compassionate.

"Make way for the king!"

Jeering shouts ran ahead of the litter. Bowed beneath the weight of the dead king, Jakim and three other slaves stumbled toward the Nadaarian command tent at the heels of an officer while slave masters lashed them from behind. On all sides, soldiers jostled and shouted and shoved, drunken with conquest. Some bowed mockingly. Some spat and hurled curses. Others mobbed around them, clashing spears on shields as they howled their victory to the stars.

The stars looked down in silence. Jakim tilted his chin toward those pale lights, and a hollow ache opened in his chest. His people believed that the stars wept for the horrors unleashed upon the earth, so surely, they wept now. Maybe if men could hear the weeping of the stars, wars and oppression would cease.

Someone shoved him and he tripped.

"Watch your footing," the slave next to him snarled. It was the sailor he had met unloading on the docks, forehead wound now healed to an angry scar that sliced through one eyebrow. "That is my king you carry. Don't drop him."

Jakim did not speak. He was shaking with exhaustion, sick with his own stench after digging through the dead, and his heart was a raw, bleeding mass inside of him. By the time they reached the command tent—a massive thing made of fluttering red-and-yellow silks, shaped like a sprawling mountain range with multiple peaks and ridges and lit from within by strings of hanging lamps—and the officer barked a command for the sentries to let them pass, his limbs felt as limp as a rotted mango leaf and his feet were stones weighing him down.

Would this day never end?

He ducked beneath the silk hanging into a packed space and froze. Just inside the entrance crouched a muscled beast with an orange hide streaked with black. His pulse tripped. *A stone-eye tiger.* His first up-close sighting. Ink-tipped tail lashing, it snarled, baring teeth like the needles Scroll Enok had used to mark his skin.

Meeting its eyes would be dangerous.

So of course, like a complete fool, he did. Stared at it head-on for the full three seconds it took the officer to argue his way past the tiger's handler—a priest, judging by his lofty gold headpiece and those chains running from wrist to neck—before he realized that it was blindfolded. Made sense. Like sheathing a sword or storing arrows in a quiver, it was doubtless wise not to leave the ferocious man-eating beast untethered.

His vision foggy, he shuffled through the press of bodies, following the officer deeper into the tent. He was delirious. The exhaustion was getting to him. Or maybe it was the warm, stuffy air exhaled by hundreds of officers, priests, and soldiers, representatives of a dozen nations that had been absorbed by the empire and now glutted the imperial armies with tributes. Maybe it was the heady reek of wine flowing from flask to goblet and ale foaming from cask to beaker. Maybe it was the coils of incense dangling from the tent ceiling, emitting a faint smoke that stung his eyes and a sweet floral scent that tickled the back of his throat. Whatever it was, he could have curled up on the ground and slept right there.

"Tsemarc Izhar." The officer bowed to a tall man who stood with his back to them and wore a helmet crested with an enormous orange-and-green skaa-ryn plume that trailed to his knees. The plume was thicker than a stone-eye's tail—thicker than the tails of the dead horses Jakim had clambered over in the pits. Never had he seen a skaa-ryn so large, but clearly one existed somewhere in the world. Or had. Before it was killed for its plumage.

Breaking off his conversation with a burly priest in flowing scarlet robes and an even more elaborate headpiece than the tiger's handler, the tsemarc turned, and the officer impatiently gestured for the slaves to lower the litter.

It landed with a sickening thud.

"Sir, we have the king."

Snaking whips herded them out of the tsemarc's way, and Jakim found himself jostled beside the sailor again. He ignored the man's scowl–studying under Scrollmaster Gedron had given him lots of practice–and tried to ignore the cold lump of the signet ring under his tunic and his fear over what they might do to him if they spotted it.

Tsemarc Izhar was a craggy mountain of a man in gold scale armor with a scar that scored the right side of his face and forced his lip downward into a sneer–as though the chisel that had carved him from a boulder had accidentally slipped. He tapped a ringed finger against his goblet. *Clink. Clink. Clink.* "The head, Adaan. Where is it?"

That was the voice of a man deaf to excuses.

Judging by how the officer bowed even lower than before, lank hair swinging forward to cloak his thin face, he knew it too. "It is missing, Tsemarc. But this armor bears the king's emblem and his helm was found beside his corpse."

Clink. Clink. Clink.

"Beside the corpse. Minus the head. Unusual, don't you think, Adaan?"

"Tsemarc, the slaves are still searching. But without someone to identify the head if we find it . . . well, there were many corpses . . ."

A sharp jab to the ribs distracted Jakim.

"Scroll." The sailor jerked his chin toward the Nadaari. "What are they saying?" He spoke in a harsh whisper barely lower than his normal voice. It snagged the attention of an overseer, and a whip flicked casually toward their legs in warning.

"Many corpses indeed," Tsemarc Izhar rumbled. "And where is the man responsible, the champion of today's battle? Ah, there he is! Come, Khilamook, drink to the triumph." He raised his goblet, and Jakim stretched his neck to see who he had addressed. His Nadaarian accent had butchered the name, but it was still unmistakably Canthorian, as misplaced in this foreign land and foreign army as Jakim.

Riotous celebrants parted like water around a rock, skirting one man standing still. Candlelight gleamed against his gold skull markings and glinted off the beaded front of his robe. It was the scholar. He advanced toward Izhar with startling, tigerlike quickness, and swept an upturned palm toward him in the Canthorian manner of greeting between equals. Jakim watched in surprise, but the tsemarc did not seem offended.

"Some say victory favors the brave. Others that she is fickle. But I say that she kisses the cunning." Izhar tipped his goblet toward the scholar who stared at him in an unblinking silence for so long that Jakim shifted uncomfortably and the priest coughed and the tsemarc broke off with a curse. "Silent One Alive, has he left his translator behind again? Deprive him for a moment of his machines and designs, and the man is helpless as a child." He scowled at Adaan. "Where is the engineer's translator?"

"Dead, Tsemarc. Struck by the arrow of a sky-demon."

Izhar swore again and abruptly downed his wine then tossed the goblet into the hands of an attendant, gesturing for a refill with a flick of his wrist. His knotted brow and rock slab of a jaw reminded Jakim of his first master, a brute who had enjoyed wielding a whip for maximum damage. Not the sort you wanted noticing you. Which was exactly what had happened, Jakim realized, as Izhar's gaze hardened on him.

What was his problem with eye contact tonight? First a stone-eye, now a tsemarc? So much for keeping his head down and biding his time.

Still maybe that was a flawed plan . . .

It wasn't uncommon to stumble across a chance to run away,

but running like that usually got you caught. The opportunity to truly escape never just appeared. You had to hunt it down. Jump in its path. Greet it with a grin and catch hold with both hands like a python wrestler–yes, according to his brother Yath, some people were crazy enough to tangle with snakes for fun.

Before fear–or common sense–could kick in, he stepped forward. Not toward the slave master or the officers or even the tsemarc. Toward the scholar, Khilamook. Was that a spark of recognition in his eyes? The man had seen him weeks ago on the docks and had seemed intrigued. Maybe that would act in his favor. "Master," he said in Canthorian. "I speak Nadaarian. Allow me to translate for you."

Khilamook pursed his lips, eyes deep-set beneath a tall forehead exaggerated by the elaborate gold markings. Those were clearly a work of art with their delicate whorls and interwoven letters and embellished symbols. They made the simple lines of script that Enok had inked on Jakim's arms seem childish and clumsy by comparison.

Jakim fidgeted. "Master–"

Overseers seized him and dragged him back. He bit back a yelp as a lash snaked around his neck. Well, he had made his move and snatched the python, only to find himself gripping the tail and not the head.

"Wait." Khilamook's lofty, commanding tone halted the overseer, even though it was doubtful the slave master understood Canthorian. "You may translate, slave."

Reluctantly, the overseer released Jakim, leaving him alone beside the dead king. Jakim blew out a breath and wiped his sweaty palms on his filthy trousers before bowing to the tsemarc and priest and explaining his intent in Nadaarian.

Izhar nodded brusquely, and the work began.

The tsemarc spoke first, congratulating Khilamook on the victory. Apparently, he had not only engineered the war machines used in the battle but also the pit and stakes beneath, and it had been his specifications that enabled the platforms to support the

Nadaari soldiers yet collapse beneath the hooves of the Soldonian steeds. The man was clearly brilliant. And deadly.

Jakim had never before translated a conversation like this one. It involved complex ideas as well as strategic and technical terms he barely recognized let alone knew how to convey in a different language, so he was forced to improvise, racking his brain for simpler ways of relaying the necessary information. Caught between the ruthless stare of the tsemarc and the calculating eyes of the scholar, sweat trickled down his back, stinging the raw lash marks that wrapped around his ribs, and his tunic clung cold and damp to his spine by the time he finished translating the tsemarc's words.

Khilamook nodded abruptly, rocking forward on his toes. "This was nothing. Greater designs and greater victories await once I have secured the rest of my belongings that the imbecile Adaan in all his vast wisdom insisted on leaving behind. When should I expect my manuscripts to arrive?"

Jakim translated his words. Minus the insult, of course.

Still, Adaan's face reddened, but he did not speak until Izhar flicked a lazy hand, inviting his response. "I told you before, engineer, your trunks will be on the next transport ship to dock and the first reinforcements to march inland will bring your manuscripts."

"Only think had they been allowed aboard with me how much delay could have been avoided," Khilamook observed. "We might be standing over the corpses of all the war-chiefs of this wretched land and not just their king. Short sightedness has been the fatal flaw of many a Nadaarian invasion, second only to an appalling lack of ingenuity which is, of course, why I am here."

Jakim's jaw dropped, and he awaited an explosive response . . . only to recall that he alone had understood.

The scholar met his shocked expression with the cold, flat gaze of a Canthorian spine snake and a calculated grin that touched only his lips and did not affect the rest of his face. Despite his words, his tone remained smooth and calm. "No matter. I am here, and I shall require a team of my choosing to assist me." He paused, expectant.

Jakim coughed to hide his hesitation. He could not relay those words directly. Khilamook would be able to deny them, blame him for mistranslation or an attempt at sabotage. He would be whipped. Maybe killed. He would never deliver the ring. Never return home. Never fulfill his purpose.

The butt of a lash clipped his head. "Speak, slave."

So he did, breaking eye contact and blurting the first thing that came to mind–the engineer's request to select his own workers–and skipping the rest. It was a decent lie. Better than the one he had told Gedron. This time he didn't even feel the need to be sick, though that could have been because he had already emptied his stomach twice in the pits.

"It will be done." Izhar raised his refilled goblet toward Khilamook, wine sloshing over the rim to spatter the breastplate of the dead king. "To triumph, engineer. To the Dominion of Murloch and the fall of nations."

Khilamook swept a hand palm down toward himself in acknowledgment, regarding Jakim with that same amused smirk. It sent a tingle of alarm all the way to his toes. Somehow, the scholar knew what he had done. Was it the difference in length between the original and the translation or the tsemarc's calm response that had given it away?

Would he be furious or maybe–

"This one I will take." Khilamook turned and strode away, crowd parting before him. "Come, slave!"

–intrigued.

Jakim started to follow, but the sting of a lash reminded him to relay those final words. "I am to go with him. He is my new master." Aodh grant that he was kinder than the others.

Somehow he doubted it.

TWENTY: RAFI

The jungle remembers.
– Mahque saying

Rafi did not dare blink. He hardly dared breathe. Was this . . . really happening? Or like the voice of the ghost in his head, were images from his past invading the present? He dug his fingernails into the bark of the tree and felt them catch–real, that was real. As Sahak's chariot neared, he could see the knives gleaming in the baldric on his cousin's chest, could make out the cruel glint in his eye and the proud slant to his mouth, and knew he was moments away from joining his brother and sister and mother and father in death.

But the chariot rattled past without stopping.

Within moments, the thick of the jungle had swallowed the soldiers and their torchlight too, and the whine of insects replaced the steady tramp of feet. Rafi sagged and clenched his fists to his aching skull.

"Who was that?"

Iakki's attempted whisper grated painfully on his raw nerves, but he managed to keep his voice steady. "You saw them?"

"Hard to miss it."

Rafi swallowed a wave of nausea. That meant it was real then. Sahak–assassin, priest, and the usurping Emperor Lykier's illegitimate son–was here in Zorrad. "I told you not to move."

"Since when do I listen to anyone?"

"Just net your tongue . . . and let me think."

It was a struggle. His mind felt murky, his skin prickling with a heat that was not entirely from panic. He pressed a hand to his side and felt the bandages squish wetly beneath his fingers.

That was probably bad.

One thing he knew clearly: Sahak hunted him. The fishing village lay at the far end of nothing on the road to nowhere. What else could draw his cousin so far from the Center of the World? But maybe, if he surrendered, Sahak would spare the village.

Like he spared me, his own flesh and blood? came the ghost's voice.

No, Rafi had to admit, mercy was not in Sahak's nature, but cruelty was as innate to him as salt to the sea. Surrendering would not save the village. Sahak would only force him to watch the slaughter. He always had enjoyed twisting the knife in the wound, so to speak.

"Nahiki?" Iakki tugged at his arm. "Get up. We got to go home."

"We can't."

"Sure you can. I can help you. Kaya says I'm strong as–"

"No, Iakki, we can't go home."

Speaking it out loud hammered the truth into his own mind. Maybe if Sahak arrived, only to be informed that Rafi had been there and had fled down the coast–he would never believe that Rafi had drowned, not again–he would set off in pursuit without waiting to destroy Zorrad. Running was not always the coward's way. Sometimes, it was just the only way.

First, he needed to deal with his wound. "I need your help again, Iakki. There's a satchel hidden in the lightning scar on this tree. Can you get it?"

No response.

Iakki gone quiet? Never a good sign.

Rafi reached for his shoulder, and the boy shrugged away. He bit back his frustration, trying to recall how Delmar had reassured him on that night that had changed their lives, not to mention their quarters in the palace. He hadn't been much older than Iakki when the sudden death of his parents and sister to a mysterious illness had "forced" his father's brother, Lykier, to stage a "bloodless" coup, resulting in his and Delmar's permanent relocation to the dungeons. There, as far as the empire knew, they had sadly fallen to the same illness.

"It's not for forever, Iakki," Rafi promised and hoped he wasn't lying. "We will go home. But for now, you must trust me. Can you do that . . . cousin?"

Silence stretched long, broken only by the sound of Iakki's toes scuffing the dirt.

"Fine." Iakki sighed, then whirled around and raced off, mood shifting as swiftly as the sea. "Guess what the last one to the lightning scar is!"

"I know, I know, a turtle's egg."

It seemed a turtle's age before Iakki bounced back and dropped the satchel on Rafi's chest. He clamped down a scream and the urge to strangle the boy. Treating the wound proved only slightly less painful. Sev–or most likely Kaya–had packed one of Torva's salves, and at the first whiff of the pungent scent, Rafi imagined the old fisherman dabbing at his wounds, mouth crooked in concentration. Iakki, unfortunately, wasn't nearly so gentle. His hands were better suited to climbing vines and wrestling oysters from the ocean bed than applying ointments or wrapping bandages.

"Careful, Iakki, you're not trying to gut me."

Iakki tied the final knot with what felt like a savage twist. Rafi caught a hanging root, hauled himself up and ventured off with the boy into the Mah jungle. Into the humming, hooting, howling dark.

The jungle remembered Rafi. That was what the ghost whispered in his mind as he stumbled through the dense tangle of vines, trees, and enormous sprawling leaves–some bigger than Iakki, some big enough to serve as sails for the fishing boats of the Alonque, only they would split at the first stiff gust of sea wind. This forest was old. Old in a way that the sea-washed coast and storm-shaken outskirts could never comprehend. The deeper he went, the older it seemed, and the more it oozed memory, like poisonous sap wept from the knots of a saga tree.

What of you, Rafi? the ghost asked. *Do you remember?*

Oh, yes, he remembered. With each step, the years seemed to unravel a little more, their weight plucked from his shoulders by the delicate brush of dark purple mollusk moss tendrils dangling from the canopy above. Had it really been years since he and Delmar plunged into the wild wood, desperate to escape? Or only days? Rotting leaves squelched as he planted his foot, and he looked down, half expecting to see overlapping footprints–his and his and his again.

Was he walking in circles? Or just stuck living the same cycle over and over and over. Running. Hiding. Discarding identities. But never able to slip free of the one he truly wanted to forget. It drifted behind him like a half-shed skin.

Rafi . . . do you remember?

Night melted into day into afternoon. When exhaustion threatened to crush him, Rafi called the halt. Iakki was snoring before Rafi could ease himself to the ground. For once, it was not screaming sea-demons that broke his sleep, only the jungle coming alive at dusk with the cackling of monkeys, the croaking of tree frogs, and the warbling calls of asha birds. Still, he lay, wracked with fever chills, until Iakki stirred and together they plodded on.

He blinked and saw Delmar walking alongside, brow pinched in that too-serious expression he had inherited from their father, from a man accustomed to sitting enthroned at the Center of the World. Rafi had inherited his mother's crooked smile and that quirk to her eyebrow that always made her look like she was on the verge of sharing a joke. Or a secret.

Come on, brother, just a little farther . . .

"How much farther, Nahiki?"

Iakki's voice came from behind, startling Rafi out of his daze. Sunlight pierced the canopy and scattered in shards across the jungle floor, stinging his eyes. He shook off his disorientation and did not break stride. Somehow, their feet had swallowed the night. But if he stopped, if he even slowed, he would collapse, and Ches-Shu only knew if he would be able to risc again.

His lips were cracked, his voice rasping. "Not much farther."

"But where are we going?" Iakki caught up. "Why won't you tell me? Sev would."

Rafi looked at him.

"Okay, maybe not. But Kaya would. You know it's true."

The boy chattered on, but Rafi had stopped listening. He swiped a bead of sweat from the tip of his nose. His limbs were shaking, his teeth starting to chatter. Maybe Iakki should know their destination. Just in case. "Tehorra Peak."

"Huh?"

"Where we're going. You wanted to know."

"Sure, but why?" Iakki's forehead puckered in confusion. Even on the remote Alon coast, he would have heard of Tehorra Peak. It was the tallest, most inhospitable mountain in the Hanon range, located where the earth rose in steep folds beneath the Mah jungle and a hundred rivers clashed and spilled in bounding waterfalls toward the sea. A lopsided grin crossed the boy's face. "We're joining the revolution?"

Rafi startled at this leap. "How did you . . ."

Iakki shrugged. "Just a hunch. So, why didn't you say so?"

Because revolution was the *last* thing on Rafi's mind. He had never shared Sev's belief that the Que tribes would reclaim their autonomy, despite the mixed Alonque and Nadaarian blood in his veins. Or maybe, because of it. He had witnessed the strength and ruthlessness of the empire firsthand. To this day, he couldn't grasp what shred of conscience or cowardice had stopped his father's brother from slitting his and Delmar's throats on the night of the coup, but it hadn't stopped Sahak from eventually murdering Delmar. It wouldn't stop Sahak from hunting him down now. He needed better shelter than an assumed identity and a new village could provide. The Que Revolution offered that.

More than that, it offered hope.

Six years ago, two frightened boys had discovered their prison door open, their path cleared before their feet, and a cloaked man waiting to guide them. He had perished with one of Sahak's knives in his throat, but not before whispering the name of their mysterious benefactor: Umut of the Hanonque. Rafi mumbled that name to himself as the land swelled beneath his feet and he pressed doggedly upward, and both the ghost and the jungle echoed it back.

No, the jungle did not forget. Nor did it forgive. Mind swinging from past to present, vision blurring between what was there and what couldn't be, Rafi wondered if he would find Umut and the Que Revolution just in time to die.

"Nahiki . . ."

Rafi emerged to the sensation that hours, maybe days, had passed and he had been drifting through them like a leaf caught in the current of a stream. Dull throbbing pulsed behind his eyes. His tongue felt thick and dry. Iakki was shaking his arm, eyes as wide as oysters.

"Nahiki," he whispered, "someone is here."

Rafi stopped, but the earth seemed to keep moving. His knees struck first, and he crumpled. Mud crusted his lips. He felt Iakki pulling at him and tried to rise, but his limbs refused, no more his to control than when he'd been trapped by the stone-eye.

Shapes separated from the jungle, and he could only watch as they crept nearer, blinking until they came into focus. Not soldiers. Not priests. Not even Sahak. But tribesmen, dark-haired and armed to the teeth–there, the flash of a spear tip; here, the creak of a bowstring or the slither of a net coiled to throw.

This was the Que Revolution, come to kill.

"Nahiki, do something!"

Rafi coughed and spat out mud, then willed his hand to rise, palm out in token of peace. "Umut." He coughed again, dragging his voice up out of that flaming pit of pain inside of him. "Take us . . . to Umut of the Hanonque."

Voices murmured and clashed in whispered dispute. Iakki shrank against Rafi, and he held white-knuckled to the boy and to consciousness until one of the tribesmen gestured with his spear. "We will take you to Umut."

Rafi sagged in relief.

Then someone yanked a hood over his head from behind. "If you live that long."

TWENTY-ONE: CERIDWEN

Of all fireriders, Uthold the Bold was most renowned for his ferocity and will be forever remembered for his brazen strategies, impossible victories, and reckless valor.

Ceridwen rode with one ear to the wind, listening for pursuit. On foot, the Nadaari could not catch them, but astride their solborn steeds, the four hundred traitors of Ardon could. Any moment, she expected to hear the rumble of hooves, sense the waver of movement that presaged a shadower attack, or feel the deadly bite of an arrow in her spine.

Snorting, Mindar pawed the ground. It rammed a spike up her wounded leg. Once in the saddle, the pain dulled to a throb, but any action that stretched the muscle sparked it afresh. With all his anxious prancing, her restless steed was no help, but since leaving the hollow at dawn three days ago, she'd been on high alert, which always fed his agitation. She sensed the tension coiling his limbs, the flames blossoming behind his ribs, and slid her hand to Mindar's neck, to settle him before he ignited the plains of Lochrann.

"How is it?"

Startled, she glanced at Finnian. He had caught her rubbing the ache, but the concern that furrowed his brow and softened his tone implied more. *How is it?* What, her injury, her father's death, or his assumption that the war-chiefs would welcome her return when not even he wished to ride at her side? She was nothing more than a gaping wound, flesh ripped open and exposed, to be torn and irritated and scraped raw again and again.

"It is nothing," she said, and knew he sensed the chill in her tone.

Stiffly, he set his face forward and started whistling. They had spoken little since setting out. There was little to say. For now, they rode the same path, and for now, that path led toward Rysinger. There the remnants of the war-host would gather, no matter how scattered or splintered by the retreat. It was the great stronghold, the final defense, and the last place Ceridwen wished to be. If Aodh was merciful or the warrior spirits kind, she would locate Apex Markham and see Finnian freed without needing to enter those shadowed walls.

But she dared not hope. Hope was as elusive as a dawnling.

As if kindled by the thought, Finnian's whistling took shape as the mournful ballad of an archer named Harrigan, cursed for shooting one of those legendary steeds. Ever after, whatever he sought turned to ruin, until at last, as he slept in a wasteland of his making, his own hand throttled him. Not all of the ancient warriors were remembered as heroes. Some lived on in infamy. That fate she feared even more than dying forgotten.

"Must you whistle that one?" she asked.

Finnian broke off and fell silent, victim to her reckless tongue. In this she and Harrigan were alike, forever doomed to ruin all they touched. Once Finnian was free, she would convince Markham not to assign her a new partner.

She rode better alone.

Hefting her apple core in one hand, Ceridwen whistled softly. Ears pricked toward her, Mindar's head swung up from his grazing a few feet away, forelock cloaking his emberlike eyes. Snorting puffs of smoke, he tilted his head to track her hand. She whistled again, a sharp ascending note, pointed to guide his blast, and tossed the core in the air.

Mindar did not flame.

Not until she whispered the word.

Whistle then word, that was the cue, and she was proud of her restless, volatile steed for remembering it. He flamed too late to roast the core midflight, but he chased it to earth and crisped it to a fine charcoal black, inedible for all but a fireborn. Still, he had flamed on her command. Timing was another issue entirely.

"*Shades,* that was a neat trick," Finnian sounded rightfully impressed. He sat beside his grazing shadower, both barely visible in the shade of a clump of thorny seaberry shrubs. Such partial ghosting, he'd explained, was camouflage against attack. It left Ceridwen feeling exposed in comparison as she sprawled back in the grass to stretch her sore leg, but she was in no hurry to return to the saddle, still less to continue their journey, and their steeds did need the rest. With the race to summon the Outrider patrols, the tension of the battle, and the speed of their flight since, both shadower and fireborn had been pushed hard for weeks. Solborn were magnificent creatures but not indestructible.

"Does it have a purpose?" Finnian asked, digging out his own apple from his saddlebags.

"Just a new skill." She could have left it at that, but a part of her wanted to share this breakthrough with someone . . . anyone. "Remote flame on command. He was late, but he'll master it."

"Remote flame?" Finnian repeated. "You mean with a rider dismounted? Thought he'd mastered that already. He took those crossbow bolts in the poacher's trap handily enough."

"Not just dismounted, cued from a distance."

Most fireborn were trained to flame only with a rider in the saddle, some to flame on rein commands from a rider on the ground, but flaming on cue from a rider beyond rein reach? That was a skill never before mastered, so of course, she had decided to attempt it.

Finnian whistled softly. "Thought that was impossible."

"Never been done before, but that is not the same thing. 'The unachievable is often but one stride more from reality.'"

"One stride, huh? That sounds like a quote, tor Nimid."

She sat up abruptly, staring at him in disbelief. "It *is* a quote, and you should know it. Or do the words of Uthold the Bold no longer carry weight in the kingdom he forged?"

"Uthold?" He tilted his head, considering. "You admire him then?"

"He was a great warrior, a firerider, a legend."

"He was reckless."

"And my ancestor. His blood flows in my veins."

Finnian laughed aloud, expression cracking wide with the first full, honest, and wholly transparent grin he'd ever shown her. It transformed his face, like a glimpse of the sun breaking through clouds. "So your recklessness is an inherited trait then? I can see the resemblance."

His laughter carried no bite. It reminded her of Bair's gentle teasing. Bair had always adhered to more cautious ideals of warfare than their flaming ancestor too. But this was Finnian, not Bair, and their bond would soon be broken. Distance, her heart urged, and she focused on that thought as they mounted and resumed the smooth traveling pace that solborn could maintain for hours, unlike their weaker kin, tolf.

Over the next two days, her dread grew. Only a month ago, she'd crossed this same ground at a run, summoning all the stamina of her steed to deliver her tidings to Rysinger. She'd ridden headlong into the fear of that journey in defiance of what awaited her.

Of who awaited her.

But now, the king, her father, was dead, and with his passing, the world shifted. There was no purpose in defiance, no chance in proving her worth, no hope of regaining his love. She could not stand before the war-chiefs as tal Desmond.

She was only tor Nimid now. Only an Outrider. Surely that was best for all.

"Hold." Raising a fist, Finnian abruptly reined his shadower in. "Do you smell that?" His eyes flicked to her tense fireborn, to the sparks winking to life in the coppery tangle of his mane, then outward, scanning the horizon.

She shook her head.

"Heavy smoke, damp ash. Something burns."

Her hand flew to her sabre, his to his bow, and side by side they rounded a shallow hill into a stand of trees. There, trapped in the leaves, Ceridwen tasted the smoke. It had a damper, dirtier tang than Mindar's. Beyond the trees, it hung low in a depression, rising from the smoldering ruin of a village where survivors picked through wreckage and corpses littered the ground. No sign of Nadaari or Ardon traitors, so the attack seemed to have come and gone.

They were too late . . .

Finnian's hand brushed her arm. "Steady."

Too late . . .

Mindar's mane burst alight. Ceridwen smothered the flames but let him prance, hooves striking with a force that echoed her own rising anger, down the slope toward the ruin. He shied from the speared corpse of a woman with a sword still clenched in her hand.

Ceridwen shied from the smaller body lying in the shadow of her form.

"Shadows claim them!" Finnian's jaw was hard, his eyes deep and liquid as a summer night sky. He fingered the coppery fletching of the arrows in his quiver as though he too envisioned sinking steel into the ones who had done this.

"They came at dawn," a weak voice said.

Ceridwen spun to see an old man sitting in the rubble, wreathed in smoke, cradling the limp form of an elderly woman to his chest. Both so streaked with soot they blended into the background, like shadowers on the verge of ghosting. Out of the saddle in an instant, Finnian knelt beside them. His eyes flicked up, grim.

The woman was dead.

Gently, he took the old man's arm. "Come away and rest. You're injured."

But the old man just reached a trembling hand to the cut on his forehead and sat blinking at the splash of crimson on his fingers, until Finnian went to rummage for bandages in his saddlebags, and Ceridwen tried to shake off the ache of helplessness in action. She dismounted to let Mindar guzzle water from a trough while she refilled her waterskin from the well and then searched the broken earth for signs of the attackers. She found few hoofmarks. Not enough for this to be the work of Ardon traitors–not unless all rode shadowers, the only solborn capable of leaving the ground unscarred, and that was unlikely. But if not them, it must have been the Nadaari, and how could so many thousands have marched so quickly from the valley of slaughter?

"Tell me, father," Finnian was asking, "who did this?"

"Nadaari, who else?"

Ceridwen rose with ash on her fingertips from tracing a pair of wheel-marks. Too narrow in beam for a cart or a wagon. Likely one of those tiger-drawn chariots. "How many?" she demanded, and the voice she heard seemed to belong to a stranger able to look upon this ruin and not weep, to think only of tactics and the deployment of troops.

Surely that was not her voice.

Finnian's head rose sharply from the bandaging, casting her a look of reproach. "Can you tell me how many there were?" he asked, more gently.

"Some thirty . . . maybe forty? It . . . all happened so fast . . ."

Ceridwen crumbled the ash between her fingers and went to offer the old man her refilled waterskin. He took it in trembling hands. Forty soldiers must have seemed an overwhelming force to the small village, but so few would not march far from support in hostile territory. Odds stood the main Nadaarian army still trailed behind, so the attackers were probably just an offshoot of a larger host out raiding for supplies and spreading fear in flame and sword.

"We offered no resistance, and still they killed us." Voice wavering, tears coursing down his cheeks, the old man gathered up the thread of the story and carried it beyond what Ceridwen had read in the bloodstained ground. "They spared our young, chained them behind the priest's chariot, and we begged them to kill them instead." His voice broke. "Do you know why we would do such a thing, why we would plead for the death of our own?"

She shook her head, not trusting her voice.

"The priest thanked us for their sacrifice." He shuddered, and Ceridwen felt the chill of his words in her bones. Rumors told of the sacrifices Murlochian worship demanded. She could imagine few worse fates. "The priest smiled as he spoke of terrible things: of defeat, of slaughter without end, of the war-chiefs betraying one another and the *ayeds* riding over our own. He said the king was dead, the Dominion of Murloch come. Tell me . . . is it true?"

For the first time, his eyes seemed to focus, and beneath the watery gray of his grief, she found strength. It was the strength of one who had seen herds come and go, survived storm and drought, and coaxed a living from hard, windswept ground by the sweat of his brow and the blisters on his hands, and who through all had endured. There was a strength to him even now as he held his wife amidst the ruins of all he had, tattered clothes falling from withered shoulders, singed hair standing out in wisps around his age-spotted head.

He deserved the truth, raw and bitter though it might be.

"There has been a defeat." She met Finnian's eyes, and he shook his head, warning her to rein in her tongue. "The war is not over, but the king is dead."

"Oh," the old man gasped, "Aodh have mercy . . ."

Finnian straightened abruptly, snapping his saddlebags closed. She could sense his disapproval, but this village stood in Lochrann, in the chiefdom that even more than the throne should have been hers by right of blood to shield from harm. That right was denied her. The truth was all she could offer them now. *Or was it?*

It was too late for salvation. But what about vengeance?

Finnian's voice rose. Too late, his words sparked her attention. "King Desmond may be dead, but hope is not. She who stands–"

Warmth drained from her limbs.

She stood, too late to halt the words.

"–before you is his daughter and heir, Ceridwen tal Desmond."

And like an arrow loosed from the string, there was no reclaiming them. They fell around her like a rain of fire, landing with a hiss that made the survivors who had gathered in silence pull back in alarm. But no, that hiss came from her own lips, expelled by the fear clawing its way up her throat. Finnian's brow wrinkled in confusion. *Blazes,* he had no idea what he'd done. How could he without the *kasar* on his skin?

She felt every gaze on her scarf-bound forehead, confirming the weight in her stomach. But she would not shrink from shame. One step, two, to Mindar's side. Hand to saddlebow, foot to stirrup. Swinging up, she checked his restless plunge, ignoring the twinge in her leg, and lifted her voice to carry over the ruins. "The war-chiefs will not abandon you. Help will come–"

"Too late to save the dead." The old man gazed up at her. "Too late to aid the living. Tell me, Ceridwen tal Desmond, what help will come?"

She hesitated only a breath, then knotted her hand around the sabre, and murmurs rose at this mark of a blade oath. "The blood of Lochrann will come. This I swear." She repeated the words to herself as she spun from the ruin, Mindar's mane and tail igniting to release the pent-up heat in his veins. Not until the next rise did she slow, allowing Finnian to catch up. By then, at last, the way before her feet was clear. "Our paths split here, te Donal."

"What do you mean?" he demanded.

"I cannot ride on to Rysinger. I have sworn to help."

He shoved a hand through his dark hair, pushing it back from his eyes. "You will help by regrouping with the Outriders, with Apex Markham. It is our duty. Ceridwen, the war-chiefs await–"

"Let them wait. I am an Outrider, yes, but only an Outrider. Tor Nimid. Not tal Desmond. That name was seared from me by the *kasar*–" She checked herself like an unruly steed. Given loose rein, the words rolled off her tongue like a fireblast. Had she no control? "But I am honor bound to protect this people. Hunting those who harm them *is* my duty."

His brow furrowed, but her mind was already set.

"I will not ask you to stay." She brought Mindar dancing around, felt his limbs tighten beneath her, neck arched, nostrils flaring, burning to run. "Tell Apex Markham we are a pair no longer. Ride on, Finnian. I cannot."

Mindar sprang forward.

But Finnian snagged her reins. "Wait!"

His grip flew open again before Mindar flamed but it still brought the fireborn to a stamping halt. Finnian rubbed at his forehead, ruffling his hair until it stood on end like a wolf's hackles, then cast her the same exasperated and weary glance she'd received many times from Markham. "*Shades,* Ceridwen!"

"Yes?"

"Just . . . *shades.*"

TWENTY-TWO: RAFI

Only a fool watches the sky and ignores the leak in his hull.
– Alonque saying

Deafening birdsong greeted Rafi even before he peeled his eyes open to stare at the mossy concave ceiling, just as it had the past . . . however many . . . days he had been here in the rebel camp. It beat jolting awake to the screams of sea-demons.

Or it would have, if he hadn't been a prisoner.

"So, here's the deal," he remarked, not bothering to lift his head from his hammock. "I know how this goes. I demand to see Umut. You grunt. I ask for Iakki. You grunt again. I respond with something witty and you forget to laugh, killing the conversation. Again. What do you say we skip the routine, just this once, and you take me to see them both now?"

Not surprisingly, he got only a grunt in response.

Sighing, Rafi raised himself onto one elbow, ignoring the tug in his side, and squinted against the daylight that leaked through the hut's woven walls. His guard lounged beside the brightly colored cloth door, arms crossed over a leaf-bladed spear, black hair rising in a spiked wave like the dorsal fin of a sailfish.

He looked to be near Rafi's own age, but Rafi didn't know his name. Still, his voice identified him as the rebel who had yanked a sack over Rafi's head, threatened to kill him before letting him see Umut, and stood guard over him every moment since.

"So, that was a yes? Great, let's go." He slung his legs over the side, and his toes brushed mossy earth before the spearpoint tickled his ribs. "On second thought, I'll stay. It'd be a shame to have to redo those stitches, don't you think?"

His guard grunted again.

Rafi rubbed at the persistent ache behind his eyes. Really, as far as prisons went, this wasn't half bad. Oh, he complained, but he had food, air, sunlight, not to mention the breeze that ruffled the cloth door and stirred the edge of his blanket. He had a blanket. Good thing too, since he had awakened days ago with fresh stitches in his side and barely a stitch on otherwise.

He half expected the ghost to chime in with a sarcastic response. The voice had been growing more and more audible, more distinct from his own thoughts, more real. But apparently, not even the ghost was talking to him anymore and–

"Ah, good, you're awake."

That was not the ghost. Or his guard.

Rafi jolted up, ignoring the twinge in his side, eyes latching onto the burly man halfway through the doorway, one arm raised to push back the cloth. Salted hair tied at his neck, beard dusted white at the chin, sweat-stained tunic hanging loose over a frame as rugged and worn as the driftwood that washed up on the Alon coast. Sea-blue eyes studied him, weighed him. "How is that ugly wound of yours today?"

Was this the healer who had stitched it up? He had been half out of his mind with delirium then. Rafi gestured at the bandage. "Still there."

"Ah, it will heal."

"It will scar."

"And it will not be your first, Nahiki of the Alonque." Letting the cloth fall, the man lurched into the hut. His strange gait confused Rafi until he saw the man's crutch and the leg missing at the knee. "Those marks on your chest are from scadtha claws, if I'm not mistaken?"

Rafi glanced at the puckered scars that scored his ribs and considered denying it. But what was the point? *"Own it,"* Sev had insisted, and if it would buy him and Iakki refuge here among the rebels, he would do just that. "You're not."

"Sounds like an interesting story."

"Umut will think so. When can I see him?"

"Oh . . . soon enough, I daresay." Waving Rafi's guard back, the man planted his crutch and eased himself to the mossy ground where he settled his legs before him. "I hear you have been kicking up quite the storm to see him."

It might have been the twinkle in those sea-blue eyes. Or it might have been his guard's stifled snort and the blank expression that erased his habitual scowl. Somehow, Rafi knew. "You are Umut, aren't you?"

Still staring at him, the man laughed a hoarse throaty laugh. "You should have warned me he was so sharp, Nef."

The guard sullenly crossed his arms. "He's not."

"As a kaava's thorns. Give merit where it is due."

"You haven't had to watch him drool."

Rafi coughed, swinging his legs over the side of the hammock again so he could face Umut and maybe reclaim some shred of dignity before revealing his true identity to this man who had been an unknown piece of his past for so long. The blanket tucked around his waist slightly lessened that effect. Umut barked something at Nef who shoved away from the wall to retrieve a bundle and toss it to Rafi.

He caught it against his chest. Ah, clothes. Such generosity.

Gingerly, he stepped into the baggy trousers and wide beaded belt–Mahque style, like Nef wore, with symbols and patterns that told the story of its maker–and settled the loose tunic over his head. By the time he eased back onto the hammock, arm tucked against his wounded side, he was sweating, and that familiar headache had started up again, right on cue.

"That was a strange wound," Umut observed. "You shouldn't be alive, much less standing. How does it feel?"

"Hurts less than it did."

Which really wasn't saying much. Like comparing a river and

the sea. Both were capricious bodies of raging water that could kill you in an eyeblink.

"I imagine it should." Umut opened a pouch at his belt, pinched a dark curved object with the hem of his tunic, and held it up for Rafi to see. "Tip of a scadtha claw. We found it buried in your wound. It should have festered. You should have been dying from the inside. Oddly, it didn't and you didn't. Like I said, strange."

A chill prickled Rafi's arms at a flashed image of the claw on Cortovah's hand. But the priest had stabbed him with a dagger, hadn't he?

He had seen it. Or thought he had.

"So tell me, Nahiki of the Alonque, this tale I will find so interesting." Behind the claw, Umut's sea-blue eyes seemed as bright and fierce as the sea-demon's. "Tell me what winds have blown you against so many scadtha and left you alive to tell the tale?"

Swallowing, Rafi ignored the way Nef glowered down at him and grounded himself in the story he would tell. His life before Zorrad would wait until he was certain this Umut was actually responsible for rescuing him and his brother. Instead, he began with the discovery of the sea-demon in the net. Nef shifted uncomfortably at that, but he snorted at the scadtha's attack and laughed outright at Rafi's claim to have killed it.

"Oh, sit down," Umut commanded. "Stop looming like a thunderstorm about to burst."

Nef's spear dropped with a muffled *thunk*, and he sank sullenly beside it.

This was where things could get tricky, so Rafi kept the next part vague. "It all happened so fast . . ." He muddled the details of the failed sacrifice and Sev's revolt, removing himself as a key character so it seemed like he had stumbled onto the priest's dagger by accident. "I knew this would be the only safe refuge for us, so–"

Nef leaned forward, eyes hard and glittering. "So, you fled and brought your storm down on our heads? Are you even here to fight, or are you too much of a coward?" After days of grunts and stony silence, Rafi found the sudden rush of words more amusing than aggravating. "You fisher folk cling to your shores, content to woo the sea and the imperial beast too, ignoring the plight of your cousins and–"

"Peace." Umut flicked a hand at Nef but focused on Rafi. "I am more interested in how you knew our location. Knew my name. We guard those carefully to keep the Emperor's Stone-eye from sniffing us out."

It startled Rafi to hear Delmar's derogatory title for Sahak–inspired by the chained stone-eye Lykier kept close to hand, much like his unacknowledged son–in common use.

"So, Nahiki, who told you my name?"

Umut's voice was calm as the bay in summer, but Rafi caught the glint in his eyes. His answer was important, he realized. Maybe life-or-death important. But Nef's scowling presence impeded the truth. "My brother told me. I don't know how he knew."

"Convenient." Nef snorted. "And you only mention him now? Where is he? Spilling secrets to the Stone-eye? Leading soldiers down the trail you left for them to follow?"

"He is dead."

Thankfully, that quieted him.

Umut wedged his crutch and used it to lever to his feet. "Nef, why don't you take our guest outside and show him around? Get him some food too."

That was it? Rafi blinked and saw his surprise magnified to shock on Nef's face.

"Show him . . . what?"

"Everything."

"But–"

"Humor me, Nef." Umut's voice briefly took on an edge. "You know I appreciate any evidence you have some control over your rampaging temper. It gives me hope for you yet."

If Nef's scowl had been a thunderstorm before, a hurricane now churned across his expression. But he stood sharply, snapped his spear to his chest in salute, and pushed through the cloth door without looking back. Rafi followed just as stiffly, but that was because everything hurt, not because he had an iron rod for a backbone. Still, something nagged at him.

"Speaking of names"–he twisted to face Umut–"how did you know mine?"

"To borrow the Alonque expression, your cousin has a leaky hull."

"Like your brother," Nef muttered outside.

Was he lurking out there just to eavesdrop?

Umut winked as he limped to the curtain. "Clever boy, that one. Weaves a good tale."

Rafi's stomach flipped. So Iakki had been talking, had he? What exactly had he told them? More importantly, how had it differed from his story? But before he could stew in his worry, Umut flung the curtain back, and all else faded.

Rafi halted on the threshold of a lush green place where birdsong soared over the sound of rushing water. Not the ceaseless wash of the sea, but the heavier roar of a waterfall. He smelled roasting meat and tangy spices, and he heard children shrieking in laughter, voices chattering, and warriors shouting as they trained. The raw life of it all reminded him so strongly of Zorrad, it cracked the dam he had built around his grief, flooding his throat.

He hesitated and then stepped out into the sun.

TWENTY-THREE: CERIDWEN

Shadowers walk in silence and can fade into shadow, smoke, and fog, rendering even their riders invisible. This is referred to as ghosting. Beware the moonless battle.

"*Shades,* Ceridwen." Finnian dropped into the grass beside her. They sprawled atop the crest of a hill, their steeds waiting behind, combat raging below. A ragged force of solborn riders harried their quarry, the Nadaari raiders, who had drawn into a tight block formation around the chariot and chained captives. Spears jutted over the soldiers' broad shields, and their helmets gleamed crimson in the dying sun.

She shifted to see over a clump of gorse. "You said that before."

"I have a feeling I'll be saying it a—where are you going? Stay down!"

Ignoring his warning hiss, she slithered forward to gain a better view of the combatants. Of course, she would be careful. Did he think she wanted to get killed? Not yet, at any rate. Not from a distance and not without slaying many before she fell.

It had taken a full day to run down the Nadaari raiders, only to find them already embroiled in a fight and outnumbering their opponents three to one. Unhorsed warriors fought beside downed steeds while mounted riders plunged through the fray, held at bay from freeing the captives by nearly forty Nadaari. Combat under such terms could not rage long. Her countrymen were failing. They would die. Or join the captives. But she read steadfastness in their dogged, relentless advance, and pride warmed her: they would not retreat.

A riveren collapsed, speared through the gut.

Its rider rolled free of its thrashing only to take a spear in the neck.

Behind, a thrown spear carried a stormrider from the saddle. He hit headfirst.

Her sabre was half-drawn before she realized it. She would not watch them die, not as she had watched her father. Not without wielding blade or flame in their aid, though it cost her life. To her steed, she ran with Finnian at her side. He might have disagreed with delaying their return, but no one could witness that slaughter below and not know that this was right. *This* was their duty.

Mindar pranced as she seized the reins, and the smoke that roiled from his nostrils was black as tar. She sang the wild cry of the Outriders, and Finnian sang it back as they sprang down the slope. Down toward the fight. Down toward spears glistening with the blood of their kin. Ceridwen struck first. Bathing the shield wall in fire, she launched into the soldiers. They fell back screaming, beating at the flames. Mindar's hooves drummed a man and his shield mate to the ground. Her sabre claimed the next head, breaking a path into the square where she spun Mindar into a firestorm and the soldiers surrounding her fled.

She pursued, the familiar song of blade upon blade rousing her heart. It thudded and stamped a warlike beat in her chest, keeping rhythm with Mindar's pounding hooves as she felled one, then another, then two more. In the fury, she forgot the ache of her leg and the agony of loss, forgot all but the horror unleashed upon her land, and for that, she demanded blood.

Until a roar like tumbling stones shattered her focus and her enemies parted in a wave before a chariot drawn by two enormous beasts with coats the color of ash and flame. Stone-eye tigers. Muscles bulging like cords, they lunged into their traces, goaded on by the charioteer, a man in flowing robes with chains dangling from his neck and wrists, jingling against the haft of his spear like a rain of coins. This must be the priest.

Reeling from a blow, an unhorsed warrior staggered into the chariot's path and froze. Body twisted to the side, one arm drawn back, weaponless. Beneath his helm, Ceridwen glimpsed brown eyes widened in terror as the tigers stalked forward.

He was trapped in their gaze.

Ceridwen cursed beneath her breath, already on the move, Mindar responding to the slightest adjustment in her position and reins, forging a path in a whirlwind of hooves, blade, and flame, not toward the front of the chariot where she too could be trapped, but toward the rear. Mindar hurtled over a slain riveren and flamed as he sprang.

The priest spun into a torrent of fire. White heat replaced the air in Ceridwen's lungs, smoke the breath in her nostrils, and a riot of color consumed her vision, blotting out a glimpse of the priest's flailing legs as he dove headlong from the flame. Hooves struck wood, jolting Ceridwen back to her senses, to the chariot straining beneath the weight of her fireborn's forelegs and the pull of the tigers. Their coats were singed only in patches. She could remedy that. On cue, Mindar tucked his nose, but the warrior stumbled into view, shaking his head.

Why was he still there? "Run!"

Startled, he looked up and their eyes locked. Then he knelt clumsily, seized a discarded spear, shielded his eyes with one arm, and ran *toward* the beasts.

Blazes, no! She twitched her reins and Mindar swallowed his flames. She dared not risk hitting the fool, even if he was determined to get himself killed. Claws slashed toward his chest. Missed by pure luck, since he didn't even dodge. Yelling, he rammed his spear into the stone-eye's throat, releasing a flood of crimson.

The beast roared and flung its head.

Knocking his grip loose.

Throwing him at the feet of the second stone-eye.

His muscles stiffened again, immobilizing him in a sprawl.

Defenseless like Bair before the stallion. No time for thought; it always yielded to action in the end anyway. Ceridwen rose, sabre in hand, set one boot on the saddle's seat–and for once, her unruly steed stood still–planted the other on the saddlebow, and leaped. Both hands found her hilt as she soared, rotating the blade downward toward the stone-eye's neck.

She hit and rolled, elbow striking something with bone-numbing force. It jarred the sabre from her grip. The earth knocked the breath from her lungs. Gasping, dust clinging to her lips, she got an aching knee under her and reached for the weapon.

Yellow eyes stared unblinking at her.

And she was able to look away. The power had gone out of them. *Blazes*, that had been close. She stood, eying the six inches of steel visible beneath the tiger's throat, pinning its head to the ground. The other beast was still twitching feebly, but copper-fletched arrows bristled along its spine. It wouldn't be rising anytime soon.

"Is it dead?" the warrior panted, scrambling back. "It is . . . isn't it?"

Ceridwen scanned him–alive, uninjured, but clearly shaken–and limped to retrieve her sabre, half-healed wound twinging at each step. Wincing, she planted one foot against the tiger's ribcage and pulled her blade free. "It's dead."

"Oh . . . good." Shuddering, he yanked off his helm and dropped it, braced his hands on his knees and bent double, chest heaving. "Oh good, good, good . . ."

She caught his arm as he swayed and eyed his lanky limbs and sharp elbows, his twiggy hair, his hearty spattering of freckles. *Blazes*, he was young–maybe fourteen? "Easy there. I'm Ceridwen. And you are?"

He looked up at her. "Uh . . . Liam."

"Stay with me, Liam. You'll be fine."

Everywhere, the battle dwindled. Their charge had been so surprising, so forceful, it had turned the tide. Riders loped across the valley, chasing fleeing soldiers and dispatching the enemy wounded, many who'd been felled by Finnian's copper-fletched arrows. Others freed the captives, and instead of blades clanging on shields, the air rang with breaking chains.

"Not dead yet, I see."

That voice brought a smile to her lips. "Nor you."

She turned slowly, wary of her aching leg, and barely caught the reins Finnian tossed her. He'd retrieved her steed. Mindar snorted contentedly as he ambled over to graze beside the dead tigers, ignoring the blood-tinged air that would normally spark him into combustion. Always a mystery, her wildborn. Calm one moment, an inferno the next. Unlike Finnian who surprised her only in his steadfastness, in his sense of duty that could lead him miles out of his way to ride to battle at her side, *kasar* brand and all.

Finnian slung a knee over his saddlebow and casually rested an elbow on it. Sweat streaked his shadower's hide, and his quiver was empty, arrows spent, but neither he nor his steed seemed injured. Relief was fresh air, a draught from Markham's flask, and apparently, it went straight to her head. She found herself grinning at the copper-fletched arrows–four of them–bristling from the stone-eye's back. "Somewhat overkill, don't you think? Unless you were aiming at me and kept missing."

"Of course I kept missing. Hitting you would mean patching you up again." He noticed the fresh bloodstain on her bandage and sighed. "Looks like I have to do that anyway. Clearly you don't need my help in almost getting killed. You have honed that skill into an art."

"Why attempt anything if not to master it?"

Shouts rang across the valley, and Finnian straightened abruptly, slinging his leg from the saddlebow. "Speaking of not dying, it appears you are not the only one." He took off toward two warriors who dragged a struggling form over to the clustered survivors.

It was the Nadaarian priest.

Cursing her leg, Ceridwen mounted and chased after Finnian, Liam jogging at her stirrup. The boy had reclaimed his helmet and the spear he'd used to kill the stone-eye. She felt strangely proud at that. Both freed captives and dismounted riders had formed a ring around the priest in the center of the battleground, but at the first puff of Mindar's heated breath against their backs, they parted, allowing her to pass.

Chains clanking, the priest crawled to his knees, his tattered robe catching under one foot and tearing as he rocked back to his heels, revealing burned skin beneath. So he had tasted Mindar's flames. That gave her a savage sense of satisfaction that fled as a tall woman stepped forward, face like flint, and the warriors bared the priest's throat for her knife.

He was the only survivor.

Instinct drove Ceridwen forward. "Hold! We should question him."

"Question him?" The woman raised an eyebrow but did not lower her blade. Hers was a blunt stare that took in Ceridwen's sudden appearance on her ash-streaked fireborn, the bloodied bandage on her thigh, and the crimson scarf on her forehead, and dismissed it. "How? I don't suppose you speak Nadaarian?"

Heirs of kings and war-chiefs learned such things. Outriders did not.

Ceridwen closed her eyes, forming the sentence before speaking it. "Can you understand me, priest?" It had been long since she had spoken Nadaarian, and the language felt rough on her tongue, but rattling chains told her the priest lifted his head.

"I understand you, woman."

She found him staring at her with an interest that did not match his sullen response. Instinct it seemed had not failed her. This was no mere underling. Those chains that ran from his neck to his wrists would signify his devotion and years of service to Murloch—so much she recalled from lessons on Nadaarian culture, religion, and government. His dark beard and smooth forehead marked him a young man, but already his chains were long. He might be able to tell her what the invaders planned if she questioned him carefully.

"Tell me, priest, why do you invade our land and slaughter my people?"

"The Voice has spoken."

That made her pause. Had she misunderstood? She had always

heard Murloch referred to as the *Silent One*. "And what does the voice say?"

"That if you yield now, you need not die."

"Strange since you are the one facing death." She nodded toward the woman's unsheathed knife and the two warriors braced on either side of the priest, and then dismounted carefully, so she did not wince and reveal her weakness. "But if you answer now, I may kill you quickly. Where is the army headed?"

"Everywhere." The priest gave a bloodstained smile. "It has marched on from the valley of slaughter. One column heads south. One marches north. The main column brings sword and ruin through the heart of your kingdom, and dozens of parties like this one were dispatched to lay waste ahead of it. Murloch stirs from slumber. He rises to dominate the world, and the world must be made ready to fall at his feet."

So much he offered so readily?

Ceridwen eyed him skeptically. "Soldonia is not the world."

He tilted his head, running his tongue over cracked lips. "No . . . it is not."

His hand snaked out so fast she had no time to react. Something stabbed into her wrist and for an instant the world darkened and became cold, her breath fogged before her, and a thunderous voice splintered her to the bone:

Prepare yourself, woman, for the falling of all nations.

Sparks struck her back, and she came to herself to find her fireborn in flames behind her and the priest still clutching her wrist. She jerked free as the two warriors restrained the priest and turned to calm Mindar. He snorted, pawing the ground. Blood trickled down her glove from a puncture wound. She clamped it with her other hand, but it was not deep. It barely stung.

But that voice. That *Voice*.

"What was that?" she demanded.

The priest pressed his lips together. She nodded at the warriors and they forced his arm over, revealing a curved claw attached to his palm. Chitinous and colored a dark blue above and mottled pale red beneath. No, not attached–embedded, with the skin grown around it. *Blazes*, the sight of it made her feel sick.

She seized his chains and dragged him close. "What was that? Answer me."

"The Voice speaks as it wills. All nations must bow or fall. Soldonia, Rhiakkor, Hurron, Venyamar–"

"Venyamar?" Ceridwen repeated, collecting her scattered wits. He had spoken first of bordering nations, but Venyamar was a vast and frozen wasteland far to the north. "It is far from here to Venyamar, and it is far from Idolas to all of Soldonia."

The priest raised his chin. "Have you ever seen a scadtha devour its prey? It cages it within its legs, then drives its claws into its flesh, one after another." His eyes flicked down to her wrist. "Then when it is paralyzed, blood draining from numerous wounds, only then does it lower its head to feast. So the armies of Nadaar will spread across your land, draining the lifeblood of your warriors, your steeds, your children, and only when your nation lies bleeding from a hundred wounds will you be devoured."

She released him and backed away. Her skin seemed afire but with cold not heat, and even her sabre offered no comfort. No strength. No stability against the shivering of that Voice.

"The Eyes have seen it. The Ears have heard it. And the Voice has–"

The swish of her sabre stole his final words. She turned and walked blindly to Mindar's side. "I am finished with him."

Behind, the body toppled with a thud.

TWENTY-FOUR: RAFI

There is wisdom in the cry of a songbird for the one who has ears to hear.
– Hanonque proverb

Rafi emerged into an airy cavern that flashed with the bright blue and yellow wings of a hundred darting songbirds, shimmered with waterfall-tossed droplets, and rang with the hollow clanging of bells on the necks of goats scampering precariously along the cliff-like walls. His beehive-shaped hut stood apart from a cluster of similar huts all woven from rattan, crowned with blue flowering moss, and surrounded by people going about their work. But it was the waterfall that claimed his openmouthed attention.

Ahead to his left, water and sunlight poured together in a shimmering, thunderous stream from an enormous hole in the ceiling, showering his face with cool mist before plunging past his feet through another hole.

"Beautiful, isn't it?" Umut called over its roar.

And Rafi had no reply but a laugh, for how could words begin to describe such a sight?

Umut breathed deeply, head tipped back, sea-blue eyes vanishing beneath heavy lids. "Lykier may sit in his palace, atop the hoarded riches of the kingdoms he has claimed, surrounded by the thousand waterfalls of Cetmur, but not even he can boast a view so grand."

Rafi inched to the edge where he saw another cavern below. Huts and people speckled the rim of a third hole through which the waterfall continued to plunge. Down. Down. Down. It was dizzying.

For a heartbeat, a trailing scream drowned out water and birdsong. Delmar?

"If you're done gawking, Alonque . . ." Nef's surly voice yanked him into the present.

Wiping the mist from his face, he left Umut leaning on his crutch, gazing into that rippling curtain of light, and followed as Nef rounded the waterfall and angled toward a massive opening in the cavern wall. Another gaped in the side of the cavern below, just visible through the hole. The sheer scale of this place was confusing. Only now did Rafi realize it wasn't actually a cavern but a gorge that ripped through the earth.

Three natural bridges connected the two gorge walls, forming rings around the waterfall that created the ceiling above, the cavern he stood in, the one below, and beneath that . . . no telling. From here, the massive openings between bridges looked like windows. One open to the sky above, allowing the waterfall to pour through as if bled from the cloudless blue; one–on his level–gaping toward the rocky upper cliffs of the gorge; and one–below–offering a sprawling overview of the verdant valley beneath, where the Mah jungle boiled up to stake its claim.

Instead of crossing the bridge, Nef turned toward the hole, ducking beneath teardrop-shaped woven nests dangling from a low overhang, and swung out onto a slat-and-rope staircase that zigzagged down the gorge wall into the cavern below.

Rafi jerked to a stop, mouth dry. He didn't trust Nef not to "show him" a shortcut to a long fall. "So . . . where are we going?"

"Down."

His reluctance had everything to do with his injury, of course, and nothing with nightmares of falling–so he told himself as he inched out onto the staircase. At least waterfall mist had not slicked the slats, so slipping would not be a problem. Then again, he had tripped over flat ground before, and a fall from here would be far less forgiving, so he kept a tight grip on the waist-high rope. Unlike Nef who was practically jogging.

"Keep up, Alonque!"

"It's *Nahiki*." Clamping one hand to his side, Rafi limped faster. He stood a head taller and his legs were longer, so Nef had to be deliberately setting such a blistering pace. And he showed no signs of slacking once they reached the bottom and wove through the people scattered along both cavern and bridge. Men, women, children. Some in Mahque beaded belts and earthy colors, some with Alonque bead strands knotted in their hair and shell necklaces heaped around their necks, some wearing Hanonque feathered vests and colorful woven armbands. All going about their daily lives, working, eating, and playing together. On the far side, three children climbed the cavern wall, clinging with fingers and toes. Their laughter reminded him of diving with Iakki and his twin cousins. It was all so ordinary, so peaceful, so unlike what he had expected from the secret camp of the Que Revolution.

He quickened his pace to reach Nef's side. "How many rebels are there?"

"Enough."

"For what?"

"To tear the empire down."

Rafi glanced at a group of women pounding blue moss in a pestle while a man stirred a mass of thread in a bubbling cauldron. Farther down the cavern, another group wove cloth of varied shades of blue on small frames. Still farther, potters slung clay, netmakers twisted ropes, and as they crossed the bridge, he could see where Mahque soil tenders had carved a field out of the jungle on the gorge floor to grow fruits and vegetables. There were hundreds of people here from all three Que tribes.

And it was not nearly enough.

"Are we thinking of the same empire?"

Nef shot him an unpleasant smirk. "What, Alonque, are you afraid?"

"Hoy, Nef!" The man who loped up to tower over them was tall as a neefwa tree but twice as broad. His hair was shaved around a healing wound that carved from his right eyebrow to the back of his skull, and the tip of one ear was missing. The rest of his hair was knotted on the back of his head, but a strand of red and yellow beads dangled behind his left ear. Alonque, then, but from a different section of the coast than Zorrad.

"Hoy, Moc." Nef greeted him with a clasped wrist.

"Any news from my brother?"

To Rafi's surprise, Nef's manner softened. "Moc . . . you know it's only been three weeks. It takes time to get reports from the outposts."

"I know, I know." Moc pocketed his fists and scuffed one foot. His features looked like they had been carved with a blunt knife, except that scar, which had clearly come from a very sharp, very large object. "I just worry about him. Out there without me. But the healers say I'll be fit for fighting again soon."

He actually looked hopeful.

If he had any sense, he would run before the revolution finished the job and got him killed. There was no doubt that the more the rebels resisted, the more trouble they stirred up for themselves, and the more the empire–and Sahak, as its chief weapon–sought to crush them. Then again, Sahak never needed much excuse to make someone squirm.

Nef gripped his shoulder. "That, Moc, is the spirit that will win this war for us."

Rafi rolled his eyes at the jab as Moc went away grinning and they resumed their rushed march across the bridge. "So, where is his brother? Out on a raid?"

Not even a grunt.

"Some tour this is. Is this what Umut meant when he told you to show me around?"

"He said nothing about talking."

"What about feeding? I could eat."

Nef tossed him a withering scowl and moved around the curve of a wide alcove in the cavern wall. Steam struck Rafi in the face as he followed, carrying the distinct spicy tang of boiling cala root. So, this was the kitchens. Chopped vegetables awaited roasting in clay bowls, skewers of goat meat sizzled in stone ovens, and colorful soups simmered in massive pots. Until that first whiff, he hadn't realized just how hungry he was.

Clunk, clunk, clunk. Rafi startled at the slap of a knife on a board. His focus on the food had kept him from noticing the cooks: a girl with shining dark hair that reminded him of Yeena deftly wielded the enormous blade, a boy no older than Iakki skewered goat meat one-handed, and a stocky man with shoulder-length hair like Sev scrubbed dishes with ash soap in a cauldron.

The boy glanced up, and Rafi gave him a grin.

"Here." Nef snagged a cala root cracker from a stack and slapped it in Rafi's hand. "Food." He spun to leave and knocked into an elderly woman with a graybeard monkey on her shoulder and a clay jar on her head. The monkey screeched and launched at his face. He jerked back, jostling the woman, and the jar slipped.

Rafi caught it before it broke. Luckily, it was empty. He straightened and found the woman staring at him. Her skin sagged with deep wrinkles like the . . . hide of a shelled turtle. Like Torva. The lump in his throat took on the sharp edges of a sea urchin. It wasn't enough that he heard the ghost's voice, now he had to see reminders of lost loved ones everywhere. Maybe Sahak wasn't the only crazy one in the family.

He shook his head when the woman reached for the jar. "Let me help."

She patted his elbow, then balanced another jar on her head and left. Rafi eyed his jar, tempted to try it, if only because his many stints in new villages had taught him that the sooner he faded into the local way of life, the better. Still, his limp impeded his balance, and breaking things seemed a bad start, so he hugged it to his chest instead.

Shaking off the chattering monkey, Nef blocked his exit. "What are you doing?"

"Helping. You should try it." Rafi shouldered away from his grasp. "With your own jar. Don't worry there's more." He netted his amusement as Nef yanked a jar from the ground. "After you."

Cool water lapped at Rafi's toes as he dipped his jar into the pool at the waterfall's end. It was dark here in the lowest cavern, but the sunlight that reached so far cast shimmering reflections off the water where gossamer strands of luminescent threads spun by silk spiders drifted beneath the surface. No songbirds flew, no huts ringed the pool, but there was life still. Herbs grew in vines from woven planters hanging on the moss-covered walls, and farther down, where the pool drained into a stream, women scrubbed clothes on the bank while children splashed and played.

Rafi let his hand sink into the water. So smooth, it felt, without the swirl of salt and sand.

"Don't even think about it." Nef dunked his jar. "This pool is reserved for drinking. Washing happens downstream." He glanced at Rafi. "You could use it."

Rafi ignored the gibe. "Where does the stream go?"

"Underground."

"And then?"

Nef turned abruptly. "Who knows?"

But his manner told Rafi that he, at least, knew well enough.

Strong fingers gripped his elbow, stopping him from hefting his jar. The woman, Saffa—he had pried her name from Nef on the way down—nodded at his head, then made sure he was watching before settling her own jar without spilling a drop. Clearly, she wanted him to imitate her example.

"I can't do it, Saffa."

Her face scrunched in confusion.

"Sorry, I can't," he repeated louder, tugging up his tunic to reveal his bandage. Not the only reason, but the simplest to explain.

Behind him, Nef scoffed. "She may not speak, but she can hear just fine."

Right. He let his tunic fall, and Saffa patted his arm with a patient smile before beginning her slow, steady climb. Nef chafed at his heels all the way, but with his aching side and weak legs, the pace suited Rafi. Even so, his breath was coming in gasps by the time they neared the kitchens, and water had sloshed down his tunic, sopping his bandage. Voices overhead drew his eye to the three climbers now scaling a wall dotted with hanging nests while songbirds darted anxiously around them. But he spared only a brief glance before again watching the ground under his feet.

"Careful, Iakki!"

Startled, Rafi wheeled toward the climbers: a girl with curly hair in a tail, a boy with wide ears and a triangular face, and ten feet higher, wearing a pieced-together outfit of Alonque cropped trousers, Mahque belt, and Hanonque vest, Iakki. The boy clung with one dusty foot swinging free, stretching to grab a nest. "Iakki?"

"Nahiki?" Iakki twisted, face splitting into a grin. "Cousin! You ain't dead!"

His foot slipped. Rafi lunged, but Iakki's handhold slammed him into the wall where he hung, laughing hysterically. The nest rocked back and two blue eggs spilled out.

The climbers gasped. Iakki's laughter died.

But somehow, Nef managed to catch both eggs in his water jar without spilling a drop. Meanwhile, Rafi was soaked after his lunge, and to add injury to insult, his skull was pounding again. Saffa raised a wry eyebrow as she shuffled toward the kitchen, leaving him to wring out his tunic while the climbers scrambled down to stand sheepishly before Nef.

Nef shook his head. "You have some excuse, Iakki. You are new to our ways. But you two"–to the boy and girl–"are not. The songbirds are a gift from Cael herself to the Hanonque. They sing at our births, weep at our deaths, shelter us with cast-off feathers, and watch our skies for danger. You will respect them."

Rafi had expected more harshness and less solemnity from him. He was Mahque, wasn't he? What did he care for the gifts of Cael when Cihana was favored of his people? But Nef waited until all three nodded their understanding before instructing the girl to return the eggs.

Once she started climbing, Iakki ran to Rafi. "Where have you been, cousin? I have been swimming, climbing, chasing goats and–"

"Speaking of that," Nef interrupted, "Hald says to stop before the goats eat you."

Iakki laughed. "Goats don't eat *boys*."

"Ah, but Hald does."

Was that a hint of a smile on Nef's face? Rafi felt disoriented. "Iakki–" He caught sight of the bruises smudging the boy's face and tipped Iakki's chin so he could inspect the black eye. "What happened?"

"It's nothing." Iakki pushed his hand away. "I waited for you for *ages*."

"I was preoccupied with not dying. Sorry it took so long."

Iakki opened his mouth to speak, but Nef pressed his jar into his arms. "Here, run the water to Saffa." He motioned the other boy to take Rafi's. "Quickly now. And see you stay out of trouble."

Both ran off without complaint, Iakki without even looking at Rafi. Since when had the boy not argued about a chore? He seemed to be settling in well.

Why did that needle Rafi so?

"Come, Alonque," Nef called over his shoulder, striking toward a sloping path that ran up the side of the gorge to the next level. "Umut awaits."

The songbird fell still, melody stolen by strong hands. Holding the tiny corpse before him, Umut leaned on his crutch, but he did not look a weathered piece of driftwood now with a cloak of iridescent blue feathers tenting his rugged frame and a crown of gilded beaks wreathing his salted head. He stood on an open grassy stretch where the highest cavern floor extended past the natural bridge and ran along the side of the gorge, a place where rebels trained with spear and sling and bow and where the families of the lost were gathered for this final farewell.

Some weeping. Some stone-faced. Some raw with anger.

Rafi's pace slowed as he and Nef approached the outskirts of the group. This was not a moment to disturb. Tears shone in Umut's sea-blue eyes and ran down the seams of his rough-wood face as he lifted the feathery mass to his lips and whispered something Rafi could not hear and then plucked the feathers one by one, breaking them, and passing one half to each family who took it in silence and then left.

The songbird did not sing. The families did not speak. But the voice of war roared behind them in the shouts of trainers and the grunts and yells of warriors struggling in the sun, sweat glistening on bare backs and slicking weapon grips.

"What is it?" Nef jeered. "Is the sound of combat so offensive?"

No, it just felt wrong somehow.

No relief for the grieving from reminders of the fight. No relief for the warriors from reminders of their fate. Only broken feathers from a broken bird bestowed as a blessing from their . . . suddenly, just as he had known before who Umut was, now he knew what he was. "Umut is their leader," he muttered.

Seeing him now as a figure resplendent in the sun, it made sense: Umut was the head of the Que Revolution. Of course, he had expected the orchestrator of that long-ago escape to be someone important–who else could have coordinated infiltrating the capitol to break the sons of the old regime out of prison? But he hadn't expected *this*.

"What, Alonque, your brother didn't tell you?"

Somehow, Nef's tongue always transformed "Alonque" into an insult, but that bite had been missing when he addressed Moc and Iakki, so clearly it wasn't Rafi's heritage he despised so much as *him*. "Tell me, Nef, why am I 'Alonque' and my cousin is 'Iakki'?"

"Your cousin is a fighter. Like them." Nef jerked his chin toward the trainees. "They are the old, young, sick, and injured, yet they come to fight. You want to know how Iakki got his black eye? He fought like a terror to see you." He held up his hand so Rafi could see the scabbed-over toothmarks. "You lazed on that hammock for a week and merely asked about him."

So that was how long it had been. Rafi only remembered snatches of their journey here–tied into a sling, delirious with fever, blind inside that sack–and little more of his recovery. But he could imagine Nef filling Iakki's head with notions about his uncaring cousin, and his knuckles cracked as his fists tightened.

Someone stepped up behind him. "So we honor those we have lost." Umut stood there, and Rafi could not tell if his words were a rebuke or merely commentary on the ritual. Seen up close, Rafi realized his cloak fluttered with hundreds of broken feathers, matching those given to the grieving. "What think you of our camp, Nahiki?"

Rafi swallowed. "This is more what I expected." He gestured toward the warriors training and the craftsmen fashioning arms. "Though you might consider separating your fighters from your grieving widows. You must see a lot of desertion."

Nef threw up his hands in disgust and stalked off to join those sparring.

"That is the purpose." Umut eyed him thoughtfully, surprisingly regal with his crutch and cloak and crown. "So, what do you say, are you ready to join our hopeless fight?"

"This is your recruitment speech?"

"I have enough fiery young fools under my leadership."

As if on cue, Nef let out a roar, startling the trainee he sparred against. The boy stumbled, dropping his spear, earning a lecture as Nef tossed it back to him.

Umut raised both eyebrows and shook his head. "Cael knows passion can be harnessed, but I need warriors who weigh the cost against our cause and know it to be worthy. Only such warriors will be able to rise and rise again when all seems lost. And all will seem lost, Nahiki of the Alonque. I won't lie to you about that. I can't."

Rafi almost revealed his identity then and there. The words flooded his tongue, desperate for air. But if the head of the Que

Revolution could admit the cause was doomed, he was better off remaining Nahiki a while longer. Forever, if possible. Shrugging, he indicated his side. "Not much good for fighting right now."

It was a poor excuse, and he knew it.

Clearly, Umut did too. But he only nodded slowly and summoned Nef with instructions to see Rafi settled–he interpreted that as "given some preoccupying task"–and then left. Beneath his cloak, Umut's shoulders seemed bent lower than before.

Panting from exertion, sweaty hair plastered to his forehead, Nef leaned on his spear to inspect Rafi before pointedly glancing at the trainees. Rafi followed the look. They were indeed the old, the young, the sick, and the injured.

And they might fight.

But they would die and the empire would barely notice.

"Go back to Saffa." Nef scoffed. "The kitchen is all you are fit for."

TWENTY-FIVE: CERIDWEN

Of all stormriders, Briead the Farseeing soared highest and shot farthest and never failed to strike her mark until the day she fell like a bolt from the sky and smote the earth.

Ceridwen grimaced as Finnian plucked out the torn stitches from her inflamed wound. She shifted to hide her discomfort, pressing her back against the sturdy saddle propped behind her, and breathed deeply. Something about the familiar scent of horse mixed with the earthiness of oiled leather and the sharp tang of ash calmed her. It helped her breathe easier, despite the pain and the echo of the Voice whispering in her ears.

"Does that hurt?" Finnian's eyes flicked up.

"Yes, *blazes*, it does."

"Good." The corners of his mouth twitched toward a smile. "Maybe that will teach you not to pull such a stunt again. Not while wounded at least. You're not invincible, Ceridwen–"

"Really? I had no idea."

"–and there's the proof in case you hadn't noticed." He drew her attention to her leg.

She glimpsed raw flesh and violet bruising before an image of Bair's broken body invaded her vision, and she had to force her eyes away to the survivors setting up camp around them instead. The tall woman had taken charge, directing some to tend wounds, others to unsaddle steeds and release them to graze, still others to begin building a pyre for their fallen, while a bearded man tended a skillet over the flaming ruin of the chariot. Both warriors and freed captives worked willingly. Snatches of their conversation drifted to Ceridwen. Murmurings of fear. Vows of retribution. Prayers of hope and despair. It all scraped against that raw wound inside her and demanded a response. She knew what she must do, and it made her heart rattle unevenly against her ribs until her fingers picked up the beat and drummed it into the packed earth.

Onward, onward, onward.

"Saved me from being eaten by stone-eyes, she did." Liam passed by, tailing a lean man with curly hair and a crooked grin to the fireside, only twenty paces from Ceridwen. "Rained fire and freed me from the beasts' spell so I could stab one of them with this very spear I hold in my hand. See? There's blood on it still. And here, see where its claws nicked me? Why, another inch and–no, here, see? But she leaped in the air and–"

"Save the tale for later, lad." The woman clapped Liam's shoulder in passing and gently spun him around. "When it can be best enjoyed over meat and a cup. Let your tongue rest awhile, and set your hands to work instead, eh?"

"Oh, but Aunt–"

"Now, lad."

"I'm going. I'm going." Liam jogged off, spear bouncing on his shoulder. Ceridwen winked as he passed. His face reddened, but he grinned back.

"I swear that lad could talk a stone-eye to death." Sighing, the lean man crouched to sneak a taste out of the skillet and narrowly evaded a swipe of the cook's spoon. He juggled the meat in his fingers before tossing it in his mouth. "Now that . . . that's good. But do you think it's wise to light a fire? Mightn't it draw more raiders upon us?"

"What if it does?" The woman tugged at the straps of her archer's bracers to tighten them. Her blue, quilted, hooded clothing and boiled leather harness and greaves accentuated the strength of her build and marked her a stormrider. "I say let them come. The earth has yet to drink its fill of Nadaari blood, I think, and I have yet to sate my appetite for spilling it. What say you, Hab?"

Grunting, the bearded man gave the skillet another stir.

"Now that was well put. Speaking of appetite, I'm fair starved and that smells almost edible. Done to blackness, is it? Nold, would you pass word that supper is past ready and like to burn if not eaten?"

Chuckling, the lean man strode off into the twilight.

"Done," Finnian announced, tying off a fresh bandage and wiping his hands on his knees. "You need to stay off that leg as much as possible, unless you want to tear the muscles further and wind up with permanent damage. Or risk a soured wound."

That was a sobering thought. It would be just her pit-spawned luck to escape Kilmark's ambush only to die from infection. There could be no glory, no atonement in such a death. Then again, she had no hope for glory or atonement anymore. "Stay off the leg. Got it."

"I mean it." He busied himself gathering the soiled bandages. "We should take it easier on our ride back. Travel slower. Rest more."

"And let the kingdom burn?"

Finnian's jaw tightened. She had relayed the priest's words to him but not the words of the Voice. No one else had heard it, and she could not begin to explain. Maybe that was why she read only unease in the lines of his face and nothing to match the horror of the chill rooted deep inside her.

"We should stay, Finnian, and fight. You know that we should."

"I know our duty is clear. The war-chiefs should hear what we have discovered."

"You ride on then. I will stay." She felt the heat of the words rolling off her tongue and embraced it, banishing the chill. "On my last return, I spent weeks in a cell for breaking the *kasar*. The war-chiefs do not want me alive. They certainly do not want me as heir. But there is a threat here and now, and I can fight to save our people. Who knows, maybe I can slow the Nadaari, give the war-hosts time to regroup."

"All on your own?"

"Certainly not. Mindar counts for at least three."

"So that's how it must be, is it? Just you and your fireborn and all the world arrayed against you?" Muscles taut as a drawn bowstring, he shoved back on his heels. "All hail the final ride of Ceridwen tal Desmond as she blazes out to glory. Is that what you wish?"

Already he knew her so well.

Her fingers found the horse-head pommel of her sabre, the dip in its nose worn smooth by the rubbing of her thumb, and she did not try to deny it. "I wish to know I've done something to save them."

"Then you will not ride alone, Ceridwen tal Desmond," a woman said.

Startled, Ceridwen jerked her head up to see the tall stormrider standing over them. A thick brown rope of a braid wrapped over the woman's head and down one shoulder, framing a square jaw around a smile that broke like a beam of sunshine stretching broad and warm over grassy plains. It revealed a slight gap between her front teeth.

"Iona tal Vern," the woman said, holding out a hand. "Of Lochrann."

Ceridwen made no move to take it. "You know my name?" Flames take Finnian and his ill-tamed tongue. She shot him a withering glare.

"Oh, don't flame at him." Iona shook her head. "I knew it already. I was there, you see, at Rysinger, the day you carried your brother across the drawbridge."

Solid earth melted beneath her.

Ash on her tongue, down her throat, in her lungs . . .

With an effort, she relaxed her fingers from her sabre. "What do you want from me?"

"I have two sons. My sister keeps them safe in her village to the east. I *had* a husband." Iona's voice fractured, and she looked down, adjusting her bracers. Not soon enough to hide the gleam of tears. "He was . . . killed . . . at Idolas. I still have my nephew Liam. Only because I rode to save him, and once we got out, we kept on riding."

Iona nodded at the nine warriors clustering around Hab's skillet to eat now that the freed captives had been served. "What you see here is all that remains of four patrols from three separate units and two chiefdoms: Harnoth and Lochrann. We were all of us cut off in the rout. I bear no rank at all, yet somehow, I found myself responsible for them."

Too easily, Ceridwen could forget that sorrow was not hers alone, that the world was full of suffering and they all rode beneath the shadow of death. "Why are you telling me this?"

Iona drew in a steadying breath. "Because our leaders are dead or fled, and I daresay there are hundreds more like us. Scattered, maybe, but willing to ride if it means protecting our own." Her eyes lifted, and something in them made Ceridwen straighten, heedless of the ache in her leg or the crushing exhaustion she always felt after a fight. "Ride here, Ceridwen tal Desmond, and we will ride with you. You will be our war-chief, and we will be your patrol, and together, we will drive those cursed Nadaari back into the sea."

Ceridwen's throat tightened. "Why? You saw what I am."

"I did. I saw you fighting atop that pit-spawned steed, and *sky's blood* but I would sooner have you by my side than all the rest of the war-hosts."

For an instant, Ceridwen breathed and did not taste ash. She looked down, and the crater did not gape before her. She closed her eyes and did not see Bair lying broken at her feet. But it only lasted an instant. Leveraging her good leg beneath her, she stood, spurning the hand Finnian offered, lest it reveal the lie in her words. "I ride best alone."

"Maybe." Iona eyed her flatly. "But we will save more together. Think on it."

Together. The word hummed in Ceridwen's ears, rattled in her bones, and pranced an off-beat rhythm in her chest as she sat beside Finnian on the outskirts of the fire, watching the others eat and talk, laugh and sing. Invaders stalked across their land, traitors devoured their own, and the slain still smoldered in their pyre, but for a time, together, they could forget.

With a breezy sigh, Iona dropped beside Finnian and kicked off her boots. She rubbed her feet, wincing. "Good to be free of those!"

"Wrong size?" Finnian asked, nodding at the boots.

Iona laughed ruefully. "Wrong feet, I'm afraid. Never yet found a pair of boots that didn't hurt by day's end. Anyone seen that nephew of mine?"

Nold snorted. "With any luck he's still riding the perimeter." He laughed at Iona's reproachful glance. "What? I needed a breather. He kept going on and on, chattering my ears off with that wild claim he slew a stone-eye. As if!"

The bearded cook and a few others chuckled along.

Over the flames, Ceridwen spied Liam trotting up on a dappled gray riveren, spear resting casually on one shoulder. Too far to know he was the brunt of their laughter, he rode with a swagger that would have put Markham to shame. She raised her voice. "It is true, you know."

"What is?"

"Liam killed a stone-eye." Granted, Finnian's arrows had helped, but the boy had attacked when any other–wiser–warrior would have fled.

Nold's eyes widened, and he choked on his drink. "He did?" His gaze slid past her, and he leaped to his feet. "Would you look at who it is? The great Stone-eye Killer himself!"

Face crimsoning, Liam dismounted to applause and strutted over to Iona who yanked him down into an embrace. Seeing them shoulder to shoulder, the resemblance became clear. Same brown hair, long limbs, freckled cheeks, and bluff openness of expression.

Iona said, "Now you can tell your tale."

"Aye, and spare no details," Nold added.

"Oh, but would you believe it?" Liam's face was aglow with firelight, and he leaned forward basking in the attention. "I'd only just been knocked from my steed by a sneaky spear swipe from a *shardaar* of a Nadaari–"

"Mind that tongue, boy!" Iona interrupted. "What would your mother say?"

"–when I heard the unutterable sound of a stone-eye roar!"

His was a dramatic storytelling style, full of weighted pauses and changes to volume and cadence that invited his listeners to hearken to every word. Caught up in the inventive retelling that little resembled her recollection, Ceridwen missed the moment Finnian glided away, but she noted his absence and followed.

She found him near the picketed steeds. So far from the fire's glow, his shadower was invisible to her, but she could hear the faint creak of tack being tightened and buckled in place. "You're not leaving tonight, are you?"

Finnian tensed at her voice. "Someone has to carry word to the war-chiefs." His cloak brushed her as he moved to adjust the shadower's bridle. "Come with me, Ceridwen. Ride on to Rysinger, talk with Markham–"

"I will, as I swore I would. Once I am finished here."

"Not about the pairing. Do you really think that still matters? About the kingdom. You have a duty to the war-chiefs. Why won't you come?"

"I have already said why–"

"No." He shifted to face her, frustration crackling from him like energy from a stormer's hooves. "Say what you like, but I see the truth in you. You're afraid, Ceridwen tal Desmond. Of what, I don't know, but I do know this: cowardice does not run in the blood of Lochrann."

That blood boiled within her now, hotter than all the fiery streams of Koltar. She did not trust herself to speak. Would not deign retreat. So, she stood as he mounted and trotted past, shadower's hooves falling noiselessly as always.

"I only do my duty, Ceridwen. What are you doing?"

His words haunted her long after he ghosted into the night.

TWENTY-SIX: JAKIM

Aodh restores.

"Imbecile!" Khilamook hissed, lashing out with his cane. It struck the slave's back with a crack, and the man groaned as he bent to retrieve the shards of the ceramic sphere that had slipped from his hands onto a rock instead of into the cradle of the war machine. "Have you sand for wits and reeds for hands?"

Jakim stifled a sympathetic wince, his own back already aching and bruised. He shuffled to balance the armload of loose papers and scrolls Khilamook had crammed into his arms before leaving his tent. Some of the loose sheafs stuck to his sweat-slick skin, and he could only hope the ink didn't start running or—

Khilamook was staring at him, eyebrows raised expectantly.

Jakim felt a flood of panic. What had he missed? The insult? He hadn't bothered to translate it. The cane seemed to relay the message clearly enough. "Uh . . ." He racked his brain for the closest approximation in the slave's native Soldonian and ended up making up a word for lack of an alternative.

Scrollmaster Gedron would be shocked at how easily that lie came.

He caught a hint of a knowing smirk on Khilamook's face before the engineer darted away around the wheeled war machine with a gait that resembled a long-legged slythe. There was something of that seabird in the way he held his head too, tilted slightly and tucked forward, and in his darting eyes and sharp movements. Jakim hurried to keep up. One week in the engineer's service had inspired ample words in several languages to describe the man, and kind was not one of them. Or patient. Jakim had served many masters but none as unpredictable as the engineer—and in a master, unpredictability was a terrifying trait.

Over that week, the army had moved sluggishly on from the valley of corpses, and the engineer had spent hours poring over manuscripts in his cart when they marched and hours more in his tent when they halted and fortified their camp against cavalry attacks, tinkering with strange cylindrical devices that he inserted carefully into those ceramic spheres. Only the engineer knew their purpose, but Jakim recalled wading through broken warriors and steeds, and his stomach upended. Khilamook had promised the tsemarc even greater victories to come.

"You on the cranks, rotate those evenly or . . . and you, sledgehammer here . . ."

Jakim caught up to Khilamook in time to catch the cane between his shoulder blades before he began translating the barked commands to the team loading the war machine. Somehow, the engineer's tongue never broke stride.

"Careful with that, or I'll replace it with your head!"

This at the slave muscling a ceramic sphere into the cradle. Thick neck, lean arms, jagged scar. It was the sailor. Jakim broke off his translation, but Khilamook had moved on. He seemed in a state of frenzied distraction, issuing strings of half-uttered instructions that Jakim had to interpret and translate, all while keeping up with his mad dash. Translation was challenging on its own, but the technical knowledge required here far exceeded Jakim's skill. By the time the war machine was ready, he had a dozen new bruises from the cane.

Khilamook halted and flung open the high collar of his tapestried robe against the sun's warmth and rolled the wide sleeves up past his elbows, revealing thin but muscled arms covered in waxy scars. Jakim blinked away, not wanting to be caught staring. "Ready the hammer. Potter, with me." The crisp commands summoned a wiry man in a clay-smeared smock who fidgeted nervously at

Khilamook's elbow while a slave squared a sledgehammer over the trigger block.

"Hoy, Scroll . . ." a voice hissed.

Jakim turned around and spied the sailor lounging against a handcart piled with ceramic spheres. The sailor tossed a wheel chock in the air and caught it. What was he–*ow*! His distraction earned a sharp jab in the ribs from the engineer's cane.

"Release the trigger!"

The hammer struck with a crash. The ropes groaned. The war machine's arm shot up and slammed into the crossbar, and the sphere shattered overhead. It was echoed by a louder crash behind. Jakim bent over his scrolls. Stinging shards pelted his neck and something wet trickled down his spine. He freed a hand to swipe at it, expecting blood but finding mostly water.

Khilamook drew in a hissing breath and deliberately wiped his face with his sleeve. "Congratulations, potter. You have killed us all."

Or . . . maybe . . . not water.

Jakim's lungs hitched in panic. Was it . . . poison? He didn't feel like he was dying. Aodh knew he wasn't ready. Not with the lies he had told. Not with his vows unfulfilled. Not without seeing his brothers. A whack of the cane stung a stumbling translation from his lips that made the potter blanch and tighten his fists around his smock.

"Or you would have"–Khilamook's tone was scornful–"if this were not merely a test. I believe I made my specifications for the design quite clear. It required a highly complex bit of mathematics, and I am not prone to miscalculation." He held out one hand. "Bring out the diagram, slave, and show this imbecile his error."

Jakim shuffled through his load, unsure which diagram the engineer meant. A sketch of the war machine and a scroll filled with strings of letters and numbers were dismissed out of hand. Nothing else seemed to fit. "Could it still be on your desk, master?"

"Only if you failed to bring it as instructed."

If instructed, he would have brought it. But Khilamook had

selected this stack, so if it was anyone's fault, it was the engineer's. Of course, "fair" was also not a word that described the engineer, so there was no point in protesting. "I will check, master."

As he dashed off, papers fluttering against his chin, his gaze snagged on the handcart where the sailor had been sitting. It had tipped over, scattering broken spheres on the ground. That must have been the second crash he had heard. Should he say something?

No. Better not to be the bearer of bad tidings.

Jakim shouldered through the silk hangings, dumped his armload on the engineer's stool, and rifled through the mass of papers on his campaign desk. More sketches of war machines, more undecipherable strings of numbers and . . . there. He lifted a single sheet containing multiple drawings of the spheres surrounded by a spiderweb of notes.

It was immediately plucked from his fingers.

"Many thanks, Scroll."

Jakim gaped as the sailor lowered the paper to the oil lamp he had forgotten to extinguish before leaving the tent. He yelped and yanked the burning paper away, dropping it into a pile of dirty clothes and using them to smother the flames. "What are you doing?"

"Sabotage, obviously. Or you know, not helping those who enslaved me."

"You think burning one page will make a difference?"

"Huh." The sailor pursed his lips. "Good point." He kicked the stool over, scattering Jakim's stacked scrolls and papers, then reached for the oil lamp.

Jakim grabbed it, burning his fingers in his haste. "You tipped the handcart, didn't you?"

"Of course, I did."

"But how did you get in here without being seen?" Half a dozen overseers constantly prowled around Khilamook's tent and the testing yard on the edge of camp whenever the army's delayed march provided opportunity for his experiments. Their constant presence dampened Jakim's hopes for escape. How had they missed the sailor sneaking in?

The sailor snorted. "I may be no shadowrider, but when you live on a floating tub where the work never stops, you learn how to make yourself scarce."

Shouts broke outside, and Jakim spun toward the silk hangings. That was Khilamook's voice, and his inability to communicate without his translator would not improve his temper before Jakim could get back. Things just kept tumbling from bad to worse. The sailor was gone when he turned around, but the burned paper still sat in the pile of dirty clothes. He retrieved it, hastily straightened the rest, and rushed out into the chaos where slaves scrambled around the toppled handcart, whips cracked, and overseers growled curses.

Khilamook's face whitened at the sight of the singed scrap in Jakim's hand. His bones seemed to press against his skin, accentuating the hollows in his cheeks and around his eyes. He demanded no explanation and Jakim offered none, just squared his shoulders for a beating. His stomach churned when the engineer raised his hand instead of his cane, summoning an overseer with a long black snake of a whip slithering behind him.

Maybe it was feverish to look on a lash and fear a snake, but the snake was suddenly all he could see. He had stepped on a snake once. Felt its fangs pierce his foot. Only Aodh's mercy and Siba's remedies had saved him, and as he lay with his leg swollen so thick he feared his skin would burst, she had whispered that Aodh's hand was upon him, preserving him, guiding him—

Calloused hands shoved him to his knees and tore the tunic from his back. Shivering, exposed, he clenched his teeth. It was not his first whipping. Before he had endured with only anger to ground him. Now he was rooted in purpose and in hope.

Through the war machine's frame, he met the sailor's eyes.

Crack. Fire streaked his bare back. Gasping, he dug his nails into his palms. *Crack*. *Crack*. The third strike coiled around his ribs, blazing a stripe across his stomach. *Crack*. The fourth drove something hard and cold into his chest. He looked down and gold flashed. The ring. The king's signet. Freed from his tunic, swinging loose for all to see. He caught it, hand to throat, and snapped the cord, hiding it in his fist.

Crack . . . Crack . . . Crack.

"That is enough," Khilamook said, sounding bored, and though Jakim could not unclench his teeth to translate, the overseer began coiling his whip. Jakim flinched as the tip flicked inches from his eyes. But it did not sting him again. "Get up, slave."

Those words struck his ears strangely, but he couldn't latch onto why. Not with his senses reeling and his back on fire and humiliation tightening his throat. It was Scroll Enok's voice he imagined whispering calm into his ears. Scroll Enok's hands steadying him. Scroll Enok who had also worn a slave's collar and knew the shaming bite of a whip.

"Come," Khilamook demanded. "There is work to be done, and I require you to translate. Consider the matter forgotten." But something about his words sounded wrong. Not just his flippant, arrogant tone, though that raked against Jakim's spine, but the words themselves sounded strange coming from the engineer . . . because . . .

Because he had spoken in *Nadaarian.*

Jakim stood, slowly, and lifted his gaze to the smugness staining Khilamook's smile, confirming that yes, indeed, he knew full well what he had done. Then the engineer strode away at a pace that made Jakim's back throb when he stumbled after him, the king's ring digging into his palm. At least he had not lost that. At least he could fulfill his vow.

At least he could pretend that mattered, even if he only lied to himself.

Wincing, Jakim wobbled up to Khilamook's desk, barely managing to keep the tureen, filled to the brim with a customary Canthorian hearty meat and vegetable soup, from sloshing spicy broth onto his bare feet. One whiff of the sharp spices and Jakim could picture himself back in Kerrikar, stirring a steaming cauldron in the outdoor kitchen. Apparently, the engineer's status earned meals prepared individually to his tastes.

"Master?" Jakim cleared his throat. "I have brought food."

Khilamook gestured for quiet, perching on the edge of his stool to study the cylindrical device disassembled across his desk. Pursing his lips, he scratched out notes with a gold pen fitted with skaa-ryn vanes in mimicry of a real quill. Jakim eyed the haphazard sea of papers and scrolls. Carrying the heavy tureen pulled his tunic against the oozing marks on his back, but after a week of making and breaking camp, he had learned to disturb Khilamook's research with extreme caution. Organization lurked beneath the chaos, a system no one else would understand.

He settled the tureen on a relatively clear corner where Khilamook could reach it when he was hungry. Traditional hours for waking, eating, or sleeping meant nothing when the engineer was consumed with an idea, but once he finished, he would expect to find Jakim at his elbow, waiting. Like a trained graybeard monkey.

His gut boiled with a sudden nauseating hatred, almost as strong as the anger he'd once harbored against those who had sold him. He'd thought he had escaped it when he joined the Scrolls. What was his anger compared to both Aodh's justice and mercy? Yet there it was, slithering inside him like a snake. Unnerved by the thought, Jakim started straightening up, gathering discarded robes, emptying soiled wash water, and shaking out the reed mats.

"You have been a slave before?"

Jakim's head jerked up to see Khilamook digging into the tureen of soup. His quill sprawled atop his notes, leaking ink. The engineer had never shown interest in his story before. Was it . . . maybe . . . a good sign? "Yes, master, in Canthor." He debated halting there. "I . . . I was given my freedom."

"Indeed? Less than one in fifty slaves is freed."

It was not outright disbelief in the engineer's voice, but Jakim tugged the ripped neck of his tunic down to reveal the triple diamond mark of freedom on his chest and instantly regretted how the fabric scraped his raw back. "I . . . had a kind master," he explained, swallowing a lump at the memory.

But Khilamook barely glanced up, spoon clicking the rim of his tureen as he slurped his meal. "And who was this kind master?"

"His name was Ha Sian."

"Ah." Disdain soured the engineer's tone. "That tallies."

"With what, master?"

"Oh, the depth of your Canthorian accent."

Jakim pried his fingers from his tunic, letting it conceal the mark again. It seemed the world had not changed since he was last a slave. It still offered no justice, and he would offer no more of his tale. That was an honor Khilamook had not earned.

"Your pronunciation is hardly flawless," Khilamook continued, "but it carries the ring of authenticity. You should be grateful it has earned you such a comfortable position in my service." Grasping the tureen in both hands, he downed the last of the broth.

Comfortable. The welts on his back declared that a lie. Like Khilamook's need for a translator.

Jakim's ire rose again. "My Canthorian is passable," he said, then impulsively switched languages mid-sentence, studying the engineer's expression. "But it is nowhere near as good as my Nadaarian."

A knowing expression quirked Khilamook's lips. "So, you noticed," he said in the same tongue before morphing into another. "I did wonder. Still, I think my Soldonian is better than yours." It was. "So long as you avoid today's errors, you will not find me a hard master. What thrice-slave could demand more?"

Those last words pricked at Jakim. "Thrice-slave? What does that mean?"

"Twice to men," Khilamook said deliberately. "Once to your god."

Jakim stiffened at the sound of his own language, Eliami. Once he would have wept to hear those rolling, earthy tones. But not from this man. Not uttering such untruths. In all the years since the caravan had dragged him away, only the Scrolls had spoken it. His nation was broken, his people were nomads in a land no longer theirs. Who would learn their dying tongue?

"I recognized your markings. The mythos of your religion fascinates me," Khilamook mused, reverting to Canthorian. "Tell me, how long did you wait to take the Scroll's seal after the slave's collar was struck from your throat? It is ironic to consider. And here you are a slave again. Yet Aodh supposedly shields his own. That is the origin of his Eternal Scars, isn't it?"

Flustered, Jakim studied the script on his forearms, the most basic tenets of the holy writ. If he had completed his mission to Broken-Eliam, he would have carried even more truths back to the Sanctuary on his skin. If he had not left the Sanctuary, study would have increased his understanding. But now, this was all he had. He cleared his throat. "Aodh promises restoration. That his hand mends all things."

That concept was woven through the fabric of the holy writ and history itself. It had freed him from bitterness and drawn him to face the journey home to the purpose that awaited him. That purpose still drummed in his heart. Without it, he had nothing.

Without it, he was nothing.

"Ah, so it is good that you are a slave again?"

The drumbeat faltered.

Jakim licked dry lips. "If I were not, I could not serve you, master."

"And you consider that good?" Khilamook leaned forward abruptly. "Recite your truths all you will, I see the lie in your eyes. You hate me. And not me alone. You should hope your Aodh is less perceptive, or he would surely renounce you as his own."

That resonated inside Jakim, like a string plucked until it snapped. He felt stripped bare by the engineer's words. And he knew that was how he stood before Aodh too. He tightened his fists, watching the script shift on his arms. Everything had seemed so simple when Scroll Enok inked his skin. Trials behind him, purpose ahead, answers only a flick of the eyes away. Until he lied his way onto the mission to Broken-Eliam, only to wind up here.

There was nothing simple about his path now. Or this man he served.

Maybe Aodh *had* renounced him.

Khilamook settled back on his stool with that snakelike smile. He seemed satisfied, as though he'd gained something in the discussion. But what? It nagged at Jakim as he collected the empty tureen and pushed through the silk hangings. He paused and looked back. "What does it matter to you, master, what I am?"

It was a bold question. He risked another whipping.

Khilamook just snorted and purposefully resumed his work. "It does not matter. And you are nothing. Only a slave." But if eyes revealed the truth, surely his concealed a lie.

TWENTY-SEVEN: CERIDWEN

Of the sol-breath, little is written and much is whispered. But the change wrought by the sol-breath upon a rider is at once instantaneous, mysterious, and profound.

"Fire-demon–"

Ceridwen's sabre splintered the Nadaarian's cry. On all sides, her warriors thundered across the plain in loose formation, chasing survivors of the supply column and felling them as they ran. Clusters formed shield-and-spear walls, but without war machines or devious stratagems, foot soldiers were no match for solborn. Their corpses littered the plain in splashes of scarlets and golds, like autumn leaves after a storm.

It was not a battle anymore. Only retribution.

She slowed Mindar, watching the fighting dwindle. Scouting stormers had spied the column's march from the coast days ago, granting her time to summon her force which had been scattered in patrols spanning the main Nadaarian army. Two thirds had mustered today in the shadow of a pair of hills to descend upon the convoy and drive them out onto the plain where her riders could run them down.

Stormer alighting with flared wings and stamping hooves, Iona flung the fur-lined hood from her head, baring her flushed, glowing face. "Victory! We have won the day!"

"Victory!" Ceridwen repeated, though the plain was strewn with fallen and the day's fight was not yet done. "And the survivor?"

"Nold brings him now."

Rumbling warned of Nold's approach before she saw the earthhewn bearing a bound and blindfolded soldier across the saddlebow. Nold tossed him before Mindar. Warriors swept in, ringing the soldier with jostling steeds. Others milled in concentric circles around them, a formation designed to conceal their numbers. The soldier backed blindly away until Ceridwen summoned a spurt of flame to blaze past his ear.

He went still, cringing.

She slid from the saddle in a jingle of spurs and tore off his blindfold, revealing a weathered face with a crooked nose and gray-stubbled jaw. Blood trickled from his split chin. His narrowed gaze roved the circle, taking in the array of solborn surrounding him. Kneeling limited his view to the first row and the waves of dust stirred by the circling steeds behind, hopefully giving the impression of a greater host than answered her horn.

Loose riders of every breed had been trickling in over the past three weeks, raising her force to three hundred strong, though she was war-chief of Lochrann in name only unless the seven chieftains chose to swear to her banner. Too few to oppose the Nadaarian advance, but enough to strike fear into scavengers and stragglers if wielded to effect.

"You will return to your masters to deliver my words," Ceridwen said in Nadaarian. Out of each of the past twelve skirmishes, she had spared only one survivor. Stripped of weapons, boots, and armor, and escorted within bowshot of Nadaari scouts–spotted by a stormer fly-over–to deliver her threat.

Ever the same words: "Look for us in the shadows, in the sky, in the ocean and rivers. Seek us behind every sunrise, around every tree, and beyond every hill. But we will not be waiting to be found. Death rides for you all."

She flicked her reins, and flames warmed the soldier's face. He fell back, cursing.

"Careful, rabbit," Iona remarked. "You'll want your legs fit for running, though not until you've delivered our words. Try to enter the camp before and you will find an arrow in your spine. The first two tried it. The other ten proved wiser. Tell me, Nadaarian, are you wise?"

Wise enough to understand her meaning if not her Soldonian tongue. Still, Ceridwen pressed her sabre to his throat. "You know the words?"

His reflexive swallow left blood on the blade. "I know the words."

"See you do not forget."

Blindfolded again, the soldier stumbled after Nold's patrol while the rest disbanded at Iona's command to search for wounded, leaving Ceridwen alone among the slain. She knelt to clean her blade. It was always eerily quiet following a battle, as though her senses struggled to adjust after the cataclysmic shock of noise and killing and the pressure to survive. No longer the ring of metal, the jolt of Mindar's hooves, the rasp of breath in his throat, the ragged pulse of her own. No rush of flame, no enveloping warmth. In their absence, only a void.

"My lady!" Liam urged his riveren toward her, armor askew and dirt spattered. His right eye was swollen shut, a bruise darkened the side of his face, and his helmet was missing. Again. He never could seem to keep it on. But he was alive and still grinning, tiger-slaying spear propped on his shoulder, and just the sight of him lifted her spirits. *Blazes*. She was so relieved.

Dangerous, her heart warned.

But not even it could steal her smile. "What have I told you, Liam?"

"To . . . keep my helmet on?"

"Aye, *and* . . ."

"And . . . to call you tor Nimid?"

"That would be it."

"Right." He nodded, eyes gleaming with excitement. "You won't believe what we found. We were just poking around, Coritza and I." He broke into a smile. Whoever Coritza was, young Liam was clearly smitten. "Scavenging the supply wagons, and there it was, tucked away in a hidden compartment in a trunk and–"

"There *what* was?"

Once Liam had hold of a tale, dramatic emphasis ran roughshod over details. Reining him in was as challenging as coaxing the bit from a runaway steed.

"I'm thinking you should see it for yourself, my la–I mean, tor Nimid."

"Liam–" She broke off, distracted by a thudding beat that resonated in her chest and rattled her senses alert.

Those were hooves.

The eastern hills beyond the plain came alive with the sound. Ceridwen snatched the war horn hanging at her side and loosed a blast on the run to her grazing steed. His head came up. She gripped the saddlebow, kicked up one leg, and wheeled to face the threat as her warriors abandoned their work and fell into formation behind her.

Iona snapped her hood up. "Kilmark and Ondri?"

"I don't know."

"The war-hosts?"

"I don't know."

The words broke sharper than intended, but Iona simply loosed her reins to ride. "Shall I dispatch a scouting pair?"

Ceridwen shook her head. "We wait."

Solborn appeared over the crest of the hill and poured down onto the plain. One line in loose traveling formation, then two, then three. Ceridwen flexed her blade arm, counting as more and more came. Not one unit, or even three. This was an *ayed*, maybe two. Over five times the size of her force at least.

A wolfhound dashed out ahead of the line, streaking low to the ground, drawing her gaze to the familiar figure behind it, cloaked in gray and riding in a loose-limbed, relaxed manner that made it look as though he glided across the earth on a sea of mist. Beside Finnian, Apex Markham raised his voice. The shout was carried from line to line, and riders checked their steeds, slowing to a halt, while Markham and Finnian rode forward.

They had come for her, but why?

Markham's arrival with two thousand riders at his back boded something significant. She had survived Idolas, so did the war-chiefs now demand her life? Did Markham hold her Outrider oath forsworn since she had not returned? Or were the war-hosts mustering to crush the Nadaari once and for all?

Whatever it was, she must face it. Alone.

"Wait here," she commanded, then urged Mindar onward to meet them halfway, her fireborn prancing and snorting as the wolfhound sniffed at his heels, while the two shadowers stood motionless but visible in the noonday sun.

"Not dead yet, I see." Finnian offered a faint smile she did not return.

"No thanks to you, te Donal," Markham drawled. With that familiar sardonic grin sprawling across his face, he seemed glad to see her–in his own way. "I swear, tor Nimid, if we'd found you dead or wounded, he would have been demoted to mucking stalls, oiling my saddle, and refilling my flask for the rest of his miserable days walking the earth." His grin widened. "But you're too fire-blasted stubborn for death, aren't you?"

If he was pleased she lived, her death could not be his mission.

Relieved, she laughed outright at his words and was shocked to do so while the blood of friend and foe still dampened the soil. "I thought Finnian was stubborn and I was *reckless*."

"Aye, that too." Markham shifted in the saddle, expression clouding. "Well," he drew the word out between his teeth. "It is time."

She braced herself.

His saddle creaked as he swung down, his boots scuffed the dirt, then he knelt awkwardly before her. "Hail, Ceridwen tal Desmond, Heir of Soldonia."

Markham was kneeling to *her*.

Smoke flooding her throat, Ceridwen stood, at a loss for words. "The king did not name me heir." She lingered over the sting of that admission, knowing because of it that it was true. Truth was a harsh and bitter thing, like a wintry wind that slapped a warrior to wakefulness. Lies promised warmth and comfort and lulled a warrior into deadly sleep. “I bear the *kasar*. The war-chiefs would never accept my rule.”

And the king had not forgiven her for Bair’s death.

Still, Markham knelt.

“Stand up. Please.”

He rose, toeing aside the wolfhound who whined and shimmied toward his legs with his tail wagging until whistled to heel by Finnian. Markham started toward his steed, but Ceridwen shot Mindar across his path, forcing a halt.

“Tell me, Apex, why you dare to call me heir.”

Out of the corner of her eye, she saw Finnian stiffen at her tone.

“Pardon my rudeness,” Markham drawled, sidestepping to rummage in his saddlebags. “You seemed so certain, I didn’t realize there was a question in there. Thought I’d let you spew the denial from your system so we could move on to more pressing matters.”

“Such as?” His hand flicked, tossing something. She caught it one-handed and found herself looking at a vial of dark viscous liquid. Costly stuff to treat so casually. “Skivva oil?”

“Your saddle needs oiling. Gear too. Thought I taught you better.”

“I have been preoccupied.”

“Yes, you have. Beheading priests. Hunting Nadaari. Leaving one survivor to carry the tale. Who knew you had a flair for the dramatic?” Sarcasm fairly dripped off his tongue as he signaled Finnian away to see the *ayed* settled, then nodded at her. “Go on then, you oil your gear and I’ll oil your oars, and maybe we’ll save this kingdom yet.”

Sighing, she dismounted and untacked her steed. Markham was right, of course. She had run out of oil a week ago, and the toll showed in minuscule cracks that splintered the outer layer of leather, eerily reminiscent of the fire-filled cracks that crisscrossed the floor of the crater of Koltar. Dangerous for any rider when combat put gear under strain. More so for a firerider. She watched as the leather greedily drank in the oil, sun-washed tan deepening to a gleaming brown.

It was easier than meeting Markham's eye.

He cleared his throat, settling beside her. "It is true your father failed to name an heir, and so the mantle of regent has fallen to Lord Glyndwr. That, at least, he had the foresight to will, though it would have been better left undone. Glyndwr is a kindly man"–the bite in his tone made it an insult–"but not up to the task."

She waited for him to elaborate.

Instead, he launched a different lead. "While you have been 'preoccupied,' we Outriders have been tracking the Nadaari. Overall, their advance seems delayed by that subtlest foe: logistics. It's reasonable to assume their slowed pace and widespread scavenging means their rapid march drained their supplies. But I suspect it is strategic too. They know our strength resides upon the backs of our steeds, and our mobility requires carrying limited supplies and restocking as we pass through."

"So," Ceridwen realized, "they would seize what they can and scorch the rest, starving our steeds or chaining us to supply trains. Either cripples our advantage."

"Aye, cunning devils, aren't they? The force you harass here is the largest of the three that separated after Idolas. The one that split north aims to join another force that landed in Cenyon opposite Craignorm and struck inland, where it has been beating its head against a wall of earthhewn backed by Eagan's shadower kill-squads, so I dispatched two Outrider *ayeds* to intercept. It is unlikely to make much headway."

"And the one that marched south?"

"Kilmark and Ondri rode ahead of it, opening a path into Ardon. I harp on te Donal for returning without you, but his information proved useful. It's kept us from being wholly blind in the midst of this."

"And is this where you harp on me for not returning?"

"Why would I do that?"

Ceridwen looked up from her oiling. "Honestly? I thought you would hold me forsworn from my duty. Abandoning my partner, failing to muster with the war-host." She had earned the *kasar* for matters less under her control.

"There's duty, tal Desmond, and then there's *duty.* The moment your father died, everything changed. Surely you can see that. Besides"–Markham drew his flask, took a long pull, and swiped his hand across his whiskers–"there's no war-host to muster with."

Oil dripped from her stilled rag as she eyed him. "What do you mean?"

"The treachery at Idolas shattered the cohesion of the chiefdoms. In the retreat, each of the war-chiefs fled to their own. Eagan battles in the north, Telweg upon the coast, Rhodri has ridden south, vowing to return with Kilmark's and Ondri's heads on poles. Never seen him so wild with rage. Reckon that sort of betrayal is personal."

That left only Craddock, Ormond, and Glyndwr.

Craddock's lands in the mountains of Gimleal lay farthest from threat. With the inhospitable Gauroth range shielding his western border, he could withdraw into his fortress and watch the rest of Soldonia fall. The soft green lands of Ormond's Ruiadh would be threatened if Ardon caved, but lacking his mother's commanding presence, Ceridwen doubted if the young war-chief could muster even his own chieftains to the defense of the kingdom.

"You see the danger we are in?" Markham's eye twitched. He had been watching her mental calculations, no doubt knew where she had landed. "Divided, we haven't a pit-spawned chance against the armies they can field. Idolas proved their cunning, and mighty as the solborn are, it will come down to numbers in the end. We will need aid, sure enough."

"Aid from where?"

His eye flashed with a wolf's craftiness, and Ceridwen sensed she had stepped into his catch-rope, corralled in the direction he wished. "Rhiakkor. Hurron. Mabassi, if need be. Your father was a good king once, and my friend, but ruling the kingdom became too great a burden. He allowed alliances to lapse, ignored old treaties. But you, Ceridwen tal Desmond, can convince the inland nations to join us and halt the Nadaarian tide before it seizes their soil. You must lay claim to your title to save your people."

"Lord Glyndwr–"

"Is regent of a splintering kingdom." Markham's voice dropped to a growl. "He has less power than I, for the five Outrider *ayeds* answer my horn, and he has only the few of Harnoth. We retreated with him to Rysinger, shielding him for the muster. But he failed to command it then, and now the war-chiefs pay him no heed for all his bluster."

"Nor will they heed me." Discarding rag and vial, she stood. "Not until the *kasar* is broken." She reached for her saddle, but Markham gripped her arm.

"Continue as you have begun, but fight not only as war-chief of Lochrann but in the authority of the heir. Riders will flock to your banner. When the war-chiefs emerge, you will have the nation behind you, as Uthold did when he rode from the east. The *kasar* will mean nothing then."

Ceridwen retreated from his scrutiny. "Maybe not to them. But to me?"

"No," he said quietly. "You forget that I know you. You rode to Rysinger in defiance. You broke down the doors of the great hall, rode that pit-spawned steed before the king's own table, and spat fire at him in his own fortress. You forget that I saw you when that brand was raw and the smoke of the crater hung thick about you. You rode that wildborn into a gauntlet of trained warriors without a breath of hesitation. And you rode out of the melee, clinging to the flaming mane of your steed, undaunted still. It is not the *kasar* nor the war-chiefs that you fear, is it, Ceridwen tal Desmond?"

His question hung between them, demanding a response.

"No." Her voice faltered.

"Then what is it? The truth."

"Myself." She released it in a breath and knew that it was indeed the truth. "Once, the ambition to be heir flowed hot in my veins. I sought to prove my worth to the blood of Lochrann and lost all instead. I dare not risk such ambition again."

Markham leaned forward, weathered face cast in taut lines, and all hints of laziness vanished from his posture. He was a fireborn restrained, a force barely controlled. "Ambition be blazed. Look beyond your own shadow, tal Desmond, and rise to the challenge for the good of your people." His voice was hard, his words more so. But there was a hint of something more than harshness in his one blue eye. "This is the true test of blood. Not the Sol-Donair. Not your naming as heir. *This*. Would you know if you are worthy of the blood of Lochrann?" The weight of his hand settled on her shoulder, both burden and support. "Become worthy. Lead."

TWENTY-EIGHT: RAFI

Conquest is not a means to an end. Conquest is the end.
– Nadaarian maxim

As soon as Nef blew into the kitchens like a wild breeze threatening havoc, scattering workers from his path, Rafi knew the moment he had been dreading had come. Of course, Nef couldn't just leave him alone. Of course, confrontation was inevitable.

"You, with me." Nef tossed a spear at Rafi's feet, barely missing his toes.

And of course, he would still try to avoid it.

Rafi glanced at the spear and pointedly went back to work. "Sorry, got a job to do." His hands were sticky from scraping out gourds so Saffa could add them to the soup already bubbling in three enormous cauldrons, throwing up a fragrant steam scented with rich spices and sun-warmed vegetables. Saffa's kitchen fed the wounded, the trainees, and the newly arrived refugees until they settled in and could sustain themselves. Four weeks since Rafi's arrival, three since joining the cooks, and his side had mostly healed, he had found his place–and what did Nef care if it meant wielding spices rather than spears?–and life in the rebel camp had fallen into a peaceful monotony broken only by Iakki's persistent pleas to return home.

"When, Nahiki, when?"

But surely it was safer for the village if he stayed away and kept Sahak engaged in futile pursuit. Sometimes, he could convince himself that was true. Other times, he wondered if he had been running too long to stop.

Most times, he tried not to think.

Rafi kept his voice light. "You're welcome to help. Jasri can show you."

The girl chopping leafy greens to his left shot him a glare beneath the shadow of her hair. She always tilted her head just so, so the sweeping strands concealed her scars. "He can show himself out if he's going to be tossing spears around."

Saffa shuffled up to inspect Rafi's work and claimed the cleaned gourds. Basket on her hip, she pointedly eyed Nef and his spear, then pressed a broom into his hands and nodded at the floor. Rafi coughed to hide his smile. Not even Nef dared speak back to Saffa. All the kitchen crew carried scars. Jasri had lost her right eye, the boy his left hand, and the burly armed man who reminded him of Sev had barely survived losing both legs. Saffa had no voice, but her hands could speak, and she conveyed more with an expression than Rafi could with words, and no one could look into those wise, stubborn eyes and not know her for a warrior.

Nef stood rigid, waiting until the gourds sizzled as Saffa roasted them on hot stones, then he dropped the broom and yanked an alarmingly familiar sack from his belt. But instead of trying to stuff it over Rafi's head, he stuffed it with cala root crackers, roasted meat, and dried saga fruit rounds. "It is time, Nahiki, to earn your keep and prove yourself one of us."

Rafi eyed him warily. "I thought I was doing just that. But if stealing food is the key, count me out. Saffa and her crew work hard enough."

"To feed the revolution. This is revolution business. It's hardly stealing." Nef tied off the sack, slung it over his shoulder, and swaggered to the exit. His hair was spiked back, sleeveless leather vest hanging open, beaded belt slung low to accommodate a *chet*—the wide, heavy blade the Mahque used to tame the jungle. He glanced over his shoulder. "Come on then."

"You're going on a raid?"

"No. We are."

"You don't want me. You don't trust me."

Nef's eyes gleamed. "Admitting you can't be trusted?"

"No, but–"

"It's settled then."

Rafi took a deep breath. He wasn't going anywhere with Nef. Not for all the pearls on the Alon coast. "Where is Umut?"

"Out." Nef stepped closer. "This is simple, Alonque. I need a seventh. It can be you. Or it can be your cousin, Iakki. Your choice."

Those words were the prick of a hundred scadtha claws beneath his skin. Rafi gripped his spoon like a harpoon, heedless of the seeds and juice dripping down his arm and spattering his feet. No one else was close enough to have heard the threat. No one would believe him if he repeated it.

He was a leaf blown adrift here. Nef had roots.

"He's just a boy."

"You think that will matter to the Nadaari?" Nef arched a brow. "Don't forget the spear. I hope you know how to use it."

And what choice did Rafi have but to drop the spoon and retrieve the spear? To leave the kitchen and follow Nef out of the alcove to meet Moc grinning at the head of four warriors? To fall in line as they descended to the waterfall's end, jogged through the undergrowth, squeezed through a crack in the gorge wall, and broke out into the jungle? No choice at all.

"You are sure about this, Nef?" Moc's hushed voice rumbled above the chirrup of crickets and the rustle of leaves stirred by the evening breeze that seeped from the clearing ahead where Mahque soil tenders farmed to feed their village.

Where Nef would launch his raid.

It had taken them a full day's walk to reach it. Kneeling beside the scowling rebel, dampness seeping into his trousers, Rafi could just see the huts built among the sprawling branches of a cluster of banyan trees to his right. Bright curtains fluttered in doorways and windows, and graybeard monkeys—clever creatures that Sev had claimed the Mahque trained to retrieve fruits and nuts from treetops—swung from railings and rope ladders. But the huts stood empty, tools lay idle at the base of the trees, and the voices that spilled from the clearing bore the rough edge of Nadaarian laughter.

"I am sure." Nef bristled. "Listen to them. They have feasted on our labor long enough. Let them taste our blades now and see if it is a meal to their liking."

Rafi carefully lifted a pale jar-sized leaf that blocked his view of the clearing. The Mahque stood in stiff groups watching while Nadaari soldiers lounged on the grass and gorged themselves on cala root cakes, saga wine, and roasted goat, surrounded by baskets laden with the bounty of the earth. Substitute fish for fruits and oysters for root vegetables, and tribute collection day looked almost the same here as on the Alon coast.

Irksome, yes, but the Que were still fortunate. The empire never had considered them worthy opponents, so unlike other conquered nations, their tribute filled only the army's stomach, rather than its ranks, which had always struck Rafi as surprising. When the empire stretched out its hand, it took and took and took, and the beast of war had an insatiable appetite. How long before their tribute was expanded from food for the army to fodder for enemy archers?

Not long, Rafi thought, if the revolution kept prodding the sleeping monster.

Moc scratched the scar that carved across the side of his head. "Umut doesn't like us raiding so close to camp. What if we are caught?"

"Kill them all and we won't be." Nef lifted onto the balls of his feet, giving the clearing a final scan, then hefted his spear. "Rapid rush. Don't let them rise. Plant them in the soil." His eyes flicked to Rafi. "You just keep up."

Only thought of Iakki netted Rafi's tongue. It had been years since he trained for combat with Delmar, but wielding the harpoon had kept him sharp. He could keep up, but that was all he planned to do.

He firmed his grip on the spear and joined the others in their slow creep to the jungle's edge.

Nef attacked first, bursting from the underbrush and ramming his spear into a lounging soldier's gut. He left it standing like a flag while he drew his *chet*. That was the cue. The rebels broke upon the soldiers like a wave, silent and deadly, leaving corpses in their wake. Slowed by food, drink, and surprise, the soldiers made easy targets. Nine left. Then six. Rafi sidestepped a falling body and ducked out of Moc's way.

Someone bellowed. Rafi glimpsed a blur of scarlet and gold and brought his spear up to block. Caught the soldier across the chest and sent him stumbling into a basket. Crimson saga fruit tumbled around him as he tried to get to his feet.

Rafi's hovering spear stopped him.

"Oh, Murloch, mighty one . . ." the man mumbled.

Rafi scanned the clearing. Soldiers moaned and died in the wreckage of their spoils while the rebels claimed their weapons and armor. It was done. His arm quivered, and he did not strike. He had faced a sea-demon, skewered a scadtha, and stared his brother's murderer in the eye. He had never killed a man.

Could not, would not, it made no difference. Did it?

"What have you done?" One of the villagers stormed up to Nef, *chet* in hand. His wide, beaded belt wrapped thrice around his waist, rising to his ribs. It was a sign of rank among the Mahque. This must be the village elder.

Nef tugged his spear from the corpse. "I have freed you from fear, cousin. Severed your last restraints. You can stand and fight or die a Nadaari slave. It is your choice."

He kept using that phrase. Rafi wasn't sure he understood it.

Screams suddenly rent the air. From across the clearing, soldiers boiled from the jungle, followed by a man in a chariot, wearing a priest's robes, a tsemarc's breastplate, and an assassin's baldric of knives. Sahak. His cousin sprang from the chariot, eyes fixed upon him in surprise, and then smiled in triumph. Years vanished in seconds, and Rafi was once more a boy weeping as his brother died.

He stumbled back. How?

Something yanked his ankle, snapping him to the ground. His skull struck. Blinding light shot across his vision. He kicked out, felt a crack, heard a grunt, and glimpsed blood seeping from the downed soldier's nose.

Run, brother. Run!

Rafi hauled himself to his feet, to chaos. Tigers roared. Soldiers crashed through the field. Rebels and villagers scattered, fleeing into the jungle in a dozen different directions. Nef shoved against the tide. "*Chets* out, cousins! We can take them!"

"No!" Moc dragged him back. "There are too many. Run. Run!"

Rafi . . . RUN.

"Rafi!" Sahak's distant shout slung him into motion. "Rafi Tetrani!"

Clutching his spear, he sprinted into the thick jungle after Moc and Nef. Crashing through heavy leaves, slapping aside vines, fighting through dizziness. Violent pain surged behind his eyes, like the entire sea was encased in his skull and raging to be set free.

"This way!" Moc hissed.

He hurried to follow and jammed his foot under a root. His ankle twisted and he struck the ground, cringing as soldiers crashed nearer through the brush. Oh, Ches-Shu, how had Sahak found him here? Was that Sahak still shouting his name? Or the ghost screaming in his mind?

"Up, up, get up!" That was Moc, seizing his tunic and heaving him up.

He gasped as his foot struck, but Moc yanked his arm over his shoulder and hauled him, zigzagging through dense underbrush, across earth that grew steadily damper until they slogged across soggy ground that spurted water underfoot.

"Rest," Moc gasped, letting him slump on the bank of a sluggish river.

The setting sun piercing the leaves stabbed into his eyes. He curled over, clutching his head. Their pursuers would be slowed by heavy armor, giving them an advantage if they could keep running. Running. *Running.*

Rafi vomited into a clump of grass.

"What's wrong with him?" Nef demanded.

"I don't know." Moc. "The others get out?"

"They split west. Except Rik. Took a blade in the back. We should have fought." Nef's voice stretched taut. "You shouldn't have dragged me away."

"We should keep moving. Your turn to drag him."

"Leave him. He will slow us."

"And if he's captured? He knows the camp."

"I'm fine," Rafi muttered through waves of pain.

Nef yanked him up. "You'd better be able to keep up, Alonque." He splashed into the river and waded toward the far bank, half dragging Rafi. Reflected sunlight made Rafi's head spin until he could hardly see, but somehow, he managed to latch onto Nef's ferocious glare when the rebel abruptly halted in chest-deep water.

"I know who you are," Nef whispered.

And thrust him beneath the surface.

Brackish water stung Rafi's eyes. He jerked back. Strong hands gripped his neck, forcing his head down. Planting his good foot, he tried to push up to the surface, but Nef kicked it out from under him and jammed a knee against his spine.

No. No!

He had no leverage.

But he thrashed until the ache behind his eyes flared to white-hot brightness. Until his injured foot struck the riverbed and he almost blacked out. Until panic set in and numbed his limbs. Alonque blue might run in his veins, but he could drown. He would drown.

Only . . . his lungs weren't screaming yet.

He'd never held his breath this long before. He counted the seconds in the rapid pulse in his throat and knew his lungs should be straining but weren't. Instinct made him stop struggling. But not immediately. Too suspicious. He twitched feebly, then fell still and let his limbs sink.

Nef shoved him away and sloshed ashore.

He remained motionless, ignoring the ache just starting in his chest.

"Nef . . . what did you do?" Moc's stunned voice drifted down to him.

"What I had to," Nef rasped, breathing hard. "We couldn't drag him the whole way. We'd all be caught. But you said it yourself. He could lead them to our camp, willingly or tortured into it. Tell me a quick death isn't more merciful?"

"This was not mercy."

"I didn't see you trying to stop me. Come on."

Rafi waited until his lungs flamed, until he was convinced they must be gone, before he finally dared surface to breathe. Dashing the water from his eyes, he scanned both banks and found no one. He let himself float, sucking in breath after breath, his head tipped back and his eyes closed, until his pounding pulse eased and he could think again. He was alive and he was free, but Sahak would come, and no faked death would satisfy him, so Rafi started swimming, following the river's sluggish course downstream.

Thus, Nahiki of the Alonque died by drowning.

Ironic? Yes, *yes*, it was. It amused Rafi, probably far too much. Hours later, he crawled ashore and collapsed on the damp riverbank. The sun woke him the next morning. Shivering from sleeping in soaked clothes on soaked earth, he shrugged out of his tunic and used it to bind his injured ankle. It had swollen to twice its size, like Iakki's hand that time he brushed against a specter jellyfish and almost died. Rafi had never seen Sev so terrified.

Not until the priests selected Iakki for sacrifice.

That thought sobered him. He hadn't begun to consider his future, but dead or not, he would haunt the rebel camp until he reclaimed Iakki. He owed Sev that much. If not more. But he could not be sidetracked by concern for Zorrad when Sahak was here—

Something snapped behind him.

He stilled, fingers on the knot of his makeshift bandage, as heavy steps crunched nearer. Then a damp, snuffling breath struck his neck, flooding his nostrils with the tang of salt. Slowly, Rafi turned and met the familiar blue eyes of the sea-demon colt.

It snorted and tossed its head, seaweed-tangled mane slapping its neck.

He clumsily rose, palms out. "Shh, shh." He whispered it like the sea. "Shh, now." So Alonque mothers sang to their children. So his mother had sung to him. Long ago.

Nickering, it nudged its nose toward his hand. He tried not to wince as coarse whiskers brushed his palm. It blew out steaming breaths, and he found himself breathing along with it.

Where had it come from? Was it . . . following him?

He studied the sweep of its broad back and the scales that speckled its spine. The Alonque had many tales of Ches-Shu appearing as sea creatures to save drowning sailors who had earned her favor. But sea-demons were not of Ches-Shu. They came from Soldonia. Still this colt had saved his life by towing him ashore, and Soldonian warriors rode such beasts into battle. Ruefully testing his ankle, he envisioned the grueling hike back to the rebel camp. Comparatively, how hard could riding be?

The colt watched as he planted both hands on its back. That felt awkward. He gripped its mane instead and tried to swing a leg over. Instantly, the colt transformed from a flesh and blood steed into a whirlwind of mist and storm that hurled him into the river. Or so it felt when he surfaced, spluttering, to see the beast calmly munching riverweed.

"Grueling hike it is." Shaking his head, he slogged ashore and started limping toward Tehorra Peak. Overnight, the pain in his skull had slackened to a dull throb, but now his ankle burned like it had a knife rammed through it. Cracking bushes told him the sea-demon followed, and when the colt ambled alongside to pluck leaves from a vine, he reached over to scratch its jaw. Before he knew it, his elbow was crooked over its neck, easing the strain on his ankle.

"For a sea-demon, you're not half bad," he muttered.

So, of course, it snorted mucous in his face.

TWENTY-NINE: JAKIM

Aodh is wise.

"Aha, I have it!"

Jakim jolted awake at the cry and fell over. He'd fallen asleep with his back to a tent pole while the engineer toiled over his notes long into the night. Judging by the gloom lurking beyond the fluttering silks covering the entrance, it was still night, but Khilamook was on his feet, clothing rumpled and eyes red-rimmed in the glow of his oil lamp.

"Up, slave!" Khilamook snatched a scroll from his desk and rolled it feverishly. "We must see the tsemarc at once. I have solved the problem of dispersal. And Carpaartin said it couldn't be done. You heard me, slave. Up!"

"Won't the tsemarc be asleep?" Jakim ventured.

"Nonsense! It is . . ." Khilamook swept the silk hangings aside. "Ah, I see. Perhaps it can wait. Prepare my wash basin and bedroll and see that you wake me early."

Both had been prepared hours ago, but Jakim just nodded and stumbled through his duties until the engineer snored beneath silk sheets and he could collapse on his own mat in search of sleep that was slow to arrive and brought no peace when it came.

"You, Jakim, will save our people."

Siba came to him in his dreams. He knew it was a dream, for though it was her hazel eyes glistening with concern, her high cheekbones dusted with rose, her dark hair curling beneath her colorful scarf, it was Amir's voice that fell, mocking, from her lips.

"You, little brother? How would you *accomplish that?"*

It sounded so wrong coming from dear, kind Siba who had cared for him and their ailing father since their mother died that Jakim thrashed against the dream. Until the voice changed, and it was his own, whispering that Khilamook was right. Aodh had renounced him. He had no purpose. He was only a slave.

Only a slave . . .

"That's right, little brother . . ."

He surged awake to the echo of Amir's laughter in his ears, throbbing ribs, and an up-close look at the detailed embroidery on the engineer's soft leather shoes—a tangle of sosswyrms with beads for eyes—before Khilamook drew his foot back for another kick. Jakim shot to his feet, wincing as the action pulled on the tight, itchy skin of his healing back. He forced himself not to scratch—that would only worsen the scarring—and rubbed his sore ribs instead.

Good thing Khilamook's refined taste in clothing prohibited boots.

"I said to wake me early! The sun is up, a messenger has come and gone, my discovery gathers dust, and you, my slave, lie abed. Quickly!" Khilamook flung out an arm, pointing. "Clothes, cane, scroll." Jakim scrambled to fetch what was wanted. "And come, to the tsemarc!"

Once on the move, the engineer was a boulder rolling downhill, scattering all in his path. Only one guard attempted to halt his entrance to the command tent, but Khilamook scowled and barked a command, and before Jakim could translate, the man awkwardly pulled back to let them pass. The curtains fluttered behind them, stirring up a whiff of the burning incense coils and bringing back memories of shoving through the disorderly mob, stumbling beneath the weight of the fallen king. Today, the reek of drink was gone, and with it the sense of celebration. Officers stood at attention in clusters around a large table where Tsemarc Izhar braced his fists, studying the map laid out before him while a burly priest with a gravelly voice droned on. The tsemarc's helm perched on the table's corner, skaa-ryn plume brushing the ground. Jakim hesitated, expecting the engineer to wait, but Khilamook marched straight up to the table and slapped his scroll down.

Izhar eyed him narrowly. "What is this, engineer?"

Jakim hurried over to translate for Khilamook, even though the infuriating man understood well enough on his own. "This," the engineer said, "is victory. I have means to halt the Soldonian charge in its tracks, to decimate their forces in a single blow, to unleash utter annihilation. I hold that power here in my hands. Or I will, as soon as the trunks with my manuscripts arrive from the coast." His eyes glinted. "Tell me, when shall I look for them?"

Jakim could see the map up close now, and though it was unfamiliar, he guessed it represented Soldonia. Coins of mixed denominations formed patterns and groupings across the map. The tsemarc pinched one between his fingers as Jakim relayed Khilamook's words and tapped it against the table. *Clink. Clink. Clink.* "Annihilation, you say?"

Khilamook nodded eagerly. "Indeed–"

"Tsemarc Izhar." The guard burst into the tent. "Soldonians!"

Officers reached for swords, but the priest forestalled them with a command as the silk hangings parted wide, fabric ripping, allowing four warriors and four massive horses to enter. One horse nipped at another, teeth clacking dully off a hide of stone. Jakim caught his breath, jaw dropping. These were the legendary solborn. He had never seen a live one up close before. The massive black on the left looked like it had torn itself from a mountainside. On the right, a steed that already seemed somehow less real, less there, sidestepped into shadow and nearly vanished. Behind it, light glinted on the silvery scales surrounding the eyes of a sleek steed, and in the center, a compact blood-red horse with embers flickering in its mane snorted a wisp of black smoke that made Jakim jump in awe.

A fire-breathing horse.

"You are late," Izhar stated without lifting his gaze from the map.

"And you are slow." One of the warriors sauntered forward, dropping the lead for his steed–the fiery one–on the ground. His boots deposited clumps of dirt on the woven floor mats. "How far have you marched from Idolas? I thought to find you in Rysinger already." Wheat-colored hair had been shorn close along the sides of his skull, leaving a broad strip that was gathered in a braid down his back. Sweat and ash streaked his face, but gold bands gleamed in the braid, giving him a fierce, almost kingly look.

He dragged a chair across from Izhar and dropped into it, folding his arms over his boiled leather cuirass. "War rides us all, I suppose."

"Out." Izhar flicked a hand, and his officers filed out until only the priest and the engineer remained. Khilamook stubbornly stood his ground, and Jakim hovered at his side, stealing glances at the mighty steeds. Who were these warriors? Captives? No. Emissaries? Unlikely. Or maybe . . . traitors like those in the pit.

"You *are* still fighting the war?" the warrior asked in a voice of spider silk, smooth but weighty. He spoke Nadaarian with an accent, but Jakim had no difficulty with the translation when Khilamook's cane jabbed his side. "Victory seemed assured after Idolas. Yet here you sit."

"Victory *is* assured," the priest intoned in a voice like scraping stone. He had a round face with a scruffy shadow of a beard, eyes that seemed perpetually squinted, and a muscular build like the massive black horse. "The Voice has spoken it from the Center of the World."

"True as that may be, Nahrog," Izhar acknowledged, "it has not yet come to pass." He leaned toward the warrior, voice lowering to a growl. "You promised us a nation broken. Chiefdoms splintered. War-chiefs divided. Forces scattered. Instead, we find foes behind every rock and tree and your demon-steeds descending from the skies. They trample my scavenging parties and vanish, leaving a single survivor to deliver the same message each time."

"Death rides for you all." Nahrog's voice filled the tent.

The warrior shrugged. "The war-hosts are scattered. Your scavengers are harried only by a few hundred stragglers who conceal their true numbers."

"Those stragglers, as you call them, have managed to carry out a number of organized, strategic assaults that threaten to cripple our advance," Izhar said. "Even now the supply convoy we expected from the coast is late."

Khilamook straightened, scroll crinkling in his grip. "But my trunks, my belongings . . . my manuscripts? What will those barbarians do with them?"

Jakim translated, and the warrior snorted. "Oh, they will put them to good use: padding saddles, rubbing down steeds, lighting cookfires. As barbarians are wont to do."

"By the thirteen orders," Khilamook whispered, "you are all mud-born imbeciles." His face had whitened. He looked like he was about to be sick. "Those manuscripts are life, death, victory, *everything*. I need them and–"

"The convoy may only be delayed." Izhar's raised hand cut Khilamook off before Jakim could translate. "We have no way of knowing"–this with a glance at Nahrog, who nodded–"and more pressing matters to discuss. Tell us of the woman, son of Soldonia."

For the first time, the warrior's composure slipped. "The woman?"

"She that rides the fire-demon." The priest could make anything sound like an incantation, but something about his voice now made Jakim shiver. His eyes were distant and his body unnaturally still. "She that leads hosts to battle and dares set her will against the Dominion of Murloch."

"Ceridwen tal Desmond," the warrior said slowly. "That is who you mean?"

Izhar nodded, clasping his hands behind him. "She was supposed to die at Idolas."

"She was. Kilmark regrets his failure."

That earned a sniff from one of his companions who still stood beside the steeds. Jakim had been so focused on those legendary creatures and the one traitor that he had skimmed past the others. He recognized the king's two killers: the axeman with long dark hair and the one built like a brick with a face like a mallet. He had never before seen the woman, but he could not look away. The hair that spilled beneath her gray cloak shone with the iridescent gleam of a hummingbird's wings. Mesmerizing. She was beautiful and fierce in her armor, and even his memories of his sister Siba seemed suddenly ragged and humble in comparison.

But the warrior was still speaking. "She has laid claim to her father's throne, and the Outriders answer her horn. What more must you know? Surely one woman has no hope of hindering Murloch's Dominion?"

Spine tingling, Jakim felt for the lump of the ring beneath his tunic and inched closer to listen. He was neglecting his translation, but all eyes had shifted away from Khilamook. Finally, he had a name for the king's daughter: Ceridwen tal Desmond. He repeated it silently to himself, folding it in his mind. He knew what else he wanted to know. Where was she? How could he find her? How could he fulfill his vow and pursue his true purpose?

Of course, Izhar asked none of that. "You assured us your ascension was certain."

"It is. It will be."

"And if the war-chiefs unite behind her?"

"She is flame-bent and reckless. They do not trust her."

"And yet . . . she is a threat?"

"She is *the* threat. She must be defeated."

"Then see to it. You have baited us with promises long enough. Emperor Lykier would know if your oaths have teeth."

The warrior just calmly sat back in his seat. "I cannot lead forces against her. You need me in position to negotiate. I hold to my agreement. You would be wise to do the same."

"You misunderstand our purpose, son of Soldonia." Izhar straightened and retrieved his helm, settling it on his head with both hands, each movement weighted with intention. "Negotiation alone could save your would-be kingdom. But we are here to conquer." He drew the word out, let it lie between them. "You have given us little indeed to make demands."

Slowly, the warrior stood and adjusted his sword belt.

Contrasted with the tsemarc's gleaming helm, golden scale armor, and cape like a river of blood, the warrior's earth-hued cuirass seemed rugged and worn. "I gave you the king." His voice was still quiet but edged like a blade. "The victory at Idolas belongs to me."

"The victory at Idolas belongs to those who bloodied steel in the guts of their enemies. Where were you, son of Soldonia, when the killing began?"

"Where were you, tsemarc?"

Izhar smiled, and it was the first time Jakim had seen him with anything other than a scowl. Only the left half of his face responded, accentuating the scar on his right cheek. "This arrangement grows tiresome. The Dominion of Murloch will advance, with Soldonian aid or over Soldonian corpses. You may choose. The demon-steeds are your strength, and the world knows it. Reveal to us their weaknesses. Equip us to defeat them and to fold their power into our armies. Then you will have your throne."

The warrior worked his jaw. His gloved hands flexed. "It is impossible. Only a Soldonian can share the sol-breath." Suddenly the cloaked woman stood at his side, and his expression softened as he drew her hand to his chest. It hardened again as he focused on the tsemarc. "No, this I will not do."

King, nation, and honor, this man betrayed. Yet not the secrets of their steeds?

Jakim should not care. This was not his country. But only once before had he experienced treachery so sickening, when the slave caravan hauled him away from the sound of Siba's weeping. And he had held the dying king's hand, had seen his severed head tossed carelessly in a sack. Hatred uncoiled inside his chest.

Beside him, Khilamook stirred, eyes sharp with cunning. "That is your steed there, is it not, horseman?" The words were slow to register with Jakim. He searched for a translation before realizing why. The engineer had spoken Soldonian.

The warrior started, muscles tightening.

"Truly, a magnificent specimen." Lifting his cane, Khilamook twisted his hands and withdrew a long, thin blade concealed within.

He squinted down its length. "Scholars could learn much from the blood drained from its veins, its muscles flayed, its guts strung up to dry. It is not my field of study, but many are learned in such things."

With a look, the warrior halted his companions from advancing. "You would die before touching Vakhar. His flames burn hot."

"Enough to halt a volley of ballista bolts?"

"And reduce you to ashes where you stand." Disdainfully, the warrior turned back to the tsemarc and spoke in Nadaarian. "I gave you the king, his daughter, and the kingdom. You will give me my throne."

Izhar pursed his lips, considering. "His head could not be found, you know. His corpse lies in the valley, but if his spirit is restless, it wanders without a head to guide it."

Something flickered in the warrior's eyes. "That is a pity."

"Tormark likened him to your father."

"I have a father."

"And how is he these days?"

"He is dead."

"So Tormark said." Izhar held his gaze and something seemed to pass between them. "I will allow that you have given us the king. But you have not given us his daughter yet. Or the kingdom."

"It is a simple matter." The warrior's eyes shifted to the panels of scarlet and orange that fluttered in the breeze, revealing glimpses of the camp and countryside beyond. Jakim wondered if the man realized how much he revealed in that naked stare. Simple or not, this cost him something. "She is of the blood of Lochrann and sworn to defend her own. Strike there. You will draw her out."

"You can offer better than that."

He hesitated. "Her cousin is chieftain at Soras Ford. She cares for him."

"And the kingdom?"

"Will be mine soon enough."

That, at last, seemed to satisfy the tsemarc, and in a whirl of motion, the warriors and their steeds were gone, though the echoes of their hooves still rumbled in Jakim's bones. His forehead was suddenly damp with sweat.

"What of my manuscripts–"

Izhar forestalled Khilamook with an upraised hand. "You speak Soldonian, engineer?" He asked it in Nadaarian, and it took a jab of the cane to remind Jakim to translate both it and the engineer's less-than-truthful reply.

"Only some, tsemarc."

"Pity mine is so poor, or we could dispense with all this." Izhar waved vaguely at Jakim.

"Indeed, a pity." But like the warrior, something flickered in Khilamook's eyes, and Jakim had no doubt his calculating master had already known exactly how much Soldonian the tsemarc spoke. Khilamook spun to leave, and something squelched under his foot.

It seemed one of the legendary steeds had dropped a fresh pile of manure in the command tent. Talk about sabotage. It was almost unbearably funny.

"Master . . ."

Snarling, Khilamook stepped out of the shoe and flung it at Jakim who tried to catch it too late. It struck his chest and fell. "Clean it, slave."

Wrinkling his nose at the smell, Jakim picked it up and followed after Khilamook. At least he had learned something today. The king's daughter had claimed her father's throne . . . and she was surrounded by traitors who wanted her dead. Suddenly both ring and vow weighed down his neck. But at least he finally knew her name.

THIRTY: CERIDWEN

And this truth is held by all the horsemasters of yore: only a true son or daughter of Soldonia can bond a steed and share the sol-breath.

A thousand, thousand stars pierced the night sky over Ceridwen's head as she sat on a rock beyond the Outrider camp, listening to the rustle of two thousand steeds grazing and the hum of night riders making their rounds. Their song drifted softly before them, reminding her of long-ago night trainings under the horsemasters with Rhodri and Bair. On the march, Outriders could hobble their steeds beside their bedrolls or loose them to roam in their unit's herd overnight. Patrols watched from sky and shadows to give advance warning of enemies so they could saddle if necessary.

Still, Ceridwen chose to keep her fireborn close, unbridled though not yet untacked. Sabre and steed alike should never be far from hand—so Markham had taught her.

Of course, his list had included "spirits" too.

Beside her, Mindar breathed a contented snort, flaming the grass with a soft *whoosh*, the glow highlighting the strong lines of his nose and the burning coals of his eyes. Once the flames dwindled, he ate the singed stalks. Eventually, ashweed would grow in the scorched soil, displacing the natural grass. Maybe that was why fireborn were feared most of all solborn. Even in grazing, they left their mark on the world.

Whereas she struggled to effect any change at all.

Claiming the throne should have been a moment that hummed

with weight and purpose. But after she stated her intent to the *ayeds*, mounted on her fireborn with the stain of battle yet clinging to her leathers and his hide, after Markham had dispatched relay riders to the seven chiefdoms, after wounds had been tended, the dead burned, and the third Outrider *ayed* arrived, war simply plodded on.

Slowly, the Nadaari crawled inland, marching one day out of three and crouching behind fortifications the rest, while soldiers trained and scavenging parties ravaged the land. These the Outriders hunted. Once more, her forces were scattered in units and *ayeds* that patrolled for miles surrounding the line of march. Each night on the move, the Nadaari halted hours before dusk so workers could fortify the camp with palisades and trenches. These the Outriders targeted until a stormrider diving for a shot spied the iron collars marking them as war-slaves.

That night, Ceridwen had ridden off alone and spurred Mindar into such a firestorm, that even with the bond, she could hardly breathe for the sizzling heat.

Whistling neared and her hand fell to her sabre. A tall figure emerged from the night with a wolfhound gliding at his heels, and in that rustling grass, the hound made more noise than the man. Such was the gift of the shadowrider sol-breath.

"Any word from the war-chiefs?" she asked.

Finnian eased onto the rock beside her, settling his bow on his knees and plucking a knife from his belt while the wolfhound circled twice before dropping at his feet. "Not yet, I'm afraid."

It had been two weeks. No war-chief had answered the summons. No war-hosts had been mustered. No response had come even from the chieftains of Lochrann.

Yet was too hopeful a word.

"More warriors come every day," Finnian said in the same gentling tone riders used to calm agitated steeds. Her claim had unleashed such a torrent of activity that in two weeks their paths had scarcely crossed, so his parting words formed uneven ground between them still, leaving her wary of her footing. "Lochrann will respond. You fought for them when the war-chiefs fled. You are fighting still."

Was that admiration in his voice?

He had questioned her decision, called her reckless and a coward. Those barbed words had penetrated deeper than any arrow, deeper than the brand on her forehead. Sidelong, she glanced at the interplay of shadow and moonlight catching and glinting off the bones of his face. Why had he changed his mind? Or had he? She had sworn to free him from their pairing. Much had changed, but she would hold to her word.

The scrape of a blade on wood distracted her. "Are you whittling . . . in the dark?"

He shrugged. "Not so dark for a shadowrider."

Ah, yes, it was easy to forget the less visible effects of other sol-breaths. Hers granted her resistance to flames and smothering smoke. Night vision also would have been a handy skill, though it was strange to know in this moment that he could see her clearly as she could not.

"It is a pipe," he added, offering the chunk of wood so she could inspect its shape. "Markham's shadower fell in the retreat. Snapped his pipe inside his saddlebags."

"Lucky it wasn't his leg."

"Or his steed's."

"So . . ." She returned the pipe and kept her voice light. "Is it a bribe then? To barter for a new partner? You needn't go to such lengths, you know. I have not forgotten my promise."

"It's a *pipe,* Ceridwen."

"Still–"

"It's an old habit."

She blinked. "Smoking?"

"No, whittling. I can't sit still. Need to be doing something with my hands. *He* drilled it into me." His voice dropped, and she did not have to ask who *he* was, the man Finnian did not call his father. "Markham noticed after I joined up, taught me to carve, put that restlessness to use. Looked after my mother too, made sure she was cared for when I was gone, until I was old enough to see to it. He is a good man. Deserves a good pipe."

Silence drifted between them as his words took root. How old had he been when he rode the gauntlet? Younger than she by the way he spoke. The Outriders were his all. His home and his hope for the future. They were only her atonement from her past.

She cleared her throat. "Still, I swore to speak to Markham, and I will. The Outriders may ride with me, but you could rejoin your war-chief. You could be free."

"Free to hide in Craddock's ranges with him? I think not. Anyway, it's too late for that." Finnian reached down to scratch Cù's ears and paused, evidently reading her confusion. "You haven't heard? Markham appointed me your back-rider."

"Markham is . . . full of surprises."

Back-riders rode at a war-chief's off flank in battle, and she was a war-chief now—or nearly one—so the appointment made sense, even if the appointee caught her unawares. But Finnian's voice revealed nothing of his thoughts, and the dark concealed his expression.

"And what say you?" she asked. "I will hold to my oath if you will it."

Finnian spun his knife and sheathed it. "My oath has already been given. I will ride at your side, Ceridwen tal Desmond, and I will be your back-rider if you will it."

"Aye," she said quietly. "I will it."

Though she wanted to demand why. Nothing had changed since that night by the fireside when exhaustion and sorrow had bled honesty from both their tongues. He had been open then. Was he being open now?

"Good. Because Cù likes you. I can tell."

She shook off her doubts and eyed the shape sprawled at his feet. "Does he?" Ever the wolfhound kept his distance. "He did attack me in Rysinger's stable."

"Only after you attacked me." He raised his hands, stifling her objection. "In his eyes, at least. You can come across a bit threatening." With the toe of his boot, he scratched the wolfhound's back, prompting Cù to yawn noisily. "Still, I think you've grown on him since."

His eyes met hers, and for a breath, she dared wonder if he still meant the hound. Something in his gaze set her heart pounding as it did before battle. Before life and death clashed and the world hovered on the brink of eternity.

Only a breath.

Then she retreated from the thought and from his starlit gaze. Both were inherently dangerous, like charging blindly into the crater of Koltar, and she would sooner do that than risk . . . whatever this was. Or wasn't.

"My lady . . . I mean . . . tor Nimid . . ."

Flames kiss you, Liam.

Ceridwen rose abruptly, grateful for the distraction, as Liam approached with a dark-haired girl carrying a bundle tucked under her chin. "What is it?"

"Only that I've remembered something, you see." Sheepishly, Liam fumbled his spear and lurched to keep from dropping it. "Something important. Or rather, to tell it true, Coritza remembered it and . . . sorry, but what are we to call you? Is it tal Desmond now or—ow!" He broke off, glaring at the girl who'd poked him with her elbow.

"Would you stop jabbering already and just tell her?"

"Fine!" Liam rubbed his ribs. "I found something in a Nadaarian supply cart weeks ago. You remember, don't you? I tried to tell you, only—"

Hooves thudded toward them, shattering the soft song of the night riders. Ceridwen spun to bridle Mindar even as Finnian swung smoothly into place beside her, arrow nocked. Taking his new role seriously, it seemed.

Liam sighed. "Only I was interrupted then too."

Iona's stormer skidded to a halt in a spray of earth, and the woman rocked back in the saddle, flinging the hair back from her face. "Come quickly, Ceridwen. You must see this!"

She was in the saddle before Iona had finished.

"What is it?" Finnian stood taut while his wolfhound streaked away to fetch his steed. "Have the Nadaari been sighted? Do we ride to battle?"

"Oh, it's better than that." Iona broke into a grin. "Lochrann has come."

Lochrann has come. Those words hummed inside Ceridwen, warming her from within, as she rode after Iona into the heart of the camp. But nothing warmed her more than the sight of Gavin te Annamark standing foremost among the chieftains and their patrols–the rest of their forces no doubt waited outside the camp–ringed by a dozen torches held by her Outriders.

Markham bowed with a wolfish grin. "Hail, war-chief and queen."

Solemnly, Gavin knelt and led the chieftains in swearing blade oaths in her name. Ceridwen answered with an oath of her own, vowing her blade and flame to the chiefdom's service until the last drop of blood had spilled from her veins. Mindar loosed a spout of fire toward the sky when she relaxed, startling muttered curses from several chieftains.

She dismounted, dropping her reins to ground tie her steed, and stepped into Gavin's hug. A silent cough rattled his chest, and his dusky-blue tunic seemed to hang even more loosely from his shoulders than before, but his arms were firm and strong. She heard the murmur of the other chieftains and ignored them, stepping back to grip his forearms.

"It is good to see you, Wen," he said.

"And you, Gav. How are Fiona and the boys?"

His smile broadened. "Fiona would have ridden at my side, but we welcome our third child soon. If it is a son, we will call him Desmond after your father. We grieve your loss."

It shamed her to hear him speak of her father with more feeling than she could muster. She still felt numb. But the blade at her side provided the answer. Vengeance was ever an acceptable response. "We will make the Nadaari regret setting foot on our soil."

Gavin nodded. "To that end, I offer three units of riverriders."

"And I bring three hundred and sixty-seven riders." Silver-haired and grandmotherly, Yianna tal Rorych spoke without pride or hesitation, though her holdings were small and such a force would require mustering every rider capable of bearing arms, leaving few to guard her range. She fingered the twin long-knives belted at her waist. "You don't sit on the nest when a predator prowls through the eyrie. Your cousin is persuasive. He thinks you can save Lochrann. Maybe even the kingdom. Why do you think we are here?"

Gavin smiled at Ceridwen's raised eyebrow. "Oh, I have battled you in too many strategy games not to bet on you now. You prefer desperate measures against long odds."

"Yet you beat me every time."

"Less and less, as I recall."

His memory must be failing him. But he only winked as he stepped back, allowing the other chieftains to come forward. Raw-boned Ballard te Bronwen offered four units, and his even taller, soot-haired sister Kassa promised three more. That left only scowling and bearded Doogan te Owen, ears gleaming with silver rings, neck arching defiantly.

"One hundred and fifty," Doogan declared, as proudly as if his range was not twice the size of Yianna's and his offering less than half.

"Please," Markham drawled. "Don't overtax yourself. We are only at war."

Doogan sniffed and turned away, but his arrogance sparked Ceridwen's ire. She blocked his path. "Tell me, Doogan, how many warriors you lost at Idolas."

"I don't see how that's–"

"How many?"

"*Floods*, woman, I don't have to answer to–"

"Your sworn oath says otherwise."

He stiffened and straightened his mail coif. "Sadly, my muster arrived too late."

"Too late," Ceridwen repeated. "Yet you send only one hundred and fifty—"

"Earthhewn," Gavin interrupted, thin hand on her arm. "One hundred and fifty earthhewn *and* a full unit of riverriders." Out of the corner of her eye, she saw Markham track the hand and scowl. He disliked anyone even seemingly encroaching on her authority. Save him, of course. "Isn't that what you told me, Doogan?"

Behind her, Mindar snorted smoke.

Doogan's eyes shifted to the fireborn, and his throat bobbed. "I suppose . . . I forgot to mention the riverriders."

Markham regarded him. "Let's hope their blades are sharper than your memory."

Ceridwen allowed Doogan to pass, mentally calculating the additions to her forces. Only five of Lochrann's seven chieftains had come. She looked to Markham, and he leaned closer. "Forrold fell childless at Idolas—his holdings must be reassigned. Callum was injured and carried with Glyndwr to Rysinger. He is there still. But a majority of the chieftains can confirm a war-chief. It is enough."

Nodding, Ceridwen dismissed the chieftains to settle their steeds while she saw to Mindar, then summoned them again for a meal and war-meet around the fire. She listened long to the relentless cadence of tongues striking and parrying over their strategy, then stood to speak, and they fell silent. Gavin nodded encouragement. Her voice resonated in her ears as she delivered the plan she and Markham had envisioned: forces divided for harassing tactics, avoiding pitched battles where war machines could decimate their ranks, retreating often, forever on the move. They would wield the land itself and all the mobility of their steeds against the invaders.

"We will sever them from the coast," she finished, "strand them inland, and when the war-hosts muster again, we will destroy them."

And the chieftains cheered as if they believed it possible.

But their offerings only raised her host to seven thousand strong, and her forces were already divided over a dozen different fronts. Recent losses had been minimal, but war was an untamed steed, more volatile than her own. And still, the war-chiefs sent no word.

She sat, feeling strangely deflated, as Markham detailed their plan to stock hidden stations to resupply the *ayeds*, reducing their reliance on villages the Nadaari might plunder. At the next fire, Liam slumped dejectedly with his elbows on his knees, spear discarded. He even ignored the girl, Coritza, sitting at his side, bundle still hugged to her chest.

Ceridwen stood, nodding for Markham to continue, then strolled over to sit beside the boy. "All right, Liam, what did you find?" His expression brightened, but she told him, "Straight to the point this time."

He gestured to Coritza who pulled a manuscript from her bundle. Ceridwen took it and leafed through crinkled pages of foreign script–not Nadaarian–full of sharp symbols and broad sweeping lines.

"You said you found this in a Nadaarian supply cart?"

"Aye, and six more," Liam said. "I'm no scholar, but Coritza's traveled wide and seen all sorts of creatures. Graybeard monkeys, scadtha, even sosswyrms in the wild." He started to go on but faltered at Ceridwen's stare. "Well, she said it's written in Canthorian."

Ceridwen eyed the girl. "You know Canthorian?"

She smiled boldly. "Speak? Aye. Grew up sailing with my dad, a shipmaster of Cenyon, and my ma of the Alon Coast. Read? Not so much. Saw a name–Carpaartin–but most is too complex to translate. It was the diagrams caught my eye . . ." She trailed off as Ceridwen turned to a detailed drawing of a war machine.

"Aye," Liam said. "It was the diagrams convinced us to show you."

Ceridwen nodded slowly. Historically, the empires of Canthor and Nadaar had maintained a stance of uneasy neutrality toward one another, but the existence of these manuscripts along with the war machines at Idolas seemed to prove the connection between the two now extended to military assistance, if not more.

"A ballista," a voice mused behind them. "Where did you find that?"

Ceridwen turned to see the completely incongruous sight of Astra tor Telweg afoot, wearing the dull gray cloak of a shadowrider, hood thrown back to reveal dark hair loosely knotted at the base of her skull. She felt a thrill of hope. *Cenyon has come.* "Astra, you're here!"

"Oh, but I am not here. Not officially." Astra casually lifted her trident in salute. "Not even your scouts saw me. Speaking of which, you might consider increasing your patrols. There are a few gaps."

Of course. Cenyon would be the last to come, if it came at all.

Ceridwen tried to squelch her frustration, but it boiled through her words. "So why are you 'not' here then, when you could be 'not' anywhere else?"

"Happenstance, what else?"

"The fate of the kingdom perhaps?"

Astra seated herself gracefully. "My errand is urgent and elsewhere, so I will speak plainly, if I must, for I have little time." She accepted the ale skin Liam held out and took a delicate sip, though judging from the dust coating her gear and her torn and bloodstained cloak, her journey had been arduous. "Pride flows in the blood of Cenyon no less than in the blood of Lochrann, but we are struggling. Alone, we cannot hold out. Yet my mother would never come here. She would never allow me to come here. And yet, if you would go to her . . ."

"She would cast me into the deeps."

"Or she would listen. You risk life and limb for the kingdom. Will you risk pride too?" Ceridwen shifted uncomfortably at that, but Astra merely left the question hanging and glanced at the manuscript. "You say this was taken from the Nadaari?"

"Aye." Ceridwen tilted the manuscript so the fire illuminated the drawings of joints and levers and the notes in the margins. Leafing forward uncovered illustrations of mangonels too, as well as several war machines she had not seen at Idolas. "If we could translate this, we could know how their machines work–"

"And how best to destroy them," Astra said. "*Floods.*"

"I knew it!" Liam crowed. "I knew this was important, didn't I, Coritza?"

Ceridwen snapped the manuscript shut. "You've had it for two weeks, Liam. If you knew it was so important, why did you delay?"

His face reddened. "I . . . uh . . . forgot."

"You . . . forgot?"

"It was all so chaotic, what with the *ayed* arriving, so I stowed them in my saddlebags for safekeeping, only I forgot and have been using them as a pillow."

"Sleeping on our enemy's stratagems?" Astra's lips twisted wryly. "I don't suppose any of it seeped in?" She ruffled Liam's hair, and he pushed her hand away with a scowl.

"It doesn't work that way."

"Oh?" Astra fluttered her lashes innocently. "No matter. I can translate it."

Ceridwen regarded her curiously. "You can?" This confident woman scarcely resembled the shy girl she remembered. Of course, she herself was a far cry from who she'd been too–a child desperately pining for her father's regard.

"I am fluent in several languages. It comes from living in a center of coastal trade like Tel Renaair. But more so from living as tor Telweg." Astra's voice dropped as she leaned in. "Stormers struggle to soar as high as my mother's expectations. But this I can do and more too. I noticed no war-chiefs ride with you."

"Not so," Liam cut in defensively. "She is our war-chief."

"Your pardon." Astra's lips twitched in amusement. "No other war-chiefs, I should say. I carry a message from my mother to Glyndwr in Rysinger. Should I deliver this manuscript as well, it might provide the impetus needed to summon them back to arms."

The war-chiefs shouldn't need any impetus to defend their country.

If Ceridwen were the acknowledged heir, her summons would

have sufficed, but until they recognized her claim, Glyndwr remained regent, and they might answer his horn when they would not answer hers. That was reason enough to consider Astra's suggestion, but this captured manuscript might also provide proof of her capability. It could only aid her cause and the kingdom's, so why did she hesitate? *Blazes*, was it so hard to yield the reins to another?

She swallowed. "Aye, it's a good plan."

"Aye, it is." Astra's eyes gleamed like waves in moonlight as Coritza bundled the manuscripts and handed them over.

"Wen?" Gavin called, peeling off from the fireside gathering. Behind him, the chieftains were rising, pounding shoulders and clasping wrists before dispersing for the night. Ceridwen caught Markham's longsuffering glare and realized she probably should have been present to dismiss the war-meet she'd called. Too late now. Coritza elbowed Liam to move, creating space for Gavin to lower himself beside Ceridwen. "Or should I say Queen Wen?"

"Best not say that too loudly," she warned. Yet.

A smile creased his eyes. "As you wish. Though you've no idea how long I have waited to say it." His shoulders shook with a muffled cough. "I must return to Soras Ford tomorrow to complete the muster. Only half my forces are here. I would send a rider to fetch the rest, but Fiona's time is soon, and I would be with her."

"Of course–" Ceridwen began, but Astra interrupted.

"If you ride eastward, perhaps you would consider escorting me to Rysinger? I did not set out alone, but I alone am left." She laid her hand protectively atop the manuscripts. "Soras Ford is not far astray, and with my errand, safety matters more than speed."

Gavin glanced to Ceridwen for approval before nodding courteously. "I would be honored to offer my services. Once I know Fiona is well, I shall see you safely to Glyndwr. We ride at first light." He bent closer to Ceridwen, eyes twinkling as he lowered his voice. "You might send someone to oversee Doogan's muster, ensure he keeps his oath. Until we meet again, Queen Wen . . ."

"May Aodh be with you," she finished, daring to hope the prayer fell on listening ears.

Astra rose gracefully, embracing the manuscripts. "And until we meet again, consider what we spoke of first."

Ceridwen raised an eyebrow. "When you were not here?"

"So much for secrecy," Astra said ruefully. "Delivering the manuscripts does spoil it. Still, I suppose the needs of the kingdom supersede the will of even Telweg tal Anor—though floods take me if she learns I said that."

Stars dimmed as daybreak hovered beyond the horizon, when Ceridwen found Markham lounging beside a dying fire, smoking his new pipe. He propped one boot on the other, giving her space to sit, and the straight knob of his spurs—shadowriders avoided roweled spurs that clinked and jingled—glinted in the embers' glow.

"Not bad." He saluted her with his flask. "You are a war-chief in truth now, and nothing the others do can negate that. It is a stride toward our goal. A good stride."

"But only a stride. We still need them."

"Aye." Pursing his lips, Markham gazed up at the fading stars. "Glyndwr is the sort of man who thinks twice before donning his boots. I hoped your claim would spark action, but the stubborn fools wait to see what the others will do. Meanwhile, we delay the Nadaari for a fight we cannot win on our own."

It was one of the basic tenets of war: delaying tactics only served if decisive action followed. But for action, Ceridwen needed more. More warriors. More steeds. More war-chiefs behind her. She needed the Nadaari cut off from reinforcements and starving in their own camp. She needed Cenyon with its command of the coast and the inland paths.

If Astra's gamble paid off, she would get all that and more. But it was not in her blood to sit idly waiting. It was in her blood to risk.

Life, limb, and yes, pride.

Ceridwen stole his flask and took a swig. "Tomorrow, I ride west."

Briefly, she explained the discovery of the Canthorian manuscripts, the implications she feared, and Astra tor Telweg's suggestion. Markham took it all in, and she wondered how much aligned with the threads of information always swirling in his mind.

But all he said was, "So that's why tor Telweg was among us."

"You knew?"

"Of course, I knew. Scouts spied her miles away, chose to monitor her steps. She wasn't more than one misstep from death if she'd proved false." He snorted. "Gaps in my patrols indeed. You are right to go though. Unlike her daughter, Telweg favors straightforwardness, and the coast is vital to our defense." He scratched his weathered forehead with his thumbnail. "Reports show Nadaari reinforcements spilling from Tel Renaair through Idolas, trying to turn one of the abandoned camps beyond into a fortified outpost. Could be an attempt to secure their supply line. Meaning . . ." He eyed her, waiting for her interpretation.

"Our efforts to contain them are working. They begin to feel the strain?"

"Dead center, tal Desmond. And?"

"We should destroy that outpost. You will see to it?" She fiddled with the flask. It felt strange to issue a command–even in question form–to her Apex. But this was the role she had accepted when she stated her claim.

Markham bent his head. "I will, my queen."

His words hummed in her ears long after the sun broke and night fled.

THIRTY-ONE: RAFI

Once cracked, the shell cannot be uncracked.
– Hanonque proverb

One look at Rafi's face in the moonlight and the two young Hanonque guards drifted back, eyes widening, hands tightening on their spears. Their reaction confused Rafi. He might be a scadtha slayer, a lost prince, and a ghost three–no, four–times over, but right now, he must look more ragged than old Hanu's net. Trousers wrinkled and torn, bare chest streaked with thorn scratches and mosquito bites, shirt forming a makeshift ankle wrap, and his arm–

The colt snorted a sharp, salty blast that sent the boys reeling back.

Well, his arm was crooked over the neck of a live sea-demon with glistening scales, eyes like gems, and breath that reeked of fish. Maybe that was what had them on edge.

Or just the fact that he was supposed to be dead.

They silently gave ground as he limped through the narrow crack that separated the rebels' cavernous hideout from the world. With his injury and his certainty that Sahak hunted him still, hiking back had taken a painful two days, but the biggest challenge had been retracing his steps once he neared Tehorra Peak, to locate the entrance through jungle so thick it was nearly impassable and across ground that unexpectedly climbed and dropped in steep folds. In the end, finding it had been the result of sheer luck.

Neither guard hindered his march across the gorge, but one ran ahead while the other trailed at a safe distance. From this angle, the three caverns looked like stacked rings strung on the glistening silver thread of the waterfall. His initial plan to sneak in and sneak Iakki out had been foiled by the beast crashing at his side. Hours of trying to lose it and flapping his arms to scare it away had proved useless, so he had amended his plan. Deprived of stealth, he would stroll in boldly and hope for safety in the attention he drew.

After that, his plan was simple: Get in. Get Iakki. Get out.

Then run as far as he could from both Sahak and this doomed revolution.

Lamps flickered along bridges and staircases, and voices mingled with the roar of the waterfall when he passed into the cool, shimmering luminescence of the lowest cavern. Armed rebels awaited him, massed around the pool. Rafi scanned for Iakki and spied the guard who had run ahead whispering to Umut. The colt plodded on, ignoring his attempt to restrain it, and the tribesmen parted, allowing it to splash into the shallows. Huffed breaths rippled the water, and the colt backed away without drinking, lips curled back from its teeth.

"Nahiki!" Iakki cried, and Rafi glimpsed his broken-toothed grin bobbing through the crowd as he squirmed around arms and legs. Someone caught his shoulder as he broke free.

One glimpse at that scowling face made Rafi's blood boil. Nef.

"Get off me!" Iakki kicked out, catching Nef's shin, and the rebel loosened his grip, distracted. Rafi didn't hesitate. He stepped up and let fly a punch that caught Nef full on the nose. Cartilage crunched, and Nef stumbled back into Moc, eyes wide with shock. Rafi shook out his stinging fist as spears jabbed toward him, hands seized his shoulders, and Iakki's arms squeezed his ribs.

He hadn't even split his knuckles. Definitely worth it.

"Nahiki?" Umut's tone warred between bafflement, irritation, and maybe a little relief, as he waved the rebels back. "What is the meaning of this? We were told you were dead."

Iakki was clinging so tightly Rafi's ribs ached. He had been missed.

Suddenly, Rafi wanted to punch Nef again and again. And maybe once more for good measure. For threatening Iakki. For trying to kill him. For that perpetual scowl. One excuse was as good as another. "Not quite dead." He released Iakki and squared up to denounce his would-be murderer, but one glimpse at Nef's glare as he shoved free of Moc and swiped the blood from his lips cut him off.

"I know who you are . . ."

Nef had tried to kill him for who he was. What if the others agreed?

Rafi fixed his gaze on Nef, raising an eyebrow to convey the bargain: silence for silence. "Just a misunderstanding." He touched the still-tender knot on his skull and didn't have to feign a wince. "Hit my head. Woke up alone. Must have looked like I died." Moc bowed his head, looking ashamed, and Rafi grinned at Umut. "Lucky for me, I'm not so easy to kill."

"I'll bear that in mind," Nef cut in. "Next time."

"You do that . . . and good luck with it." Rafi needed to get out of here. Confessing to attempted murder didn't seem the sort of thing you did voluntarily, but maybe killing a Tetrani prince, like slaying a scadtha, earned you status in the revolution.

He tried to move on again, but Nef shouldered away from Moc's restraining hand and blocked his path. "How did you survive?"

"What can I say? I'm Alonque."

"Part Alonque. Not enough to save you, now that we know who you are."

Rafi flinched at the hatred in his eyes and fear pricked his spine. He clutched at the unraveling threads of his plan, eying the sea-demon now contentedly grazing on the luminescent blue moss that slicked the floor, and ducked over Iakki to whisper in his ear, "Get ready to run."

"Who exactly is he, Nef?" Moc demanded.

Satisfaction deepened Nef's snarl. "This waterlogged rat," he announced, "is none other than Rafi Tetrani, prince of Nadaar, nephew of the tyrant Lykier and cousin to our mortal enemy, the Emperor's Stone-eye himself."

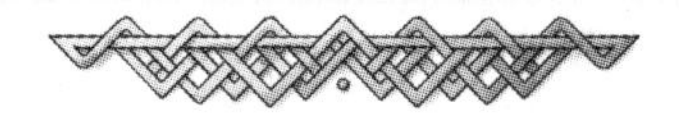

"Huh." Moc's forehead wrinkled. "I thought he was dead."

With all eyes on him, Rafi wished he was dead. *Run, brother,* the ghost whispered, and how he itched to do it. Shocked voices surrounded him. Some marked the resemblance to his father's coin-minted likeness, others saw only the strong Alonque facial bones he had inherited from his mother. Some demanded proof, others his head, and Nef's rang out the loudest. "He must answer for the crimes of his kin . . ."

Iakki's voice drowned it all out. "Nahiki?"

Rafi reached for him, sick at the hurt in his eyes, but Iakki knocked his hand away and tore up the staircase. Snared by the angry mob, Rafi could not follow. So much for his plan. Getting Iakki out would prove challenging if he got himself killed now.

Umut rapped his crutch for silence. "Leave us," he growled, and to Rafi's surprise, the rebels immediately began to disperse, muttering, grumbling, but obedient. "Not you." He caught Nef with a hand to the chest and lowered his voice. "But you will cease your blustering. You are all thunder, boy, and no lightning."

Scowling, Nef dropped beside the pool to wash his face. His nose was broken. Rafi hoped both eyes swelled shut too and turned blacker than an engorged leach.

Petty, maybe, but he didn't care.

Once the cavern had emptied, Umut sighed and started to speak, but Nef cut him off. "All thunder and no lightning?" He stood, flinging water from his hands. "I am the only one not afraid to take action. I am the only one actually fighting–" Umut's crutch slammed into his knee, knocking him flat. His groan startled a snort from the sea-demon. Nef was up again in time for the crutch's return swing to catch him in the chest. He fell on his back, wheezing, and the colt sailed over him and skittered downstream.

"Wait!" Rafi darted after it. Loosing a wild sea-demon on the rebels would only reinforce their hatred of him. His hand snagged in the colt's tangled mane. Teeth grazed his forearm, and he jumped back, cursing. "Ches-Shu!"

"Easy," Umut called out. "You're not grappling a python."

No kidding. This was *way* more dangerous. The colt halted, ears pricked, flecks of blue moss clinging to its whiskers. "Shh, shh." Rafi eased up, hands raised, and it suffered his touch without trying to eat him this time. Progress.

Nef picked himself up, spitting blood. "What was that for?"

"If you don't know, there's no point telling you." Umut shook his head pityingly. "Launching a raid without my permission? Forcing our kin to rise or be killed?" A knife flashed in his hand, blade pressed to Nef's cheek who stood stiff as a spear. "Trying to kill one of our own? Did you expect to be commended for your actions?"

"He is a Tetrani. He is not one of our own."

Umut's voice cracked sharply. "He is if I say he is." He flicked his blade away and Nef fingered the blood beading along the cut. "I expect better of you. Return to your hut. You are relieved of duty until you prove worthy of it. Go!"

Nef worked his jaw then snapped a crisp salute and stormed off, though not before shooting Rafi a murderous glare from the stairs. Clearly this was far from over.

Umut leaned into his crutch. "And what shall we do with you, young Tetrani?"

Rafi casually planted his elbow on the sea-demon's neck. "Feed me?" *To what?* his own voice whispered inside. What a twisted sense of humor he had. "Feed *me*, I mean. Not *feed* me to something else like worms or pythons or sea-demons." He eyed the colt sidelong and found it eying him too. "They eat humans?"

"Rarely." Umut lowered himself beside the pool and patted a seat beside him. "But I am sure we can arrange some food later to negate the risk."

He was probably joking.

Just to be safe, Rafi gave the colt a wide berth as he limped over to join Umut. "Great, I'll have some seaweed tea." That brought to mind sleepless nights chatting with Torva. He'd have given anything to be back there in that time. Before his past came crashing into his present. "Maybe some cala root crackers? And whatever it wants." He jerked a thumb at the colt who had begun grazing again.

"Never seen one up close before." Umut's voice held admiration. "Never heard of one coming so far inland either."

"It's following me, I think, so I must be cursed or something."

Which, honestly, came as no surprise.

"That's Murlochian superstition talking. We of the Que know better. *Anhana Lasha* such beasts are called, heralds of the Three, omens of fate, good and bad. Seeing one is sign enough. Befriending one marks you a man of destiny." Umut regarded him with a penetrating gaze. "Clearly that is true. Few escape death once. You have evaded it three times."

"Four, I think, but I keep losing track."

He kept avoiding the topic at hand too, and had been, ever since his arrival. Umut had orchestrated his long-ago escape, and Rafi still didn't know why. Maybe it was time he stopped running long enough to get some answers.

Umut scratched thoughtfully at his salt-gray beard. "Can't deny a small part of me wondered. You and your cousin sang much the same tale, but there were oddities. Snarled threads, as it were. Snags that didn't line up. Should have known when you asked for me by name, but it's been, what, six years? What happened? Riku sent word the escape was on, then confirmation of success, and then . . . nothing."

Rafi's throat filled, recalling how the rush of the escape, of leaving their cell, of realizing that the outside world had not forgotten them, had vanished in an instant, drained by the blade that sliced their guide's throat before they even learned his name. Riku, apparently. "Why did you get us out? How did you even know we were alive?"

"I am the head of the Que Revolution. I have my sources."

"Like Riku? He's dead. My brother too."

Umut nodded as if this was expected. "Your loss is ours. We got you and your brother out because we need you."

"For target practice?"

"For a distraction."

Rafi shifted uncomfortably. "I can juggle. Tell a joke. Some people think I'm funny." Judging by Umut's expression, he was not one of them. "Does Nef know you need me? He hates my Tetrani innards, and I get the feeling he's not alone."

"He is not. Your uncle is a blight upon the world, and your cousin—"

"Is a monster. Believe me, I know."

Umut dipped his head, conceding the point. "But your father was far more temperate. There are factions among the territories that still mourn his loss, even among the Que. However much they chafe under Nadaar's rule, they know rebelling alone is suicide."

"You might tell Nef that," Rafi muttered.

"I have tried." Umut rubbed his forehead. "Nef is an idealist. He would limit our fight to the Que's war for freedom. I would share the casualties and spare my cousins. If the empire could be shaken by turmoil within, by the rise of a claimant to the throne who could counter the official story with rumors of murder . . ." He let his voice trail off, inviting Rafi to picture it. "As the face of our revolution, you could drive a wedge through Nadaar and inspire the other territories to resist. You see? A distraction."

Delmar had often speculated that poison had been the root of the "mysterious illness" that claimed their parents, but that theory had broken down in the face of their survival. If Lykier had been willing to kill, why not kill them all? Still, Rafi knew how quarrelsome the Nadaarian court could be. Rumors had caused many a rift before.

"I probably could," Rafi conceded. "But why would I?"

Umut twitched an eyebrow at him. "Self-interest? Surely ridding the world of your hunter would let you sleep better at night."

Rafi's vision fogged and he was falling, grasping vainly toward a dying scream. He snapped back to reality and shrugged. "Not so interested in myself. You'll have to do better."

"Iakki then. Fight for his safety if not your own."

"Not so convinced your revolution can succeed, even with my help, and that's the only way you could guarantee his safety. More likely, I'll get myself and lots more killed when the empire retaliates." Rafi narrowed his eyes at Umut. "And they will retaliate."

"Fair," Umut grunted, leveraging to his feet. "I did ask you to weigh the cost of resistance on your arrival, but you should weigh the cost of passivity too. Whether or not you believe this fight is worth it, we already wade through accumulating losses. Your brother. My leg. Saffa's voice." Rafi started, horrified. "Oh yes, her too. She protested when they took her son, so they took her tongue as well. Think on it, Rafi Tetrani. The world drowns. Will you stand by and watch?"

Saffa still puttered about the kitchens, monkey on her shoulder, when Rafi limped in and slumped into a chair beside the stone ovens, catching his forehead in his hands. His stomach ached, his ankle throbbed, and his head felt like someone had driven a spike through it from temple to temple. Saffa's calloused fingers prodded his wrist until he lifted his head and accepted a cup of tea and a stack of cala root crackers. He sniffed the reddish liquid. Not seaweed tea, but it smelled good. A little sweet, maybe, and hot enough to scald his tongue.

He drank it anyway. The monkey dropped into his lap, eying each bite expectantly and poking about for crumbs. Something about its tilted head and sharp expression reminded him of Iakki who he had passed tossing pebbles over the side of the bridge. A quiet, stubborn Iakki who had refused eye contact and stormed away when Rafi called out to him.

Rafi let the monkey eat the rest of his food.

"Will you stand by and watch?"

Umut could not have known how deeply those words would strike, how they would summon memories of helplessly watching Delmar fall, Torva bleed, and Iakki almost drown. Now, Rafi's secret was out. Soon the whole camp would know his identity, and his life would be cheap indeed unless he fled or committed himself to their cause. But the odds of Iakki fleeing with him now seemed no greater than the revolution's chances of success.

It came down to this:

If he ran, he would run alone.

If he fought, he would die in company.

He did not know which was worse, but neither offered any hope of freedom. In his place, Delmar would have embraced even a doomed fight, relishing any opportunity to repay Lykier's empire in blood for the horrors it had committed. But then Delmar had been destined to rule and right the wrongs of the world. Rafi was destined only to cheat death at the expense of others.

The rhythmic thumping and scraping of a stone grinder drew him from his thoughts. Saffa, he realized, worked alone. The others were probably sleeping. Or trying to. The sea-demon hadn't taken kindly to being left below, and its shrieks had chased him all the way to the kitchens. If he focused, he could still hear it screaming.

Now everyone would sleep as poorly as he usually did.

Saffa's head swayed as she worked, not hustling, yet somehow, each time he looked, she had accomplished more. This he need not stand by and watch. This he could help. He stood, pushing the scolding monkey aside. "Show me what I can do, Saffa."

She considered him, then backed away from the grinder, motioning him to wait, and shuffled to the corner where brooms lodged in a tangle. But instead of a broom, she pulled out a spear and held it before her, firelight catching on the blade and reflecting in her eyes. Rafi swallowed reflexively as she set it in his left hand, folded his fingers around the haft, and shook his grip with the strength of her own. And he did not know if the voice in his head was hers or the ghost's or his own conscience. *This*, it cried, *you can do.*

"No," he said, "I can't."

The wrong brother had survived six years ago. Rafi Tetrani was not bold enough to face the beast in its den. But he would swear to the revolution if it would keep him and Iakki alive for a few more days, and he would break his oath later if he must, and it would not be the worst thing he had done. Gripping the spear, he limped off in search of Umut.

THIRTY-TWO: JAKIM

Aodh is lifegiver.

"I am sick of this place." Khilamook halted abruptly to let a cart rattle by inches from his toes. He had unbuttoned his collar and rolled up his sleeves, but his skull–newly shaved by Jakim that morning–still shone with sweat, despite the fringed shade Jakim held over his head. After wielding the razor for Khilamook, Jakim had tried to shear the bristly new crop on his own head and nearly sliced off his scalp. It was harder than it looked. His ears were hot beneath a bandage as they wove through the chaotic camp.

Soldiers quick-marched past. Whetstones rasped against spearheads. Tents fell and slaves bundled them. The army had been stationary nearly a week, the longest halt since their victory. But the engineer had not yet ordered Jakim to pack their tent, and only one square section of the camp seemed to be mobilizing now, so perhaps they were not yet marching on.

"The dust, the incessant noise! I ask you, slave, how can a scholar be expected to labor under such strenuous conditions?" Without breaking stride, Khilamook lashed out with his cane. It smacked Jakim's shins, alerting him that he had accidentally let the shade dip.

Ow. Strenuous conditions, huh?

"And yet, I have labored and solved the problem of dispersal . . . which is meaningless without something to disperse. Without my manuscripts, I am immobilized and bored out of my wits." Khilamook sighed. "Clearly, since I am talking to you." He skirted a dismantled tent, and Jakim swerved to follow, mind lagging on his own forced immobilization.

Aodh's hand was supposed to be upon him. He had felt the summons from Kerrikar. But each night, he dreamed of the engineer's suggestion that Aodh should renounce him. Each morning, he awoke feeling a little more dead inside. No closer to escape, to fulfilling his vows, or to his purpose. Maybe Khilamook was right. Aodh was true. He was not.

How could he be a Scroll?

"Engineer, I did not expect to see you here."

Jakim's head shot up, and he spilled a rushed translation. Crimson cloak streaming in the wind, Tsemarc Izhar stood with his hands clasped behind his back, observing the departing forces, flanked by the officer Adaan, the priest Nahrog, and a dozen soldiers.

"Have you abandoned your calculations and machines to bid our soldiers farewell?"

Khilamook raised one eyebrow. "The army marches?"

"They march," Nahrog said, "carrying the Dominion of Murloch with them."

"Silent One Alive," Khilamook murmured, his expression reverent, his tone anything but. It gave Jakim pause. Was that not why the engineer fought? The scholarly in Canthor tended to worship the mind itself with intellectual achievement as the highest goal, while the lower classes sought hope in legends and myths and magical superstitions. But he had never before considered what had drawn the Canthorian scholar here to support a foreign army on foreign soil, if not shared beliefs. Riches, perhaps? Or political gain . . . or transferred allegiance . . .

The cane twitched, and Jakim hastily translated the sentiment, minus the sarcasm.

Izhar nodded sharply. "I have only just issued the command. Demon-riders doubtless watch us from the skies, so the movement of our main force is meant to distract from the departure of a splinter force that Adaan will lead to strike at the heart of Lochrann."

"Indeed? Clever." Khilamook sounded distracted, which explained the rare compliment. "Have you received word of the convoy? What of my manuscripts?"

"Sadly, engineer, a survivor has confirmed the loss of the convoy and the regrettable destruction of all supplies weeks ago." Somehow, Izhar's clipped tone sounded neither sad nor regretful. "You will have to make do without, but surely what you have invented once you can invent again."

Khilamook's knuckles turned white on his cane. "It is not as simple as that, Tsemarc. Discoveries like these are complex . . . and without my notes . . ." Suspicion filled his eyes. "How long have you known and delayed telling me?"

Izhar ignored the question. "Without your brother's notes, you mean."

The engineer stiffened but withheld a response until Jakim translated Izhar's words. His commitment to the farce was as impressive as it was baffling. "Tsemarc, I don't–"

"It could only be so simple if you were the true inventor, and you are not, are you?" Izhar's smile reminded Jakim of a drawn blade. "The survivor brought me two messages. One verbal, the usual demon-rider threats. One written, bearing the royal seal of Canthor. Evidently, it reached Nadaar after our departure and was carried over with the convoy, though fortunately it was kept with the messenger instead of the supplies and was accompanied by a translation."

Nahrog unfurled a parchment. One glimpse drained the blood from Khilamook's face.

"It would seem you are a thief and impostor, and your manuscripts are the work of your brother, Carpaartin. He sends his regard and demands their return and recompense. He also denounced you to the Supreme Chancellor who demands your return and removal from the orders of scholars, effective immediately."

Khilamook lifted a trembling hand to the symbol on his forehead. He looked so stricken by the news that Jakim couldn't completely quell his pity. "Tsemarc, the invention is mine–"

Izhar cut him off. "Fortunately for you, I am not interested in scholarly politics or familial disputes. You have been of use. Continue to prove your value, find me an edge over these demon-riders, and you will remain under my protection, striving for the Dominion of Murloch." His voice deepened. "Fail and your brothers can have you. Pack your things. We march."

His cloak snapped in the wind as he strode off, soldiers clanking at his heels. Nahrog studied the engineer through narrowed eyes, then dropped the parchment and followed.

"Pick it up," Khilamook snarled and spun away, and by the time Jakim retrieved the parchment and wrestled the shade closed so he could run without it turning into a sail, the engineer was halfway to his tent, moving with sharp, punctuated steps that made his shoes slap against his heels. "Hold your tongue!" he ordered as Jakim caught up.

"Yes, master . . ." Jakim stopped.

But his error went unnoticed as Khilamook burst through the hanging silks, hurled down his cane, staggered up to his desk and pressed both hands to its cluttered top. "Ahaz blot out their names," he muttered beneath his breath. "Blot them *out*!" He lashed out, scattering scrolls, cylinder pieces, even his stool. It cracked into a tent pole. Loose papers fluttered down around him as he shook with fury–and perhaps also with fear.

Jakim avoided eye contact as he righted the stool and began gathering the ink-splashed, crumpled sheets. It reminded him of the sailor's vandalism attempt weeks ago. Ironic that he needn't have bothered. Khilamook had done worse damage in less time, and Jakim probably wouldn't even be lashed for it. Probably.

"Do you have brothers, slave?"

His eyes darted up.

"Older brothers?" The engineer slumped at his desk, fists to his temples.

Jakim shuffled uncomfortably at the question, but something about the way Khilamook's collar was ruffled around his ears reminded Jakim of the fledgling he'd returned to the nest that fateful morning in Kerrikar when this all began. It stirred him to pity. He fidgeted with Siba's cord behind his back. "Six of them."

"Older brothers can be . . . cruel." Khilamook lingered over the word, rolling it over his tongue. "I was the youngest of four and that was three too many. Still, opposition forces a man to hone his wits and will. For that, I thanked my brothers the first time I saw fear in their eyes." His voice softened. "And I will thank them again when I see them dead."

In his strange, thin face, his eyes seemed gaping pits with the broken bodies of horses and warriors reflected within, and Jakim felt his own widen in shock. Khilamook's lips twitched into a smile. "Oh, come, you have never dreamed of such a thing?"

"Never." But it came out as a strangled gasp. Jakim wasn't sure he believed it.

"Then your brothers were nothing like mine."

"They sold me!"

Khilamook raised an eyebrow.

Jakim hadn't meant to blurt it, but now the tale boiled from his lips. "I spent seven years a slave because of their jealousy over the words–" He cut himself off just in time. Those words might not concern a Canthorian, but they could be taken as a threat to the empire of Nadaar who undoubtedly preferred the Eliamites as exiles far from their home. He shifted tack, hoping the abrupt change would seem the result of emotion rather than calculation. "I was headed home when my ship was taken."

"I stand corrected. It is a pity you have been deprived of your opportunity to take revenge." Khilamook actually sounded sincere, and part of Jakim wanted to leave it at that. To retreat from this uncomfortable conversation. To bury himself in the mindset of a slave before the fear that he had no purpose as anything but a slave could kick in.

Instead, he caught himself shaking his head. "Justice belongs to Aodh."

So it was written. Twenty-seven times to be exact. But now the words fell flat, lacking the vibrant echo of truth he had clung to with each blistering step at the back of the slave caravan. Only among the Scrolls had he found any comfort in promises of divine mercy as well as divine justice.

"Oh come, you would claim that the thought of your brothers comfortable, satisfied, free does not gnaw at your insides? I have told you before: lying does not become you."

It did gnaw at him. Not all the time, but in moments of inaction when all he could do was think, and thinking of Amir's grin made his fists clench, of Siba's tears made his gut twist, and of his father—who had not been fully mentally present since his wife's death and would never comprehend what had become of his youngest son—made his chest ache.

But Aodh help him, his purpose did not lie in revenge.

It lay in something infinitely harder, and this, his life as a war-slave in the Nadaarian army, must be only a detour on the path Aodh's hand had sent him down. He just wished Aodh would hurry up and lead him home again.

Khilamook snorted in disgust, arms and forehead sinking to rest on his table. "Your inability to see the truth is both comical and sickening. Fetch me food and drink—fine food and strong drink. And be quick. You have packing to do."

He nodded, swallowing. "Yes, master."

But as soon as the silks fluttered behind him and he waded into the rush of the packing war-camp, he veered off track from the cooking tent. Chaos simmered with opportunity. Without the engineer at his side, he could scout potential escapes while the soldiers were preoccupied. But he'd have to be careful. Fast steps could be purposeful. Too fast would be suspicious.

Sentries patrolled the outskirts of the camp, which were marked by a ditch and rampart of piled earth and lined with machines that Khilamook called *ballistae*. Apparently the Nadaari feared the king's daughter—"Ceridwen," he uprooted the name from his memory—would venture from attacking scavengers to the camp itself. One of the sentries glared at his approach, and Jakim ducked behind a barrel of projectiles.

"Oh, aye, that's not suspicious," a familiar voice drawled.

Still crouching, Jakim spied the sailor folding the canvas of a downed tent while other slaves stacked poles and an overseer lounged in the shade of the rampart. He had not seen the sailor since the whipping, which suited him fine. Troublemakers like him were leaky vessels that tended to spill pain and suffering over everyone within reach. It was too late to avoid him now though, so Jakim strolled over to him as if he had nothing to hide. "What are you doing?"

"Dismantling a tent." With his forearm, the sailor wiped the sweat from his scarred forehead. "Keeping my head down. Biding my time. As advised."

"Right." Jakim grinned despite himself. "And I am a sosswyrm."

"About as useful as one. New look?"

"What?"

The sailor tapped his head. "Your shoddy disguise?"

Jakim reached up and felt his bandage. "Oh . . . uh . . . just a cut."

"Uh huh, so you going to stand there watching or help?"

He should finish scouting so he could fetch Khilamook's meal and start packing. Instead, he grabbed a corner. "What are you really doing?"

"Well, I was watching those sentries until you stumbled up and drew their attention." The sailor smirked. "How fares consorting with the greats and helping that tsemarc and his pet scholar destroy my people? You're worse than they are, you know?"

Jakim started at his harsh tone. "I took a whipping for you."

"You're also an idiot. Congratulations. Did you expect gratitude?"

"Not such an idiot." Jakim pulled the canvas too hard, yanking it from the sailor's hands. He wrestled it into a square as a soldier began harnessing a team of dirt-brown horses to a cart-mounted ballista. Their coats shone in the sun as if slicked with oil, but they seemed somehow less than the mighty beasts the Soldonian warriors had led into the command tent. Could a cart lessen a steed as a collar could lessen a man? "Are those them? Solborn?"

"*Floods*, have you no eyes?" The sailor snorted and shook his head. "Those are tolf and half-starved ones at that. If you haven't even the wits to distinguish the two, you've no hope of escaping." He spoke as if there was no question about Jakim's intentions.

Jakim still considered denying it.

"Still, you're better dead trying to escape than living to serve those beasts. I'm almost tempted to help you get out of here. For a price." The sailor seized another square of canvas and shook it out until Jakim caught the loose end. "It would drastically improve your chances. Seamus te Douglas has never been kept anywhere against his will."

"And Seamus is . . . ?"

"Me, of course."

"So, you're still here because you want to be? Why not escape if you can?"

Seamus's flat scowl told him he'd focused on the wrong thing. "Forget it. Stay with your scholar. Just don't forget to scrub the blood from your hands each night." He bundled the canvas beneath his arm and turned away.

"Wait!" Jakim said, unintentionally snagging a sentry's attention. He bent over his work, hastily piling tent stakes. "Sorry," he said, more quietly as Seamus joined him. "But I need your help. What do you know of Ceridwen tal Desmond, the king's daughter?"

"I know who she is. Not much else. What do you know?"

"That I need to find her." He chose his words carefully, mindful of the ring against his chest and the oath he had sworn. Seamus was undoubtedly a troublemaker but not likely to be a traitor. Could he be trusted with that knowledge? Whispering a plea for guidance, Jakim forged ahead. "That she is in danger."

Seamus snorted. "Aren't we all?"

"That"–Jakim hesitated–"I have information to aid her."

"Oh, you have more than that, Scroll. You have access to the mastermind of death himself, that Canthorian engineer." Seamus tipped his chin and pursed his lips, considering. "Could be we could reach an accord: your aid for mine."

That actually sounded more concerning, but if Seamus could help him escape and locate the king's daughter, it might be worth the risk. "What do you want from me?"

"First tell me what *you* got. Convince me it's worth it."

Jakim pasted on a knowing grin. "Not such an idiot, remember?"

"Suspicious for a Scroll, ain't you?" Seamus grunted begrudging approval. "Shows you've some sense at least."

Nearby a whip cracked, and a slave cried out in pain. Time to go.

Jakim dropped the canvas, plotting out how long it would take to sprint to the cooking tent so he could avoid a similar punishment from Khilamook. "We'll speak again?"

"Maybe. Get out of here."

He started off then turned back. "Jakim Ha'Nor." Seamus spread his arms and shrugged, so he jabbed a thumb toward his chest. "My name!"

"What do I care? Scram."

But the tugging feeling in Jakim's gut told him all he needed to know. This was not coincidence, this meeting. This was the start of everything. Surely this was Aodh's hand leading him onto the path laid before his feet. All he had to do was follow. Elated, he broke into a run.

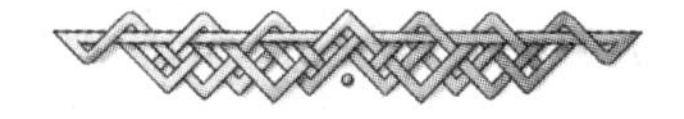

Bottle of saga wine in one hand and a plate of flatbread and spicy grua dip in the other, Jakim raced all the way back to the engineer's tent and burst inside. "I am sorry—" He broke off. It looked like a windstorm had swept through, shuffling half of Khilamook's belongings onto the floor and the other half into an open trunk. His stomach sank. How long had he been gone?

Would the engineer be furious?

"Good!" Khilamook breezed past and snatched both food and drink from his hands. "You're back. Get packing." He lowered himself onto his stool and began to eat. No anger at Jakim's delay. No threatened whipping. No hint of curiosity.

Aodh was merciful.

Jakim jumped into his work. "When do we leave?"

The engineer shrugged. "I have no idea. Once you finish, find Adaan and ask him."

Hadn't the tsemarc said Adaan would be splitting from the main column to march to battle? Jakim paused, halfway through folding a beaded robe. "We are going to fight, master?"

"Not just to fight, no." Voice crisp and brisk, Khilamook picked up two vials from his desk and held them toward the light coming through the parted curtains. One held a thick silvery liquid the light did not penetrate. The other contained a coarse white powder. He uncapped one of the cylindrical devices and poured the silvery liquid inside. "We are going to prove that my designs are behind this army's success. We are going to grind my brother's name into the dust of this country. We are going to win."

THIRTY-THREE: CERIDWEN

Riveren may appear less striking than their ocean kin but are capable of sensing water tabled within the earth and humming to summon streams to the surface.

"*So Roland fair, with the blazing hair,*
Did fall, by countless foes surrounded . . ."

Curly head flung back, Nold sang to the rhythm of his earthhewn's hooves, and his melody rose above the clatter of Ceridwen's fireborn and the rumble of the three hundred steeds who followed. They were her first followers, her faithful warriors, those who had answered her call to battle before her claim to the throne, now rounded out by Kassa tor Bronwen leading several patrols of her earthhewn and Ballard's fireborn.

After five days of steady riding, they had awakened to a Cenyon sunrise. Solborn could maintain a swift traveling pace, and routine rests had conserved their steeds' energy for fight or flight, and the riders' energy, apparently, for song. Cheerful, rangy Nold did most of the singing. He had a pleasant voice and a keen ear, but his lyrics left something wanting.

"*And 'neath the deeps in twilight sleeps,*
Oh fireheart, by oceans drownded."

"*Drownded?*" Iona's tone was sardonic. "Have you nothing better to sing?"

"I wrote it myself, you know," Nold said, without a hint of ire. His ability to greet an insult with a shrug and turn aside a slight with a quip reminded Ceridwen of Bair, whereas she had ever been quick to flame.

Iona eyed him. "Well that explains it."

Kassa rode with her helm tucked under one arm, mail coif slapping against her shoulders, soot-colored hair braided and coiled at the base of her skull. She towered over them all, jogging alongside on her massive bay earthhewn with its distinctive bald face, creamy horn, and streaks of white in its otherwise black tail. "What about *Harrigan's Hand*?" she suggested, aiming a warm, dimpled smile at Nold, though she towered over him too.

"No." Finnian coughed pointedly on Ceridwen's left. "Not that one."

"We could sing of 'Ceridwen fair of the blazing hair!'" Liam piped up from the second row where he clutched the spear he had used to kill the stone-eye. It seemed his badge of glory. Ceridwen expected that he slept, ate, and washed with it in hand.

"You would consign her to a watery grave?" Finnian asked.

Ceridwen shook her head vigorously. "Oh, *blazes*, no." Drowning was one of the worst deaths she imagined. Sundered from heat, from flame. Consumed forever by cold.

"What? No! That's not–"

Iona cut Liam off. "Then use your wits, lad, or hold your tongue."

"All I meant, Aunt, was that we have a legend of our own to sing about. Mayhap, Nold, you could sing *Beloved Isil*, only use our fine war-chief's name instead?"

Kassa's bold laugh rang out. "The lad aims high–you've got to grant him that!"

But Ceridwen's face warmed at the notion of her name inserted into the couplets of a love song. She twisted in the saddle and found Liam grinning, completely unabashed. "What would Coritza say?" Only then did she notice the girl's unusual absence from his side.

"Sadly, we've come to a parting of ways. 'Tis a long, tragic tale, full of weeping and wailing, of a romance not meant to be." Liam pressed his lips together, but from the glint in his eyes, he was bursting to tell it.

"Oh, lad. Lad!" Iona's eyes flicked skyward. "You've your mother's heart and none of her sense. And to think I thought hers the heavier bargain. She has care of my two boys, ages four and seven, and I her one." She aimed this toward Ceridwen, smile widening as it always did at talk of her sons. "The younger is a terror for his own way, and the older is a quiet sort of rebel, but I am finding young Liam more trouble than the both of them."

"I heard that, Aunt."

"Only because you were meant to."

Laughter rippled down the line. Stride lengthening, Mindar nosed ahead of the others. Warmth pooled in his ribcage; dark smoke puffed from his nostrils. Ceridwen longed to let him run purely for the rush of the earth falling away, for the wind in her ears, for her head held high. But the sheen of pain behind Iona's smile was sobering. Being parted from her sons clearly weighed on her. To mend this splintering of families and diminish the blaze of funeral pyres, Ceridwen needed the war-chiefs to commit swords and steeds to the fight. For this, she would swallow her pride, even before Telweg–but not without a strategy.

She called the halt and dismounted, setting off a ripple of creaking saddles, jingling spurs, and crunching boots as the three hundred followed.

"Full rest?" Iona inquired.

Ceridwen nodded briefly, releasing warriors and steeds to be watered and fed. Riverriders began milling about in search of groundwater near the surface, while earthriders waited to carve depressions for the summoned springs. Kassa plucked dainty white daisies and wove them into her braid, occasionally voicing her loud laugh as Liam and Nold sparred with stories, entertaining her with increasingly exaggerated tales. It was encouraging to see one of Lochrann's chieftains meshing so well with this motley crew. It gave Ceridwen hope for their errand.

She unbridled Mindar to graze and worked an oil-treated rag down his neck as she planned. Thinking came easier on the move.

Action had ever been her strength, but words had been Bair's. She would need his skill today.

Mindar's ears flicked, and he paused mid-crunch, alerting Ceridwen to the presence behind her. Someone she had not heard approaching. "You know, Finnian, being my back-rider doesn't mean you have to stand behind me."

"*Shades.*" Finnian stepped up beside her. "How did he sense me?" He eyed her sidelong. "Also, I'm fairly certain standing behind you is in the description."

"Only if you take it literally."

Enormous hooves struck the earth. Once. Twice.

It splintered, showering them with dust. Over Mindar's withers, she watched the riveren swarm the newly created depressions, humming a deep throaty sound so unlike the piercing screams of their ocean-born kin. Water seeped into the basins, forming pools where the Outriders took turns watering their steeds and filling their skins, including the large reservoirs carried by the five earthhewn pack horses. Traveling with a variety of solborn had its advantages. She had never eaten or drank so well on solo trips for the Outriders.

Finnian brushed dirt from his jerkin. "Let us hope our enemies are too far to notice a little earth shaking."

"No scout reports, so the odds are good."

Long before crossing into Cenyon, she had dispatched patrols of shadowers and stormers to scout for signs of friend and foe. She counted on them to find Telweg since Astra had only been able to offer a general location for her mother's ever-moving camp.

"Or they could be dead," Finnian countered.

"What, all of them?" Ceridwen tossed the rag back in her saddlebags and wiped her hands on her leathers. "Since when are you such a pessimist?"

"Since Markham threatened to strand me afoot in Gauroth if you die."

A smirk tugged at her lips. "You should have whittled him a better pipe."

Finnian let out a laugh, an honest laugh that warmed her through and through. Something bumped her knee. She looked down to find the wolfhound snarling up at her—but no, his tail wagged hesitantly, and he nudged her again, the snarl an illusion created by his twisted upper lip.

"I told you he liked you," Finnian said.

Carefully, as though approaching her flaming steed, she lowered her hand to Cù's misshapen skull, feeling the odd ridges of bone beneath the shaggy coat. He suffered her touch for only an instant before flopping at Finnian's feet. "How long have you had him?"

"Since he was a pup."

"What happened to him?"

Finnian's jaw tightened and he knelt beside Cù. "Life."

His voice was elusive, his expression more so, so she did not press him. Not yet. Instead, she dug in her saddle bag for dried meat but found only apples. Instantly, Mindar's ears swung forward and he nickered. "Fine," she sighed. "You can have one. But let's see what you remember." She let him take a whiff then pulled back before he could flame.

Whistle and name. That was the cue.

She tossed the apple.

Mindar blasted it midflight then scooped the charred remnants from the ground. Ceridwen laughed in delight. "He did it! Remote flame." Once again, her "ill-tamed" wildborn had proved the impossible wrong. "Did you see it?"

"That spout of flame that seared my eyes? Can't say I did."

"You sound like Markham."

Finnian winked, ruffling the wolfhound's ears.

"That wasn't a compliment." But Mindar had already finished crunching and was snuffling expectantly at her hands, so she dug out another apple and cued him again. He flamed too late. Unsinged, the apple dropped and bounced, and Cù streaked past in a blur and caught it. Ears flapping, he loped it back to Finnian.

"Hmm, still didn't see it." Finnian pried the apple from Cù and tossed it to her. "Again?"

It reminded her of those frustrating early days of training her wildborn, where failure frequently rode roughshod over success. He had learned then, but it had taken time. Unfortunately, time rode against her now, and she needed words to convince Telweg, not fireborn tricks. First though . . . She threw the apple back to Finnian.

He caught it one-handed. "Is this a bribe to hold my tongue?"

"Or loose it to tell me about your hound."

"Sadly, I cannot be bought. Comes with rising to the rank of back-rider. Scruples and honor and all that." He bit off a chunk and grinned, and in his grin was warmth. She found herself inching closer.

Mindar's snort shook her free.

Distance, her heart warned. Safer for her and him.

She shut her saddlebags and turned away to bridle her steed, but beating wings stirred the air, and a stormer alighted a dozen yards away.

The scout whirled her white-feathered steed and dipped her head. "My queen! Telweg and the Cenyon combat a Nadaarian force only a few hours west from here. The battle is well in hand. It should be won before our arrival, but with haste, we could aid the pursuit."

"Shall we ride?" Finnian reached for his horn to give the command.

Before Ceridwen could respond, a second stormer howled overhead, banked hard, and landed at a run. "Reinforcements march from Tel Renaair," the stormrider cried. "Three thousand strong. Their pace is swift, their weapons ready, their course northeast."

"Northeast?" Concern flashed in the first scout's eyes. "I know the terrain. That will allow them to fall on Telweg's force from the rear."

Finnian swore under his breath.

Ceridwen pushed down her panic, ignoring the murmurs of the warriors massing around them, drawn instinctively to rumor of war. "How many with Telweg?"

"Seven hundred against"—the woman grimaced—"two thousand spearmen?"

"And how long until those reinforcements reach them?" She turned to the second scout, but he shook his head, shrugging.

The first scout met her gaze. "Maybe three hours."

Ceridwen set her jaw. Time was an untamed beast barreling away while three thousand Nadaari stood between her and her goal. Three thousand. No aid could come from the *ayeds*, so fight they must. She swiveled toward Finnian. He stood beside his wolfhound, and his steed could have ghosted into the shadow of his eyes. He had fought in Cenyon before Idolas. She recalled his haunted look when he spoke of the overwhelming Nadaarian tide.

"Finnian."

His gaze darted to her.

"Dispatch a stormer to warn Telweg." With a strong wind, a stormer could fly swifter than run. Without it, the stormer and her forces would reach Telweg around the same time. "And ready the host to ride."

He nodded sharply and jogged off without a word.

Mindar danced when she set foot to stirrup, sensing the drums pulsing in her chest. Sparks shot from his tossing mane, flaring into coils of flame as Ceridwen whirled him to face her faithful three hundred already forming up into a column. She drew her sabre and let Mindar's restless energy carry him into a rear. Fire shot down his mane and tail, and the heat of Koltar burned in his eyes. She could see it reflected in the eyes staring back at her.

"For Cenyon," she cried. "For Soldonia. We ride!"

They took up the call and made it a song as Mindar's hooves touched the earth and he shot forward in a streak of flame, and three hundred sets of hooves rang behind.

THIRTY-FOUR: CERIDWEN

For the firerider, the sol-breath grants partial invulnerability to flames and the ability to withstand levels of heat and smoke that would fell any other rider.

Concealed behind a dune, Ceridwen whispered to quiet her stamping fireborn, though her own ears burned with the roar of battle: screaming seabloods, clashing weapons, the shock and thunder of steeds and soldiers colliding and hitting the ground, the groans of the dying. Her three hundred had ridden like a wildfire, arriving to wait in ambush before the Cenyon could claim the victory and the Nadaari reinforcements could arrive to steal it.

But her scouts warned those reinforcements would arrive soon.

Mindar shifted, jostling against Finnian's shadower. Ash flaked from his coat as Ceridwen rubbed his neck. The tension-charged atmosphere unnerved him, crammed as he was alongside three hundred warriors in two dense columns behind the dunes bordering the roadway from Tel Renaair. Earthhewns at the front, fireborn then shadowers next, riveren in the rear. Stormers waited a furlong back, needing the long gallop to reach flight.

Three hundred all told. Against three thousand.

Was it madness to attempt it? Uthold had often won against greater odds. Many of her other ancestors had not. But the Cenyon were already embroiled in battle. Pulling out now would weaken and scatter their forces, not to mention allowing those reinforcements to reach the main column that Ceridwen sought to leave stranded in Lochrann. She closed her eyes, listening. On all sides, hooves crunched, tack creaked, and steeds snorted anxiously. The close quarters magnified the sounds, but with the wind rustling the salt grasses, she doubted the Nadaari would hear over the tramp of their own feet.

"Makes your blood boil, doesn't it?" Nold muttered in front of Ceridwen. "Hearing that and sitting idle. It's unnatural."

"Silence." Finnian's growl sounded strangely like Markham's.

Despite his warning, his fingers twitched a nervous beat on the horn slung from his neck. In the dune's shadow, his steed blurred, melting into its surroundings unless Ceridwen focused on it. The rest of the shadowers trailed the fireborn to ghost in their smoke, but as her back-rider, Finnian rode at her side. There, he would shield her and watch for her signals and relay them by horn to her warriors. His gear had been treated with skivva oil, but there was no such protection for his steed. He would need to avoid direct contact with flame.

Mindar's ears perked and his muscles tightened. His head swung away from the battle, toward Tel Renaair. It seemed ages before Ceridwen heard it too: the crunch of sand beneath thousands of feet, the jingle of mail, and the rattle of spears and shields. This was an ideal location for an ambush. The opposite edge of the road leveled off into a broad, flat expanse with space to wheel and maneuver, offering her warriors their first advantage—

Three hundred.

Against three thousand. *Blazes.*

Her hand tightened on her sabre as soldiers appeared past the dune. Garbed in scarlet and orange and gold-tinged steel, attention focused on the battle ahead, they marched at a rapid half jog parallel to her forces, heedless and confident, as though the land was already theirs. That arrogance was her second advantage.

She drew her half mask up, counting rows of soldiers, waiting, waiting, waiting, until a scout banner flared, signaling that half the Nadaari had passed. Energy shot through her veins. It was time. The massed earthhewns accelerated slowly. Her fisted hand restrained the swifter fireborn and her own dancing steed. Not leading the charge felt wrong, but only a fool would run ahead of earthhewns in full tilt. Their maximum speed required maximum halting distance, and anything in their path would be crushed by an avalanche of horseflesh. Gradually gaining speed, the twin columns parted around the dune.

Offered slack, Mindar shot over the shuddering ground and Ceridwen beheld the ranks of orange and gold rippling in confusion. Shouts rose. Gongs crashed. Soldiers wheeled, bringing up spears and shields and falling into stance.

But spears and shields could sooner halt a rockslide then an earthhewn charge.

Ten abreast, the massive steeds slammed into the army with an impact like cracking stone. Straight through, they tore with Kassa in the lead, barely slowing as armored chests flung soldiers aside and iron hooves trampled the fallen, and the fireborn raced after them.

Engulfed in smoke, a war cry in her throat, Ceridwen rose in her stirrups as Mindar cleared a pile of corpses. She spun out to the right in the center of the enemy column, sabre raised in a signal that Finnian's horn relayed, and the fireborn at her heels spun with her. Stirrup to stirrup, they charged the Nadaari. Ceridwen rolled her spurs, blasting them with flames. More fireborn fell into place, forming a ring of flames that consumed the heart of the column.

Bowstrings twanged behind. Arrows zipped past.

Soundlessly, the shadowers had filled the ring of fireborn and were shooting through the gaps. Stung by arrows and flame, the Nadaari lines melted. Some fighting. Some fleeing. Some caught between the two. It was working. Raising her blade, Ceridwen voiced the Outrider yell and hundreds of voices sang it back to her.

But the soldiers of Nadaar were disciplined and battle-hardened, forged by an empire that had consumed nations, kingdoms, and tribes. They did not yield. Shouting a rhythmic march, spears and shields clattering, those behind rammed those in front against the fireborn. They fell, screaming, to hoof, flame, and blade. But still they came. And no fireborn could maintain a blaze forever, especially not wearied by an extended run. Once their fire dwindled, it would take time to rekindle. How long depended on the energy they continued to expend.

On her right, a fireborn's smoke faded from gray to white and puffed out. Soldiers surged forward. Spears took the steed. Blades took the rider as he rose. Farther down the ring, another fireborn collapsed. Then a rider. Then three more.

Mindar's flame sputtered, smoke puffing to gray. Soldiers lunged toward Ceridwen, stumbling over their dead. One of Finnian's coppery arrows took a spearman in the throat. Her rearing steed struck another down and crushed him, while her sabre caught a third in the neck. On either side, the fireborn ring shuddered and bowed inward before the weight of numbers.

Thunder shook the earth, and within the Nadaarian column, soldiers shot into the air. Destruction swept a swath through their ranks and arced past the fireborn, giving Ceridwen a glimpse at the second earthhewn column before it punched through the far side of the army. Their sheer strength took her breath away. Even the Nadaari stood stunned after their passing.

Into that breathless silence, Ceridwen and the fireborn exploded, slashing with swords, axes, and hooves. They did not flame, allowing their steeds time to rekindle. It took longer when they were on the move, but momentum was all in mounted combat. Halting risked becoming vulnerable to attacks from the ground, to soldiers disemboweling or crippling their steeds.

So Ceridwen rode.

Rode to kill. Rode to survive.

Teeth bared, she brought her sabre down again and again, slicing through spears, beating past shields, hammering helm and breastplate and flesh beneath. Each breath dragged a thousand scents down her throat: the tang of blood, the stench of sweat, the reek of viscera, and over all, the choking thickness of ash.

"Ceridwen!"

Halting mid-swing, she twisted in the saddle, and Finnian materialized at her elbow, gesturing with his bow, an arrow already nocked. His shout could have been horror or fury or excitement; the clamor swallowed any nuance of tone.

"Lady Telweg is . . ."

The scream of a dying man drowned out the rest.

Ceridwen pulled back, allowing the fireborn to push ahead and the shadowers–only faint impressions of steeds and riders vanishing and reappearing in the swirling smoke and sand as they harried the Nadaari–to sweep around her. The air felt muted and heavy, the noise of battle dulled within the mass of shadowers. She rose in her stirrups to scan the battlefield over the mesmerizing, shifting sea of mottled steeds.

The earthhewns had done their work, barreling through the army on crisscrossing paths until the column splintered. Soldiers clumped in uneven squares, harassed by arrows loosed by riveren racing along their flanks and by the stormers soaring overhead.

It almost looked like her three hundred were . . . *winning.*

"Ceridwen, the Cenyon!" Finnian jerked his chin toward what had been the front of the Nadaarian column before chaos shredded it. "Lady Telweg!"

She saw it then, a mass of blue-gray steeds engaged against one of the largest squares. How long ago had the Cenyon joined this fight? Long enough to push in deep. She spied the smaller mass cut off and embroiled in the center. Too deep. Soldiers pressed in from all sides, forcing them to a standstill. Three riders fell in a blink. Then two steeds. Blades slashed across hocks. Spears pierced guts. *Blazes*, they would be consumed.

Not if she could help it.

Finnian spoke again, but his words drifted past her ears. She leaned forward slightly and felt Mindar tense for the spring. Black smoke coiled from his nostrils. His flames had returned. Finnian's horn blared, opening a path through the shadowers, and Ceridwen launched into the Nadaari spearmen, a terror of flame and hoof and deadly steel pressing onward, ever onward, toward the Cenyon.

With each stride, Mindar's inferno grew. The heat radiated through the layers of saddle leather. Grasping tendrils blew back with the speed of their passage, warming her mask and hood. Her blade arm shielded her eyes from sparks.

None stood in her path.

All were beaten back by the heat.

Mindar no longer seemed a thing of flesh and bone. She rode upon fire itself, as though the molten heart of the crater of Koltar had risen in four-legged form and raged forth to unleash destruction upon the world. His blast slammed into the Nadaari ringing the Cenyon, crackling against shield, armor, and spearhead. She drove him into their midst. Beneath the pressure of her heels, he swung left to right, clearing a path, giving her room to wield her sabre, and bringing his hindquarters to bear against any who ventured too close.

Something slammed into her foot, twisting it outward and wrenching her knee. Spears thudded hollowly against her cuirass. Something raked her arm, numbing her grip on the reins.

She ignored it.

She was aflame without and within.

She would not–*could* not–be quenched.

Like a wave, the Nadaari broke and fled, and three dozen fireborn swept past in pursuit. Their appearance startled her. She had thought herself alone, though doubtless she would have been killed were they not close upon her heels. Breathless, she slowed Mindar and surveyed the slain surrounding her. A tall warrior on a dappled blue seablood raised her trident in salute before wheeling with the Cenyon and charging after the soldiers.

"They flee!" Blue-black wings flaring, Iona's stormer skidded up beside her. One of her pauldrons was missing, blood ran from a gash above her eye, and still she grinned. And well she might. Even a superficial glance told Ceridwen that everywhere the solborn surged victorious across the field of battle. "Your orders, my queen?"

"Take to the sky." Her voice was a dry rasp, but her will was strong. "Hunt them down. Let none reach the columns inland."

"I swear it will be done." Iona peeled off and the stormer unit followed.

"We did it, Ceridwen!" Finnian reined to a stop in Iona's place, soot-streaked face breaking into a smile. "We did it. We won!"

She could only nod. We won.

Mindar circled restlessly, flames still licking across his skin. Drained, Ceridwen pried her stiff fingers from the reins and dropped her stifling mask. She reached down for Mindar, wincing as his flames curled around her weakened glove and heat penetrated the cracked surface. Soothingly, she stroked his neck.

He snorted, blasting a corpse. Once. Twice.

Unease rippled through her. She snapped to catch his attention, but he did not heed her. She reined him back, but he set his stubborn neck and ambled forward. His ribs expanded with amassed flame. He had never ignored her before.

But she had never before demanded such a blaze.

One end of her reins snapped loose in her hand. Mindar blew another spout of fire that licked over a slain Cenyon warrior. Ceridwen bailed from the saddle, discarding her blade, and rounded his head, palms up, forcing him to halt. His eyes were dying embers, dull red within a cloud of ash white. Heat shimmered around his nostrils. She tensed. Her leathers could not withstand a direct shot, not in their current brittle condition. Bair's face invaded her thoughts. His broken limbs and seared skin and–

No. She lifted her gloved hand to the soft patch of skin between Mindar's nostrils and breathed out a long slow breath. The red in his eyes flared, burning the ash away, and he leaned into her hand. Smoke coiled cold and white around her. Only then did Ceridwen realize how she trembled.

Finnian breathed out a soft whistle behind her, and she turned slowly to face him. "*Blazes*, Ceridwen." He reached up to brush away sweat before it dripped in his eyes, leaving a smudge on his forehead. Ashes sprinkled his dark hair and cloak like snowflakes.

Her ears still pulsed with the roar of battle, of fire, of her own lifeblood. She could not identify the tone of his voice, but he'd seen her struggle to control her steed. Too weary to engage with the judgment that would surely come, she turned back toward Mindar and halted. Her saddle hung crooked, cinch singed and partially torn. If it had given out during the battle . . .

Hands numb, she let the reins slip and leaned over, willing her chest to rise and fall.

"Tal Desmond." Telweg's imperious voice jarred her back to herself. She straightened as the war-chief dismounted, mail skirt clinking like sea-chimes in a stiff breeze. Telweg removed her helmet and tucked it beneath one arm, and though her hair was plastered to her head, she still managed to look regal. "Where is the rest of your force?"

That question was a spear-blade to the heart. Her three hundred had ridden against three thousand and survived. But at what cost? Dreading the sight, Ceridwen rounded to survey the battlefield. Riders hunted the remaining soldiers while the dead lay in heaps amidst pockets of flame and uprooted earth. Sword and bowstring no longer sang, but the gasping cries of the wounded rose to fill the silence.

"I see only a few hundred Outriders here," Telweg continued, and finally, Ceridwen understood. It was not the fate of her force that concerned the war-chief, only its size.

"This is all," she said, voice still rasping in her throat. Not since her first trip to the crater had she passed through such fire. "We rode with haste to offer aid."

Telweg rolled a slain Nadaarian over with her foot. She wiped the tines of her trident on his back, then scanned the edges, pursing her lips. "It is long past time for aid. What the other war-chiefs have done is shameful, retreating to protect their own and forsaking the kingdom when wisdom demands unity."

And this was the opening Ceridwen needed, the argument she

had readied to convince the war-chief, offered by Telweg herself. "That is why I have come to speak with you."

Telweg arched a sharp eyebrow. "A message would have sufficed."

"A message could have been ignored."

"That would depend on its content." Telweg drew in a breath, and it seemed the marble cast to her face softened slightly, though that might only have been the light fading with the first brush of evening. "Still, I will hear you. You have ridden far to aid my people. An attack from the rear would have been devastating. This boon I will grant. Speak, and let us be done with it."

But words fled Ceridwen's tongue. All her strategies and arguments vanished. She knelt and retrieved her sabre, wincing at the ominous creak of her leathers, then wiped her blade on a cast-off cloak. On the battleground beyond, warriors tended wounded riders and offered swift death to wounded soldiers. Such was the nature of this brutal war. They had no means to care for captives and no desire to leave wounded invaders roaming free. It still sickened her.

Telweg cleared her throat.

Sheathing her sabre, Ceridwen found the war-chief's eyes fixed on her forehead. She reached for her scarf. Still there. It was an intentional slight then, a reminder that she should remember her place. Heat bristled in her chest, and she knew: no words could ever speak louder than the charge blazoned across her forehead.

But she was a war-chief, if not yet the acknowledged heir, and she had ridden and fought and ordered her three hundred into battle to convince this woman through action and not speech. Her warriors had given her that chance. They deserved her attention first.

Ceridwen gathered up her reins, looping the broken end over one shoulder. "See to your forces, Lady Telweg, and I will see to mine. Then we will speak."

She turned away, and Telweg did not recall her.

Finnian slid from his shadower to walk beside her. "I can have Nold look at your gear. He has some skill as a leatherworker.

Should be able to replace what cannot be salvaged." He hesitated and lowered his voice. "She is a proud woman, Ceridwen, and powerful among the war-chiefs. Was it wise to dismiss her so?"

Not by Astra's reckoning. Antagonizing the Cenyon war-chief would not aid their cause. But Ceridwen had ever heeded instinct over wisdom or caution, and instinct told her that Telweg tal Anor was a woman of steel and salt water and frost-bitten spray. Strength was the only language she knew.

"We will see."

He whistled beneath his breath. "*Blazes,* Ceridwen."

But she could hear his tone now, and it sounded strangely like respect.

THIRTY-FIVE: RAFI

What is the jungle without the seed, the leaf, the twig, the log, and the loam? Remove but one, and the jungle itself will be no more.
– Mahque saying

"So, *this* is revolution?" Rafi hauled on the shoulder straps so his basket of saga fruit rode higher on his back as he limped after Moc through the bustling market town. Built on the border of the Mah jungle, it was a five-day hike from the rebel camp, and his ankle was still sore. Luckily, the swelling had finally diminished, and the bruising was fading from violent purple to a hideous, yellowish green.

"Sure is." Moc grinned down at him. He really was a giant for an Alonque, among whom Rafi had often felt overly tall. Did he have Choth blood in him? His hazel eyes were too pale for Rafi to see the yellow flecks that marked that western people, who had long since been folded into the empire. "What did you expect?"

Rafi dodged a flock of sheep guided by Eliamite herdsmen in colorful scarves, long white coats, and sand-colored trousers. Located near a meeting of rivers, the town was a natural hub for trade and boasted both an imperial infantry garrison and Murlochian temple–and knowing that made his skin crawl as though he were being watched. "I don't know. More spear waving and grunting. Less hauling fruit to market."

"You've spent too much time around Nef."

"Oh, trust me, no disagreement here."

Rafi would have been grateful that Umut had refused Nef's

demands to round out Moc's team of five, only Umut had also insisted that Rafi go and prove his commitment–which, apparently, translated to hard labor. Still, swearing to the revolution had bought him time. Whatever plans had been intended to capitalize on his long-ago rescue had clearly been abandoned, leaving Umut scrambling to organize new strategies. That left Rafi time to work (in the kitchens) and train (with the spear) and think (far too much), dreaming up ways to make amends to Iakki while inventing new jokes to help him bond with his rebellious cousins, all in hopes that he might, someday soon, set off in pursuit of freedom again.

Judging by the scowls thrown his way by the rebels on their hike here, that bonding wasn't going so well. He'd been relieved when Moc instructed the others to await their return on the outskirts of town. Moc, at least, seemed to be warming to him–though, granted, that might be due to guilt over not preventing Nef's murder attempt. Still, with Iakki avoiding him, Rafi's standards for friends were rapidly declining.

Rafi instinctively lowered his head as he passed soldiers clustered around a stall hawking cala root crackers topped with slices of raw blood-fin and diced simba fruit. Odds stood against anyone recognizing him, but he had avoided large towns for years, and here the breezy treetop Mahque dwellings and the rounded moss-covered Hanonque huts were dwarfed by a stolid Nadaarian stone wall. With it looming over him, he felt a prisoner again. Sweat trickled down his face, and he dashed it away with his arm, ignoring the ghostly prodding to *run*.

"See, revolution isn't all raids and killing," Moc said, reviving the conversation. "Sometime it's spying for information. Sometimes it's delivering trade goods. Sometimes it's working the fields or mending nets or forging spearheads, but we all pitch in to aid the cause. And sometimes"–he raised his voice as he thumped his basket down before a woven mat stacked with neat pyramids of vegetables, where a stocky boy slouched on an overturned basket, elbows on his knees, head in his hands–"it's kicking your brother's tail for sleeping on the job."

The boy jerked to his feet. "Moc?"

"Lowen!" Moc boomed, looping an arm over his neck. The boy looked like a younger, shorter version minus the scars and muscle, with a mass of curly hair restrained by a blue forehead band. "We bring reinforcements for your depleted ranks: saga fruit, bushka beans, and other things." He winked broadly, hinting at the spearheads concealed in the bottom layers of their baskets. Subtlety was not his strength.

"It is good to see you, brother." Lowen disentangled himself with a squirm and began carefully positioning Moc's fruit atop his piles. "Even if you are a thorn in my big toe."

Moc clutched at his chest. "You wound me!"

"But we are about to launch a raid so—"

"Oh, and you usually sleep on duty before raiding?"

"It's called being inconspicuous." Lowen rolled his eyes, shooing a fly from a stack of overripe ishna melons that oozed juice from cracks in their rinds. Rafi watched their banter with a lump clogging his throat. It reminded him of Sev and Iakki and . . . Delmar. "Seriously, we have trouble."

Moc's teasing smile vanished. "What kind of trouble?"

Rafi lowered his basket, freeing his limbs for action—preferably of the running variety, if Ches-Shu regarded him with favor. Lowen's eyes darted toward him, but Moc waved him on. "He's one of us."

"It's our informant. Got himself rounded up in a sweep two days ago. They're marching him to the coast today with the next batch of tribesmen."

Moc grimaced. "Time to find a new informant then."

"Ah, but he has promised us vital information. 'Earth shattering,' he called it. We must free him if we would learn it."

"No, you must be careful, little brother."

The boy straightened with a frown. "I'm not little anymore."

Moc held a hand out over Lowen's head to measure and made a noncommittal sound then hastily ducked the simba Lowen lobbed at him. Rafi snatched it from the air, saving a passing woman from being hit.

"If you're worried, we could use another spear or two," Lowen suggested.

"Make that"–Moc caught Rafi's eye–"five."

Rafi squelched the impulse to run, rubbing his thumb across the simba's hairy rind. "I don't understand. The tribes don't supply soldiers to the army, so where are they taking them?"

Silence.

The fly buzzed over the ishna melons again.

Moc coughed, ignoring an incredulous look from Lowen. This, it seemed, was common knowledge among the rebels if not the fisherfolk of Zorrad. "Not soldiers, no, but armies need labor, and ships need rowers . . ."

And the beast of war was never sated.

Rafi grimaced at the thought, but the warbling cry of a nearby asha bird awoke hope in him like a bracing breath of sea air. Though the world was war and horror and death, it could also be seaweed tea and pearl diving and birds singing in the trees. Somehow, he would get back to that. Someday, he would be free.

"That's it!" Lowen sprang into action, dragging a spear out from under the mat.

Moc spun, looking for danger. "That's what?"

"The signal. I was watching the west gate. Rin, the east. He's spotted them heading his way so we're clear to join my team in the jungle." Lowen waved a Mahque girl about Iakki's age over from the next stall, selected a cala root, and flipped it to her. "Watch the stall today, Ava? Pack up tonight, and you can have three more."

The girl nodded, seemingly familiar with the request. Was she a rebel too?

"Starting them young," Rafi muttered, recalling Nef's threat to drag Iakki on that first raid. Ches-Shu, Cael, and Cihana together grant this did not go as poorly as that.

Lowen jogged off backward. "You coming?"

"How can I say no?" Moc followed, grinning at Rafi over his shoulder. "Come on! You wanted spear waving!"

Rafi sighed. "Actually, I didn't."

He really, really didn't, but since when had that mattered?

Ambushes, Rafi decided, made him wish he could crawl out of his own skin. Crouched on damp earth beneath an enormous leaf, insects skittering over his toes, sweat tickling his spine, and Moc's barely muffled breathing roaring in his ears, he gripped his borrowed spear and ran over the plan of attack. Again.

It was fairly simple: distract the soldiers, free the informant, and run.

His part was even simpler: follow Moc, wave his spear, and don't get killed.

Moc didn't seem nearly concerned enough with that last part, considering he would have to explain Rafi's fate to Umut. Either he thought Rafi invincible–an unfortunate side effect of his habit of surviving–or he hadn't warmed up to him as much as Rafi had thought.

Rafi shifted his weight off his sore ankle. After exiting the town, they had raced off at an angle through the jungle for a solid hour, gathering the rest of Moc's team and gradually folding into Lowen's as they all merged toward an eastward rallying point. There, the dozen Mahque, Hanonque, and Alonque that made up the combined crews had melted into the undergrowth on either side of the coastal road, after dispatching five graybeard monkeys to the canopy above. Tilting his head let him see the monkeys waiting in a row, eerily still.

"Creepy, isn't it?" Moc said in a hushed voice, or rather, attempted to, but his natural resonance carried. The others hissed for quiet, and Moc rolled his eyes, but Rafi stiffened.

He could hear them coming.

Holding his breath, Rafi peered through the worm-bitten leaf. Splashes of scarlet and gold pierced the thick green foliage, along with daubs of washed-out blue, muted tans, and drab whites that resolved into the shuffling shapes of prisoners marching on a line, flanked by a dozen soldiers in white-plumed helms. His mouth went dry.

"Those are royal guards," he whispered.

Moc's forehead creased in confusion, but Rafi bit his tongue to keep from being overheard. Once soldiers in such garb had died to prevent Lykier's minions from locking him and Delmar in the dungeons. Now, they were surely all traitors, sworn to the new regime. But why would royal guards be assigned to escort laborers to the coast? Why be here if not for him? Or Sahak? But no chariot followed, and Rafi could not imagine the Emperor's Stone-eye walking in line like a common soldier. It made no sense.

Ahead, a chattering call rang out, startling the soldiers. Rafi had known it was coming—one of the rebels had demonstrated it on their arrival—but it still made his hair stand on end. Instantly, the graybeard monkeys sprang from branch to branch, shaking the canopy, and screeching like miniature sea-demons.

Distraction, complete.

Gazes and weapons raised, the soldiers did not see Lowen roll out from the underbrush and melt seamlessly into the line of prisoners before it moved off again. Rafi felt Moc stiffen. He had wanted that job, until Lowen pointed out his size, too big to move so smoothly and silently. Lowen would cut the informant's bonds, then as the group rounded the next bend, the rebels would strike from both ends, distracting from the escape, and then . . . they would all run.

Rafi's legs cramped. He gritted his teeth. Soon . . . soon.

Muffled grunts broke out ahead, and the line of prisoners rippled. Rafi tried to see over a web of fingerlace vines but could not pick out the back of Lowen's head. He did see a soldier step toward the disturbance, spear raised, demanding answers.

Someone broke from the line.

The spear flashed. *Thunk.*

A ragged scream.

Moc bellowed Lowen's name and burst from his hiding place, and Rafi lingered only a stunned heartbeat before leaping after him, waving his spear and yelling like mad. He had stood by before. He had watched Delmar fall. He would not again. Crashing broke all around as the rebels leaped into action. Moc rammed into a soldier, knocking him flat and grappling on the ground. Rafi slipped past a spear thrust, searching for curly hair and a blue band and . . . *there.*

Lowen scuttled toward thicker jungle, half dragging an Eliamite in a sand-colored overcoat that flapped at his heels, a soldier in pursuit. Rafi raced to catch up, arms and spear pumping, as Lowen turned to block a sword with his spear. It cracked and split in two.

The soldier raised his sword again. Hesitated, sensing Rafi's approach.

Rafi screamed Delmar's name as he rammed his spear like a harpoon up into the unarmored patch beneath the soldier's arm. He stood there, panting, as bloody spittle burst from the man's lips and his breath expelled in a groan.

The toppling weight dragged the spear from Rafi's hands.

Slowly, he turned, as if in a fog. Freed prisoners scrambled past, scattering into the trees. Those still on the line yanked at it, weighed down by their slain. Rebels screamed and fell. Rapid strike, rapid retreat–that had been the plan. Instead, their attack had been ragged, disorganized, and the soldiers were predators trained to isolate and surround and kill.

Run, Rafi, the ghost whispered.

But he had had enough of running. He was a Tetrani, was he not?

Running from it did not make it untrue. He had slain a scadtha and killed a man. He would stand. Rafi seized the fallen soldier's sword, planted his feet, and as his blood stirred within him, loosed the ancient war cry of his ancestors.

It tore from his lips as a roar.

It raged and gnashed its teeth.

It parted the fight and silence fell in its wake.

Soldiers stilled and stared at him, stunned by his use of the old Nadaarian tongue. Few understood it anymore. Fewer still spoke it.

But these were not ordinary infantry or levied foreign troops. These were royal guard. They knew the war cry of the Tetrani.

They knew *him*.

With a yell, the last prisoners broke free and joined the rebels, falling upon the confused soldiers, beating them with hammered blows, crushing them with the weight of numbers. Rafi's voice fled. He lurched forward, hand raised. To stop them. To join them. He did not know. But it was too late, the deed already done. The soldiers lay in tangled heaps, their blood watering the earth, and his secret died with them.

Rafi let the sword fall and sank to his knees. He did not shake but everything inside him felt shaken, like a boat smashed ashore until it was torn apart.

"What was that?" a voice demanded behind him. "How did you make them stop?"

He took a breath, sensing eyes shifting toward him and rebels crowding around with hostile expressions. "I . . . told them a riddle. They were waiting for the answer." That did not seem to satisfy them, but they scattered when Moc burst through their ranks and flung a log-like arm around his neck, clapping him so hard on the back that his teeth rattled.

"That is for saving my brother!"

Rafi winced, rubbing his neck.

"My brother has strange ways of showing his gratitude," Lowen called out, approaching with the long-legged Eliamite trailing behind him. The man had eyes so pale they nearly matched his sand-colored overcoat, minus the jagged spray of blood across the front.

"Not mine," the Eliamite said, noticing Rafi's focus. He raised bloodied hands and eyed them with distaste, then scanned for somewhere to wipe them.

"What happened back there?" Moc demanded, crossing his burly arms.

Lowen shifted uncomfortably. "Once I freed him, I figured I would free the others too, but some idiots weren't content to wait their turn."

Moc shook his head in disbelief. "You're the idiot, brother. You nearly got all of us killed. You and Nef make a fine pair, you do." He turned a suspicious eye on the informant who had gingerly shrugged out of his stained coat and was now vigorously scrubbing his hands on a clean corner. "This vital information had better be worth it, Eliamite."

"His name is Yath Ha'Nor," Lowen put in.

"Fine. Yath, what can you tell me?"

"Much I do not understand." Yath straightened and balled up the ruined garment, fingertips still leaving rusty stains on the damp cloth. He discarded it and nudged it away with his foot. "Not yet. But perhaps others will." And Rafi could have sworn Yath's eyes flickered briefly to him as he began to speak.

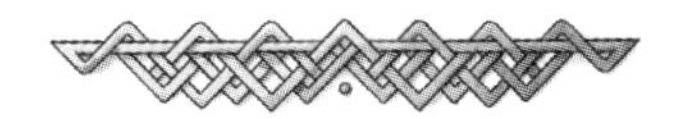

"What about knives, Rafi?"

Caught off guard by the question, Rafi looked up at Lowen, who scaled the staircase to the second cavern above him, and almost missed a step, prompting Moc and the others behind to roar in laughter. The five-day return hike had not diminished their victory-fueled spirits, and so it was a boisterous crew that had delivered Lowen's report to Umut and now ascended to the kitchens to celebrate. "What about them?"

"Could you juggle them?"

On the march that morning, Rafi had amused his companions by demonstrating his skill on everything from saga fruit to fish heads. It had seemed innocent enough, but the others had been dreaming up increasingly wild challenges for him since. Knives, however, seemed extreme . . . and a touch too reminiscent of Sahak. "Why would I want to?"

"You said you could juggle anything."

"Anything!" Moc caught up as they turned onto the bridge and slung an arm over Rafi's shoulder. "What about–" He broke off.

Nef stood on the center of the bridge ahead. His stare raked across them, and Rafi couldn't deny a twinge of satisfaction at the sight of his nemesis with two black eyes and a basket of kitchen refuse in his arms.

"Nef!" Moc shouted, flinging his arms wide. "We are celebrating! Join us."

Nef ignored him and stalked away in the opposite direction.

"Maybe he didn't hear you . . ." Lowen smirked.

Rafi was fairly certain Cael of the Sky-Above, Cihana of the Earth-Below, and Ches-Shu of the Deeps-Beneath had heard Moc, and Nef needed no prodding to hate him.

Moc scowled. "Oh, net your tongue." But his humor recovered by the time they entered the kitchen alcove and caught the familiar wave of heavy spices and oven warmth across their faces. "Saffa! Your finest wine for the hero of the hour!"

Saffa discarded the enormous paddle she had been using to stir soup and began to set out food and drink. Rafi tried to help, but she waved him to a seat, and one did not argue with Saffa, so he found himself wedged among the others as they feasted and swilled saga wine and roared with laughter. In exchange for fewer scowls on the return hike, Rafi had traded in jokes, burying his sickness over the raid and his part in it. Now such humor felt forced, and when Lowen stole Saffa's knives and sent them spinning across the table toward him, he feigned panic for laughs and seized the opportunity to flee.

Saffa was waiting for him outside the alcove. She pressed a bowl of dried simba fruit into his hands with a nod at the stairs. For the sea-demon? Since he hadn't been able to drive it away, he had built an enclosure on the gorge floor to keep it from trampling the rebels' crops or following him on his mission. He'd coaxed it inside with moss and darted out again, leaving it trapped and screaming. He'd felt a traitor then and now, as he emerged from the lowest cavern into twilight and tried to catch its bright blue eyes over the woven rattan fence.

The colt did not look at him.

Rafi raised his voice. "Still mad at me?"

"What gave it away?"

Iakki? He found the boy perched atop the fence, chin in his hands. It had been weeks since they had spoken, and part of Rafi wondered if it was for the best. If Iakki, like Zorrad, might not benefit from his absence. He slipped inside the enclosure, holding the bowl up in explanation. "Saffa sent fruit for the colt."

"It doesn't eat fruit," Iakki scoffed. "Sea-demons like seaweed and fish and stuff. Saffa knows it too. She's sent down scraps before."

"Oh. You want some then?" Rafi offered the bowl but a whiskered nose knocked it from his hands. Snuffling, the colt lipped the scattered fruit up from the ground and seemed to be enjoying it too, despite Iakki's claim.

"Not anymore I don't."

Iakki started to climb down, but Rafi swung up beside him. "Cousin–"

"You're not my cousin. You're . . . what . . . a prince? You shouldn't even have that." He jabbed at the bead strand still knotted in Rafi's hair.

"Look, I didn't want to hurt you or–"

"You got Torva killed!"

The pang of that truth stole his breath. "If I could fix it–"

"You could bring me back!" Iakki gripped his arm, pleading. "Back to Zorrad."

"Bored with cliff climbing and goat chasing already?" It was a lame attempt at humor, and Iakki pulled back, eyes glistening wet.

"I want to go home."

Rafi hesitated. Only a second, but it was a second too long. Iakki jumped down and ran away, and Rafi did not call him back. What more could he say? Sighing, he dropped beside the grazing colt and scratched at the scales running down its throat. Was it the waning light, or had their color dulled while he was gone? "At least I can still talk to you."

Chewing, the colt raised its head and snorted down his arm.

"Some spirits are not meant to be tamed," a warm, rugged voice said.

Rafi glanced up to see the Hanonque leader emerge from the

streamward side of the cavern and come toward him at a surprisingly fast clip on his crutch. He wiped his arm on his trousers. "Some things were born to be free."

Umut's eyes glittered with mirth as he rested his elbows on the fence. "I was speaking of your cousin. This beast is another matter altogether." Rafi's face must have revealed his surprise because Umut chuckled. "Soldonian warriors wield such steeds in battle. Never heard of others doing so, but then I've never heard of others bonding one."

"Bonding? Not so sure we have so much as a mutual understanding."

Umut laughed his deep, choking laugh, but trailed off, expression turning grave. "Speaking of understanding, what did you think of the Eliamite's report?"

Most, Rafi had not understood: rumors of a new harbor on the Alon coast, of more Eliamites seized by raids, of increased demands for labor, and of talk of the Center of the World–something he had been taught referred to Cetmur, capital of Nadaar, though Yath claimed it meant something else, something hidden. No news of Sahak, so the only real matter of interest to him had been sighting the royal guard, which was probably of less importance to Umut.

"Not sure I know what any of it means."

Umut's expression narrowed thoughtfully. "It means the world is changing more swiftly than I thought. We must make our move soon. I am working on a plan still, but I do think your time could be well spent here." He nodded toward the sea-demon. "Think of the surprise element such a steed could give you on a raid if the legends are true."

Ride the sea-demon? Could such a thing be possible?

Rafi rubbed his face. "I wouldn't even know where to begin."

Umut's sea-blue eyes twinkled. "I might be able to help with that. Drove a team of horses once–not like that, grant you–but how much harder can riding a sea-demon be?"

"Are you asking me?"

"Should be simple enough." Umut quirked a smile. "Like falling off a log."

The colt's ears twitched, and Rafi had a sneaking suspicion it could understand them. "Yeah, I've a feeling you've got the falling part right."

THIRTY-SIX: CERIDWEN

Both seariders and riverriders gain increased lung capacity and the ability to withstand significant underwater pressures, enabling them to launch submerged attacks while their steeds use the force of streams or waves to propel themselves in aquatic combat.

On a dune washed in moonlight, Ceridwen let Cenyon's salt-tinged air sink into her lungs to cleanse the taint of scorched flesh. Below, warriors ate and slept and tended gear while the soft song of the night riders rose on the breeze. Beyond, scouts patrolled both dunes and sky for signs of the enemy, though Iona's pursuit had left few survivors. On her return, Iona had delivered the death count: two hundred and eleven of Cenyon, sixty-one Outriders, countless Nadaari.

Even the mightiest of her ancestors would have found pride in such a victory. When diminished to numbers on a scale, human lives could seem little indeed. But she knew the void a single loss left behind, like the shock of destruction following an earthhewn charge. Heart and hope shattered into ash and dust.

She thought of Bair.

She thought of the king, her father.

She thought of the imperial soldiers who had sailed lusting for conquest in this kingdom and a dozen others, of the priests who lashed them on in pursuit of the Dominion of Murloch, and of Emperor Lykier seated on his throne amidst the thousand waterfalls of Cetmur. They had brought this horror upon her land. Would that flames might take them all.

Sand crunched behind her. Hand resting on her sabre, she turned to see Lady Telweg, armor-clad and glinting silver in the moonlight. Ceridwen had sent her leathers for repair along with her saddle, leaving her only a loose tunic, leggings, and Finnian's cloak. Yet she could have been crowned and enthroned and still felt unworthy before Telweg's gaze. Only from the back of her flaming steed could she feel equal.

But Mindar grazed below, and the war-chief stared at her in silence, face pale and impassive as the moon itself. The wind crept through the cloak's loose weave while the passing moments seemed to crawl across her skin, and still no words came.

"Here, child." Telweg held up a pouch of dried meat and fruit. "Eat."

Her voice was neither condescending nor kind, but it bore a hint of the dragging weariness Ceridwen felt, so she forced herself to eat, though the food tasted like ash and stuck in her throat.

Eventually, Telweg spoke again. "We battle an empire with standing armies and levies supplied by conquest. It is small wonder our forces wear thin." Her voice sounded thin as well, stripped of pretense. Unusual since Telweg wore composure like an armored hide. "So long as they possess our ports to receive transport ships, we will not win this war. A hundred times, I have demanded the war-chiefs muster their hosts to our aid, and still, they have not come."

"I have come—"

"You are not enough."

She never had been. Not enough to satisfy her father, save her brother, or earn the respect of the war-chiefs. "Yet I am here," Ceridwen said. "The war-chiefs may fear treachery but we must be united. Kilmark and Ondri's betrayal continues to cost us each day we stand apart."

"Kilmark and Ondri? Oh, it goes deeper than that. Did it never occur to you to wonder how Cenyon had no warning of the invasion when seariders patrol our waters? They were all slaughtered. Or so

I must assume since no trace has been found. Nadaar's spies are either far more effective or had far more aid than we thought."

Ceridwen's blood chilled. She had assumed the two chieftains' treachery had been a response to the invasion, an attempt to curry favor with the presumed victors by betraying their own. But this meant it had been planned. "I cannot fathom how any could do such a thing."

"No more difficult, I suppose, than abandoning one's kin to die." Telweg's eyes were dark pools frosted with ice. "But you ask the wrong question. Ask not how but why, and you shall have your answer. For example, why do I cast your brother's death in your face, why do I speak so to you, why–"

"You test me."

"Perhaps. And perhaps I merely despise you."

This time, Ceridwen expected the blow. "And yet, you need me. You said it yourself, our strength wanes while our enemy's is renewed. We must unite if we are to make them spend such a price in blood that they rue the day they sailed for our coasts and–"

"Why are you here, child?" There was a sad, almost mocking twist to Telweg's lips. "I received tidings of your claim. Have you come for my oath? You will not get it. I have seen little in the blood of Lochrann worthy of rule. Your father was a strong king once, but your brother's death destroyed him. It weakened the seven chiefdoms for Nadaar's attack. For that, I hold you responsible."

Brutal, relentless, those words shattered the steel forged around Ceridwen's heart, exposing the void inside. "I did not kill Bair." Her voice seemed swallowed by the night, and yet, the truth was both flint and steel casting sparks to warm and strengthen her. "I did not kill him," she repeated, louder. "But for his death, I will spend the rest of my life seeking atonement."

The cold steel of her sabre still filled her palm, marking it a blade oath.

"Yes." Telweg's voice broke soft as the wind over the salt-grass. "You will. If you would rule, you must know the responsibility. Countless lives rest upon your choices."

"And upon yours, Lady Telweg." She released her grip, meeting the war-chief's gaze with no weapon but conviction. "My claim stands, but I will not demand your oath. Not now. If our nation is to survive, we must change tactics together."

"You have a strategy in mind?"

"I do." The compelling words came, as if breathed into her mind by her brother. "Do not fight to reclaim Cenyon yet. Fight to contain the coast. No supplies or forces dispatched inland can be allowed to reach the Nadaari. With your *ayeds* and mine fighting in unison, we can leave them stranded, harassed, and starving in their own camp."

"Before that, they will break through and lay waste to the countryside."

"And we will yield before them, but they will control only the earth beneath their feet." The heat of battle filled her again, warming her limbs to action, and for a moment, she thought she saw an answering light flicker to life in the war-chief's eyes.

Then Telweg shook her head. "You ask too much of Cenyon. You would have us regard our land as lost and ignore the suffering of our own. I will not have it. I cannot."

Her breath left her in a rush.

Ceridwen opened her mouth to explain Astra's visit, to reveal the discovery of the manuscripts, to beg if it would convince the war-chief to reconsider. But the words suffocated in her throat. They, like her, would never be enough.

Hoofbeats approached, dulled by sand, and a seablood crested the dune followed by a lathered riveren that stumbled and trembled with each heaving breath, sweat spattering the earth. Only dire need would drive a rider to demand so much from a bonded steed. "Messenger from Lochrann," the searider said, but Ceridwen had eyes only for the girl dismounting the riveren to fall to her knees, as exhausted as her steed. Only for the tears shimmering in her eyes beneath the mass of her curly black hair.

"My lady," the girl whispered. "Soras Ford is under attack."

Her heart stilled. Gavin. She closed her eyes, breathing deep to ease the fear cracking open her chest. "Has Apex Markham been summoned?" He had ridden out at the same time as she to destroy the fortified outpost the Nadaari were building beyond Idolas. His forces would be closer than hers . . . but close enough?

"Messengers rode for him and the other chieftains of Lochrann too, but no word had come before I left. 'Do not spare your steed.' Those were my orders, and I swear I didn't." The girl's eyes darted anxiously to the spent riveren. "What say you? Will you ride to their aid?"

The night sank heavy around her. Ceridwen's mind raced with the thought of all that must be done, but it was the unsteady, shambling gallop of an exhausted steed. "I will ride," she said, though her voice was thick and dull, and she had no hope for what she would find. There was no time for hope or for fear. She would not fail at this. She would not lose Gavin, Fiona, and the boys, not if strength of blade or steed could save them.

Telweg halted her departure. "I make no oath of allegiance nor of alliance. Nor will I yield the coast as lost. But your strategy merits testing. Cenyon will vow to blockade the Nadaari from their fleet if Lochrann will vow to help reclaim Cenyon."

Warmth kindled in Ceridwen's veins, for beneath the demand lurked the subtle acknowledgment that she was, if nothing else, a war-chief. That was more than she had truly expected from Telweg. She met the woman's eyes. "I have already vowed that and more. I have laid claim to this kingdom, and whether you offer your oath or not, I have sworn to every man, woman, and child of this nation. By blood and blade, I have sworn it."

And though she was no closer to wearing a crown, still she felt its weight as she turned from the war-chief to lift the exhausted scout to her feet and then descended to the war-camp. Finnian received her commands with grave sympathy and sent Cù darting to retrieve his steed so he could issue the muster to the remnant of her three hundred. At dawn, they would ride.

THIRTY-SEVEN: JAKIM

Aodh does not slumber.

It was wrong for such a beautiful dawn to end in killing. Sunlight warmed Jakim's upturned face, and wildflowers sweetened each breath as he hiked up the slope and halted beside Khilamook to overlook the meandering river where soldiers and warriors faced off on either bank. All clutching weapons, breathing silent prayers, and thirsting for blood.

Tonight, the stars would weep once more. He whispered a prayer of his own. "Aodh have mercy on us all."

Chariot wheels scythed through the grass carrying Nahrog, the priest, past. Clad in gilded armor shaped like massive overlapping scales, he raised his spear. "Murloch smiles upon us!" he bellowed toward the descending soldiers, and dozens echoed his cry. "To battle!"

"This is no battle," Khilamook said, stabbing the earth with his cane, clearly still seething over Adaan's refusal to use his war machines. Only reluctantly had he left his cart behind in the baggage train and continued on foot to watch the "disaster," as he put it, unfold. "Where are the clever tactics? The devious feints? There is no more subtlety here than a boulder careening downhill. No skill. Only velocity."

Below, soldiers swept forward, shoulder to shoulder, shield to shield, armor clanking in unison, and gradually gained speed as they neared the ford. Mist rose from the river, partially obscuring the dappled steeds and riders in dusky blue waiting on the far bank.

Jakim guessed there were nearly a hundred. Piercing the creeping gray beyond them, a wooden palisade surrounded a cluster of thatched cottages and a larger manor house where Ceridwen's cousin lived and would die—unless Aodh intervened.

"Refusing to wait for ballista to soften the crossing?" Hands clasped behind him, Khilamook paced feverishly. "Fording a river head-on into the enemy? However much he craves the tsemarc's ear, he is a fool to deny me the victory and, like my brothers, will soon learn his error." His voice cracked like splintering twigs. "Even now, their jaws split to swallow him, mark my words, and I have half a mind to let it happen."

But no attack came as the Nadaari charged across the ford, shields lifted against arrows that never fell, spears shredding the mist, throats roaring a challenge over the din of their splashing. They made it halfway across before the river heaved.

Jakim caught his breath. Was that a wave . . . or . . . ?

Silvery steeds burst from beneath the river in a torrent of white-flecked water that churned as they emerged from the deeper sections bordering the ford and crashed into the soldiers from all sides. Khilamook crowed in delight, and Jakim gasped in awe. How had the riders survived underwater? It defied reason.

But so did the mighty steeds.

The river itself seemed to act in concert with them, sweeping soldiers from their feet and lifting horses and riders in impossible leaps. It was a beautiful, fierce, unnatural—and yet, somehow wholly natural—manner of fighting. At Idolas, Jakim had seen only the gruesome cruelty of war. Here, he saw also its deadly beauty, even as Adaan unleashed archers with flaming arrows and the slain clogged the river.

"Aodh have mercy," he whispered and did not know who he prayed for.

But soon, like a beast rolling over itself, the mass of Nadaari soldiers began pulling back. Weary, half-drowned, they slogged ashore beneath the covering fire of their archer reserves, and the riders did not pursue them, seemingly reluctant to leave the watery battleground that was their element.

Where they could win.

Jakim was suddenly sure of it. And if they did, and if he made a break for it and begged asylum, maybe he could fulfill his oath to the king. Maybe this was Aodh's purpose for bringing him here. Slipping into the confusion below might prove his best chance. Muscles tingling, limbs jittery with anticipation, he inched away.

One step. Two.

"Oh, Ahaz take him," Khilamook exclaimed before he could break into a sprint. "Hurry, boy, to the ballista–" He broke off, staring, and Jakim tracked his gaze to a figure that emerged from the palisade and dashed down to the river on foot.

Moments later, a horn rang out, and a single rider streaked toward the manor. Confusion rippled through the remaining riders. Some seemed on the brink of scattering, others pressed closer together, a few threw down their weapons. Surrendering? Baffled, Jakim hopped anxiously from foot to foot, straining to see.

They had been winning, right? Why not keep on fighting?

Khilamook seized the front of his tunic and hauled him away. "Ballista now!"

An echoing gong halted them in their tracks. That brief moment of chaos proved the only catalyst Adaan needed to turn the tide, and it was a howling, screeching, bloodthirsty mob of soldiers that turned and dashed across the ford, and it was only a disorganized scattering of riders that met them and pitched hoof and steel against shield and spear until the slopes rang with the clamor of the slaughter.

Until both river and bank were painted red.

Until the last steed and rider fell and with them, silence.

Then cheers erupted from the battlefield, gongs clashed, and spears clanged on shields as the Nadaari celebrated their victory. Jakim's head sagged along with his hopes.

There would be no asylum, no escape, no fulfilling of his vows today.

Khilamook released Jakim's tattered tunic and pulled out a silk handkerchief to mop the sweat from his own brow, and though the sun beat upon Jakim too, he shivered as his insides turned to ice. "Well," the engineer sighed. "This was a supreme waste of my time and talent. Come. We have work to do."

Jakim fingered the worn cord knotted around his wrist and tried in vain to call Siba's comforting face to mind as he forded the river, picked his way across the corpse-littered bank, and followed Khilamook toward the open palisade gate. Lately, the details he recalled of his long-lost family and home seemed more and more blurred, until only Amir's laughter rang clearly in his memory. But soon he would find his way back.

He clung to that blindly, hopelessly, even as each step seemed a descent back into the horror of the killing pits, and the scene revealed when Khilamook broke through the mob on the manor's greensward was no better. Nahrog stood enthroned in his chariot, Adaan at his side, watching as two soldiers dragged a warrior over and threw him at their feet. Something snapped, and the warrior's helmet flew free and rolled to a stop before Khilamook, who prodded Jakim to retrieve it.

"Priest Nahrog," a crisp feminine voice called.

Still bent over, fingers slipping on the helmet's wet steel, Jakim raised his eyes to the woman descending the shallow manor steps, clad in a long cloak of shimmering blue that rippled behind. Dark hair spilled loose across her armored shoulders, and blood streaked the blades of the trident in her hand. On the lowest step, flanked by the king's two killers, she halted and inclined her head. "Priest Nahrog, Soras Ford is yours."

Belatedly, Jakim realized he was still bent double, still gaping. He fumbled the helmet, caught it, and passed it to Khilamook, cheeks burning. He had seen this woman before. She had accompanied the traitor that day in the command tent, and she was here now, complicit in the day's slaughter. That made her beauty edged and deadly, like a knife. Or a kaava's thorns.

Khilamook muttered to himself as he turned the helmet over to inspect it. He removed a strange mask ending in a long, thin tube that had been attached inside.

"And who are you?" Adaan demanded, pointed chin jutting. But for all his stiff bearing, he lacked the tsemarc's sense of weighty authority, and the woman scarcely glanced at him.

"The priest knows who I am."

"The priest is not in command here."

She turned slowly to face Adaan, grounding her trident with a rap on stone. "I am Astra tor Telweg, betrothed of Soldonia's future king and therefore, future queen. You owe this victory to me. Without my aid, you would have found barred gates awaiting you, not the trussed form of Gavin te Annamark." She gestured at the warrior sprawled in the dust, Nadaarian dripping smoothly from her tongue with an accent so flawless it baffled Jakim.

"Tor Telweg?" Adaan's voice betrayed surprise. "Not related to Cenyon's war-chief, surely? Her sea-demons remain a barb in our flesh, and, it is rumored, may soon swear to she that rides the fire-demon. Wouldn't that set a wrench in your plans for a crown?"

Her lips curved. "Where do you think the rumors came from? Cenyon has not and never will swear allegiance to Ceridwen tal Desmond." She spun the trident and caught its haft in both hands. "By blood and blade, I swear it."

Ragged coughing drowned out Adaan's response. Head dangling, gasping with effort, the warrior—Gavin—pushed up to his hands and knees, then rocked back onto his heels. River water dripped down his battered armor, staining the earth beneath the color of rust. He lifted hollow, pleading eyes to the woman. "Astra, my wife . . . my children . . ." Coughing wrenched his body, and bloody spittle speckled his lips. The whole right side of his breastplate had been dented in by some massive blow.

Nahrog's cracked lips parted in a ghastly grin. "Dead, demon-rider, as you will soon be."

"Oh Aodh . . . no." Gavin sank forward with a soul-wrenching groan, spine yielding like a severed rope, and Jakim found himself echoing his plea with a prayer for justice.

"Not too soon, I hope." One of the king's killers—the burly brute with a head like a lump of clay—commented in response to Nahrog's threat. "Don't tell me you'd kill him outright after we went to such trouble to take him alive. Seems wasteful."

"He means nothing to Ceridwen dead," the axeman added.

Their mocking voices swirled around Jakim, a blend of harsh tones he knew all too well. So Amir had spoken to him. So his brothers had laughed. Oh Aodh, could he do nothing for this broken, weeping man now watering the soil with his blood and his tears?

He stepped forward, but Khilamook's cane shot in front of him, blocking his path. The engineer shook his head, a bemused expression on his face.

Gavin raised his head, face awash in pain. "You swore, Astra," he choked, and though his voice was barely audible, it silenced the two traitors. "The messenger who gave me this"—he raised a clenched fist—"swore that if I surrendered, they would live." Planting one foot, he started to rise, but his guard snapped the butt of his spear between his shoulder blades, dropping him with a groan. His fist flew open, fingers splaying to break his fall.

The soldier raised his spear again but stopped at a barked command from Adaan.

"No one touches a hair on his head without my word." Astra's haughty air dared a challenge. "He is our means to draw Ceridwen out. She is reckless and uncontrollable, a force to be reckoned with, and yet, she can be baited like any wildborn."

Nahrog's heavy eyelids rose. "And how do you propose we sink the hook?"

"We are not fishing, priest, only herding her into our catch-rope." Astra descended onto the greensward, pointedly nodding for her two escorts to follow the soldiers Adaan directed to drag Gavin away. "In any case, that is your task. Not mine."

"You are certain of that?" With the tip of his sword, Adaan prodded something small and bloodstained left in the dirt then pierced it and lifted it up, an expression of distaste on his face. "Tell me, did you kill them before or after sending your threat?"

Oh Aodh . . .

Oh, Bearer of the Eternal Scars . . .

It was an ear.

Jakim's insides twisted. He fought the urge to be sick, but the woman did not flinch. She only shrugged casually. "Before, of course."

"Cold, demon-rider, cold indeed." Shaking his head, Adaan sheathed his sword.

"Half measures are worthless in threats and negotiations." This, she directed toward Nahrog. "Sadly, this is a truth my betrothed has yet to learn."

Adaan seemed to take that as an opening and proffered his arm with a clipped bow. "Then perhaps you will consider a mutually beneficial arrangement?"

She regarded his arm as Jakim might a snake, and he withdrew it after an awkward pause.

"I deal with the priest now. Not with you or your tsemarc."

Nahrog stepped heavily down from his chariot and leaned on his spear, eyes hooded with a blank gaze that Jakim found profoundly unnerving. It was like he stared into nothingness and there saw something none other could see. "Then you have done it?"

In contrast, Astra's gaze was as sharp and glinting as fallen stars. "The ship sails as discussed. Consider it a guarantee of more to come, provided I receive assurances that *he* has the power to fulfill his promises."

"He is the power." Nahrog squinted one eye at her. "But I am curious what your betrothed thinks of our arrangement?"

"He will be king and I will be queen. What else matters?"

Khilamook chuckled softly, startling Jakim with the reminder of his presence. He realized that all this time, he had been only listening and neglecting to translate. Cringing, expecting a blow, he turned to fulfill his role in the engineer's farce, only to find a strange masked face staring back at him. His pulse skipped, and only slowly did his mind catch up. It was the mask Khilamook had removed from the helmet. It sealed over both mouth and nose and a long, flexible snakelike tube emerged from the side and hung down to his waist where it ended in a ragged tear as if ripped from another piece.

"Oh, this is quite remarkable," Khilamook muttered, voice muffled. "I wonder . . ." He gripped the mask where it sealed beneath his cheekbones and peeled it away with a slight sucking sound, leaving faint red lines on his skin. "The mechanism within is based upon Canthorian technology surely. Some sort of breathing apparatus. But this membrane is most peculiar." He tapped the mask's exterior inquisitively. "Solborn perhaps?"

This seemed directed at Jakim, so he shrugged.

"What my brother Vishna wouldn't give to possess this . . ." Khilamook's lips spread into a lazy but distinctly unnerving smile that vanished as shouts rang out for "the engineer," and three soldiers pushed through the mass dragging a struggling slave with straw-colored hair and corded arms that strained against restraints. One soldier kicked the slave's legs out, dropping him to his knees. Breathing strenuously between clenched teeth, the slave raised his head.

His nose had been broken and one eye was swollen shut, but Jakim could have recognized him by that furious, hate-filled stare alone: Seamus.

"Caught this man trying to escape, engineer," one of the soldiers explained.

Without him? Jakim tried to meet Seamus's gaze, but Khilamook's cane stung him to translate as the soldier raised a sack and dug through it. "Had this with him. It would appear he ransacked your cart before making a break for it." Crumpled papers emerged first, then one of the strange cylindrical devices.

All the blood drained from the engineer's face. "Give it here," he snapped.

Rattled, the soldier fumbled the device, but Khilamook snatched it before it shattered. He froze in that position, and Jakim could see the pulse hammering in his throat.

What exactly did those devices do?

And was this theft what Seamus had wanted his aid to accomplish? Could they have succeeded together, or would Jakim have been caught too? He tried again to catch Seamus's eye and turned to find Khilamook standing too close, eyes narrowed suspiciously at them both.

Oh Aodh, did he suspect?

"Just kill the thief and be done," Adaan barked impatiently. "We have a trap to plan."

"Yes, yes we do," Khilamook said to himself, weighing the device in his hand.

"You should move on from here first," Astra suggested, scraping clean the tines of her trident in the grass. "Ceridwen must reflect upon the horrors of this scene before receiving news of her cousin's capture if you would taunt her into recklessness."

Adaan's expression tightened. "And of course, *you* know where we should go?"

His ill temper failed to quell the serenity of her cold smile. "Of course."

"Of course," Khilamook repeated, eyes assuming a fevered gleam. With a savage twist of his cane, he prodded Jakim forward to translate. "And I know just what we should do. I will need space to mount a mangonel and"—a sweep of his cane indicated Seamus—"I will need that imbecile alive."

"Ready the ranging shot . . . and release!"

Once more, Jakim translated Khilamook's command and held his breath as a ceramic sphere thumped into the war machine's cradle. Seconds later, a sledge fell with a crack, releasing the arm and launching the sphere. It whistled on descent and this time shattered directly on target, scattering shards across the far bank of the pool below and summoning cheers from the crowd gathered to watch. They stood in the war machine's shadow within the crater atop the cone-shaped rise Astra tor Telweg had selected for their trap. It had taken a day's march to reach and a day's work to fortify, so that now with the sun setting, the mangonel's spiked elbows reared into a bloodstained sky.

"Finally." Khilamook pushed back from the folding table that served as his mobile workspace, already cluttered with papers, vials, cylindrical devices, and spheres. "Ready the trial, and bring out the imbecile."

Only as the translation left his lips did Jakim comprehend. Oh . . . oh Aodh . . . no. Shouting rang out in a familiar voice. Gut sinking, he turned to see two guards dragging Seamus to a stake planted in the pool below. He looked back to the engineer and found his lips twisted in a mocking smile.

"Master . . . what is this?"

"This is winning. Not just one battle but thousands, and it begins today. Even the wind is in our favor." Khilamook nodded toward the spear-mounted banner planted beside the war machine with its many streamers all rippling in the same direction, away from them and toward the pool below, and his smirk deepened. "Perhaps Murloch does smile upon us."

What did the wind have to do with anything?

A cold sweat broke over Jakim's back, and he shivered in that breeze. Hadn't there been enough killing? Why, oh Aodh, *why* must there be more? Worse, why must he be made complicit in it, forced to translate the commands to unleash death?

Then again, wasn't he already complicit?

For weeks he had translated every instruction needed to complete Khilamook's work. Maybe his hands were already so stained by death that Aodh should renounce him a thousand times over for the consequences of his actions.

"Come here." Khilamook meticulously inserted one of the cylindrical devices through a hole in the ceramic sphere and then dusted the inside with white powder from a vial before sealing the hole with wax and wiping his hands on the front of his embroidered robes. "I'll need a spare pair of hands with this, and I wouldn't advise dropping it."

Jakim swallowed. "Master, this is wrong."

"Wrong?" Khilamook pressed his lips and shook his head. "Calculations can be incorrect. Designs can be flawed. Strategies can prove lacking. But actions cannot be quantified on any measure, save effectivity. You would do well to remember this."

That contradicted all Jakim understood of the holy writ, despite his incomplete studies. Still, he knew one thing for certain. "I cannot help with this."

No matter the cost.

He expected a whipping. He feared something worse.

He did not expect Khilamook to nod calmly as if he had expected this. "You aided the theft then. I thought so. The truth was in your eyes."

Rough hands gripped his shoulders, stifling his objections. Jakim flinched as two soldiers flanked him while the engineer reached for the strange Soldonian mask sitting on his table. It looked different somehow than before, bulkier perhaps.

"Exactly when do you plan on performing this test, engineer?" Adaan called from within the restless crowd. Nahrog would be there too, along with Astra and the king's murderers.

Not exactly the sort you kept waiting.

Khilamook raised the mask and eyed Jakim. "There is but one more thing to prepare . . ."

"Such an idiot." Seamus scoffed as the soldiers bound Jakim beside him and then hastily slogged out of the pool and ran back up the rise. "Don't try to deny it. Only an idiot earns a death sentence like this."

He hawked up blood and spat it out. "And what's with the riverrider mask? Those things are rare, you know."

They were both idiots, Jakim thought. Strapped into the clinging mask, he gasped hopelessly for breath. It constricted his face and squeezed his eyes half shut while the tube wedged between his teeth that was supposed to allow airflow from the attached bladder-thing tasted strongly of river mud and made him gag.

"Breathe in through your mouth and out through your nose," Khilamook had instructed after shoving the mask on him. But though he wanted to savor each breath and marvel at each moment painted in the sky as it burned out from sunset's fire to the charcoal of night, his lungs refused to fully expand. Tears blurred his vision.

Gone were his vows, his purpose, even the prophecy Siba had spoken.

He had lived and would die a slave in a foreign land. He would never again see his home.

Jakim closed his eyes to concentrate on breathing and wound up listening intently instead. *Crack.* That was the war machine. *Whistling.* And that was the sphere singing of his death. Soon . . . too soon . . . he would know the truth of Aodh's mercy or justice firsthand. Panicked, he flung himself into a recitation of the truths that were supposed to bring peace.

Aodh is true. Aodh is compassionate. Aodh is–

The sphere shattered on the bank, pelting them with stinging shards and clods of dirt.

His eyes flew open. *Oh, Aodh, I cannot die now*!

Seamus let out a relieved laugh, but this, Jakim knew, was not the end.

It began as a gray wisp rising from the impact, almost like a puff of dust. But instead of dissolving, it thickened into a coil that expanded into a boiling fog that crawled down the bank, seeped across the pool, and surrounded them in an eyeblink. The world beyond vanished. Seamus cursed and thrashed against the ropes, but the knots were tight. Horrible gasping sounds came from his throat. His eyes latched onto Jakim, and the whites were stark with fear.

"Seamus . . ."

His eyes were still open, but he sagged limply in his bonds.

"Seamus!" Somehow, Jakim managed to scream the name through the mask. He screamed it again and again, and then he was gasping and sure that this was his end too. Until the fit passed and he could hear only his own smothered breathing echoing within the contraption. He dimly noticed the fog was dissipating, and though it seemed to have lasted for an eternity, the sky still burned the red of dying embers above the angular limbs of the mangonel and the figures grouped beneath it. The wind that was the "blessing of Murloch" carried their voices to him.

"See how quickly it kills and then disperses?" Khilamook was saying. "With it–"

"So then, we have our trap," Nahrog spoke over Khilamook. If the engineer wanted to be heard, maybe he shouldn't have disposed of his translator. "We have our bait. Now remains only the question of our prey."

"That," Adaan said, "is easily solved."

Whatever solution he referred to was apparently evident to the others, for the voices lapsed into silence broken eventually by Nahrog's rumble. "Your boon will be granted. By the Silent One Alive, I swear it."

"Then you will have your prey," Astra tor Telweg said. "By blood and blade, I swear it."

No one came to release Jakim, so he remained in the pool, bound to the corpse of the closest thing he had to a friend, and longed for the fall of night when stars would sprinkle the sky like the tears they shed for the deeds of men.

THIRTY-EIGHT: CERIDWEN

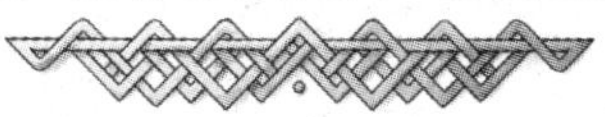

Of all riverriders, Asher the Silent was ever after recalled in verse for his heroic defense of the streams of Soltain against a thousand foes, culminating in their ruin and in his tragic demise.

Neither blade nor steed was any use here anymore. Ceridwen knew it before she crested the hill overlooking Soras Ford and saw the pyres blazing on the bank and the riders and steeds in the garb of Outriders milling through the billowing smoke below. She had felt it in Mindar's agitation, despite the exhaustion coating his hide with pale streaks of ash, tasted it in the faint scent of decay carried upon the wind. She was too late.

The enemy had come and gone.

Only the slain of Soras Ford remained.

Heedless of the comfort Finnian tried to speak in her ear, she spurred Mindar on. He fought her at the river crossing, tossing his head and backing away, and she dismounted to lead him across by hand, too numb to be frustrated, too impatient to ease him into obedience as she ought. Saddles creaked and boots thudded to the ground as her warriors followed without question. Her skin was flushed from weariness so the shock of that first step into the rippling current was dizzying. Surely it was that and not the pulsing fear that left her breathless as she emerged onto the far bank and wove around the pyres on foot, ignoring the grim-faced Outriders she passed in her search for Markham and answers.

She found him slouched over his knees on the manor's shallow steps, unlit pipe cradled in soot-stained hands, drained flask tipped on its side beside his dusty boots. His head lifted at her approach, revealing a face that looked older and more weathered than ever before. "Sit, tal Desmond. I'd offer you a drink but . . ." He nudged the flask, and it clattered down the steps into the dust at her feet.

Ceridwen drew in a breath. "Gavin?"

"No sign of him among the dead."

She let out the breath, achingly relieved. Gavin had intended to escort Astra to Rysinger after overseeing the muster. Had the messenger said he was at Soras Ford? She could not remember. Maybe he had ridden on before the attack came. Maybe he yet lived.

Markham cocked an eyebrow at her. "No sign of him among the living either, if that's what you're thinking, because there wasn't a sand-blasted soul left alive in this place. By the time we received their call for aid, they were already dead." He shoved his sweat-stiff hair back from his forehead. "Somehow with all our scouts and counterstrike forces and more than a full *ayed* shadowing the Nadaari, we missed it."

Not a soul left alive . . .

Those words seared into her mind, drawing her focus to the darkened doorway above. She dropped Mindar's reins in the dust and took a step forward, swaying.

No . . . oh . . . oh, no.

"I don't understand," Finnian spoke up from behind her. "Why fight here? Why not ride on with their families when the Nadaari came? They would have gone slowly, sure, but—"

"Slower than you think," Iona said, "if there were many young ones."

Ceridwen turned back to Markham, feeling like she moved through water that dragged at her limbs, dulled her perceptions. "What of Fiona and the boys?" He hesitated only an instant before flicking his gaze up the steps toward that yawning doorway, but that instant confirmed her fears. "I . . . I must see them."

Finnian gripped her elbow. "Ceridwen, are you certain?"

She stared at him, unspeaking, until he released her, and then scaled the steps only dimly aware that Markham thwarted his attempt to follow. Her commander knew her well. Spurs clanking dully, she strode through the eerie chill of the too-silent hall, past tapestries torn down and candles overturned. Her boot caught on a fallen bowl caked with the remnants of a meal and sent it skidding ahead to wobble and then fall still. Nowhere did she see signs of ransacking. Only of lives interrupted and cut off.

This had been a rapid assault with one intent: death.

She had never been to Soras Ford before, but she followed the trail of ruin to the central chambers where the carved doors hung from twisted hinges, hacked open by an axe, and a bloody handprint stained the frame, and within . . .

Oh, Aodh above.

She dropped to her knees, one hand pressed for support against the bloodstained floor. It might have been a lifetime she knelt there or only a breath, but when she stood, her eyes were dry, and when she descended the shallow steps to her waiting forces with the beat of war ringing in her stride, all the air in her lungs seemed turned to fire, and the voice that left her throat was forged of steel. "Burn the manor to the ground."

No other pyre would serve Fiona and her sons.

Its flames would rise, visible for miles, and her enemies would know she rode for them.

"As you will, my queen." Markham stood, pocketing his empty flask, and as streams of fire consumed the manor and her warriors withdrew beyond the gates, leaving only riverriders to limit the fire's spread, Ceridwen spoke the litany of Fiona's deeds and then led her steed out. She told herself she would have ignited the manor herself, but the race from Cenyon had left Mindar drained, reserves cooled to dangerous levels. He must rest for the next battle.

To her, it could not come soon enough.

So she told herself, and she almost believed it.

"Ceridwen, wait." Finnian strode quickly toward her, wolfhound and shadower following. She halted, and the sympathy in his eyes nearly destroyed her fragile façade of strength. "I wanted you to know you're not alone." He broke off, staring over her shoulder.

"My lady, look who I found!" Liam's voice rang out.

She turned to see the lad escorting a limping seablood with a coat that shimmered like burnished steel in the blaze of the pyres. On its back, as worn and battered as her steed, Astra tor Telweg. Ceridwen broke into a run, Finnian at her side. "It is good to see you alive!" she called. "What of Gavin? Is he safe?"

Astra dismounted wearily, steadying herself on the saddle. "He is alive." Her voice was hollow, her face streaked with blood, dirt, and tears. "Or he was before they released me. It has been . . . two days . . . I think. They gave me a message, Ceridwen, for you."

Ceridwen's feet ground to a halt. The Nadaari.

"What message?" Finnian demanded, pulling up alongside.

And though she was still reeling from the knowledge that Gavin was alive and in danger, she already knew the answer to the question. It was the only thing that made sense.

She met Astra's pale blue eyes. "Where? When?"

"Tomorrow at sunset. I will lead you there." Astra hesitated, voice quavering. "Hear the words of the Nadaari: 'His life is in your hands. Should you fail to arrive, he will die. Should you launch an attack or seek to rescue him, he will die. Should you doubt these words, let what you have seen here serve as your reminder.'"

It would. *Blazes,* it would.

But Gavin alive meant there was still time to save him.

"We will leave tonight." And somehow, her voice remained firm and her hands steady, despite the knowledge that she held Gavin's life in a grip that had already failed once.

Astra shook her head pleadingly. "Tomorrow, Ceridwen. Your warriors are exhausted, your steeds spent, and while they will kill him if you do not come, they will not kill him until after sunset. We can leave tomorrow and arrive in time."

"Now that sounds like prime sea-sense, tor Telweg." Markham stalked up and fixed his withering gaze on Ceridwen. "It would be fire-blasted reckless to go sprinting off into danger without asking a few questions first." Voice lowering to a growl, he slid his attention to Astra. "Starting with how in blazes the Nadaari slipped past my

Outriders, and why you alone survived the slaughter. Until then"—his gaze snapped back to Ceridwen—"no one is going anywhere, tomorrow or otherwise."

She met his challenge with steel in her spine. "Ask what you will, Apex. That is your duty. But tomorrow, we ride. That is mine." She turned to retrieve her steed, and Markham's response rang after her as she led him away.

"Your duty is to lead, tal Desmond. Remember that."

As if she could forget when that responsibility was a catch-rope tightening around her neck. But never again would she stand helpless while those she loved suffered. Never again.

Ceridwen drew a treated rag across Mindar's hide, leaving a trail of twinkling red sparks behind, and received a contented snort in return as he grazed beside the tack she'd laid out to dry from a fresh coat of skivva oil. Behind, the manor burned long into the night, casting a lurid glow across the camped *ayed* to the river where she had led Mindar to graze. Water rippled serenely below banks lined with trampled rushes and pitted with hoofmarks. If she closed her eyes, she could envision the conflict that had raged.

Could hear the *shiiinng* of blades drawn, the hiss of bated breaths, the crash of steeds and riders wielding the current to fight with the strength of the river itself.

With an effort, she shook free. This was not why she was here. She had come for Mindar, hoping unpressured exposure to running water might help him overcome his fears, and for herself, hoping it was the last place anyone would expect to find her.

They found her anyway.

She saw them approaching with torches in the moonlight. It was only a week until the Fire Moon rose to hover enormous and red and casting a dawn light over the earth all night long, and already the moon seemed larger and brighter than usual. It glinted off their eyes as they surrounded her in silence: Markham, Iona, Finnian and his wolfhound, the three she had come to trust most in all the years since the *kasar*.

"Where is Astra?" she asked, working the rag across Mindar's hide again, rubbing from his withers down his spine, hoping to ease any sore points where the saddle might have weighed heavily during their journey.

"Resting, the wee lamb," Iona said. "She's had quite the ordeal."

Ceridwen couldn't imagine anyone but Iona referring to Telweg's daughter as a "wee lamb" and surviving to tell the tale. "Then she has convinced you?"

"For now." Markham lowered himself with a groan, stretching his long legs before him. "I dispatched trackers to retrace her steps, but so far, her claims confirm my suspicions: Kilmark and Ondri are here in Lochrann."

"Here?" Finnian repeated. "I thought Rhodri hunted them in Ardon?"

"Must have slipped his rope. Not for want of trying, I am sure."

Ceridwen squeezed the rag in numb fingers. "You think they were behind this?"

Markham stared grimly up at her. "Like the hands that bend the bow. This was a calculated strike, tal Desmond, aimed by someone who knows you." He continued, theorizing that Kilmark and Ondri had interrupted the communications between his *ayed* and the one shadowing the Nadaarian army, but Ceridwen scarcely heard a word.

All within her had gone cold. She was a chasm's mouth, an endless pool, a starless void filled with voices all taunting her with the truth: Fiona and the boys had died because of her.

She had known it already, but hearing it stated so baldly left her reeling.

"And what of the manuscripts?" Liam's eager voice drew her back to reality. Always, he was fresh air to ash-choked lungs, but when had he joined this midnight war-meet? More to the point, where was he?

Iona turned sharply toward the shadows. "What have I told you about skulking, lad?"

"I am not skulking, Aunt!"

"Oh, and what do you call it? Spying? Aye, so much better."

He stepped into the torchlight, indignant. "You're always telling me to stay close. *Floods*, Aunt, I'm only doing as you ask."

Iona threw up her hands. "Forgive the lad. He can be a mite dim."

"Actually . . ." Markham scratched his grizzled beard. "He's on the right track."

Liam flung his arms wide. "Of course I am!" Glaring, Iona stabbed a finger at the ground, and he flopped down while Markham explained that the Nadaari had taken the Canthorian manuscripts from Astra. Now more than ever, Markham seemed troubled by the idea of an alliance between Nadaar and Canthor, and with good reason.

If they allied in this war, Soldonia would be lost.

"Mustering the war-chiefs must be our foremost aim if the kingdom is to survive." Markham regarded Ceridwen with a wolflike tilt to his head. His shaggy hair, long and unkempt from months in the saddle, only heightened the likeness. "You are backed against a crater here. Show weakness, and all is over. Forsake your cousin, and who will ally with you? Yield for his sake, and the kingdom dies. You ride the gauntlet again, and your *ayeds* with you. This offer from the Nadaari is undoubtedly a trap, but we will ride tomorrow, if that is your will. We will fight and die on your command. You are our queen, Ceridwen." It was, she thought, the first time he had called her by her given name, and it sounded strange coming from his lips.

He straightened, and in his voice was the force of an earthhewn charge, the crack of a stormer lightning attack, the menace of a shadower stalking prey. "But that means you have a responsibility to all your people too. Remember that."

She gripped her horse-head pommel. "I do, Markham. I do."

Always he challenged her: *Become worthy. Lead.*

And she would. For Bair, for Gavin, for her father too.

Markham nodded slowly, still holding her gaze. "Aye, I know you do." Sighing, he settled back on one elbow, drew his pipe from his pouch, and lit it on a smoldering twist of grass ignited by her steed.

"That's it?" Finnian looked from her to Markham. "You know it's a trap." At his tone, Cù's head shot up, and the wolfhound crouched, growling low. "They would ambush you and you would ride blindly in, like the earthhewn at Idolas?"

His words hung between them, heavy in the ensuing silence.

"And . . . we will take our leave," Iona interjected. "Come, lad."

"Oh but, Aunt–" Liam's objections faded as she towed him away into the night.

At the mention of Idolas, Ceridwen felt a flicker of the fire within her return, burning away the chill from before. She clung to it, stoked it to fury. She would need that flame soon. "I have no intention of riding in with my eyes closed."

"Still, this feels reckless, even for you," Finnian insisted. "Surely you agree, Apex?"

Markham removed his pipe from his lips and shifted to a sitting position with one elbow on his bent knee. "Agree with what, te Donal? That you can whittle a fine pipe? Sure, I can agree with that. For indeed it is."

"But you must have an opinion on this."

"Eh, I try not to take sides in matters like these."

"Matters like what?" Frustration bled into his voice. "We are talking *strategy*."

Markham's one eye glinted. "Are we?"

That seemed to throw Finnian off his stride. His forehead wrinkled. "Of course. What else would this be? And since when do you not take sides?"

"Since her steed is so much sand-blasted meaner than yours," Markham drawled. He shoved to his feet, dusted off his clothes, and started back toward the camp, calling over his shoulder, "But by all means, carry on, te Donal. I enjoy watching a good roasting."

The echoes of his tramping died away, and they were alone on the riverbank.

Finnian sank down with his wolfhound sprawled beside him. Still seething, Ceridwen gathered her tack and steeled herself to reenter the camp, to sleep in the lee of the pyre that had claimed her kin.

"You asked about his scars."

Ceridwen halted.

"He was half dead when I found him, torn to shreds and only a pup. I knew *he'd* be furious"—that he again—"he despises useless things. But I took Cù home, stitched him up, and once he healed enough to hunt, it seemed okay." Finnian's voice tightened, and the wolfhound shifted to rest its head on his knees. "The skull though, that was the day I finally stood up to him. That blow would have killed me if Cù hadn't jumped in. It nearly killed him instead." Finnian's eyes flicked to meet hers. "But he is a survivor."

Her anger had dissipated like steam.

She sank down beside him. The story was a peace offering, so she offered one in return, before she could feel the full ache of the words she would speak. "You asked why Gavin fought here. His wife, Fiona, was having their third child, a son. He was to be named Desmond after my father."

Understanding flooded his expression.

He raked his hair back from his eyes. "What will you do if they demand you in exchange for Gavin?" She did not answer, but he nodded as if he already knew, and maybe he did. "You would do it. You know, most in this war-host wish to survive for more than the opportunity to ride in the next battle, but I've seen the way you fight. Always at the front. Forever throwing yourself into the thick, like you've no regard at all for your own skin."

She met his gaze head-on. "Better my skin than another's."

What was truth but bones laid bare, stripped of flesh and covering? There was truth in sunrise and moonset, in a man's dying breath, in a fireborn's flame, and in that moment, in her eyes, she knew. Of what worth was Ceridwen tal Desmond alive if she could not save her people where she had failed Bair?

If she could not atone for the *kasar* in death if not in life?

This was truth, and it burned to be spoken.

"You may be the Fireborn, Ceridwen. But you need not ride or die alone." His voice was soft, his eyes softer still, and it took a moment for his words to take hold.

She tilted her head. "*The* Fireborn?"

"You haven't heard it yet? The Outriders started it on our ride back from Cenyon. The way you tore through the Nadaari–I've never seen anything like it. Surrounded by flame, billowing smoke, the heart of an inferno. You and Mindar seemed one. Fireborn." His eyes met hers. Dark fathomless eyes, full of stone and shadow and deep wooded places where the wild yet reigned. Something about the moonlight and the dark and his voice had her head spinning as though she had drained Markham's flask. In that moment, back-rider, Outrider, and warrior disappeared, and he was simply Finnian.

He gave a wry grin. "Reckless," he said. "But the breed of reckless that winds up immortalized in song, spun into legend, and carved into the paneling of great halls. If it doesn't get you killed first."

THIRTY-NINE: RAFI

Some plants must grow deep before growing tall.
– Mahque saying

"Rafi," Moc shouted, "catch!"

Rafi looked up from his waterskin and half-peeled simba fruit to see a spear flying toward him. He snared the fruit between his teeth and grabbed for the spear. It slapped into his blistered palm. The basket of fruit beside him teetered, but he caught it with one foot and hopped to set it right, both hands still full.

"Oh, now you're just showing off!"

Crisis averted, Rafi shifted the spear to his elbow's crook and shook the sting out of his hand before plucking the fruit from his teeth. "Maybe a warning next time?" he suggested as Moc loped up, grinning.

The big Alonque had traded his hoe for his own spear and carried it slung behind his neck, arms looped over both ends. "You ready to begin?"

Rafi grimaced, glancing over his shoulder at the laborers tending the gorge fields, chopping out weeds, digging up root vegetables, and collecting fruit from the cultivated trees that created a border against denser jungle. He had been slaving among them since sunrise, earning new aches to complement all the muscles he had strained working with the colt over the past few days, so why exactly had he agreed to spar during his afternoon water break?

Moc snorted. "Don't tell me you'd prefer weeding?"

"Less likely to be stabbed there."

"I wouldn't count on it." Moc jerked his chin, directing Rafi's gaze.

He straightened as Nef strolled past through the glistening grass, a hoe gripped low and tight in his hands, and he shifted instinctively into a defensive stance, coiling his hand under the spear like a harpoon. Movement blurred in his peripheral vision, and Moc's spear darted at his side. He jumped back, tripped over that inconvenient basket of fruit, and barely blocked and bound Moc's next thrust, the clack of spears jarring his arms. Focused on the spear's gleaming tooth, he circled as it thrust and spun and thirsted for his blood, and was pleased to find that blocking and striking felt less awkward now, though he still struggled to position his feet and–

Something drove into his legs and swept them out. He landed in a sprawl, and Moc's boulder of a head loomed over him. "Planning to play dead every time you are outmatched?"

Rafi sat up, wincing. "Well, if it works, it works. So . . . same time tomorrow?"

"Try today, my friend. We are not done yet. You need the practice."

Ever blunt of word and deed, Moc was, but this time, he had a point. Rafi had survived so far by avoiding head-on engagements. He could not count on such luck to continue. Groaning, he picked himself up and limped to retrieve his spear. It had rolled beneath a sprawling simba tree where graybeard monkeys scampered to pick fruit. Somehow, they had been trained to select only ripe fruit and deliver it to a handler waiting with baskets below–how, he had no idea, since his own efforts to tame the sea-demon were proving as much an exercise in futility as the Que Revolution and just as likely to get him killed.

Over the week since he had begun, he had taken so many falls, his hide would soon be dappled with bruises to match the sea-beast. Umut had taught him how to knot a halter, how to groom the colt, how not to get kicked when he approached it, but next to nothing about how to stay on when its heels punched the sky. Sighing, Rafi toed his spear into the air and snatched it neatly, only to slip on a fallen simba with the next step. He lurched to avoid planting his face in the ground and the spear in his chest.

Moc bellowed a laugh. "You, who killed a scadtha!"

"There might have been some luck involved." Not to mention the sea-demon. Over Moc's shoulder, he searched the woven fence for a glimpse of the colt and was disappointed again. So far, food had proved the only way to gain its attention.

Moc followed the drift of his eyes. "Have you sat on it yet?" Concern tinged his voice. Not all Que shared Umut's dismissal of Nadaarian superstitions about sea-demons.

"Sitting is easy. Staying is not." So far, a count of four was all he had managed. Just long enough to curse the sea-demon's ancestry before he was sent hurtling.

"Ah, it is your balance, cousin, that must improve." Moc fell into his stance, knees slightly bent. "You must ground yourself, see?" He stamped his feet and shifted between them. "On foot and on your beast. Root your weight low to keep from toppling. And watch for both ends of my spear." He adjusted Rafi's position, widening his grip and nudging his feet to narrow the target of his body. "I swept your feet last time because you were fixated on the point."

"Yes, because it's pointy."

"Complaining, Tetrani?" Nef's voice broke in.

Rafi dropped his stance and let his spear droop idly before turning to meet the rebel's scowl and the eager expressions of the five others at his back. Trouble in the making. He pasted on his mother's smile, knowing it would needle them.

"Missing the comforts of the palace, *prince*?" Nef pressed.

"Oh, yes," he said wryly. "Those dungeons, I tell you, *so* comfortable."

That won a chuckle from some of the rebels and a full-bodied laugh from Moc, but Nef's scowl only deepened. "You know what, Tetrani? It is good you are here."

"Why is that?" Rafi eyed the rebel's knotted fists. "Closer target?"

"To taste what awaits your kin." Without breaking eye contact, Nef thrust an open hand expectantly toward Moc whose eyes widened as he backed away, shaking his head.

"Cousin, I–"

Nef rounded on him, eyebrows raised, and Moc clamped his mouth shut. Reluctantly, he relinquished his spear, and Nef spun it between his hands and up over his shoulders before assuming a deep fighting stance reminiscent of a stone-eye tiger crouching to spring. Chin lowered, eyes smoldering, he sneered up at Rafi. "And to show my cousins how easily you Nadaari can be beaten. Consider it your contribution to the cause."

"I am all for contributing," Rafi said. "In fact, I'm told it's one of the more charming aspects of my personality—but what would you know? I have work to do—"

Nef snapped his spearpoint up. "This won't take long."

One of the others snorted. "That's for sure."

Rafi looked to Moc but could not catch his eye. No help there. Or from any of the others. "So, I guess I have no choice in the matter?"

"Oh, you have a choice," Nef said, "fight or run."

And Rafi could only laugh, somehow—ridiculously—at the irony as he wiped his clammy palms on his trousers. "You really need to learn what that word means." Still, one choice did remain: timing and terrain. This, he would seize. So, he feinted a jab and then took off at a sprint, leaving the rebel guarded against a nonexistent attack.

Looking the fool did not bother him, but it would infuriate Nef.

Crashing broke out behind as Rafi angled through jungle overgrowth and skidded to a halt before the sea-demon's enclosure. Seconds later, Nef burst from the thicket, and Rafi struck, harboring a faint hope that his left-handedness might throw off the rebel. No such luck. Nef flung himself sideways to avoid the spear and then sank into his stance, chest heaving. Rafi was panting too, sweat dripping from his hair and stinging his eyes. He tossed his head to clear his vision and sensed rather than saw the attack coming. His instinctive reaction deflected a skewering strike, then Nef was on him like a whirlwind.

But he had seen Nef train. He knew what to expect. So, he met the barrage of rapid, relentless strikes and did not back down.

Ten seconds, he held his own.

Ten seconds, he matched weapons and survived.

Then blows began to slip past his defense, bruising with the haft rather than cutting with the blade: a sharp rap to the gut, a crack to the thigh, a clip to the ear that made his head spin. He staggered against the enclosure and felt it sag beneath his weight.

Nef sneered at him. "How could *you* kill a scadtha?"

Rafi tried to straighten, but Nef caught his chest and shoved him back. Warm breath suddenly puffed against the back of his neck. He moved his head to catch a flash of blue through a gap in the weave.

Run, brother . . .

But he didn't need the ghost's warning to know what to do.

He dropped, crouching, and covered his ears as an unearthly shriek rent the air. When heard keening across moonlit shores, it was only eerie. Heard up close, it was deafening, unmaking, as if the very fabric of the world was being torn asunder.

It caught Nef full force, and he staggered.

Rafi struck, whipping his spear up to smash Nef's fingers and break his grip, then slammed into him with the force of a storm wave, throwing him to the ground. Pinning Nef's writhing shoulders, he gritted, "Want to see?"

Nef seethed up at him, going still. Only then did Rafi hear the murmur of shocked voices and realize the rebels watched. Moc was gaping at him, and Rafi felt a twinge of anger, recalling how the man had clapped him on the back and called him brother. Then Nef kicked his knee out from under him, and the world flipped. Like the scadtha, Nef twisted impossibly, rolling until Rafi was trapped, one arm caught beneath.

Punches rained from above.

Rafi blocked and caught one fist, but the other cracked against his jaw, once, twice, snapping his head against the ground. White-hot light shot across his vision. He blinked up, dazed, half expecting to see thc sea-demon nuzzling his pockets for treats like the last three times it had thrown him. All he saw was Nef's fist aiming for his nose.

It stopped mid-swing.

Someone hauled Nef from his chest. "Enough!"

Ah, Moc. So thoughtful of him to step in. Finally.

"You kill him, you answer to Umut," Moc warned in a low voice. "Go cool off."

Nef spat something in return but stomped away, and from the crackling of the undergrowth, it sounded like the others followed. Rising made Rafi's head feel like shifting, sliding rocks, so he just slid back against the enclosure and then dabbed at his aching, bloody face. At least his nose didn't seem broken. Small comfort.

Moc hovered over him. "Here, let me help."

Rafi sucked in a stinging breath and waved Moc's hands away as if shooing a fly. "Little late, don't you think?"

His face reddened. "Look, Nef is–"

"Chum? Leaf mold? Python droppings?"

"Family, Nahiki. I was going to say family."

Rafi squinted up at him. "So, he saved your brother's life too?"

"You have no idea what he has done." Moc rubbed the angry, puckered scar carved across the side of his head, then bent to retrieve Rafi's spear and slung it over his shoulders. "You hit him. He hit you. Fair and square, right?"

Minus a near-drowning.

But Rafi's head ached too much to argue more, so he just hitched his shoulders into a more comfortable position and closed his eyes.

Moc nudged his foot. "Are you coming then?"

Rafi flicked a weary hand toward the sea-demon. "You go on. I'll stay." As if he had not already tasted humiliation–and his own blood–enough for one day.

FORTY: CERIDWEN & JAKIM

With a single stamp of their massive hooves,
earthhewns can shake the earth and shatter stones.
Their hides deflect arrows like rain. Beware their charge in battle.

It was not of songs or legends or paneled halls, not even of her own death, that Ceridwen thought as she rode into the shadow of the rise, atop which the Nadaari waited, and lifted her eyes against the setting sun to survey the palisade of sharpened stakes that shielded and concealed their troops, crowned with streamered banners hanging limp in the still air. She had no banner but the steeds of Markham's *ayed* and Lochrann's muster combined, marching steadfastly behind, and yet beneath their hooves, the earth sang of their coming, and she took comfort in the knowledge that Gavin would know that they rode for him.

It was of him, she thought, and of them.

Of Markham, Finnian, Iona, and young Liam.

Of the warriors who answered her horn, though the war-chiefs did not.

Of Fiona and her sons and the pyre that yet burned, and of Gavin who might survive this day, only to wither like her father had. If Aodh possessed any mercy at all, that would not be his fate. Her grip tightened on the reins, and Mindar tossed his head, offering a glimpse of the smoldering furnace of one eye between the snapping strands of his mane. If all failed today, she would leave no mark upon the legends as her ancestors had.

But she would leave her mark in fire here yet.

Raising her blade hand, a signal Finnian's horn echoed, she summoned her forces to speed for the final approach. Not so fast it would be mistaken for a charge and spark retribution against Gavin, but enough to stir up unease in her opponents. Their lofty vantage commanded the surrounding area, leaving her to rely upon a show of strength to distract from the true threat winging through the clouded bastions of the sky.

Dust rose in swirls beneath the hooves of the earthhewn, shadowers ghosted in the coiling black smoke breathed by fireborn, and riveren raced in a seething tide, manes rising and falling like foaming waves. Of Lochrann's chieftains, Ballard and Yianna had joined the Outrider *ayed* shadowing the main Nadaarian force southward, Kassa rode with her, and Doogan–faithless Doogan–had sent only half his muster and stayed behind.

He would regret it, one day. Ceridwen would see to that.

Closer and closer, her forces poured, until the rumble of their hooves resounded off the hill, then Ceridwen raised her blade, ordering the earthhewn to slow first, before bringing the *ayed* to halt well beyond ballista-shot. Smoke eddied around her as all fell still. Even the breaths of her steed seemed loud in that silence.

On Finnian's left, Astra tor Telweg lifted her pale face and pointed toward a pool at the base of the hill, sheltered beneath two arms of the rise. "There, Ceridwen. Do you see?"

"I see."

There, bound to a stake in the water, slumped a familiar figure. His head hung limp against his chest, and he did not stir. Was he still breathing? She shifted in the saddle, but Markham seized her forearm before she could spur Mindar forward.

"That," he warned roughly, "would be the trap."

"Undoubtedly," she admitted. This too was the only thing that made sense. Why else leave him unguarded below? They meant to bait her, and she had half a mind to let them. Everything within her burned to act, to race in and free Gavin, to unleash a firestorm the Nadaari would not soon forget. If any lived to recall it.

"Surely"–Markham's eyebrows were raised–"my queen–reckless,

volatile, and ill-tamed though she may be—does not intend to ride straight into its jaws."

"Not with her eyes closed," Finnian muttered, tossing her words in her teeth.

She shot him a glare, but Markham's voice grated beside her ear. "Don't flame at him, tal Desmond, *think*. We rode upon their demands, but we must wait for their move if we are to retain any negotiating power." He released her arm but held her gaze until she nodded. He was right, of course. He usually was.

"He was sorely injured when I left, Ceridwen," Astra spoke up, her brow knotted in concern. "He might be dying now." Delaying, Astra's tone warned, might doom him, but heedless fury might doom them all, and either would be upon her command.

This was the burden of the crown she had claimed.

Setting her face forward, Ceridwen sheathed her sabre. "We wait." But they need not wait in silence. She motioned for Finnian to sound the horn again. In the echoes of the blast, each Outrider cued their steed to stamp once and then still, creating a crack like thunder that rolled toward the rise and echoed off the hill. No response from the Nadaari. No movement from Gavin. Closing her eyes, she drew a sharp breath. "Again."

She was here.

Jakim crouched instinctively as another crack shook the crater, using his chin to secure the armload of riverrider masks he had scooped up from Khilamook's workspace. From here, he could not see over the palisade lining the crater's edge, but he could hear the rumble of thousands of hooves stamping as one, and he knew.

The king's daughter was here, and she was going to die.

"Hurry!" Khilamook demanded, stinging him forward with a rap of the cane. "Our quarry grows impatient for death. We should not keep her waiting."

Jakim staggered upright and narrowly dodged a fresh pile of manure as he rounded the war machine toward the soldiers forming up before the gate with Adaan at their head. He was shaking with exhaustion as he handed out the newly modified masks to the soldiers, ten in all. Only their bloodshot eyes and restless fingers revealed any hint of anxiety as they stowed the masks in their belts, but Adaan turned his over in his hands, eyes narrowed in suspicion.

"You are certain this will work, engineer? You hold my life in your hands."

Khilamook rolled his eyes at Jakim's translation. "Oh, Murloch grant my grip is strong! Of course, it works. Otherwise my translator would not have survived to relay your idiotic whining, and what a loss that would be."

Another crack shook the earth, and Jakim's stomach flipped. He was going to be sick. He thought of Seamus's head hanging limp, eyes staring vacantly. Of the hundreds slaughtered in the raid. Of the blood of innocents staining the tines of Astra's trident.

What did the engineer know of loss?

"It will work," he said to Adaan and turned away, frowning, as he saw Khilamook's face. His altered translations never failed to amuse the engineer. He had spent a wet and miserable night bound to that stake, Seamus's corpse gradually growing cold and stiff beside him, until soldiers retrieved him at dawn. His supposed role in the theft apparently forgotten, they had hustled him back to the engineer's side to assist with modifying a set of masks like the one that had saved his life. He had considered refusing. For Seamus's sake, he nearly did.

But he had faced death with vows unfulfilled, and Aodh help him, could not risk it again.

His half-blind, unthinking steps had led him back to the war machine, so he gripped one of the support beams and scaled it like a mango tree, scrambling rapidly upward until he could balance on the crossbeam and look out over the palisade to the dusty haze rising from the sea of steeds below. He looked for her, though he did not know what he was looking for. She could be any one of a thousand faces. Soon, she could be any one of a thousand corpses. He dug his fingernails into his palms.

Oh Aodh, have–

"It *is* fortunate you survived, boy," Khilamook mused, lounging against his cart and idly tracing designs in the dirt with the tip of his cane. "Whatever would I do without my translator in this savage land of halfwits and morons? Speaking to anyone directly is certain to reduce one's own mental capacity by a disastrous seventy-four percent."

Jakim tried to smother his bitterness, but it burst out in the question he'd been longing to ask since discovering the engineer's skill with languages rivaled his own. "Why the pretense, master? You need no translator."

"I just told you."

"But you dislike relying upon anyone." Not only that, but it seemed a meaningless obstacle to conversations that determined the fates of nations.

"Ah, but I do not rely upon you. You serve me and live because of it. For now. You may consider yourself fortunate and blessed by . . . well, me. Your Aodh certainly has nothing to do with it." Khilamook's dark, bottomless eyes bored into Jakim's, then he broke into that unnerving smile. "You would know the truth of it? I am a scholar of the tenth order, honored among the learned in Canthor, a nation that existed centuries before Nadaar was spawned as a tribe, let alone an empire. My presence here is an honor. These"–he jabbed his cane toward Adaan–"should honor me in turn by speaking my own tongue."

"Of course," Khilamook added, considering him, "men also speak freely before oblivious foreigners. They underestimate you and reveal themselves. Knowledge is the truest, deadliest power. Remember that, Scroll Jakim." He lifted his face to the sky and exhaled. "Can you feel it? That shivering upon the air? The world itself takes notice. It leans in, attentive to see the work I have wrought. Mark my words, boy, this will be a day long remembered."

All Jakim felt was dread.

The crash of a gong nearly startled him from his perch. He clutched at the beam, watching the palisade gate creak open, disgorging Adaan and his men, masks swinging from their belts. Oh, Aodh above, it was happening.

"Can you feel it?" Finnian sat atop his shadower with his cloak thrown back, his eyes, like hers, carefully turned away from the dark clouds building above. His brow was taut with tension, and his gaze went to hers. "The charge in the air?" She knew from his words the night before that it was not the Nadaari's actions he feared but hers.

"I feel it," she said.

Though in truth, she felt nothing but the heat of her rage and the relief that would come when she could unleash it upon her enemy. So, when a gong crashed and the palisade slid open and nearly a dozen soldiers marched down in a phalanx of gleaming steel that skirted the pool where Gavin was bound, the breath she drew was sweet with anticipation. She sought Markham's brooding eye, exchanged a determined nod, and pointedly stared at Liam until he checked his steed from following and reluctantly sank back. The lad was loath to remain behind with the *ayed*, but Iona had threatened to leave him steedless, bootless, and miles from the fight if he did not swear to obey in her absence.

He would not die this day if Ceridwen could prevent it.

Half of her wished Iona had carried out her threat, if only to prevent Liam's fate from falling to her. She had failed too often already. She *would* fail no more. Gathering up her reins, she rode out to meet the Nadaari, Finnian and the riders of her patrol at her side.

"That height advantage will grant their arrows wings," Finnian observed.

She shrugged dismissively. "Winged arrows are no less flammable."

"And if they fire ballista upon us?"

"Also flammable. We will burn them from the sky."

"Ah." His tone carried a forced lightness. "So, I take it your steed's aim improves when targeting potentially fatal threats like arrows as opposed to minor ones like apples? He did miss after all. Twice, as I recall."

"Once, and that was remote flame without a rider for aiming."

"Oh, then I feel so much better." He winked, and though his expression remained strained, his lips hinted at a smile. It was purposeful, this teasing, an attempt to steady her before negotiating for her cousin's life and perhaps her own, but though she saw through it, it worked nonetheless. Her lungs filled more fully. Her shoulders relaxed.

And that strange feeling stirring within her chest, was that . . . hope?

She halted before the Nadaarian leader, a lean man with a long nose and lank hair, and spoke before he had a chance to begin. "You are responsible for what I found at Soras Ford?"

"I . . ." The Nadaarian seemed taken aback. "I am Adaan, leader of this–"

"Then you *are* responsible." She tightened her grip on her sabre and felt Mindar's flames rising within his ribcage, responding to her emotions. "You should know, I will relish watching the flesh melt from your bones. You will die screaming, and the fires will rage until even your bones are reduced to ash. This, I swear." She met his gaze, and he recoiled, unnerved by the expression on her face.

Uncertainty flashed through his eyes, and his head twitched toward his shoulder like he had only just stopped himself from looking back toward the forces massed on the hill. This, doubtless, was not how he had expected the conversation to unfold.

Or was he, perhaps, waiting for something?

"The signal, you imbecile," Khilamook muttered. "Give the signal."

Jakim barely heard him. He could see her now, the king's daughter. There could be no mistaking the figure that had ridden to meet Adaan on a sprightly steed that pranced and danced with each step, black smoke billowing from its nostrils. Both the woman's hair and the steed's coat were of a burnished copper color that shone in the setting sun, despite the clouds gathering overhead. Realizing he was gaping at the woman's dull red cuirass, the blade sheathed at her side, and the glow of firelight that surrounded her and her steed, he tore his focus away.

"She is in range now." Khilamook moved away from his cart, hand hovering over the sledge he would wield to unleash the war machine. "Why the delay? We should fire now before she slips the noose." He caught the sledge up in both hands. Already a ceramic sphere filled the cradle. Just the sight of it made Jakim's head spin in his lofty perch.

Maybe . . . he should get down . . .

"No." Nahrog grounded his spear with a rattle of chains, halting Khilamook's swing. "She may yet surrender herself alive. She could be useful to us."

Scowling, Khilamook indicated the roiling sky. "Those clouds are troubling. If the wind changes . . ."

It would be Aodh's judgment, avenging the blood of the innocent.

Jakim dug his fingers into the wooden crossbeam. His neck ached under the weight of the signet ring. He was intensely, almost painfully, aware of it pressing against his chest. Below, the fire-breathing steed that the king's daughter rode blasted the ground at Adaan's feet with flames that coiled around his boots.

Adaan leaped back and raised a hand.

"There, the signal!"

Levers cranked. The war machine shuddered.

Jakim clambered down, scraping his limbs in his haste. His vision had narrowed to the wooden beams before him, the taut muscles rippling the script on his forearms, and somehow, plastered across it all, the face of the dying king mumbling a plea for mercy for himself, and *oh Aodh*, for his daughter, who would die like Seamus with the breath stolen from her lungs. Ten feet from the ground, Jakim dropped and felt the shock of it in his teeth. Khilamook stood with the sledge poised, eyes alight with a fevered gleam. In seconds, she would be dead. But Jakim was already moving, yielding to the tugging sensation in his chest, to the knowledge that if Aodh's hand was upon him, then perhaps this moment was why he was here.

Running, stumbling, reaching out.

His hands closed around the sphere as the sledge fell, and he snatched it to his chest and spun. Behind, he heard the crash of the sledge, the creak of the war machine's empty arm rising, the crack as it slammed into the crossbeam, and Khilamook's furious shout, as Jakim broke into a run and tore across the crater.

FORTY-ONE: RAFI

Test the vine before you leap.
– Mahque saying

Softer than wind keening over the sea, Rafi sang a song of his mother's people as he stroked the neck of the grazing colt. Starred gray splotches had begun to dapple its dark blue hide until it resembled an expanse of night sky seen reflected in a pool of water. Each individual strand separated by his fingertips felt waxy, but together, beneath his palm, its coat lay smooth as wave-washed sand.

He slipped the rope from shoulder to hand and coaxed the colt's head up with a cala root cracker, then eased a loop around its muzzle, slid one end behind its ears, and secured it beneath the nose band. That put his bruised face inches from its nostrils, and fear wormed through him as the colt huffed three loud breaths, then turned away, disinterested.

Rafi breathed again. Safe and still uneaten.

It had taken a solid hour after the fight for his headache to settle, allowing him to clambor upright and enter the enclosure, and he would not tempt fate by attempting to ride now. One of these days he might hit his skull hard enough to do real damage–as if hearing ghosts wasn't sign of damage enough. So instead, he bribed the colt into walking alongside, turning when he turned and halting when he halted, until it decided to stomp on his foot.

"Ow!" Rafi shouldered the colt away and hopped as he rubbed the ache from his toes. Someone snickered, decidedly not a sea-demon-like sound. The branches shading the enclosure rustled, and Iakki dropped and swung like a hammock, hands and knees latched on, head tipped back to grin upside down at Rafi.

"How did you . . . ?"

"Climbed."

"And here I thought you'd flown. I meant without me seeing you?"

"You get real distracted when you're focused."

"That doesn't make any sense." Rafi eyed the colt warily as the branch rattled again, but it didn't seem bothered by the boy swinging overhead. Either it mistook him for one of the graybeard monkeys forever gamboling about, or it had grown accustomed to his antics.

Iakki whistled suddenly, and the colt's ears twitched. "What happened to your face?"

Rafi shrugged. "It's nothing." Mentioning Nef would remind Iakki of why they had scarcely talked for weeks now, and that was the last thing he wanted.

"Did the sea-demon do that to you? I told you not to feed it fruit." Iakki rocked his branch from side to side. "Might not have been so mad if you'd listened."

"No, Iakki, it wasn't the colt."

"Did you walk into a tree? Or someone's fist?"

"We were sparring. It happens." Rafi tugged unsuccessfully on the rope to move the sea-demon, then dug another cracker out of his pocket to lure it forward. The colt stretched its neck first, then relinquished a single step. Its whiskers tickled his palm.

"Careful or it'll get big as old Hanu."

Contrary to Iakki's warning, the colt actually seemed thinner than before, and maybe Rafi's eyes were blurry after the fight, but he could have sworn its coat lacked its usual luster. Maybe fruit really wasn't good for its health.

Iakki unhooked his legs and hung by his hands before dropping to the ground. "Why are you bothering with the beast anyway?"

Why indeed? Not for the reasons Umut had suggested: a surprise element in battle, a secret weapon for the Que. Rafi still planned to leave the rebel camp and strike out on his own again. For now, taming the sea-demon just felt right. It had saved him, chosen to follow, refused to leave. Bonded or not, they were connected somehow.

"His eyes," Rafi found himself saying. "They remind me of my brother."

Iakki looked up. "You have a brother?"

"Had."

"Oh."

"He died six years ago."

Of course, Rafi still heard his voice in his head, though the ghost had proved less talkative lately.

"Oh." Iakki's brow furrowed. "So, what should I call you? You ain't Nahiki."

Rafi hesitated. He had offered the war cry of the Tetrani in battle, but he was grateful no soldiers had lived to carry that tale to the empire. Soon Umut's plans would deprive him of the choice, so for now, "I prefer Nahiki."

But was that even the truth anymore?

"I . . . I'm . . ." Iakki studied his toes, and Rafi could guess the words stuck in his throat.

He slung an arm around the boy's neck and hauled him close, sparing him the need to speak of apology. "Careful–speak much slower and you will be the turtle's egg."

Iakki wriggled free. "That don't make sense." But he grinned all the same.

Grateful for the grin and the absolution it offered, Rafi stepped back and inspected the colt with a critical eye. It was not just his vision or a trick of the light. Something was changing. The scales on its forehead and nose were brittle and flaking, and its hooves no longer shone like abalone but were dull and splintering along the rim. "Something is wrong with it," he realized aloud. "It's sick, maybe, or just not thriving here."

Iakki huffed. "Of course it ain't thriving." He jumped for his branch and missed, and the colt shied away, blowing, so he swung up and over the fence instead. "It is a sea-beast, like me. It is meant for the sea!" He took off at a run, bound for more mischief, no doubt.

But his words stuck with Rafi as he continued his monotonous, frustrating work, bribing the lazy beast into obedience until evening softened the sharp edges of the gorge and all the laborers trooped past, tools on their shoulders, returning to huts, hammocks, and hearths. Alone, he stilled, eying the tall fence and the pitted path worn by the colt's circling.

Not just meant for the sea. But for freedom.

This, Rafi could understand.

He let the rope slip until he gripped only the end, and shouldered the gate open. The rope went slack. Rafi turned to see the sea-demon advance a step, nostrils flared, head erect, ears aimed toward that opening. He was nothing to it in that instant. Only an obstacle in its path. Maybe he should have removed the rope first.

"Shh . . . shh . . . now," he whispered, easing to the side.

The sea-demon bolted toward the gap. Instinct drove Rafi to catch its mane as it passed in a flash of blue and silver and swing up onto its back, harnessing its momentum. It was the smooth, balanced leap Torva had taught him for boarding a boat without tipping it, and he stretched low as Moc advised, clinging to the sea-demon's neck as it tore down the gorge.

Running, running, running.

Like an incoming tide seething before a storm.

Bound for open ground, the colt did not throw up its heels but lunged into each stride, slapping Rafi's face into branches, dragging him through netlike vines. Choppy seas he knew. Blistering winds he had endured. Sheer speed was terrifying. It felt like he was falling, spiraling, out of control. A drowning man battered by waves, clinging to driftwood for life. And was that Delmar's voice in the wind shrieking past his ears?

His teeth chattered; his bones rattled. Hands, legs, and feet, he gripped that rippling form until his muscles burned. Briefly, he remembered the lead flapping loose from his hand and considered trying to use it to steer or slow the beast. But he didn't dare relax his grip. So, he held on to the colt and to life until its pace finally slackened to a gentle rocking.

Tension eased from his limbs. He caught himself falling into rhythm with the colt. This felt far more natural. Like a second language he suddenly discovered he had always known. He gradually tightened the lead, and the colt tossed its head but slowed. Snorting, it shuffled to a halt and buried its nose in the silvery bushka beans. Rafi slumped, half laughing, half shaking with thrill and delirium, and tilted his head toward the sky. Far, far above, the pale moon met his gaze.

The sea-demon shook violently, a rattling fit to loosen its hide and shake Rafi apart. He slipped to one side, tumbled to the earth, and landed on his back, looking up into twinkling blue eyes.

Was it laughing at him?

"Sure. Laugh now. I prefer the last laugh anyway." Somehow, he doubted he would ever get it, but once his limbs steadied, he stood, wincing at his protesting legs, and snagged the colt's lead before it pranced away. He retraced their destructive path through the rebels' crops—Nef would be *so* pleased—but continued past the enclosure into the lowest cavern where the music of the waterfall promised cool water for drinking and bathing.

He bent to splash his face, but the colt tugged him downstream, and it was probably best to keep it out of the water supply, so he yielded with a groan. Rounding the pool, he followed the stream deeper into the cavern until the walls closed in, forming a tunnel. Only strands of luminescent spider silk caught above the waterline broke the darkness, and Rafi hesitated as the bank narrowed to a raised footpath just wide enough to traverse single file.

Nef had rebuffed his questions about the stream that first day. Why was that?

Curious, Rafi advanced, pushing out in front to keep clear of the colt's hindquarters. In that tight space, sounds were magnified a hundredfold: rushing water, clacking hooves, his own unsteady heartbeat thumping against the constraints of his chest. How long he walked, he did not know, mind pulsing and driving his steps as he finally, reluctantly, considered the future.

Every decision so far had been aimed at survival. Now, he needed a plan.

Remaining in the rebel camp was not a long-term option. Minor victories aside, the revolution's chances were slim, and Umut would undoubtedly soon call upon him to fulfill the oath he had made. He had been clinging to a vague notion of assuming a new identity and striking out deeper into old Nadaarian territory or across the wastes of Broken-Eliam, or maybe up north into Slyrchar. Sahak would not follow him there. Hopefully. But what of Iakki? Could he drag the boy into a new life without knowing the fate of the old?

Rafi rounded a bend and stopped short. Ahead, the tunnel ended in a circular chamber where the stream poured through a gaping hole and vanished in a swirl of mist. Huffed breaths struck his neck, and he let the colt squeeze past, not wanting to stand between it and that drop. Lowering its head, it snuffled around the rim and lipped up spray from the rocks.

Swallowing, Rafi inched to the edge of blackness. Water roared below. He could almost . . . almost . . . hear the sea throbbing, soldiers shouting, boots thudding . . .

Sahak screaming for them to yield.

Delmar's voice rang in his ears: *Run, brother!*

He swayed and scrambled back, lungs heaving. Something caught his eye opposite the waterfall, on the inside of the hole. Was that a ladder? Then loose stones skidded over the edge, kicked free by the sea-demon as it coiled to jump. No! Rafi yanked the lead too late. Down plunged the colt into the cascade, and his grip on the rope betrayed him. Down, he plunged after it into churning water and darkness.

Something nuzzled the back of Rafi's head as he pulled himself up the bank of the stream, coughing and spluttering. His head pulsed with a familiar throb. Whiskers tickled his forehead, then something harder grazed his skin. Teeth?

He opened his eyes to the sea-demon. "Are you eating my hair?"

Hooves crunched closer in answer.

He swatted its head away and scrambled to his feet before it could take a solid bite and decide that, yes, he was indeed quite tasty. Water splashed from his trousers and pooled in his footprints as he circled, surveying his surroundings.

The current had deposited them in a cave that opened upon daylight. No sign of the cascade from here, but a narrow footpath bordered the stream as far back as he could see. If that had been a rope ladder above, this was doubtless what Nef had sought to conceal: a secret entrance to the rebel camp. Odds stood he could return this same way, though the sea-demon likely couldn't, but given what it had dragged him into, maybe that wasn't so bad.

Rafi shook his head, recalling the plunge. "That was without a doubt the second most insane thing I have ever done." Or maybe the third. Charging a scadtha definitely ranked up there. So did taming a sea-demon, come to think of it.

He limped to the cave opening and emerged to a familiar landscape: thick jungle foliage, interspersed with patches of sand, rustled in a gentle breeze bearing the tang of salt and seaweed and fish guts drying in the sun. The Alon coast was near, and with it, Zorrad. No telling just how near until he broke out beyond the Mah onto the beach, but this was the closest he had been since leaving.

Nickering softly, the colt plodded alongside, pink-tinged nostrils lifted to the breeze. Sunlight highlighted the ravages of its time inland: drab coat, flaking scales, listless eyes.

"It is a sea-beast," Iakki had said. "Like me."

That decided him. Or rather, decided the matter for him.

He would return to Zorrad and face the consequences of his actions, find Sev if he still lived or weep over his grave and Torva's if he did not. Surely a brief visit could do no harm. Living among the Alonque was no longer an option for him now that Sahak had found him, but Iakki deserved the chance to return to his family, if they still lived, and the colt deserved to return to its kind too. To be free as he never could. But first . . .

Rafi snagged the colt's lead as it ambled past. "Care to save me some steps?"

FORTY-TWO: CERIDWEN & JAKIM

Earthriders gain strength and resilience, their bodies and bones capable of withstanding forces and impacts that would break any other.

A resounding crack drew Ceridwen's attention away from Adaan's frenzied efforts to stamp out the flames hissing around his boots and up to the crimson-streaked sky, where she expected to see winged steeds boiling through thickets of cloud in the wake of a lightning strike. Iona had sworn that here in this arid and rugged wasteland, the atmosphere was prime for a dry lightning attack that would not dampen Ceridwen's steed. She would have welcomed it regardless. But the sky remained empty, void of steeds, lightning, and arrows.

Had Iona missed Mindar's flaming signal? Then what was that sound?

She scanned the jagged line of spears visible over the palisade, noted the lack of ballista bolts hurtling toward her, and then dropped her gaze to Adaan and the ten soldiers who were tugging masks from their belts and strapping them to their faces—masks like the ones used by riverriders and seariders for breathing during extended dives.

A prickle ran down the back of her neck.

Was this the trap Finnian had feared? She looked to him and found him lifting his horn to his lips, ready to summon the attack. *Blazes*, where was Iona? She risked retribution against Gavin if she charged now, but if she did not, she risked yielding all. Teeth gritted, she nodded, dragged her sabre from her scabbard as the horn blared beside her ear, and summoned a spout of flames from Mindar that sent the dozen soldiers stumbling back, shields smoking.

She lunged after them. Her blade caught one shield and tore it away, exposing the soldier to a strike from Nold who thundered at her side on his earthhewn. The soldier fell, clearing a path toward Adaan who backed away, sword and shield raised. Fear etched stark lines across his face above the mask as she pounded toward him, sabre extended, heat building within Mindar until tendrils of smoke whipped around them.

One of Finnian's copper-fletched arrows took Adaan in the throat.

He swayed and fell and was trampled by Nold's earthhewn. She drew Mindar to a stuttering halt, seeking Finnian across the chaos. Nocking another arrow, he nodded sharply toward her cousin's limp form in the pool to their left, refocusing Ceridwen on their goal: rescue not retribution. Not yet, in any case.

Before she could break toward Gavin, Nold's shout, "The sky!" brought her gaze to the underbellies of the towering clouds, but instead of stormers streaking toward them, she saw a swarm of arrows and ballista bolts as long as spears. Not aimed for Gavin as the Nadaari had threatened, but for her. So long as he lived, the trap remained baited. So long as he lived, they knew she would remain within striking distance.

"Loose formation," she shouted.

Her patrol veered off on all sides, leaving Mindar alone. He reared his head back and breathed forth a rushing, roaring river of flame. It engulfed the first wave, consuming arrow shafts midflight, dropping the steel heads like hailstones. But his flames could not be everywhere at once. Missiles broke through and peppered the ground around her—*them*, rather, for a familiar pained curse made her aware that Finnian had remained on her flank. He shook his head, droplets of blood spraying from a gash carved by a passing arrow.

Stubborn, her heart whispered, and all within her warmed to the word.

That rumbling she felt in her chest, deeper than the rush of Mindar's inferno, that would be Markham and the *ayed* charging to support her. Soon they would be within bowshot too. Closer, another rumbling shook the earth, and a thunderous crash sounded as a section of the palisade shattered. Solborn poured through the gap: earthhewns in front, shadowers behind, and at their head, on his massive black steed, Kilmark te Bruin.

Seeing him was like the earth settling after a quake, jarring only in its sudden stillness. Of course he was here. He tore downhill toward the pool where Gavin was bound, and in the howling wind of his coming, blew distant, echoing horns.

"*No*!" The word was a prayer, a hope, a shout of defiance.

She raced into the raining arrows and felt one, two, three pierce Mindar's fire. It diminished but did not obliterate the force of their flight. One struck her saddlebow, one hammered her side, one spilled boiling blood from Mindar's neck. Behind, deafening collisions rang out, and she dared not look but could guess the cause: where Kilmark rode, Ondri was rarely far behind, and she–reckless, heedless–had blindly led her forces into ambush between them.

Gavin's gagged head twitched and lifted slightly, his dazed eyes settling on her.

"I am coming!" she cried, and for now, that alone mattered. Steam hissed as Mindar's hooves struck the pool, and he balked on the edge, limbs stiff, head tossing. Only a breath before she forced him onward, relinquishing the protection of his flames–smoke puffing to white, fire sputtering to ash–but that breath was all it took for Kilmark to charge ahead through a burst of glistening spray, his axe swinging for Gavin.

She was still paces away when it struck with a sickening crunch.

Not close enough to save him, only close enough to see the life leave his eyes.

Jakim had never held death in his hands before. He was drenched in cold sweat. Clutching the sphere to his chest, he dodged through the ranks of soldiers, aiming toward that newly broken gap in the palisade. For the first dozen steps, all was confusion, and he slipped through it like a snake through the tall grass, unnoticed.

Then—"Stop him! Thief!"—Khilamook's shouts caught up, and Jakim barely registered the words but they must have been Nadaarian, for hands suddenly reached out for him, spears shifted to block his path, and a sword swung for his throat.

"No!" The engineer's cane dashed the blow aside. "He must not fall. Seize him!"

Surrounded, Jakim hugged death to his chest and panted as the soldiers closed in. This was it then. The king's daughter would die, and he would die with her. Was *this* his grand purpose? Was this where Aodh's hand had led him?

The hair on his arms tingled.

Lightning struck with a resounding crack, blasting the nearest soldier off his feet. He crashed into two others, and all three fell. Hailstones pinged around him, and Jakim cowered over the sphere. One struck at his feet.

Not hail. Arrows. He risked a look up.

Winged shapes boiled from towering clouds, unleashing a hail of arrows and a sizzling web of lightning strikes that hammered the crater. Soldiers crouched and raised shields for cover, eyes and weapons turned upward. Jakim raised his head and found his path cleared. He broke into a run, scrambling up the slope of the crater, jamming his bare, bloody toes on rocks that shifted and skidded beneath him. He tripped and went down. Shoved up and stumbled on again.

Something cracked nearby, the snap of leather not of lightning.

A whip coiled around his ankles, yanking his feet out. He fell onto his face, grazing his forehead and the bridge of his nose on stone. Behind, Khilamook shrieked, and another voice let out a ragged scream. Groaning, Jakim pushed up onto his hands and knees and felt the sphere roll out from under him.

Gray wisps seeped from a hairline crack.

Energy surged through his limbs like he had been struck by

the lightning that bombarded the crater. Willing his lungs to still, he scrabbled backward on his hands and heels. His foot caught the sphere and sent it tumbling away, down the slope of the crater toward the Nadaari rallying against the unexpected attack from the skies.

It bounced once, twice, and shattered on a pointed stone. *No*!

The killing mist flooded the closest soldiers, dragging them gasping and writhing to the ground where they flopped like fish in a net. The rest scattered, fleeing for high ground or choking the palisade exits. Jakim shook free of his horror as the engineer's masked figure stalked from the mist. Cane whistling furiously through the air. Steps sharp and clipped.

Jakim had no mask of his own. His lungs already burned from lack of air. Yanking the neck of his tunic up over his nose, he floundered onward. Soon the fog would dissipate. Soon he would be able to breathe freely. Ahead, daylight shredded the mist. He staggered toward it.

Oh, Aodh, he was almost out–

Something slammed into his back, knocking him to his hands and knees. Reflexively, he gasped. Only a partial breath, but it felt like frothing seawater poured down his throat, filled his lungs, and flooded his chest with unrelenting pressure.

He couldn't . . . couldn't . . .

Breathe.

Khilamook toed him in the ribs, rolling him over. "Oh, never fear, boy, you will live long enough to regret this before you die."

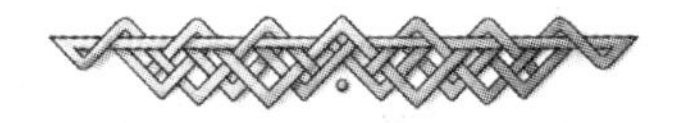

Gavin was dead. Lost like Fiona, like Bair, like her father.

Still Ceridwen dashed to his side as Kilmark charged into the fight. Still she bent over him, yanking the glove from one hand with her teeth and fumbling for a pulse. Still she pressed a trembling hand to his wound to halt the torrent of blood. But it was too late.

He was gone and she had no dawnling to recall him from the lands beyond the sun. Lightning crackled across the sky, and thunder roared in answer, but no rain spilled from those dark, churning clouds, and no tears spilled from the dry, aching eyes she raised to survey the fight.

Gavin had fallen, but her warriors had not. Not yet at least.

The rain of missiles slackened beneath the stormer attack as chaos raged through the Nadaari lines like a rampaging wildborn. Soldiers poured through gaps in the palisade and struggled to regain formations on the slope. Thinning gray smoke veiled the crater behind them. It was the wrong shade for a fireborn, the wrong shade for woodsmoke.

It was unnatural and her skin crawled at the sight.

At the base of the hill, Outriders and traitors were embroiled in a seething throng, locked stirrup to stirrup and blade to blade. It was nearly impossible to distinguish friend from foe in that tumult. Only, there–

Kilmark smashed through the Outriders, tall and imposing on his massive earthhewn, dark hair flying from beneath his helmet, axe blade dripping with blood. With a wild cry, Ceridwen spurred Mindar to meet him. Water shot up over her legs as they fled the pool. She narrowly evaded the shock of a collision with another earthhewn and slashed aside a spear thrust from a shadowrider, but she did not slow.

Her blood pulsed for retribution.

Only strides away, she summoned flame. Weak ribbons shot from Mindar's mouth and petered out in the next breath. He was still waterlogged, flames extinguished. The battle frenzy would heat his blood, rekindling the fires deep in his gut, but until it did, she had only her sabre and his speed as weapons.

Kilmark's axe intercepted her strike for his neck, knocking her blade toward the earthhewn's hindquarters where it glanced off a hide of stone. The shock numbed her arm, but Mindar's sidestep saved her from the axe's backswing. It missed her chest by a handbreadth.

"'She that rides the fireborn.'" Kilmark's voice rang hollowly inside his helm. "How can you hope to defeat me when you have no fire?"

The earthhewn swung its horned head.

Ceridwen tried to force Mindar away, but the sea of steeds held him fast. She flung up her blade arm–blocking would shatter her sabre–and slung her weight over into her left stirrup. The blow only glanced her side. But such a blow. Pain exploded in her ribs. She crashed against Mindar's neck and gasped for breath.

"Ceridwen!" Finnian's shout came from a distance, and arrows pinged off metal.

She had been separated from Finnian since she rode for Gavin, but though still cut off, he harassed Kilmark, giving her time to recover. She coughed and groaned. *Blazes.* Closing with the earthhewn had been a mistake. She might as well have tried to halt a falling boulder by standing in its path. At least she had kept her blade.

Kilmark rounded on her, breathing raggedly as he hefted his axe. His steed snorted a blast like a trumpet and stamped a hoof. "Look at you. You are nothing without your fireborn."

Ceridwen forced herself upright, gasping at her aching ribs. Her upper arm burned where the earthhewn's horn had sliced through her leather jerkin and the flesh beneath. But the pain was manageable, if she could only tear free of this riotous mess. Out into the open where Mindar could sprint circles around the massive beast, where he could not be pinned against a wall of horseflesh, where he could unleash fire without harming her own.

She ducked Kilmark's axe to charge through a break in the fray and felt the earthhewn thunder after her. Rounding the hill, she gave Mindar his head for one glorious run, soaking in the warmth spreading up his ribcage as the race rekindled his flame. Then with the battle noise dwindling behind her, she reined him back, slowing until she could hear the earthhewn's heaving breaths and the rattling of Kilmark's armor with each pounding stride. Cracks spidered across the ground as the earthhewn neared.

One breath. Two breaths. *Now.*

Heel to the inside, she whipped into a turn the massive solborn could not replicate, and, as Kilmark crashed past, summoned a rush of flame that engulfed steed and rider.

"I *am* fireborn," she said.

Out of the flames, Kilmark screamed for blood. He plunged to a halt, beating at his smoldering hair and cloak. But Ceridwen did not relent. She flamed at the earthhewn's tail and dodged a howling hoof strike as she tried to close in on its flank. Its hide could withstand all but a sustained inferno, but Kilmark could roast in his armor like meat in a cookpot.

He roared and swung his steed's massive head like a ram again, but her fleet fireborn danced aside and blasted the earthhewn's face. Startled, it reared back, forelegs flailing. Higher and higher it rose, and Mindar advanced at her urging, flames bleeding swiftly from orange to yellow to radiant white. Too swiftly.

Ceridwen recognized the signs too late. She'd demanded too much too soon after his rekindling. Mindar shuddered, stumbled, and the inferno died. They were exposed. She spun him away, to regroup–

But the earthhewn had risen too high. It teetered on its hindlegs and collapsed backward. Kilmark leaped free an instant before its thunderous crash. He hit hard and rolled.

Mindar coughed out weak, white smoke.

"You . . . are utterly . . . insane," Kilmark rasped, clutching his axe. He used it to shove himself back to his feet where he swayed, favoring one leg. Burns streaked his face beneath his helmet. "What now? Will you burn me where I stand?"

Ceridwen breathed deep and felt no pain, borne upon the winds of fury. Her steed might be spent, but an inferno still raged in her veins, demanding vengeance for Idolas, for her father, for Gavin. She had stood wounded and unhorsed before Kilmark once. Now, she could crush him as he would have crushed her, and it would be no less than just.

Kilmark sneered. "It is as I said. Without fire you are nothing."

Nothing. Never enough. Worth only the life she could sacrifice in atonement for the life that had been lost. His words stung old wounds. She let the reins slip from her fingers, ground-tying her steed, and dismounted to face him on foot.

Kilmark turned and ran.

She stared as he wove unevenly from side to side, then took off after him and caught him only strides from his struggling earthhewn. He swung for her head, but she twisted inside and slammed a foot into his injured leg, sending him down.

She waited for him to rise.

"The irony," he gasped from the ground, "is we should be allies, not enemies."

"Allies?" Her laugh sounded unhinged, echoing hollowly off the shallow rise behind her and the hill behind it, and she realized they were utterly alone, cut off from the battle, from both friend and foe. "You betrayed your country. Your king."

"I gave him a warrior's death." Kilmark struggled to one knee, grounding his axe to steady himself. "It was more than he deserved. Surely you did not weep. He branded you. You should be glad we have a chance to restore this kingdom to its former glory–not this ruin the war-chiefs have made of it. I argued that you should join us before Idolas, but he doubted your resolve. You could change his mind if you swore to our cause."

"He? Ondri?" She struggled to follow his words. Had he admitted to killing her father? "*Kasar* or no, I am no traitor. I will swear to no cause but grinding your bones into the dust."

His expression hardened. "My bones are not at risk."

Too late, she sensed movement behind. Too late, she turned, sabre rising to block. Too late, she glimpsed Ondri's hulking form charging up on his shadower, spear aimed at her heart. Then a gray blur leaped between them, intercepting the spear with a solid *thunk*, and a second shadower crashed to the ground, catapulting its rider past her head.

"Finnian." The word was a breath, not a prayer, for too often those had gone unanswered.

She leaped past the thrashing shadower and thrust her sabre into Ondri's armored side before he could recover his spear from the dying steed. He cried out, folding over the wound, and wheeled away. She spun back toward Finnian–but it was Markham who rose, blood running down his shaggy hair from a gash above his temple. He gave his head a shake, and reached awkwardly for his fallen sword.

Kilmark lurched upright with a roar, swinging his axe.

It missed Markham's chest and slammed into his outstretched arm instead, snapping bone and severing the limb. Never before had she heard her Apex scream. He dropped to his knees, and Kilmark raised the axe again, but Ceridwen was already on the move. Her blade crashed into the back of his head.

The hilt slipped her nerveless fingers, and she sidestepped his fall to catch Markham in her arms, easing him to the ground. Not Markham too. Oh, flames and floods and storms above, not Markham. His head rolled back against her shoulder.

In a blink, everything changed.

She was kneeling over Bair beside the crater of Koltar.

She was bandaging his wounds in vain, knowing that it was too late.

She was stumbling home, his body cold and stiff against her shoulders.

But then she surfaced in the present where it was not too late, not yet, and whipped the belt from Markham's waist, wrapped it tight about the stump, slid his pipe into the knot and used it to twist again and again until the flow halted. It was working. It was–

His eyes fluttered shut and his ragged breathing faded.

"Markham . . . *Markham*?"

FORTY-THREE: RAFI

We are all of us snared in the coils of a python.
– Choth proverb

Rafi only fell off three times en route to the coast. He counted that a victory, all things considered. The first fall had been the most embarrassing . . . and painful. He had overshot his jump onto the colt's back, slid off the other side, and landed sprawled in a thorn bush. A full day later, there were still barbs in his backside. Riding aggravated the wounds, not to mention being incredibly jarring. The Soldonians had built their entire culture on the backs of their steeds, so either they were insane or he was doing something wrong.

Maybe a lot of somethings wrong.

The colt sped up as they drew nigh the sea, grunting with each stride, sweat slicking its hide, until they finally burst from the Mah and its hooves sank into deep sand. Rafi whispered to it until it slowed, then gratefully slid off and crumpled to his knees, rubbing the feeling back into his legs. He knew this beach. It sat only a few hours' walk north of Zorrad.

His grip on the lead hindered the colt from bolting toward the waves. Rather than leaving the tail-end flapping, he had tied it to the nose band, creating a loop he could pull on to steer, or at least aim them in the general direction he wanted–say, within a couple miles or so. Only the Soldonians knew how many mistakes he had made, and yet, it *was* working. But now they were here, and sneaking into Zorrad would be impossible with the colt tailing him. It was time to return it to the sea so it could be free.

Stiffly, Rafi stood and reached for the knot, but the glistening water beckoned to him as it struck the beach and receded, singing of endless depths and vivid worlds waiting below. Maybe he could take one final ride first. He gripped the colt's mane and swung astride its back, then with the wind in his teeth and waves thrumming in his chest, he roared the war cry of the Tetrani and raced forward, skimming over sand, crashing through shallows, and bounding over the deep.

Saltwater welled around him.

Spray misted his face.

He flung his head back, drinking in freedom.

Then the sea-demon dove, and Rafi sucked in a rushed breath before he was pulled under. He flattened against the colt's rippling neck as it surged forward with powerful strides, and its mane fluttered across his face. Deeper and deeper, they went. Panic started to rise in his chest, but his lungs weren't straining, and his vision was clear. Like it had in the river, his single breath sustained him far longer than it should have, and he forced himself to relax as the colt frolicked beneath the waves.

It darted after silvery fish. It curved and gamboled around feathery sea fans.

Its playfulness reminded him of Iakki, and Rafi found himself grinning like a fool and throwing his arms wide as the colt finally surfaced in a shower of spray. Both he and the colt gasped in air, ribs heaving in unison, and he let out a laugh that skipped across the waves.

This could be a life worth living.

But it could not be his. Not while Sahak prowled the jungle, hunting him. Not while the Que Revolution raged against the empire's control. Not while Iakki pined for a home that might have been destroyed because of him.

Sobered by these thoughts, he rode ashore, dismounted, and untied the rope, letting it fall to the sand where it coiled like a cast-off snakeskin. Of course, the greedy colt tried to nibble on it, so Rafi snatched it back. "Is there anything you won't eat? Go on! You're–"

It took off at an ambling jog, nose trailing above the sand, strands of wispy white concealing its eyes. Abruptly, its head shot up and it charged into the surf, tail streaming like a banner. Into the heart of a wave, it dove and vanished. Rafi lingered, waiting for it to surface, but he saw nothing but roiling water and heard nothing but hissing seafoam and felt nothing but an ache in his throat as he took up the rope and turned to leave.

"Free," he whispered.

There was a soft nicker behind him. Receding waves left the sea-demon in the shallows, dripping as it regarded him wistfully. It stamped a hoof, whisking the water for an instant into a miniature whirlpool with crystalline sand visible at its center, and squealed playfully. It sounded nothing like the wails that had haunted Rafi's sleep, but still he shivered.

Rafi tore himself away but jerked to a halt, vision centering on the harpoon point hovering inches from his eyes. Spine tingling, he looked down the haft to the knotted fists, burly shoulders, and ragged black hair of the wielder.

He swallowed reflexively. "Sev?"

"Nahiki." Sev's voice was like steel on stone, bereft of warmth or welcome. He did not lower the harpoon. "Or should I say Rafi Tetrani? I thought you were dead."

"You don't seem too thrilled I'm not."

"I *hoped* you were."

"You're not the only one."

"No, I am not." Sev's lips drew tightly over gritted teeth. "So brave, I thought you. Killed a scadtha. Defied the priests. Fit to join the revolution and cast them down. Turns out, you're one of them. And even they want you dead."

"Sev, I can–"

"Net your lying tongue before I cut it out. It's done enough damage."

Sev jabbed the harpoon at his face, forcing Rafi to take a step back, hands rising defensively. He had stared death in the eye too often to mistake the wild, desperate, hate-filled look in Sev's eyes now, and the last shards of Nahiki within him broke to see it. Instinctively, he looked to the sea-demon, but it was capering about in the waves chasing fish and did not notice the threat. Not that it would have done anything if it did.

It was only a beast, after all.

"First Torva . . . then Iakki?" Sev's voice broke. "How are you the one who lived?"

Rafi had asked himself that same question for years, but this time, it seemed there was a crucial misunderstanding. He and Iakki had vanished in the chaos of the fight. It must have looked like they'd both drowned. "Sev . . ." He pried his tongue from the roof of his mouth as Sev's knuckles whitened. "Iakki lives."

The fisherman blinked at him, mouth forming soundless words.

"He is safe and with the rebels, I swear it is true."

Slowly, the harpoon dipped until its point rested in the sand, and Sev freed a hand to shove the hair back from his eyes, revealing bloodshot whites and deep shadows beneath. "But . . . how? Why should I believe you? You are a liar."

"But not a fool. And only a fool would lie about Iakki's death and risk angering his ghost." It was a jest, dangled as an overture of peace.

Sev's lips twitched briefly. "It would be a vengeful one."

"It would at that." And Rafi had ghostly trouble enough as it was.

Sev pulled back, shifting the harpoon out of the sand, and beckoned Rafi forward. "Come. Sit. Tell me everything."

"So," Rafi said, leaning in with a grin, "for days, these cala root crackers had been disappearing, and Saffa refused to blame the obvious culprit, her monkey. So, we coated the next batch in ground sniffle pod and traced the sneezing to find not only the monkey but Iakki covered in crumbs. Somehow, he'd trained the beast to steal for him!"

Sev only grunted and prodded the fire so it crackled beneath the fish speared over the flames. Probably not the tale he had expected, but "everything" was a vague request, and Iakki's mischief-making was far more interesting than a litany of Rafi's narrow escapes. Cheating death too often made for a dull story. Stakes too low. Events too predictable. Boring.

Rafi loved boring. Just not in storytelling.

Judging by Sev's posture—hunched over his knees, harpoon inches from his hands, forehead knotted like the ridged bark of the neefwa tree they camped under—his life had been anything but boring lately. He wore the burden of each day since the priests had come like an ill-fitting skin: hard lines around his mouth, hollows in his cheeks, a restlessness that reminded Rafi of Iakki's incessant need for movement.

"He asks about you a lot," Rafi said. "He wants to come home."

Sev looked up from his cooking. "Why didn't you bring him with you?"

"I had to see what things were like. I didn't know what had happened after . . ." Rafi hoped Sev would snag the line and speak, but the fisherman just grunted again. Sighing, Rafi eyed the makeshift camp they had hiked half a mile to reach. Sheltered beneath the scant shade offered by the lanky limbs of a neefwa tree, it consisted of an oilcloth bedroll, sagging supply sack, and only a chipped pot to boil seaweed tea and a single cup to drink it. "You live out here?"

"Here. There. Wherever the wind may take me."

"And . . ." Rafi hesitated. "Does it ever take you home?"

Sev's expression darkened, but a piercing shriek interrupted them. The sea-demon had followed their trek down the beach and now pranced ashore dragging a massive clump of seaweed across the sand. Was it still hungry?

"I touched one once, you know."

Rafi turned to find Sev staring at the colt. "You did?"

Sev nodded slowly. "It was . . . softer than I expected. And those eyes . . . silver, like moonlight on calm waters. I thought myself a prince among the Alonque to survive such an encounter. Next day, my father drowned at sea. I knew then that the legends are true. Sea-demons are cursed, and they curse all who cross their paths."

Deep hurt flooded his words, the kind Rafi knew too well and avoided at all costs. Humor was his lifeline. It kept his head above water.

"When I saw you ride up on that thing, I thought you a ghost," Sev said.

"Oh, I'm fairly certain this skull-splitting headache says otherwise, unless you think ghosts are corporeal enough to feel pain." Rafi felt a tinge of that hurt seeping into his words. "You could always stab me to make sure. That was your initial plan, wasn't it? Or did you just want to kill me?"

Sev slapped his hands against the sand. "What do you want from me, Rafi Tetrani? I fought to save my brother from a danger you brought upon him. I left soldiers bleeding in the sand. That is not the sort of thing your empire forgets."

Rafi knew what it was to be hunted, to see your world overturned and everything stripped away until only fear remained. "Why not leave the coast? Come to the rebels. You and Kaya would be welcomed . . . if only because Kaya can control Iakki's mischief. She is the only one he . . ." He stopped at the pain that bled across Sev's face. He knew then, knew and wished Nef had drowned him because the cause of such suffering did not deserve to live.

"Oh, Ches-Shu," he breathed. "Kaya?"

Sev rubbed his forehead with both hands. "Half the village too, that same night. So no, Nahiki or Rafi or whatever I should call you, the wind does not blow me home. I do not even know if home still stands."

This Rafi had feared since Sahak emerged from the jungle like a monster on the prowl. He had stayed away to avoid facing it. He seized the cup of seaweed tea and downed it, not caring how it scalded his throat. "Sev, I–"

"Stop." Sev took a ragged breath and yanked the knife from his belt to prod the sizzling fish. "Keep your pity and give me back my brother."

"I can take you to him."

"No." Sev shook his head. "I want no part in revolution. Not anymore. You bring Iakki to me and then get back to your rebel friends."

This Rafi had longed for, to cast off the mooring lines of responsibility and be free. But the part of him that was Nahiki, that had dared dream of a hut by the sea and a boat named after his sister . . . or maybe his bride . . . could not imagine life without Iakki to rib him, Sev to challenge him, and Torva to anchor them all.

Rafi hitched himself closer to Sev. "What if I want no part in revolution either? I have seen both it and the empire up close, and the rebels don't stand a chance. But we could journey deeper inland, together, maybe to Broken-Eliam or—"

"You *are* mad. That is dangerous country."

"How bad can it be?"

"So bold now, are we?" Sev scoffed, turning the knife slowly in his hands. "No, you and me are through, Rafi. You are on your own. Do whatever you want, just return my brother first."

Rafi shifted uncomfortably, watching the blade. Sahak had always fiddled with knives like that on his frequent visits to taunt him and Delmar through their dungeon bars, spinning the blades between his fingers and up around his wrists before lashing out and sending them flying, unbelievably deft, impossibly fast. Delmar had caught one in the forearm to save Rafi once, and the guards had swarmed in not to help him but to retrieve the blade.

How it had bled . . . and how Sahak had laughed . . .

He licked his dry lips. "I swear."

The knife flashed toward him, and he jerked. Something tugged on the side of his head, then Sev sat back, holding the chunk of hair bound with the bead strand. "This I will hold, Nahiki of the Alonque, until your oath is fulfilled."

Cold waves flooded Rafi. "Give it back." Cutting off an Alonque's bead strand was reserved for the highest offenses. It declared him guilty of serious injury to a tribe member and demanded redress, either given willingly or taken by means of the elder's rod. That Rafi could swallow, but the strand was all he had of Torva.

Sev pocketed it. "Three days at the lightning tree. Do not keep me waiting."

Rafi knew that jaw-jutted look of defiance well. Pressing the matter would end in blows. "Three days?" He eyed the sun streaking the sky with scarlet, orange, and gold, the colors of Nadaar, as it sank toward the dark canopy of the Mah jungle. "That's not much time."

"Good thing you need not walk."

Rafi traced his nod to the grazing colt and gave a pained smile. "Ah, lucky me." He had hoped to set it free, but it seemed Ches-Shu had other plans for them both. "Best not wait to eat." He dug a chunk from the roasting fish, burning his fingertips, and juggled it between his fingers until it was cool enough to toss in his mouth, then Rafi snatched up his rope and loped off to catch a sea-demon.

FORTY-FOUR: JAKIM

Aodh is near.

Jakim felt like he was drowning.

Rough earth shifted beneath his scrabbling fingers, a stone dug into his spine, and lightning-charged air sizzled across his skin, and yet he strained as if against the weight of the sea to draw air through the flooded passages of his lungs. His panic increased with each wheezing breath, and he sensed his mind slipping away.

His vision darkening.

He could no longer recall the truths of Aodh.

Or the words of Siba, his sister. *"You, Jakim, will . . ."*

Will what? Die in pursuit of a foolish vow in a foreign land, far from his home, far from his kin, far from the hand of Aodh?

A shadow blotted out the setting sun above, yet the killing fog had long since vanished. Blinking resolved the blurred shape into the engineer. Khilamook held his cane before him in both hands, twisted, and slid the concealed blade from within. "In Canthorian custom, ink markings are meant to tell the truth of who we are," he mused. "What mark, then, should I add to yours? Exile. Slave. Thief." He bent closer, voice dropping to a hiss. "Liar?"

He slid the thin blade across Jakim's cheek, sending pinpricks of fire down his jaw. "You have ruined me, boy. You have stolen my revenge and my—" His voice cut off as a writhing snake looped around his chest and yanked him to the ground. He scrabbled in the dirt, trying to stand, but another snake snared his ankles and dropped him flat.

The air throbbed in Jakim's ears.

No, not the air. *Wings.*

Flying steeds alighted in a rush, warriors leaping from saddles to surround Khilamook and bind him with the snakes—no, ropes—in their hands. His enraged shouts were muffled by a cloak thrown over his head, then one of the Soldonians slung him over the back of a steed and prepared to dash away.

Could they be true Soldonians then and not traitors?

"Wait . . ." Jakim tried to call out, but it emerged as a croak. His limbs were heavy, his head more so, but he managed to roll over onto his side and grab at a passing cloak. The flat of a blade knocked his hand away and he crumpled, face grinding in the dust.

"What is it?" a bluff female voice called.

"Found another, I think." This, a rough male voice directly overhead.

"Not pale enough . . . though those markings are surely Canthorian."

Others spoke up then, but their words shifted and blurred, blending together in his ears. Boots and hooves crunched closer and armored figures and winged steeds closed around. Jakim's vision faded for an instant, and everything dimmed like a candle blown out on a dark night, then he came to again and willed his hand to move, trembling, painstakingly slow, to the neckline of his tunic.

To the leather strap and the lump of metal it held.

He shoved it before him like a shield. "Ceridwen . . . Ceridwen . . ."

FORTY-FIVE: CERIDWEN

Stormriders gain resistance to cold temperatures and high altitudes and are capable of acclimating to the high, energy-charged atmospheres they traverse.

Markham yet lived. His pulse throbbed rapidly beneath her fingers. Ceridwen breathed deeply in relief, though she knew his wound needed skilled care to prevent shock or infection from claiming him. She rose and only then realized she was not alone.

Brown, roan, and dun shadowers surrounded her, arrows nocked to bowstrings but not yet drawn. Her hand flew to her scabbard. Empty. She surveyed the riders. Half were clad in the patterned green-and-brown cloaks of the kill-squads of Craignorm, Eagan's chiefdom. Half bore the golden sun and dawnling of Ardon on their chests and stared at Kilmark's corpse with undisguised anger. *Blazes*, she was a thrice-cursed fool for riding on alone.

How long had they been there?

Her steed grazed where she'd left him. Her blade was still buried in Kilmark's skull. With no weapon but boldness, she straightened before the silent warriors, ruthlessly smothering her own fluttering fear. "You might have helped me save him."

Without a word, the shadowers parted before a broad-shouldered man with dark hair hanging straight to his shoulders, twin scars curving down his cheeks, and twin blades sheathed on his back. Lord Eagan himself. The Fox. His eyes were golden today like sun-scorched grass. Behind him, on a blood bay fireborn, rode Rhodri te Oengus, clad in a cuirass that gleamed with fresh oil and buffing, wearing a helmet that shadowed his face.

Her mouth went dry. Were they here to claim her life?

Eagan leaned forward in the saddle, a curious expression on his face. “So, the spirits of warriors past have seen fit t’ let ye live yet again, eh tal Desmond?”

“So it would seem.” She met his gaze steadily. Here in Lochrann, she was war-chief if not queen, and though standing alone, she would not be intimidated. “Why are you here?”

“We heard the battle on the wind an’ came t’ investigate.” His shadower shifted restlessly, stamping a silent hoof. He settled the steed with a flick of his reins. “Pity the fighting was over so soon.”

Shouting quelled her retort.

The shadowers shifted, and Finnian broke through the circle with his wolfhound and her patrol hard on his heels. Sweat dripped from his dark hair, streaking his face. He rode with his bow drawn, steering with weight placement and legs alone, until he saw her and slowed. “*Shades,* Ceridwen, I thought . . .”

His voice trailed off, eyes falling to Markham.

The bow fell from his hands, and he flung himself from the saddle to inspect the wound and tourniquet. “He is still losing blood. He needs a healer and . . . we should cauterize.”

His voice had gone cold and harsh. It was hardly recognizable.

“Bring flame, Ceridwen, before he dies.”

That stung her to action. None tried to halt her as she retrieved her steed and cued Mindar to sputtering flame, heating the knife Finnian gave her until its warmth radiated through her treated leather gloves. She offered it back to Finnian.

He shook his head and leaned his weight on Markham’s chest. “Fire is your domain.”

The edge in his voice revealed the truth. He blamed her for this as her father had blamed her for Bair, and he was right. Fire *was* her domain, for like it, she blazed through those she loved and left only ash behind.

Teeth clenched, she set the knife as he directed.

A howl tore from Markham's lips. He thrashed and fought with the strength of an earthhewn. Other warriors dropped beside Finnian, adding their weight to his, while she held the knife, jaw rigid against the sizzle of singeing flesh, until Finnian nodded. "It is done." Then she cast the knife aside and stumbled back, fighting the surge of bile in her throat.

Each inhalation carried the stench of burned flesh. Her forehead throbbed, and her muscles twitched to rub away the ache of her own branding. She should be stronger than this. But she could only stand there, shivering, as Finnian and three others made a stretcher out of spears and cloaks and lifted Markham onto it. She could only watch as Finnian whistled for his wolfhound and shadower to follow and then moved swiftly away, calling for a healer. She could not even whisper his name before her voice died and all she could taste was ash on her tongue, in her throat, in her lungs.

"Markham te Hoard is a good man," Eagan observed, saddle creaking as he dismounted to stand beside her and the few of her patrol who remained. He had the compact, lean build of a Rhiakki tribesman, shorter on his feet than his height atop the rangy shadower had led her to believe. His presence forced her to grasp the torn shreds of her composure and stitch them together. "The *ayeds* he dispatched to Craignorm proved their worth in halting the Nadaarian northward advance. Will he live, do you think?"

"If the warrior spirits will it."

Months ago, Eagan had argued for her release so the spirits might judge her in combat. It felt fitting now to cast those words in his teeth since she had no more prayers to offer for Markham's survival and even less hope that anyone listened. She stalked over to Kilmark, set her boot against his spine, and retrieved her sabre but did not sheathe it. Both the blade and her hands were coated in blood. Like always.

She looked up as Rhodri halted beside her, regarding Kilmark with his arms knotted over his cuirass and a grim expression accentuating the hollows beneath his eyes. A scruffy beard shadowed his jaw, granting a hard, rough-hewn cast to his face. The months since she'd seen him last had not been kind to him. There had been bars between them then, and he had held the key. Now he looked ragged and worn thin.

"Where were you riding from?" she asked, seeking to root out the meaning of their coming. She dared not hope they had come to answer her claim or swear their steeds to the defense of the kingdom. Hope was a cruel blade slipped neatly between the ribs.

"North," Eagan answered at the same time Rhodri said, "West."

Rhodri shoved his helmet back and wiped the sweat from his brow. "I chased the traitors from Ardon," he explained, voice raw with frustration as he detailed his futile pursuit, its abrupt end in a summons to Rysinger, coincidental meeting with Eagan en route, and their sighting of her forces on the move. It was a neat tale, deftly tied off, and so it grated upon Ceridwen, though maybe it was only the events of her life that ran wild and unchecked. "I was loath to leave the traitors' ashes unscattered, so when we heard . . ." he broke off, frowning down at Kilmark. "You have spared me that sorrow."

Was it the sorrow of missing out on retribution? Or of wielding it against one of his own?

She could muster no sympathy for either. Wisdom dictated tact and diplomacy—she needed the war-chiefs—but grief raged through her like a wildborn unleashed. Gavin dead, Markham wounded, her forces nearly routed, and though her ride to Cenyon had not been in vain and Telweg had agreed to test her strategy, still the Nadaari crawled inland, and she could not halt them alone. "Much sorrow might have been spared had the war-hosts mustered after Idolas rather than retreating to shield their own."

"As you have done here in Lochrann?" Rhodri replied. "Or did I miss your warriors riding to aid Ardon? There are multiple fronts to this war, Ceridwen, and you are not the only one fighting it."

"I know that—"

"You might take care to modulate your tone then"—even as his sharpened—"or the next time you get yourself ambushed, you might find none willing to save you."

Ceridwen tightened her hold on her sabre. "To be clear, this is you saving me?"

"Actually." Eagan coughed. "I daresay our esteemed battlemaster is referring t' the shadower kill-squads I dispatched t' relieve your beleaguered forces."

"Not a moment too soon," Rhodri added, eyebrows raised.

She knew and despised that gently reproving look, having received it too often growing up. Meeting his expectations had proved as challenging as meeting her father's. His opinion no longer mattered–she reminded herself–but Markham's did, and he had told her to lead. Instead, she had been led away in pursuit of vengeance.

"Spare your gratitude, tal Desmond," Eagan said with a flick of his hand. "'Twas nothing personal. I will hunt my enemy wheresoever he may be an' sleep the sweeter for his death whomsoever delivers it, though I'll admit I'd have paid a fair sum t' witness this." He nodded at Kilmark, golden eyes alight with interest. "Tell me did he beg for mercy at the end?"

Now that the battle was ended, weariness weighted her limbs, and her aching ribs demanded attention. "If he did, it was not to me." Nor would she have offered it. She turned to retrieve Mindar and return to her battered forces but saw Iona walking up, leading her stormer. Wisps of hair frizzled out from her braid, charged by the static of the clouds she had flown through, but it was something in her expression that made Ceridwen's heart stumble.

Oh, *blazes . . .*

Not Liam too?

If Iona was startled by the presence of the war-chiefs, she gave no sign, merely acknowledged them with a brief bow before straightening with an expression of grim satisfaction that eased Ceridwen's fear. "We've got him, Ceridwen."

"Who?"

"The Canthorian from the manuscripts. It was Liam's talk put him in my mind, and no sooner had we attacked than I saw his markings and embroidered robes, so we swooped in and got him."

Iona's eyes lowered, lips tightening into a line, and she held her clenched fist out. "There's more. He had another with him—a slave, I think. He had *this*."

Gold gleamed between Iona's fingers.

Ceridwen knew that gold. Its deep, molten red hue had been forever seared into her vision even as the *kasar* seared her forehead. On Iona's palm lay a thick ring with a circular shield emblazoned with a rearing horse whose tail and mane crackled with flames.

Eagan let out a sharp breath. "Is that—"

Her voice was thick in her throat. "It is."

The ring of kings and queens, passed down through the centuries since Uthold the Bold had ridden flaming from the east and forged the nation of Soldonia out of the warrior chiefdoms. The ring of her father, lost when he fell in the earthhewn charge. The ring that should have been hers by right of blood.

If not by her father's will.

Then the ring was in her hand, shockingly heavy against her palm, and Iona was closing her fingers around it. "It is yours, Ceridwen. Your father has named you heir."

Ceridwen followed Iona into the tent erected for the wounded and found herself standing among lines of bedrolls where bandaged forms shivered, sweated, and groaned in pain. Her gaze snagged on Finnian sitting with shoulders hunched and head bowed beside Markham, but he did not look up, and so she pressed onward, barely hearing Iona's rushed explanation of her discovery of the injured lad with the Canthorian markings who had collapsed after declaring her the heir, brought down by the mysterious fog that had decimated the Nadaari but dissipated before harming her forces.

Likewise, Eagan's brusque demands for answers were only a distant rumble broken by Rhodri's hoarse queries after the lad's health—down with fever, not looking good—for Ceridwen still held the ring and Iona's words still pealed in her ears.

Named heir?

She dared not believe it.

At the far end of the tent, Iona spun back to face them, eyes flashing a warning for silence though they all outranked her, and then stepped aside. The boy lay as still as death on a bedroll that was surely Iona's, laboring for each breath. A thin crop of hair covered his skull, an iron collar circled his throat, and the torn neck of his ragged tunic revealed whip scars crisscrossing his skin while intricate lines of script wound up and down his forearms—like the old Scroll who used to inhabit Rysinger's Sanctuary—but it was his pained face that captured Ceridwen's attention. He was so young.

Surely no older than Bair had been—

"*Blazes.*" Rhodri broke the hush. "He will be dead before the dawn."

Iona glared at him, but standing over that motionless form, straining to see his chest rise, knowing the pitiless nature of the world, Ceridwen believed it. Of course the boy would die. Of course she would be denied answers. What foolishness to dare hope. Shaking his head, Rhodri turned to leave, only to be forestalled by Eagan's upraised hand.

"Rest awhile an' we may see."

"I cannot delay my return to Rysinger." Yet Rhodri hesitated and ruefully sought Ceridwen's eyes. "You should know that Lord Glyndwr has summoned all the war-chiefs to a meeting two days hence."

"I received no summons . . ."

"No, you did not." His tone ruled out any chance of coincidence. "Yet you will come?"

She was suddenly weary of the struggle and sick with sorrow, but she could not refuse this opportunity to rally the war-chiefs. "I will come."

"There's the Ceridwen I know." Rhodri's expression relaxed, gleaming with something akin to pride, and he nodded before departing. Eagan muttered something about seeing to his riders and strode after him.

This too, Ceridwen must do.

She must walk the battlefield and gather reports. She must build a pyre for her cousin and tell of his exploits. She must tend to her steed's injuries–minor, thankfully–and then, perhaps, she could see to her own. With Iona's promise that she would be summoned if the boy awakened, she escaped the suffocating tent into a chill night that felt charged with change and ruin and the souls of the departed.

The night was waning when she returned to find torches burning low, healers shuffling exhaustedly through rounds, and too many bloodstained bedrolls lying vacant. Finnian was absent from Markham's side, but his wolfhound stood watch in his place. Cù's ears lifted at her approach, but the sight of Markham's bandaged stump stole her breath, and she pressed onward to the back of the tent where the boy slept.

She sat, turning the ring over and over in her fingers. Minutes passed. Hours, maybe. Then a sharp breath drew her gaze down. Sweat streaked the boy's brow and his skin had a dull, ashen hue in the dim light, but his eyes were open and fixed on her.

He lived. *Blazes,* he lived.

"Do you . . . know me?" she asked in Nadaarian.

"Yes," he breathed, voice barely audible. "You are the heir."

That word reverberated through her like the thunder of an earthhewn charge. Only slowly did she realize he had answered her in accented Soldonian. Ceridwen begged him to explain, and he did. His tone and cadence were those of a practiced oral storyteller, but he lacked the wind to speak for long without falling to a coughing fit. Yet the tale that unfolded was one she never could have imagined. She had thought her father dead the instant the earth collapsed, lost in glory. Instead, he had suffered long in crushing agony until his own warriors beheaded him. Had she known, Kilmark would never have died by her blade. Only an inferno could have sufficed.

"You were with him then, when he died?"

The boy–Jakim, he'd called himself–licked his dry lips. "With his dying breath, he named you heir. In Aodh's name, I swear it."

Oh, how she longed to believe it. Those words sparked a flame that rushed to fill the cold, aching hollow of her chest. "His living words told a different tale. He did not name me in life. Why would he do so in death?"

Jakim focused up at her, and the maturity in his eyes made her reconsider her impression of his age. His thin frame and boyish features appeared youthful, but his eyes . . . his eyes had seen much sorrow and pain. "I do not know the words he spoke in life, but we spoke of mercy before he died–" He broke off, wheezing, clutching at the neck of his tunic.

Ceridwen went quickly to search for water. By the time she returned with a flask and a healer, the fit had passed and he was asleep. Questions still swirled in her mind, but she would get no more out of him tonight, and if she would attend the war-meet, she needed rest before departing, lest she nod off and fall from the saddle mid-gallop.

Turning, she found Finnian behind her, drooping with exhaustion, the grime and stink of battle still clinging to him. He rubbed a hand over his bloodshot eyes and weary face. "I am glad for you, Ceridwen," he said, nodding toward the ring she carried.

It was not gladness in his voice.

She could not meet his eyes. "Glyndwr has called a war-meet. We ride in the morning."

"I should wish you speed then."

So, he would not be riding with her. She should have expected it. Nor would Iona, for she trusted none other to question Jakim when he recovered, which meant Liam should remain as well. Maybe it was best. Only recently had she become accustomed to such companionship. Only recently had she dared let herself long for it.

Now so many pyres blazed because of her.

That knowledge roughened her voice. "How is Markham?"

"How do you think, Ceridwen? He lost a limb. Injuries like that shock the body, and if the wound sours . . ." He worked his jaw. "As soon as he can be moved, I will take him to my mother's house to recover."

So not only was he not coming with her, he was leaving.

She darted a glance toward the tent flap, the enclosed space filled with the reek of the wounded and dying suddenly too constraining, too stifling for her to breathe. She needed air, and Markham would too. "He will be smothered in here. See if you can get him outside. He will sleep better under the stars."

"Now you are concerned?"

Her temper flared at his bitter tone. "What does that mean?"

He rubbed at smears of dried blood on his hands until it flaked. "You rode off alone. You threw yourself headlong into peril and drew him after you." He met her eyes and leaned in, a muscle twitching in his jaw. "He warned me you were reckless. He warned me to temper you. You, a thing as wild and ill-tamed as your fireborn and–"

With difficulty, he reined in his tongue. But he had said more than enough. Chest aching, she brushed blindly past him toward the flap. Whatever had been forged between them these past months had been too weak to withstand her destructive blast. Forever, she formed the epicenter, forever ruining those around her. Now she felt hollowed out, as if that blast had raged through her body and soul, leaving her weightless.

Something to drift away upon the next gust of wind, like ash.

FORTY-SIX: RAFI

Don't bite the hand that feeds you . . . until it stops.
– Nadaarian maxim

"Iakki . . . wake up," Rafi whispered, shaking the boy's shoulders. He bent over Iakki's hammock, watching for a reaction in the faint moonlight that streamed through the parted curtain behind him, hand raised to clap over the boy's mouth when he awoke. Curled on his side with his hands beneath his chin, Iakki looked startlingly innocent as he dreamed.

About the only time he looked innocent.

Rafi shook him harder, sparing a glance at the strings of hammock-cocooned forms crowding the hut they had shared with half a dozen other Que youths with no family in the rebel camp. One mumbled and rolled over in his hammock. Grimacing, Rafi covered Iakki's mouth and scooped him out of the hammock, then backed carefully through the curtain. Halfway through, Iakki jerked awake into a grunting mass of flailing arms and legs.

"Shh, shh," Rafi hissed in his ear. "It's me, Nahiki."

Iakki stilled but glared at him until he removed his hand. "Put me down."

"Okay, but you have to be quiet," Rafi warned before setting him down.

The boy crossed his arms, eying Rafi suspiciously. "Where you been? Nef's raised a storm about you. Overturned everything looking. And what'd you do with your shirt?"

"It's . . . uh . . . below." With the sea-demon in the cave beneath the secret entrance. Before leaving the coast, he had tied his shirt into a "bag" and stuffed it and his pockets full of seaweed. He had emptied his pockets on the trip back, then left what remained in his shirt to keep the sea-demon occupied during his infiltration. Leaving the colt had been a gamble, but it could not scale the rope ladder, and he could not risk walking in the main entrance. There was no telling how Umut had reacted to his disappearance, but Nef would assume he had betrayed them. Hopefully, that seaweed would prevent the sea-demon from screaming and alerting the rebels, and with any luck, it wouldn't have time to eat his shirt too before he returned. "Come on, we need to go."

"Where we going?" Iakki grumbled, rubbing his eyes and following as Rafi stole a flaming brand from a sputtering fire and rounded the cavern. Crossing the bridge to the staircase, Rafi moved as stealthily as possible, though few rebels should be about at this hour, save the guards who patrolled the gorge rim and jungle entrance. "And what's the hurry?"

"My shirt is in danger."

Iakki yawned. "That don't make sense."

"How about being quiet?"

"How 'bout telling me where you're taking me."

Rafi sighed heavily. "Home, Iakki. I'm taking you home."

Iakki's eyes lit up, and he bounced in excitement, rocking the entire staircase. Stomach lurching, Rafi grabbed onto the cavern wall and closed his eyes until the swaying slowed. The boy held his tongue after that, even when Rafi turned down the hidden tunnel, and only raised a curious eyebrow at the rope ladder descending into the hole beside the cascading water before scampering down it. But Iakki took one look at the waiting sea-demon and backed away.

The colt lifted its head, a corner of Rafi's shirt caught between its teeth.

"Come on!" Muttering under his breath, Rafi pried it free and examined the tattered fabric with a sigh. Still, he had nothing else to wear, so he shrugged into the damp rag and led the colt out into the misty predawn gray of the jungle, halting on the bank of the stream. Iakki followed at a safe distance. Soon, the camp would wake. Soon, someone might come looking. He knotted the lead into reins. "Time to go, Iakki."

"I ain't riding that thing," Iakki said.

"Don't tell me you're scared." Rafi stepped back to gain room to swing up onto the sea-demon's back. He landed squarely behind its withers and braced, but the colt only flicked an ear at him and let out a snuffling sigh. "See?" He held out both hands. "Nothing to worry about."

"Ain't worried. Just smart."

"Smart would know that riding is better than running behind. It gets kind of messy back there. You wouldn't believe–" He broke off as Iakki flung himself at the colt's back. He hit too low and hung there, legs churning, until the colt dislodged him with a sidestep and dropped him in the stream. Rafi shook his head. "And smart knows better than to pull a stunt like that. What do you think you're doing?"

"Climbing on?"

"It's a sea-demon, not a boulder."

"Well, boulders have the sense not to move when you're climbing them." Iakki shook himself, spraying water droplets everywhere.

"Do you want to return to the ocean or not, sea-beast?" Rafi anchored one hand and held out the other. Iakki latched on and immediately went limp, leaving Rafi to haul him stomach-first across the colt's back behind him. "You know," he grunted, "the least you could do is help."

"Fine!" Iakki kicked out–once, twice, all elbows and knees–and finally managed to sit up. "Why don't I get to be in front?"

"Two seconds ago, you didn't want to ride. Now you want to steer?"

"Sure, why not?"

Rafi glanced at the grinning boy. "You'll see." Gathering up the reins, he felt the sea-demon coil beneath him, like a wave building, readying to crash upon the shore. "You might want to hold on." He clicked his tongue, and the colt surged forward, startling a yelp from Iakki, who flung both arms around his waist. Wailing like a sea-demon, Iakki buried his face between Rafi's shoulders as the colt jogged off through the jungle.

"You got lots of scars, you know."

"What?" Rafi stirred from the daze he had been lulled into by their plodding pace and glanced over his shoulder to see Iakki flopped back with his head resting on the colt's hindquarters, rocking from side to side with each step. Iakki's fear had been short-lived, dissipating before the mist had fully burned off. Now, a full day later, and he looked as comfortable on the sea-demon's back as he was lounging in a boat or clinging to the side of a cliff or dangling from the highest branches of a tree.

"Scars. Lots. Bruises too. Saw them through the holes in your shirt."

Rafi stretched both shoulders, one after the other. "The scars are thanks to that scadtha, the bruises to the colt . . . and Nef, probably."

Iakki sat up and poked at his shoulder. "That one hurt?"

"No—stop." Rafi pulled away as the poking became scraping.

"It looks kind of like a starfish with lots of curving legs, like that red one Sev dropped in my hammock that time I slipped a grub into his seaweed tea." Iakki grew quiet, his voice small. "I miss him, Nahiki."

"Not for long," Rafi assured him. "We're almost there."

Steering the colt through this familiar jungle brought a flood of memories crashing over Rafi, all now infused with the ache of Torva's loss. It was pervasive, that ache. He felt it in the hum of aged trees creaking in the wind, in the salt tang that permeated even the damp mustiness of leaf mold, in his shorn clump of hair stripped of Torva's bead strand. Like the jagged mark seared into the trunk of the lightning tree, like the scars etched into his own flesh, this wound he would carry as long as he lived.

Harpoon resting across his knees, Sev waited at the base of the lightning tree. He jumped up as Rafi halted the colt and was on the move before Iakki made it to the ground, crushing him in a hug. This ached too, this display of brotherly love. For if Torva's death was a jagged scar, Delmar's death remained a raw and weeping gash.

Still, Rafi forced a smile for Iakki's sake as he dismounted, but no sooner had his heels touched earth than Sev tucked Iakki behind him with one hand and snatched the sea-demon's lead with the other. His burly shoulder clipped Rafi's chest, knocking him back a step. Shrieking and tossing its head, the colt reared, resisting Sev's pull.

What–

A twig snapped behind.

Rafi spun and found spears at his throat, aimed by half a dozen soldiers sneering beneath steel caps with white plumes, more flooding from the jungle behind them, vines crunching beneath their boots. No. He swiveled and saw Sev toss the lead to two soldiers who wrestled the sea-demon away from the lightning tree, away from Rafi.

Sev met his eyes briefly and then turned away. "Iakki, come."

The boy stood, eyes wide with horror, and refused to budge even when Sev tried to steer him by the shoulders. His lips moved, but Rafi did not hear him, did not hear anything but the throb of his own heart as the soldiers parted before a familiar figure in a cloak of scarlet, a breastplate of burnished gold, and a bandoleer of knives that were bloodstained, every one. Smiling, Sahak drew a long thin knife, spun it, and caught it by the tip.

Run, brother!

The ghost's scream rang through every nerve in Rafi's body and stung him into action. With his forearm, he dashed aside the nearest spear and lunged into the opening. Something slammed into his ribs. Crackling pain shot up his side. He gasped and pushed forward. A boot crunched into his knee. He went down to the other. Caught a hammered fist to the side of his head that set his skull ringing.

Crawling shreds of mist clouded his eyes. Half-blinded, he shoved between two soldiers. He crashed into the lightning tree, gripping the trunk to steady himself, and blinked to bring the world into focus.

Something whistled past and struck his hand with a *thunk*.

Pain arced up his arm like a bolt of lightning. A long thin knife–Sahak's knife–pierced his left hand, pinning it to the tree. Rafi swayed and collapsed against the trunk. Oh *Ches-Shu*. Oh, Sisters Three! Should he . . . try to pull it out? He bit his lip to keep down the boiling scream.

"Nahiki!" Iakki's strangled cry burned his ears.

Vision tunneling, he glimpsed Sev wrap both arms around the boy and haul him kicking, screaming, and clawing away. Then soldiers closed around him, spears caged him in, and Sahak sauntered toward him with a smile on his lips and knives flicking between his fingers like the darting tongue of a snake.

This, Iakki should not have to see.

"Iakki . . . *go*!" Rafi croaked, shutting his eyes, refusing to meet Sahak's gaze. Staring death in the face was far overrated, particularly when death wore the face of kin.

"Ah, cousin." Sahak's breath washed hot and rank across Rafi as he leaned in to seize the knife, grating it in the wound. Rafi groaned and his knees quivered. "The years have taught you little skill and less wisdom. You are as inept as ever. Pity. I long for a challenge. But you will never be Delmar, will you?" Bracing one hand on Rafi's chest, he slowly, agonizingly, worked the blade free.

And this time, Rafi could not hold back his scream.

FORTY-SEVEN: CERIDWEN

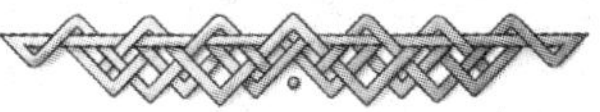

Of all earthriders, Teague the Steadfast shall forever be immortalized in song for unleashing the quake that brought the Fang of Toroth crashing down upon herself and upon the Rhiakki horde, ending their southward incursion.

Change hummed upon the evening air as Ceridwen swept through the gateway of Rysinger at the head of her patrol and Eagan's shadower kill-squad. None tried to halt them, nor would she have suffered resistance. Energy pulsed through her veins, roiled in flame across Mindar's mane, and fused her blade hand to the hilt of her sabre. It impelled her onward beyond the reach of doubt and its reminder of Gavin dead, Markham wounded, Finnian gone, and the brand forever seared into her forehead.

Onward. Ever onward.

Dismounting on the greensward, Ceridwen left Mindar with her patrol and instructions not to loosen cinches or remove bridles—even with the ring, she might be cast out again—and strode inside with Nold as her back-rider in Finnian's absence, Eagan and his back-rider, and the Canthorian Iona had captured. The prisoner shuffled along, hands bound before him, expression seething with hatred, as they descended into the heart of the great house where warriors in the livery of Harnoth guarded the seven ebony doors that led into the circular Fire Hall, one door for each of Soldonia's chiefdoms.

Ceridwen reached up and clasped the ring which hung from a strap around her neck, for she could not bring herself to wear it yet. Taking a deep breath, she seized the latch of the central door.

"Hold, tal Desmond." Eagan barred the door with a booted foot. "Let me ready the field for your arrival first. Or would ye repeat your last visit t' Rysinger?" There was no hint of mockery or a lie in his eyes that today seemed blue as the starlit sky. Still, the Fox of Craignorm was too cunning to reveal his schemes in a glance.

Within, the rumble of voices declared the war-meet begun.

She shook her head. "Hold if you will. I enter now."

Raising his hands, he yielded, and she hauled the door open. Voices broke off as it shut behind her, and she strode into the ring of war-chiefs seated on ebony thrones and halted before the central fire ring. It burned with flaming rocks from the craters of Gauroth. Her forehead throbbed beneath her scarf, and sweat prickled her brow.

There, she had knelt before the hissing flames.

There, Lord Glyndwr had pled for mercy.

There, the king–her father–had seared the brand into her skin.

Across the hearth, seated as regent in the king's place, Glyndwr's eyes widened with shock in his haggard and wrinkled face. Almost she pitied the man. He had argued so fervently for her then. She doubted he would do so again.

"Ceridwen tor Nimid, ever the fireball." His voice was weaker now than when he'd told her of the bright light that had blazed across the northern sky, only to flame out in ruin. He still thought her the same. But he was mistaken. She was fireborn, and they were far more enduring. "Have you forgotten the ban upon you? Leave now, and you may yet be forgiven."

Her feelings of pity evaporated like ice before Mindar's heated breath. "I am Ceridwen tal Desmond, war-chief of Lochrann, here to attend the war-meet you summoned. Or would you deny Lochrann its ancient right to a seat at the hearth and a voice in council?" This, after all, was the foundation of the kingdom her ancestor Uthold had forged, and if Lochrann could be excluded at will, what of the others?

She glanced at each war-chief in turn. Craddock, square-jawed and thick-necked, holding a jeweled goblet and lounging in brocaded silks bearing the emblem of Gimleal–an earthhewn depicted in the traditional *sundering* stance, sinking deep on its hindquarters, forelimbs raised to shatter the earth. Ormond of Ruiadh peered up beneath heavy eyebrows, eyes darting like a hunted beast. On the far side of the fire, standing with his face to Glyndwr and his back to her, Rhodri, and seated with an air of imperious control, offering no hint of welcome, Telweg.

In peacetime, lesser chieftains would have filled the ring of seats behind the war-chiefs, but only back-riders sat there today. Doubtless, the chieftains commanded their lieges' war-hosts in their absence, maintaining the defense against the Nadaari.

Surprisingly, Ormond spoke first. "Well, I think she is right." His confidence ebbed as all eyes shifted to him. "I mean after all she is a war-chief too . . . and all of us bear equal right to speak here in the Fire Hall, don't we?"

"To speak perhaps." Craddock yawned lazily, voice thick with wine. His hands glittered with a dozen rings bearing raw gemstones, no doubt carved from the mines of Gimleal. "But *sky's blood*, Ormond, no one wants to listen to your yammering."

The young war-chief flushed. "You insult me."

"Did I? Yes, I suppose I did. How keen of you to observe that."

"I have as much right to speak as you–"

"Indeed you do, boy, as you love reminding us. But we are under no obligation to listen unless you have found something to say that is actually worth hearing."

Ormond sputtered. "I'll . . . I'll have you know that I take offense."

"Duly noted, and you should–"

Something hit the ground with a sickening thud behind Ceridwen. She spun to see Eagan standing with a leather satchel upended and a severed head at his feet, dark hair spilling around it like a seeping bloodstain. The room burst into thunderous uproar. Without looking at the features, she knew it was Kilmark.

Blazes, why had Eagan brought that here?

"Peace! Peace!" Glyndwr's voice was swallowed by the clamor, but he hammered a fist until it quieted, leaving only Eagan's voice echoing hollowly through the chamber.

"Sure, call for peace. Call until your breath runs out. Ye should be calling for war."

Telweg leaned forward, voice stern. "What is the meaning of this?"

"This?" Eagan nudged the head with his boot and turned, spreading his arms wide. "This is a reminder of the severity of our situation, which some of you seem t' have forgotten." His voice rose, cracking like lightning off the walls, until no trace of levity remained. "We battle traitors in our own ranks, not t' mention an invading army. We cannot waste time bickering."

He could have given Ceridwen no better opening. So much of warfare was timing, and though she had restrained her tongue since arriving, this moment, at last, felt right. No longer a matter of choice or chance but of inevitability, like the shift between Mindar's inhalation of air and his exhalation of flames.

She stepped forward. "That is why I have come. Kilmark is dead by my hand. Ondri and his followers have scattered. And we have captured our enemy's engineer–the man we believe devised the war machines that decimated our forces at Idolas."

Nold thrust the bound prisoner forward into the ring where he stood, glowering.

Craddock squinted over his goblet. "Doesn't look like much, does he?"

"Still, I suppose he must be brilliant," Ormond countered, "to have built such machines."

Pride flickered across the prisoner's face so quickly Ceridwen wondered if she had imagined it. The speed of her journey had left little time to question him, and he had claimed ignorance of any language save Canthorian. Her knowledge of that tongue was too limited to glean more than that. Doubtless he had been lying.

She raised an eyebrow, letting him know she had seen his slip, before turning back to the war-chiefs. "Soon, the Nadaari will be stranded within their war-camp, cut off from the coast and access to reinforcements and supplies." She sought Telweg's gaze, hoping the words she spoke still held true, but the woman's expression yielded nothing. "But this will only be possible if we stand as one. Now is the time to strike."

"To strike, you say?" Rhodri's quiet voice cut across the ensuing silence. Slowly, he turned, and she was taken aback at the changes in his appearance that his helmet had concealed before. His hair had been shorn close to the scalp above his ears, leaving a crest braided with gold rings down the back of his skull. Oiled leathers gleamed on his chest, and firelight glanced off the ornate tooling and off the polished blade belted at his waist. His appearance made her dusty leathers and battered cuirass feel dull and weathered in comparison.

"You have done well," he continued, and he sounded sincere. "You deserve our gratitude. But there are other courses we may now pursue to prevent the reckless shedding of blood. We have held out well, but we fight a losing war against numbers that far exceed our own. Still, our resistance allows us to broach negotiations from a position of strength, and Nadaar must offer reasonable terms. This will be our victory."

His words left her stunned, unable to muster a defense. After all she had witnessed since Idolas; after the Voice had roared through her ears, heralding the collapse of nations; after seeing Gavin fall, she could not fathom the suggestion.

Surrender? Death was preferable.

Eagan snorted and tossed himself in his seat, wincing as the twin blades strapped to his back dug into his shoulders. "Why negotiate at all if they can crush us?"

"Their goals lie beyond us." Rhodri clasped his hands behind his back, outwardly calm, though his pinched forehead betrayed concern. "Why waste their forces in a bloody, extended war—which history testifies we will give them—when other means will suffice?"

"Your argument might bear merit had they bothered negotiating before launching said bloody, extended war," Telweg observed dryly, and Craddock snorted into his goblet.

"What I am hearing," Eagan put in, "is that if we destroy this force, they might reconsider before sacrificing another."

"Or field two more in its stead." Ormond's voice cracked. "This is the empire of Nadaar we speak of. They have the levies of nations at their disposal."

"And would ye have us become one o' them?"

Craddock sighed heavily and clunked his goblet against the arm of his chair. The high collar of his robe swallowed his bull-like neck, making it look like his head sprouted directly from his shoulders, and yet in his movement, Ceridwen caught the clank of mail beneath. The war-chief might be fond of ostentation and comfort, but he *was* still a warrior and not to be underestimated. "It is a simple question of mathematics. You cannot argue it both ways. Either they have vast resources–in this case, soldiers–which they are willing to expend upon our shores, or there is some point at which their losses will be too great to justify the cost."

"Then if we can just outlast them–"

"Ah, but that is just it," Craddock said. "Can we outlast them?"

"Must we outlast them?" Rhodri inclined his head toward Craddock. "At what point will our losses be too great? And should we not seize the opportunity to negotiate from victory instead of defeat?"

The others seemed to be considering his words, and that finally spurred Ceridwen to action. "We can only negotiate from defeat," she countered. "They invaded us. Slaughtered us. Murdered our king. You speak of reasonable terms. What terms could atone for that?"

Rhodri's voice remained even. "That, Ceridwen, the regent must determine."

"What, we have a regent?" Craddock blinked in exaggerated surprise. "I had nearly forgotten. He has been strangely silent of late. Ho, Glyndwr! Still with us? Someone poke the old bear and make sure he is still awake . . . and breathing."

"Confound your insolence, Craddock," Glyndwr growled. He leaned over the armrests of the king's seat, forehead in his hand.

"Ah, so he *is* alive. Bless us, we are saved."

Ceridwen studied the aged war-chief. Deep furrows scored Glyndwr's brow, and in his eyes, conflict raged. He looked ill fit to sit in her father's seat, and was so, if his control of this war-meet was any indication. It was his duty to direct the discussion, muster the war-hosts, and speak of strategy instead of surrender, but he remained silent, hunched beneath his cloak, and so like ill-tamed steeds, the war-chiefs ran wild.

This was why Markham had urged her claim.

Become worthy, he had said. *Lead.*

Ceridwen knotted her fist around the ring against her chest. "I have come to muster the war-hosts to the defense of the kingdom. I will not leave without them."

The fire sparked and crackled in the silence following her words.

Then Glyndwr stood, bowed beneath the quilted gambeson that hung loose around his withered and wasted frame. He seemed a skeletal thing now, the stark lines of bones visible beneath his frail skin. "So," he said, "we come to your claim at last. You know that in the absence of an heir, only the battlemaster or regent can muster the war-hosts, and so long as you bear the *kasar,* you cannot be named heir."

Ceridwen felt the tension in the atmosphere. It was the instant before lightning cracked, the gasp before flames unleashed, the breath before towering waves crashed upon the shore. "And yet, I have been named heir." She raised the leather strand and held aloft the signet ring where it flashed as it spun in the firelight. "Behold the ring of Uthold, willed to me by my father's dying breath." Sweeping her blade from its scabbard, she rammed it down into a gap between firerocks in the central ring. Sparks shot into the air and embers scattered hissing across the stone floor. "I, Ceridwen tal Desmond, tor Nimid, of the blood of Lochrann, claim my rightful title as heir of Soldonia and ruler over the seven chiefdoms."

She reached above the flames and clasped her hilt, treated leathers and gloves shielding her from their bite. "I swear to drive the invaders from our shores, root out treachery from our midst, and establish peace for our people once more. By blood and blade, I swear it."

The echoes of her voice faded, and for a moment, all was still.

She drew back her blade but did not yet sheathe it.

"Tell me, Ceridwen tal Desmond"–Glyndwr's wavering voice grew strong as he raised a parchment and met her eyes–"how can you have been named heir when I hold a testament in the king's own hand, sealed with his own ring, and stored in his own chambers, naming Lord Rhodri te Oengus, heir of Soldonia?"

FORTY-EIGHT: RAFI

The cost of life is death. Eventually all debts come due.
– Nadaari maxim

"Sure these ropes are tight enough?" Rafi gasped, hissing at the tingling in his fingers. "I can still feel–" He broke off in a groan, wounded hand throbbing, as the soldiers tossed the rope's end over one of the lightning tree's branches and hauled it tight, stretching his arms over his head. "That's definitely tighter."

Warmth ran down his arm from his pierced hand. Two soldiers remained to keep him upright on his toes while the rest lounged beside a fire in a clearing beneath the banyan tree's sprawl, where fish roasted on skewers, seaweed tea boiled in Sev's chipped pot, and Sev himself lurked in the lengthening shadows, refusing to meet his gaze. Tethered to a neefwa tree nearby, the hobbled sea-demon grazed contentedly. Above, setting sunlight pierced the canopy to streak leaf and loam with crimson–or maybe that was just the blood dripping in his eyes again.

"Shh, cousin, don't move." Sahak leaned in close, knife hovering a terrifying inch from his pupils, then reached down and tore the shirt from his back, used it to wipe his face with mock gentleness, and then tossed it away.

Shivering with a cold sweat, stomach boiling with nausea, Rafi sank back, scraping his spine on the tree. A soldier picked up his discarded, bloody shirt and carried it over to a cage sheltered within a cluster of enormous sheetlike leaves. Something shifted inside, and Rafi's heart faltered. Behind the bars, striped in shadow and fire glow, crouched an enormous stone-eye tiger. The soldier dangled his shirt between the bars and the beast crept forward, sniffing.

What in Ches-Shu's name were they doing?

The tiger sprang for the shirt and thudded against the cage. It held, but his shirt vanished in an instant, shredded by razor claws and dagger teeth.

He swallowed. "I . . . liked that shirt."

"Not half so much as Raas likes the taste of you," Sahak said, flicking a hand to the soldier still holding the end of the rope that looped from Rafi's hands over the branch. The soldier backed away, increasing the tension on the rope until Rafi had to balance, swaying, on the balls of his feet to resist the strain. Pain stabbed his ribs and his knee ached dully.

But it was not until the soldier bent to knot the rope to the cage's latch that Rafi began to comprehend. "Sahak . . . oh, no . . . no."

Sahak laughed soundlessly, rocking forward with his knife hand to his forehead. "It's good, isn't it? It's an old Nadaarian custom. Or Choth, maybe. I can't recall. But it's brutally effective. Keep your hands raised, the cage remains closed. Lower your arms or lose your balance, the tension on the rope releases the latch so the stone-eye can devour you alive." He tapped his blade against Rafi's chest. "I doubt you will last long. You can barely stand."

Sure enough, Rafi's limbs were already quivering. He was bleeding, concussed, and battered, but this was not how he had envisioned dying. "Not going to kill me yourself?" That, at least, might be less painful than being eaten alive.

"Oh, I didn't say that." Sahak grinned and palmed a blade from his bandoleer, flipped it, caught it by the tip, and raised his hand to throw.

And he'd had to ask . . .

Maybe the tiger could tear out his tongue first. Might save him suffering in the long run. He flinched as the knife flashed past and struck only a hair away. "Ches-Shu!" he cursed, as a creak warned of his inadvertent tug on the rope.

"Careful," Sahak chided, selecting another blade.

"Wait . . . wait . . . Sahak . . . what do you want?"

"Me? Maybe nothing."

Rafi spat out bloody spittle. "Then . . . why am I alive? Why not kill me now? Why not kill me and Delmar then? Why didn't Lykier kill all of us at once?" He was rambling, but his tongue felt slippery as a fish and impossible to restrain, and suddenly Sahak was laughing again, knife dangling from the hands he clasped before his lips.

Unhinged. He was completely unhinged.

"The emperor didn't kill anyone," Sahak said at last, humor subsiding.

"But my family didn't die of illness."

"No, they didn't." Sahak spun the knife up and caught it sideways in the air. "But you will die today. Still, you could spare yourself pain if you give me what I want."

"Which is?"

"Information."

Rafi blinked, still reeling from the confirmation that Delmar's suspicions had been correct, and missed the throw but felt the blade slice his right bicep. It required all his willpower not to flinch. "You didn't ask me anything!"

"Oh, that was for fun. Or a demonstration. You decide." Sahak inspected another knife, small with a leaflike blade, closing in and holding it up for Rafi to see. "You like this one? It came from that village you abandoned–what was its name, Sev?" he called over his shoulder.

There was a delay, then Sev muttered, "Zorrad."

"And who did it belong to?"

An even longer pause, then, "Yeena."

No. Rafi shut his eyes, breathing between his teeth as Sahak continued, "Fortunately, sweet Yeena has no use for it anymore, has she?" And Rafi couldn't contain his horror, though he knew his reaction was being measured. But what did it matter?

They were all of them dead, and so was he.

Sahak trailed the knife point across his throat. "Sea-demons never venture ashore in Nadaar, still less follow a human inland. You've managed to bond the beast—something Soldonians claim only they can do—and I want to know how."

Rafi's eyes opened wide. "That's what you want?"

The knife bit into his skin.

"But I don't know. I don't. It just . . . happened."

Of all the secrets Sahak could have demanded, such as the location of the Que Revolution or the identity of its leader, he had selected the one Rafi could not reveal since it was a mystery to him too. He repeated the words over and over as Sahak rephrased the question with the clarifying aid of a variety of knives and throwing techniques, until he had a dozen new wounds and wobbled on his feet, combating the dizziness from his spinning head. His arms had grown so heavy. They drifted down beneath their own enormous weight.

The latch rattled. The stone-eye growled.

Sahak tsked at him, and he jolted upright, forcing his arms straight despite his burning shoulders. Sahak retrieved his blades. "Your brother was ten times the Tetrani you are."

"You're not wrong." His tongue felt thick, his breath short, as he raised bleary eyes. "Pity you killed him. You know I was there? I saw him fall and—"

"Oh, the fall didn't kill him."

Rafi's pulse throbbed. "What?"

"Your brother survived the fall," Sahak said with a sickly grin. "Mostly." His tone conjured up images of Delmar's body broken beyond repair, of his mind shattered, or worse.

And yet, alive?

It couldn't be . . . he couldn't be . . .

Before Rafi could reel in his thoughts, a young soldier ran up. "Sir, it arrived! The ship! It's at the harbor but not offloaded yet. Something about the accommodations being inadequate or—"

Sahak cut him off with a slash of his hand. "Reports are to be given in private." His manner conveyed only irritation as he stalked off after the soldier, but Rafi sensed anxiety lurking beneath the façade. He was hiding something. Was it about Delmar?

Of course it's not about me, the ghost whispered in his head. *I'm dead.*

Rafi squeezed his eyes shut. *But you're not, are you? You survived.* Oh, Ches-Shu, he had survived, and Rafi had left him crippled, dying maybe, but not dead.

Unless . . . Sahak had spun the tale to torment him. But he would like to believe that, wouldn't he? Relinquish responsibility. Pretend to be free. Even if it meant losing himself, because that was what he did best.

But if Delmar was alive . . .

"Here," a gruff voice dragged his head up.

Sev stood before him, frowning, reaching up for his hands, but instead of ropes loosening, Rafi found his swollen fingers pried apart and something pressed into his uninjured palm. With the lack of circulation numbing his extremities, it took him a moment to identify the shape as Torva's bead strand.

"So, what, are we supposed to be even now?"

Sev shook his head. "I wish I could have killed you myself."

It surprised Rafi how much that stung, considering Sev had already consigned him to torture and an agonizing death. "You hate me so much?"

Sev's voice dropped to a hoarse whisper. "I would have made it quick. If it's any consolation, you don't deserve this."

"I am going to be eaten alive."

"I had no choice!"

"Then it's not too late, cousin." Rafi flicked his gaze toward the sea-demon hobbled beyond the fire where the soldiers now downed drink instead of food. "Iakki is safe, and we can be too." Whether or not the colt could—or would—carry them both remained to be seen.

But Sev shook his head again and backed away, only to collide with Sahak. His eyes bulged as Sahak clapped him on the shoulder. "Yes, Sev, listen to your cousin. It certainly isn't too late to reconsider, and just think, if you fall in his defense, he won't bother making sure you are dead before fleeing to save his own skin."

Sev pulled free and turned away, looking sick.

Sahak shook his head pityingly, sliding another knife from his bandoleer and rolling it between his fingers as he turned toward Rafi. "Now . . . where were we?"

FORTY-NINE: CERIDWEN

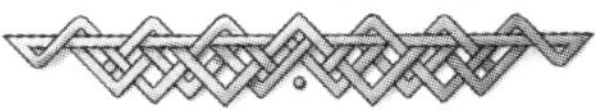

Beware the scream of a seablood. It ranges in pitch, producing a haunting, keening wail. Many seariders use this to advantage in combat to disorient and quell their foes.

Ceridwen stood stunned in the center of a cataclysmic storm as war-chiefs surged to their feet, shouting demands, and back-riders closed in, hands on weapons. Her ears rang with a long hollow note, and darkness hovered at the edge of her vision, threatening to sweep over her. Almost she wished it would. She could drown in that darkness, a speck winked out into the void. Then over the flames, she met Rhodri's gaze and saw nothing in his eyes but glowing embers.

Rhodri had been named heir, and her father had done it.

This was no mere choosing of one son or daughter over another. This was a shift in the balance of power within the nation. The right to rule had been Lochrann's since Uthold first rode from the east. For the war-chief of Ardon to be named heir in her place—how her father must have despised her. But if this bitter draught was hers to swallow, she must see it for herself. She seized the parchment, and Glyndwr yielded it. One glance and the truth smote her like a blow to the skull. There in her father's writing, sealed with the ring she held, was Rhodri's name.

For a moment, she stood again on the crater's rim, heat washing over her skin while the rattling wind pelted her with grains of sand. But the clenched ring dug into her flesh and forced her back to reality, back to the Fire Hall.

Glyndwr shook his head, eyes hooded with pity. "You were shown mercy, Ceridwen. A life for a life has always been the rule of justice, but you were granted exile, offered the chance to seek atonement through service among the Outriders. There was honor in that. But you never could be content with less than all, could you?"

Her throat burned. "But you spoke for me . . . at the branding."

"Would that I had not. I hear your followers call you 'the Fireborn' now. That is fitting, for you have no capacity for aught but destruction."

"For our enemies, perhaps." Eagan brushed up beside her and plucked the parchment from her hands, giving it only a cursory scan before shoving it against Glyndwr's chest. "Who are we t' begrudge them the chance t' perish in flame?" He spun, voice ringing out over the commotion. "Hold! We can discuss this matter as war-chiefs not rabble!"

"But what is there to discuss?" Ormond hesitantly retook his seat. "Lord Rhodri has been named heir. The matter is resolved . . . isn't it?"

His question sparked another uproar: Telweg demanded to know whether the king had outlined how to transfer the right to rule between chiefdoms, Craddock called for more wine and offered less-than-helpful commentary, and Eagan snapped at them all, while Glyndwr remained silent. Ceridwen let their voices swirl around her. Once again, her father had declared his will, and it was not mercy or vindication he offered, but judgment. Always judgment. How could she have dared hope otherwise?

"This is no simple matter," Telweg insisted, leaning forward in her chair. "Shall Rhodri yield his chiefdom? Shall Ceridwen? Shall the seat of power simply shift? These are strange waters we must traverse in a time of upheaval."

"Must we?" Eagan paced around the hearth. "Ye go too fast, I think. It has been months since the king's death, and only now do we learn of his writ? Why was it not presented when it was created or stored among the records as it should have been?"

Glyndwr raised a gnarled hand. "I have known of the king's writ for some time, and though he neglected to have it ratified before witnesses before riding to Idolas, it was his only written will. I have spent the past month drawing up the outline Lady Telweg desires–"

"Never ratified?" Eagan interrupted. "Then 'tis not binding, and we have yet the ring t' consider, willed t' his daughter with his dying breath."

"Was it?" Rhodri lifted his head, speaking for the first time since Glyndwr's announcement. His voice was quiet but edged, like a blade drawn slowly from its sheath.

"You were there," Ceridwen said. "You heard–"

"I heard the testimony of one of your warriors and saw a war-slave near death, neither of whom are here to testify today." Rhodri spoke deliberately. "I also saw you standing over the corpse of one of the traitors who orchestrated the king's death with ample time to have recovered the ring from him. I have never desired the throne, but you have never not desired it, and I must ask myself, what would a daughter of kings, disowned and dishonored, do to reclaim her place? Invent a dying will and name a witness no one can question?" He shook his head in dismay. "Your father confided in me, Ceridwen. He considered you lost and would never have named you heir."

Each word was a savage cut to her heart, draining all the hope she'd foolishly harbored in her chest. His tale made far more sense than the one she had lived. Almost she believed him.

Had the boy, Jakim, lied?

"My people have borne the brunt of this war." Telweg stood, and as if her voice had some magnetic pull, all eyes instantly swung toward her. "The coast is our livelihood and our enemy controls it, and while blood is spilled in our land, we quarrel? Enough!" Her voice rang with the clarion call of a seablood. "Would you govern chiefdoms of the dead? Lord Regent, ring or writ, it is yours to decide. I demand you name the heir."

It had become a night of sorrows following days of grief, and so it was not with hope that Ceridwen lifted her gaze to the aged war-chief as he descended slowly to stand before the hearth, but with the stubborn determination of one refusing to flee impending doom.

"Ceridwen tal Desmond, ambition boils within you. You are destruction itself, a consuming fire escaped from the depths of Koltar." Glyndwr's voice creaked like a straining rope. "Bair fell to your blaze. Desmond too, and he was my king and greatest friend. Now you seek power over the kingdom to do the same? Never while I live."

Heat fled her body, and the breath left her lungs.

"I confirm the king's writ and proclaim Rhodri te Oengus Heir of Soldonia." Without delay, Glyndwr launched into the ancient oath-swearing ritual, but all Ceridwen heard was Rhodri's voice ringing out clearly at the end.

"I so swear."

He looked kingly as he said it, clad in gleaming armor, face painted with an expression of humble nobility, leaving her painfully aware of the grime staining her gear and the flakes of ash clinging to her scarf and hair. This was it then, the end to all her striving, all her stumbling clumsily onward. Yet again, she had been declared unworthy.

Glyndwr bent creakily in a bow. "It is my honor to relinquish my burden as regent."

"And mine to bear that burden as king." Rhodri ascended to the king's chair and turned to face the war-chiefs. "I will bear this burden for the memory of Desmond and the good of the kingdom, and beside me will stand my betrothed and your future queen, Astra tor Telweg."

Ceridwen started as Astra emerged from the second row where she had been concealed behind her mother's high-backed seat. Where Telweg was frost and steel, Astra was salt spray and ocean mist and sun-warmed sand, clad in armor that shone and wearing silver strands braided into her dark hair. Somehow in the chaos of the fight days before and the grief that had followed, Ceridwen had lost track of her. She could not recall seeing her once the battle began, and watching her now ascend to Rhodri who clasped her hand to his chest with unmistakable pride, set the earth reeling beneath Ceridwen's feet.

As king, Rhodri would have authority over all seven chiefdoms, but not direct control. Yet in one masterful move, he had gained leverage in Cenyon in addition to his rule over Ardon, and with his naming as heir, Lochrann's fate hung in the balance.

What of Telweg's promises? Had every word between them been a lie?

Ceridwen's gaze shifted to the woman and found her standing as tall and immovable as the carved white stone columns of Tel Renaair. Her features were white too, so much so that Ceridwen nearly expected to see the hard edge of bone beneath translucent flesh, but she gave no other indication that anything might be amiss.

Glyndwr was speaking again. "What would you have us do now, my king?"

"Kneel." Rhodri's eyes flickered to Ceridwen, glittering with a challenge, and she realized she was shaking. "Offer your oaths. We have been divided and leaderless too long." He eased into the king's chair, armor creaking, and with that calm, assured expression on his face, it was not difficult to envision a crown resting upon his brow. "Ceridwen of Lochrann, will you speak your oath?"

Her hand had gone instinctively to her sabre, but the blade could not solve this. It had been in motion far too long–since Idolas, since her return to Rysinger, since she stumbled through the gate with Bair on her shoulders. Now, only one question remained. Could she yield to this man her father had chosen in her stead?

Never, her heart cried.

But with the kingdom at stake, could she do otherwise?

Would she let her ambition condemn them all?

Ceridwen swore beneath her breath and forced her hand from the blade. She stepped forward and opened her mouth to speak, but a disturbance at the door stole her attention. Voices raised, thudding, a scuffle. At a nod from Eagan, his back-rider started toward the door, but it burst open before he reached it and a breathless Iona entered, followed by Jakim and the burly, black-bearded Outrider, Hab, who stepped over the limp form of a Harnoth warrior.

"What is the meaning of this?" Glyndwr snapped. "How dare you barge in here?"

Iona ignored him, eyes darting for Ceridwen. "I bear an urgent message," she said in a strained voice, and Ceridwen strode toward her, heedless of the war-chiefs' demands for explanation. "Treachery," Iona said in a hushed tone when Ceridwen was close enough none other could hear. "Astra has betrayed you. She is sworn to the Nadaari and–"

"That man there," Jakim's urgent whisper interrupted. "He is a traitor too. I saw him plotting to surrender your nation in exchange for the throne."

Ceridwen's breath caught. He was pointing at Rhodri.

The world seemed to still. It had been Rhodri's battle plan at Idolas, his chieftains who betrayed them, and his the surest path to the throne. And yet, she had never doubted his loyalty to the kingdom, and his warriors had fought beside hers only days before. Or had they? She knew Eagan's kill-squads had joined the fight, but the details of that battle blurred in her mind, lost in the rush of chasing Kilmark, saving Markham, and discovering her father's ring. "You swear this?"

Jakim met her eyes unflinching. "By Aodh's Eternal Scars."

Rhodri stiffened in the king's seat, watching them–no, watching Jakim–though he could not have overheard. For a moment his eyes were unveiled, and Ceridwen felt she saw to the core of him–smoke filled, ash-choked, and violent as the crater of Koltar.

Blazes, could it be true?

She opened her mouth to demand explanation, but Astra spoke first. "She denies the oath!" Astra who had offered kindness in one hand and a knife in the other, who had manipulated her and led Gavin and his family to their doom.

Ceridwen seized her blade.

Rhodri stood and his voice filled the Fire Hall. "Ceridwen tal

Desmond, you stand under the ban of the *kasar* and refuse to swear allegiance. You are stripped of rank and title and declared traitor. You will be executed for your crimes."

"I am not the traitor," Ceridwen shouted, but her voice was swallowed by the commotion of doors slamming open on all sides, flooding the hall with scores of warriors bearing the green and gold livery of Ardon on their chests. She drew her sabre and backed away, shoving Jakim behind her.

Swords clashed. Nold cursed and jostled against her, gripping a bleeding shoulder wound while an Ardon warrior dragged the Canthorian prisoner away.

It had all gone to ruin. Glyndwr was right. She was destruction incarnate.

Hooves clattered down the passage, and Liam and her mounted patrol charged in through the open doors, leading her fireborn and the other riderless steeds. The hall reverberated with stamping hooves, shouts, and the scuff of boots as Rhodri's warriors advanced.

"I told you to wait outside!" Iona shouted over the din.

"Well, pardon me, Aunt, for thinking I'd save your skin!" Liam yelled back in exasperation as he tossed her the reins to her stormer.

Ceridwen turned aside a darting spear. "Nold, take Jakim!" She pivoted and clipped the spearman's leg as another rider brought Mindar skittering alongside. Behind, Nold's shout declared Jakim safe. With a flying leap, Ceridwen seized her saddle and swung aloft, pursuit only paces away. Warmth radiated from Mindar's ribs, but the warriors closing in were clad in protective leathers like her own with masks and hoods and metal spears in gloved hands—gear designed to withstand all but the fiercest inferno. Still, she yanked up her own hood, aimed toward the vaulted paneled ceiling, and summoned flame.

Roaring filled her ears. Sparks and burning chunks of timber rained down.

Shielding her eyes with her arm, she watched as all scrambled for cover, then quieted Mindar's flame. He dropped his head, black smoke coiling around his hooves. Sheltered behind an overturned chair, Glyndwr stared at her aghast. There were tears in his eyes.

From her father's seat, Rhodri gave a thin smile.

Ceridwen drew Mindar into a rear, then spun and retreated with her patrol down the passage lined with tapestries of her ancestors. Ashen deeds lay behind. Ashen deeds would lie ahead. She had no choice but to press onward. Ever onward.

FIFTY: RAFI

Even a coward can appear courageous if he stares a stone-eye in the eye.
– Nadaari maxim

"You were about to release me, I think," Rafi said, then dropped all levity from his voice. "Or no, you were about to tell me where my brother is."

Across the fire, the sea-demon's head came up with a snort.

Sahak spun a knife thoughtfully. "Now that is a deep philosophical question–"

Rafi cut him off. "Is he alive, Sahak?"

The knife stilled mid-twirl. "Delmar? No, he is long dead."

So casually, he tossed out those words, yet they crashed over Rafi like a wall of water. "But . . . you said . . ."

"That he survived the fall, not that he still lived. He died cursing his useless little brother." Sahak spread his hands wide, and five more blades blossomed as if by magic between his fingers. "As well he might. His sacrifice gave you, what, six more years, and what have you done with all that time? Rafi Tetrani, a fisherman? Are you certain you should aim so high?" He pointedly eyed the rope tightening under Rafi's drooping hands.

Rafi let out a ragged groan as he straightened. His spine was on fire. Cramps seized his calves, and his knees continued to shake. Soon, his limbs would give out, or in the darkening night, one of Sahak's throws would miss and strike something vital. Growing desperation lent boldness to his tongue. "And what have you done in that time? Sahak, the Emperor's Stone-eye? Have you ever truly seen the carnage left behind? The lives you've ruined?"

"Rabble and rioters."

"People trying to live in peace."

Sahak's smile was a wound carved across his face. "So, you *have* joined the Que Revolution. I heard it rumored but did not believe you would be so bold." Rafi didn't bother setting him straight. "It is fitting that it will be both Delmar's death and your survival that brings about the revolution's downfall."

"And how do you figure that exactly?"

Sahak eyed him over his blades. "I have pried secrets from mouths locked tighter than yours, and you may know nothing about bonding a steed, but you know how to raze the revolution, and in case you need a reminder of why you should speak . . ." He sent a knife spinning into the air, and though Rafi tried to track its flashing in the firelight, he caught only a glimpse of movement before a bolt of fire plunged into his thigh.

His leg gave out, and he barely caught himself with the other before the latch released. Ragged, spluttering gasps escaped his lips.

"You know . . . killing me . . . is a poor way . . . to get information."

But Sahak was right. He knew more than enough to doom the revolution. The hideout's location, for starters, not to mention the secret waterfall entrance, or how operations worked, raiders communicated, and rebels were recruited. All of which he could spill in an instant to hasten his death, and odds were, the Que tribes as a whole would be safer once the revolution disbanded, if still not free. But what would become of Saffa and her kitchen crew, or the scores of refugees who had built new lives in the gorge?

Run, run, run, the ghost whispered.

Or perhaps that was only the cowardly beat of his own heart.

Rafi let his head sag back and his voice grow faint. "You should know . . ." Sahak leaned in to hear, and Rafi smashed his head forward. Blinding pain consumed him. He floated in a luminescent sea. But when his vision finally cleared, he was still standing, and

Sahak was reeling back with a split lip and blood streaming from his nose. "I . . . won't . . . tell you anything."

Sahak dabbed at his lip with the back of his hand. "Oh, but you will."

He raised another blade, but bloodcurdling screams rang out from the Mah before he released, and the soldiers lounging around the fire scrambled upright, leveling spears.

Something rustled the branches above the tethered sea-demon. Something much larger than a graybeard monkey. The soldiers advanced stealthily toward it. But they were still paces away when a howling, flailing boy dropped from the neefwa onto the sea-demon's back and clung like a spider as the colt threw up its heels, pitched from side to side, reared around and bolted through the soldiers' midst, bowling several over and scattering the rest.

Somehow, its hobbles had been cut.

Still hooting at the top of his lungs, Iakki waved at Rafi as he passed. Sahak's shout sent the soldiers chasing to herd the colt back, but it wheeled and twisted and then plunged into thick jungle. Most of the soldiers followed, leaving only two to snap into place behind Sahak as he rounded on Sev who stared slack-jawed at the vines swaying in Iakki's wake. "That wouldn't be your–"

A dark form careened into Sahak from the side, sending both sprawling in a tangle of flashing knives, hammering fists, and flailing legs that kicked a log from the fire, scattering embers across the clearing and briefly illuminating the attacker's face.

Rafi blinked. He must be delirious. He could have sworn that was Nef.

Spears raised, the two soldiers advanced but seemed hesitant to strike. Heavy footsteps pounded and Moc's unmistakable towering form burst from the underbrush and hurtled toward them with a roar. Their collision blurred as a haze crept over Rafi's vision. Soon, he would collapse. Soon, the latch would open and the tiger would pounce.

He could no longer simply will himself to stand. His limbs were as weak as a bruised vine when they needed to be stone. He needed to be stone.

No, he needed to be *turned* to stone.

Mustering strength, he shouted hoarsely and met the tiger's gaze in its cage across the clearing. Yellow consumed his vision, and his heart thundered in his chest. Instantly, his limbs seized and became firm. His arms no longer sagged. His legs no longer trembled. Even the grunting, thudding, and frenzied scrambling of the fight faded, until all he could hear was his own uneven breathing.

Then the rope snapped with a twang.

He crashed onto his face and groaned at a dozen different pains as he lifted his head to see Nef's *chet* lodged in the branch where his rope had been cut and then lowered it to find a bloody knife inches from his bound hands. It must have slipped from his thigh when he fell. He gripped its slick hilt, wedged it between his knees, and sawed the rope from his wrists.

Freed, he scanned the clearing, gathering the strength to stand and somehow try to run, but definitely not to fight, and froze at the sight of Nef crouched over Sahak, bleeding from minor wounds, but holding one of Sahak's own blades–Rafi had seen it up close–to his throat. One soldier was down. Moc circled with the other, both wielding broken spears.

How long had he been trapped by the stone-eye?

How long before the rest of the soldiers looped back?

"Take that, Tetrani!" Nef raised the knife in both hands, readying to drive it down, and Rafi could only watch as Sahak stared unblinking at the blade that would claim his life. Then Sev appeared out of nowhere and crashed into Nef, throwing all three into a tangled knot that smashed into the lightning tree and sprawled apart.

Nef recovered first and dove for Sahak.

"No!" Sev snagged his ankle and yanked him flat, but Nef twisted around and rained punches down with one hand while scrabbling for something on the ground with the other.

He came up with a knife and flung his hand back to strike.

"Nef, no!" Rafi staggered up, then collapsed and crawled toward them instead. "No! Get Sahak!" Somehow, his voice pierced Nef's rage and propelled him away from Sev to spin in a low, sweeping circle that anticipated attack.

But Sahak was already gone.

"Where did he go?" Nef demanded. "Did anyone see?"

Moc was doubled over, gasping. No sign of his opponent either. "Got me . . . in the gut . . . got away . . . both of them . . ." He heaved in a long breath and recovered, so he must have just been winded instead of truly wounded. "We should go. Can't you hear them coming?"

Now that he had spoken, Rafi could hear crashing footsteps drawing nearer.

Nef nodded sharply. "Guess Iakki wasn't able to lead them far." He cast a scrutinizing glance over Rafi, and judging by his expression, didn't like what he saw. "Can you walk?"

"On a good day, usually."

"So . . ."

"Not today, no."

Nef's scowl deepened. Clearly his sense of humor had not improved, which was a shame, since searching for the humor in this bloody, insane, horrifying mess was the only thread holding Rafi together. "You." Nef kicked out at Sev who had crawled up onto his knees, his head clutched in his hands. "Up. Help him."

Sev lifted his bloody face, looking dazed. "Me?"

"Yes, you." Nef gave his borrowed knife a twirl, and Sev stood and grudgingly held out a hand which Rafi eyed warily before accepting. Once his weight struck his injured leg though, he gladly threw his less-injured arm over Sev's shoulder, and let him drag him into the darkening jungle after Moc who had scooped up a burning brand from the fire and used strips of cloth to craft an improvised torch to light their path, while Nef concealed their trail behind.

Only a dozen agonizing strides into the trek, Iakki dropped from a vine into their path. He saw Rafi, and dove at him in complete defiance of both their need for quiet and Rafi's need to not suffer any more injuries. Somehow, Rafi didn't mind. He hugged the boy with one hand and could barely swallow past the lump in his throat, let alone speak.

Still, he managed to promise, "Next time, you get to ride in the front."

FIFTY-ONE: JAKIM

Aodh brings peace.

"Peace, boy," Nold called over his shoulder as Jakim reflexively tightened his grip. The earth itself trembled at their passing as they fled into the night, and Jakim prayed he would not fall. His stomach lurched as the massive steed picked up speed, tilting across land lit by a moon as bright and yellow as a tiger's eye, and crisscrossed with shadows like chasms.

His own feet he would have trusted, but those of a steed?

"Solborn can see like a wolfhound at night," Nold said. "They will not misstride."

The steed leaped an uneven patch, and Jakim's gut rose and plummeted, and he clenched his teeth to keep from accidentally biting his tongue. None of the riders surrounding them seemed to bounce as he did. How did they manage it?

"You sit his back like a dead thing, you know." Nold glanced back at him, with crinkled eyes and a crooked grin despite the danger they fled. "So stiff and tense. You make it more challenging for both of you. Can you not sense the rhythm to it? Find it and move with it."

Move with it? He feared his spine would break first.

His answers to Iona's questions upon his recovery had sent them racing to deliver the tidings, but that was nothing compared to the pace Ceridwen demanded now. Out from the fortress they had thundered–his ears still rang from the echoing of hooves in those enclosed stone halls–and the guards at the gate had fallen back without attempting to halt them, allowing them to rejoin the two score other Outriders who had been waiting on the plain beyond.

"Why not stop us," he wondered aloud, in Canthorian by habit.

Nold looked over his shoulder. "What was that?"

"The guards at the gate"—this time in Soldonian—"why did they not stop us?"

"They are of Lochrann," Nold said, as if it were obvious. It wasn't. "They let her pass because she is their war-chief. I doubt Glyndwr's ruling will sit well with them. It is one thing to hesitate to place a *kasar*-branded warrior on the throne. It is another to hand the throne to Ardon."

Jakim had only understood half of what Nold said. Ardon. Lochrann. Were those people? Cities? "*Kasar*-branded?" he repeated. "What is that?"

Nold hesitated as Ceridwen slowed ahead, halting the column. Straight-backed in the saddle, she spun from east to west atop her dancing steed, surveying their route. She shifted so naturally with the horse's movements that Jakim couldn't look away. Eliami women rarely wielded weapons and never rode fire-breathing steeds into battle. Theirs was a strength of wisdom and knowledge, of healing, of recollection and memory. He tried to picture Siba in the garb of the king's daughter and found it impossible.

"It is the judgment of the blood debt," Nold finally answered.

That sounded ominous. "How . . . why?"

"She must tell you herself. But she is our Fireborn." There was awe in his voice. "It makes no difference to us." He fell silent as the column moved on at a gentler pace that allowed Jakim to relax his grip. Slightly. "And what of you, Jakim Ha'Nor? Now that you are free?"

The question surprised Jakim. He opened his mouth and found his voice gone. Was he finally, truly free again? Death had nearly claimed him not once but twice in the past few days. He had felt the breath bleed from his lungs and was horrified to find himself reluctant—or maybe, simply not ready—to face Aodh yet. What kind of a Scroll was he?

One grossly unprepared, as Scrollmaster Gedron had warned.

Yet against all odds, he had fulfilled his oath to the dying king and survived. Now he was free to sail for home to complete the call laid upon him, and if Aodh was merciful again, fulfill Enok's mission in Broken-Eliam too, so his lie might be redeemed in the truth. Knowing that should have awakened that joyful sense of purpose within him, but he felt a familiar stirring instead, and a whisper that something was incomplete. Aodh's hand?

Jakim ignored the feeling. "I am going home."

FIFTY-TWO: CERIDWEN

No fireborn can maintain flame forever. Exhaustion will win out eventually, and then, when its heart is devoid of heat and its blood is ashen cold, then the astute opponent will strike.

It was the night of the Fire Moon, and Rhodri was king.

That thought goaded Ceridwen past all limits of exhaustion as the miles rolled underfoot and the blazing orange sphere hanging low and massive in the sky dimmed behind gathering clouds. Rhodri was *king*, and what was she but the brand upon her forehead, forever doomed to seek atonement for the damage she had wrought?

"Still no sign of pursuit." Iona settled her stormer alongside, eying her with concern.

"For now," Ceridwen said curtly, for she knew it was coming.

Rhodri had called for her execution and had countless warriors who now answered his horn, whereas she had only the partial unit Iona had brought–though Iona had requested that Kassa follow when able with Lochrann's muster. One of Markham's subordinates now led the Outrider *ayeds* and would continue harrying the main Nadaarian column on its crawl inland, so she could expect no aid from there.

She glanced at the warriors riding at her heels and was suddenly aware of the tension in their postures. Did they believe her a traitor? Had they realized that she had doomed them? Still, they followed, as Bair had into the smothering heat plumes of Koltar, and Markham into the swing of Kilmark's axe. Finnian alone had turned aside. His abandonment still stung, but he had known since Markham paired them that her taint was contagious, and now it was far, far worse. The traitor's stink would cling to all who followed her.

Flames take you, Finnian, for being right.

"Where should we go?" Iona asked carefully, as though she sensed the firestorm brewing in Ceridwen's chest. "Who can we trust?"

"I don't–" Ceridwen bit off her words. "Eagan . . . maybe."

After today, she trusted him most, now that she could not rejoin the Outrider *ayeds*. Without Markham or the throne, she had no true claim upon them, and with Rhodri confirmed king, leading her warriors to join them might mean leading them to death.

Hers. Maybe even theirs. *Blazes*, she just didn't know.

Mindar snorted and tugged against her reins. His stride became choppy, rising higher and falling harder on his forelimbs. Sparks shivered from his skin. Always he sensed her turmoil and responded in fire. It raged across his mane and tail, a beacon in the night. Ceridwen cursed and drew him back. Startled, Iona called the halt. One earthhewn plunged past a full five strides before managing to slow.

Dismounting, Ceridwen met Iona's questioning gaze. "We rest here."

Iona looked relieved. She was ever concerned with the wellbeing of riders and steeds, and they were long past due for a halt. Silently, the others untacked their mounts, but the thrumming in Ceridwen's veins demanded action, and Mindar's flames had not yet cooled. Reins slung over her shoulder, she began to walk. Iona called after her, but did not follow.

Ever the beat of hooves had aided her thoughts, urging her relentlessly onward from despair. But tonight, every hoofbeat spoke of failure, of judgment, and of ruin. So she walked on foot, heedless of her warriors' confusion, not caring where she went so long as she moved.

Onward. Onward. *Onward.*

For three years, that had been her soul's cry. But tonight . . . tonight the world was dead, the fire was cold, and there was nothing but defeat.

The reins slipped from her shoulder. She left them and came to a halt, unbowed, defiant, braced against the crouching darkness. Rustling behind brought Mindar's head up with a snort, and she whirled to fend off attack, but it was only Jakim standing wide-eyed and guilty in the moonlight, a sack slung over his shoulder.

"Why are you here?" she asked. "The others sleep, and I sought . . . quiet."

Jakim swallowed, shuffling from foot to foot. "I am leaving . . . but Aodh's hand . . ." He broke off, mumbling to himself, then hefted the sack higher. "I took this from one of your warriors. Supplies for my journey home."

She raised an eyebrow. "Stole it, you mean?"

"No . . . I am telling you now, so it is not stealing, is it?" He rubbed at the markings on his arms, clearly unnerved. "I am a Scroll of Aodh. We do not steal."

Yet it sounded as if he sought to convince himself. From what Iona had relayed of the boy's story during their flight, he had saved them from some deadly new weapon the Nadaari unleashed during the battle—the same weapon that had driven the Nadaari from their own fortifications. He could have all the supplies he wished as far as Ceridwen was concerned, but she would have the truth from him first.

"You do not steal," she repeated, "but do you lie?"

"I . . ." He looked almost frightened.

She drew forth the ring. "Did my father truly intend this for me?"

"Yes . . . yes, I did not lie about that."

Yet the writ named Rhodri heir. The boy had claimed her father wished to offer mercy, but men often did strange things in the shadow of death. "The last thing my father willed me was a brand." She choked out the words. "He carried it out with his own hands, and for three years, I have sought atonement without earning it."

Jakim lowered the sack to the ground. "What . . . was it for?"

She hesitated, but there was no gain in concealing what the world already knew. "I led my brother into peril, and he died. I struggle to believe my father merciful enough to forgive *that*." She turned abruptly toward her steed. "It is good you are leaving, Scroll Jakim. You will be far safer away from me."

Mindar's ears flicked at her approach, but he continued grazing. She loosened his cinch and drew a hoof knife from her saddlebags to remove the charred earth from his hooves–anything to distract from the truths her tongue had spilled. She set the first hoof down and moved on to the second, pausing a moment to stretch her back, and saw Jakim sitting with his elbows on his knees. He was still there when she finished the third.

"My own brothers sold me as a slave."

Ceridwen's fingers tightened around the hoof knife.

Jakim tilted his head toward the moon, eyes closed, golden light bathing his face. "I was ten when the caravan dragged me away. My brothers watched. My sister Siba wept and fought, but Amir held her back. She had prophesied . . . great things . . . about me. I guess it made them jealous." He spoke with feeling, with truth and pain, absent the forced apathy or bitterness she frequently adopted when speaking of the *kasar*. "I have always wondered why they didn't just let me be taken unawares. But Yath led the slave merchants over. Amir and Isir handed me off. I saw the payment Dako received–only a dozen *teth*. He and Iben divided it while Emet stood watch."

Ceridwen slowly lowered the final hoof.

Jakim's eyes opened, meeting hers. "They wanted me to know they were responsible. So they stood there, watching, and not one helped me."

Her chest burned at the injustice of it. "You return home for retribution then?"

It made sense. More than that, it was earned.

He rubbed his bottom lip. "No." His voice was so soft it was barely audible over the wind brushing through the grass. "I return home to offer my brothers forgiveness. Aodh help me."

"*Blazes*, why?" She gripped the hoof knife even tighter. She could hear his grief at his brothers' betrayal in his voice, and yet, he would forgive them?

It was wrong. They deserved to burn for what they had done.

Jakim shrugged as if at a loss to understand himself. "Did you know Aodh's mercy is mentioned fifty-seven times in the holy writ, forgiveness thirty-four?" His mouth quirked wryly. "Yes, I counted them. It is . . . why he is named the Bearer of the Eternal Scars. He offers mercy for the guilty and justice for the innocent, and carries their suffering in himself."

She had never heard it put in such terms. Perhaps that explained his belief that her father could offer mercy. All Ceridwen knew was judgment. Wrath she understood intimately. Forgiveness was a foreign concept. "There will be no forgiveness for me." Somehow, speaking the words enabled her to grasp what had been hovering on the edge of her thoughts all night. The blood debt could only be erased in blood. *Her* blood. Saving Soldonia and defeating the Nadaari might be beyond her. But maybe . . . maybe she could keep her warriors from joining those scorched by her passage.

Of what worth was her life—or death—if she could not save them?

"Farewell, Scroll Jakim. It is time we were both on our way." She had delayed the inevitable long enough. But although Jakim nodded and hefted his sack, he promptly set off in the wrong direction. She called him back and directed his gaze to the stars where the constellation known as Hagan's Sickle forever curved toward the west and the coast. "If I could spare a rider to take you—"

"No," he said, too quickly. "I prefer walking."

Yet he hesitated as she tightened Mindar's cinch and swung up into the saddle. The fireborn plunged forward, and she checked him, reassured that his fires burned brightly still. He would need that energy before the night was done.

"Your brother's death was an accident."

Jakim's voice stilled her. "And yet, it was my fault."

"Do you believe you control all the world?" He spoke with quiet conviction. "Are you Aodh that life and death rest in your hands? Please, Ceridwen . . . think on it?" He looked very lost and very young and impossibly weary as he shouldered his sack and walked away.

Ceridwen waited until he was out of sight then gave her fireborn slack and raced away over the moonlit earth. At last, she knew what she must do. Traitor or not, Rhodri was king. He would come for her, and when he did, she could not command her warriors to lift weapons against their own countrymen.

If they fought for her, they would be doomed.

If they killed for her, they too would bear the *kasar.*

"No, Jakim," she answered his question to herself, as she skirted the camp where Iona and her faithful few awaited her return, and rode back across the gorse-clad hills toward Rysinger. "Merely death."

FIFTY-THREE: RAFI

At the start of every jungle is a single seed.
– Mahque saying

"Stop here." Nef shoved past Sev and Rafi and up the narrow jungle trail with Iakki clinging to his back, fast asleep, mouth open and head bobbing with each step. Ahead, Moc turned to face him, hovering over his dying torch to protect the flame, and Nef hitched the sleeping boy higher as they conferred in a whisper.

"You think we'll get to rest?" Sev gasped.

Rafi was so exhausted from their hours-long trek that he just grunted–which, he realized, had the unfortunate effect of making him sound like Nef. He sank to the damp ground, and Sev sprawled beside him, breathing heavily and ruffling his damp shirt. Rafi closed his eyes and barely cracked an eyelid when Moc stomped a clear space for a fire, but he pushed up onto one elbow when Nef eased Iakki to the ground and vanished into the Mah without a word.

"Where's he going?"

Moc shrugged, setting down the smoldering torch and feeding it twigs until it sputtered and smoked and finally threw up a real flame. "Nef isn't much of a one for sharing."

"But"–Rafi sat up–"what are you even doing here?"

"Oh, that? We followed you."

"You what?"

Moc sheepishly met his eyes. "You sneaked off twice in a row. Nef was suspicious. We couldn't keep up, but you left a decent trail.

We knew we were on the right track when Iakki came crashing up hollering that you were about to be killed."

"So, you decided to help me? Nef agreed to that?"

"He was concerned."

"That I'd betray the revolution."

Moc looked away. "Something like that."

Of course. "What did he want to do, kill me before I could break?" He had been half joking, but the way Moc busied himself poking the fire made him wonder. "You agreed to that?"

"What? No. I didn't, Nahiki. Honest. I trusted you."

Moc sounded so earnest, Rafi couldn't help believing him, and his reference to Rafi's false identity–not to mention the fact that they had rescued him–didn't leave much ground for indignation. "What changed Nef's mind?"

"Well–"

Trailing vines parted abruptly beside them, and Nef pushed through. He eyed them narrowly as if aware they had been talking about him, before dropping beside Rafi and scattering an armful of various leaves and roots. Silently, he stripped the skin from a root with his teeth, then spat it out onto a strip of bark where he also piled a handful of leaves. Using the hilt of Sahak's knife, he mashed it all into a poultice that he then smeared onto Rafi's many cuts, slices, and gouges. Its sting made Rafi's eyes water.

Nef worked with skilled efficiency, if not gentleness, though he took greater care with the stab wounds in Rafi's hand and thigh. Once all the cuts were slathered with the oozing green mixture, he disappeared again, only to return with a bunch of thick yellow leaves that he separated and bound around each wound with a strip of cloth cut from his own tunic.

Rafi gingerly prodded the leafy poultice on his left hand. Leave it to Sahak to aim at his dominant hand. Hopefully, he hadn't severed a tendon. "Thanks, Nef." He got the words out in a rush to avoid the sour taste in his mouth, and of course, got only a grunt in return.

Moc raised an eyebrow. "Tell me that wasn't more painful than being stabbed."

"Pretty close." Rafi grinned, then winced, lifting a hand to his head. "Not nearly as bad as this headache though. Don't suppose you have a poultice for that?" He looked to Nef who had settled beside the fire to polish Sahak's blade.

Nef snorted loudly. "For stupidity? No. What exactly was headbutting him supposed to do? Was there any thought process behind it at all?"

"Well . . . I really, really wanted to hit him."

Kind of like he was feeling right now.

Moc coughed and stood. "You know, I'm going to go retrace our path a bit and make sure we weren't followed. Can't be too careful."

Nef stared up at him. "I already concealed our trail."

"Right, but–"

"So, we are safe."

"Sure, but–"

"Unless your blundering draws attention."

Moc shrugged mildly. "Then I'll have to blunder quietly." He pushed off into the jungle and for all the talk of blundering, he moved smoothly enough through the thick underbrush. The rustle of his steps quickly faded, leaving only the crackle of flames to harmonize with the chirruping insect symphony that characterized the jungle at night.

"Why didn't you let them kill me?" Rafi asked at last.

He had almost given up hope of an answer when Nef finally spoke. "You could have betrayed us, but you didn't. I may not like you, Tetrani, but . . . maybe I don't hate you. I suppose you cannot help what you are born."

That ranked as one of the most backhanded, not-quite-there apologies Rafi had ever received. "But maybe I still hate you. You did try to drown me, after all."

"And now I have saved you. I think that makes us even."

Rafi considered, pursing his lips, and shook his head. "No, not even close."

"Ah, that's right," Nef said, without missing a beat. "You owe me a *chet*." And maybe it was the flickering firelight or the smoke in his eyes, but Rafi could have sworn Nef smiled. Silence blossomed between them, broken only by the croaking warble of frogs, and Rafi was just contemplating sleep, when Nef nodded toward Sev who sprawled motionless on his back, one arm flung across his face. "What do you plan to do with him?"

"Yeah, Rafi." Sev's bitter voice was muffled. "What do you plan to do with me?"

Rafi cursed beneath his breath. Had Sev been awake this whole time? He hadn't even begun to process the fact that Sev had betrayed him, watched Sahak carve into him and threaten to let a tiger tear him limb from limb, and the only regret Sev seemed to have was that he could not kill him quickly. Still, he knew how grief could rage like a hurricane, leaving you capsized and drowning, desperate to lash out. "Nothing, Sev, I just–"

"Nothing?" Nef interrupted, voice sharp. "I didn't stay my blade to spare his life, but because it is fitting you end him yourself. He is a traitor."

"But he is my cousin."

"He is working with them."

"You don't understand," Rafi gritted out, "so net your tongue and let me speak." Surprisingly, Nef raised his hands in surrender. Rafi took a deep breath, more wary of Sev than he had ever been of the sea-demon. "I am sorry for Kaya–"

"You know nothing about her." Sev spat, sitting up and slamming his fists against the ground. "She's not dead. Or at least, she wasn't. Not before. But after all this?" He flung out a hand, and his anger veered toward despair. "I had one shot at saving her, and now she is gone."

"Kaya is alive?" Rafi's relief faded as understanding crashed like a cold wave in his gut. "That one shot, that was me?"

"I just had to find you, find you and bring you back," Sev said, words tumbling together. "That was it. He didn't say anything about torture, and I thought . . ." His gaze darted away. "Well, you lied to me about who you were. What do I owe you above Kaya?"

"Nothing," Rafi said, voice low.

"She . . . we . . . are going to have a child."

Oh, Ches-Shu. "Tell me what happened, Sev. Where is she?"

"He took her." Sev's voice matched his hollow eyes. "Her and half the village."

FIFTY-FOUR: CERIDWEN

Like their steeds, shadowriders can move without making a sound, vanish from sight in shadow, and possess heightened night vision. They often serve as scouts, spies, and assassins.

The rhythmic fall of Mindar's hooves punctuated the stillness of a world bathed in the golden light of the Fire Moon. Ceridwen restrained him to a gentle lope, conserving his energy. With each stride, her saddle creaked faintly and her spurs jingled—sounds so familiar that ordinarily she would scarcely have noticed them. Only now, with one ear turned into the wind and her senses strained, did they strike her as ominous for they might mask a foe's approach.

In Rhodri's place, she would have sent shadowriders first with orders to locate her, determine a plan of attack, and report back to the main force which would have been slower to muster and advance. But finding her alone, unaided, and presumably outnumbered should be enough to tempt them to attack rather than pursue her warriors, and then she would unleash a reckoning upon them, Rhodri, and all the traitors she could root out before dying.

This would be her atonement.

It was the change in Mindar—nostrils flared, muscles taut—that finally alerted her to their presence. Ever he sensed what others could not. That was her first advantage. Her second was that she knew Lochrann in a way that warriors of Ardon would not. So, she rode on until reaching a wide, flat space, devoid of trees, where the Fire Moon hung low and bright in the vast expanse of the sky yet cast few shadows upon the earth. Here she would stand. She halted to settle her mask and hood and could feel Mindar's flames rising, warming his ribcage. Sparks drifted from his mane as the wind ruffled it across his arched neck.

Mindar stamped and snorted a harsh, ragged sound. They had come.

She drew her ringing blade. "Come out and face me!" Touch of the spurs, rein hand on Mindar's neck, one heel pressed to his side, and he twisted into the firestorm, spewing flame while spinning on his hindquarters. Three rotations before she halted him inside a scorched ring.

Only the breeze answered, whispering through moon-gilded grass.

Her pulse quickened. "Will you not fight?" She stabbed her blade toward the stars, involuntarily twitching the reins. Mindar sidestepped and an arrow whisked past her face so near she could have seized the shaft in her teeth. She caught her breath.

Moonlight glinted off a shadower's sweat-slicked hide as it emerged into the open, rider swiftly setting another arrow. Only one? She'd expected–

Pain ripped through her left shoulder, and a cry escaped her lips. She fell against Mindar's neck, reins slipping from her fingers, and he plunged beneath her, grinding the arrow in the wound. She groaned, twisting her fingers in his mane.

Of course, they had circled her.

Only a fool would have missed it.

She sucked shallow breaths through gritted teeth, rallying herself to strike back, yet even now it was Finnian's voice in her head that advised caution, so she waited, and like mist rising in the cool of morning, three more shadowriders materialized in the moonlight to surround her. Four in total–two archers, two swordsmen–and doubtless more scattered between here and Rysinger.

Pain pulsed down her arm and across her chest as she forced herself upright. No hail of arrows followed. The archers had sacrificed distance to close in and must be wary of hitting their own. Clearly, they sought to take her alive, advancing slowly as they did, not in a rush, and yet grouped closely enough to make attacking dangerous. What better way to seal Rhodri's claim than a public execution? Perhaps she could still gain amnesty for her warriors.

"Where is Rhodri?" she demanded. "I would speak with him."

"You will see him soon enough. Yield, and it may go better for you."

Gingerly, Ceridwen tested her injured arm. The slightest motion shifted the arrow within the wound. She could hold the reins but lacked the strength to maneuver. She could rein with her blade hand instead but would have to drop them to strike. Mindar responded to leg pressure, but deprived of the reins, she would have to wield him more like an earthhewn–blunt and forceful, lacking the crisp turns and finesse typical of a fireborn in combat.

"Surrender," the warrior repeated, "and you will–"

Ceridwen attacked, spinning Mindar sideways with her heel, broadside to the nearest archer. Her hasty strike grazed his arm and bit into his bow. Cursing, the man swung the other end of the bow at her head and missed as Mindar barreled onward another three strides before she managed to seize the reins in her blade hand.

She whipped around, narrowly evading the swordswoman's sweep. Steel passed inches from her neck. With her blade tangled among the reins, she could not retaliate, but she wove Mindar through their midst, forcing them into each other's paths, flaming when they pressed in too close. She abandoned the reins for her blade as the swordsman charged up on her wounded left and pinned her leg to Mindar's side with his shadower's chest, forcing them sideways. Three staggering blows hammered against her sabre.

She blocked at an awkward angle, body twisted sideways, and felt her arm weakening, so she yielded to the next blow, letting the tip of his sword slice across her cuirass, so his own weight would slap the flat of her blade against the shadower's head. The steed jerked, exposing the swordsman to her blade. It bit through his mail. Only a shallow wound, but he wheeled away to join the other three. They charged toward her in a solid line.

Their first rush had been scattered. They would not make that mistake again.

Mane tossing, Mindar danced as she reclaimed his reins then

launched toward the shadowers, unleashing a river of flame. Ramming them was not an option, since her steed lacked an earthhewn's hide, but few would withstand a fireborn shrieking toward them in fury.

At the last second, she exchanged reins for blade.

The shadowers split before the raging torrent. One archer broke to her right. Her strike caught him in the back of the neck. He fell headlong, and his steed loped on, empty stirrups flapping at its sides. One down.

Steel glinted to her left. She pressed Mindar away with her heel, and the swordswoman's blade gouged a line across the skirt of her saddle, barely missing her thigh. She groped for Mindar's reins, trying to swing around to engage, but they had slid down his neck, and he careened heedlessly onward. Without her steadying hand, the pressure of leg cues only riled him, as years of conditioning vanished before the reckless heat of the fight.

She abandoned her reach for the reins as Mindar broadsided another shadower, surprising the rider—the swordsman—and enabling her to catch his blade on hers, but the arc of his strike rammed the hilt against the side of her head.

Nausea shot through her.

Her vision darkened in a churning spiral.

Then his arm hooked around her neck and began to drag her from her steed. Instinctively, she seized the saddle with her left hand, and the white-hot stab of her wound shocked her alert. She rolled her spurs and fire roared from Mindar's throat. Heat engulfed her, and the swordsman bellowed, releasing her as the shadower lurched away, coat in flames, and Mindar's speed increased, consumed by the rush of his own inferno.

She lunged in the stirrups and snatched his reins, halting his torrent. Reluctantly, he ground to a halt. Grunts, gasps, and moans of pain eddied around her, but it was the crackle of fire and the hiss of sparks that captured her attention. Flames had seized the grass and ran on ahead, throwing up plumes of black smoke.

Smoke . . .

Shadowers could ghost in smoke too.

Cursing her error, she twisted in the saddle. The swordsman had been pitched by his flaming steed which raced away, a torch soon lost against the massive blaze of the Fire Moon. He lurched toward the riderless steed pacing anxiously back and forth behind the slain archer, and the swordswoman drew up between Ceridwen and the unhorsed warrior. But where was the other–

Behind her, a bowstring creaked.

She spun, cuing Mindar to flame, knowing that it was too late. Her spine trembled, anticipating the agony of another arrow tearing through flesh, but the bow snapped as the archer drew. Her first strike had done damage. She let out the shrill cry of the Outriders and charged as he flung down the pieces and drew a long knife instead. Then the Fire Moon vanished behind thick clouds, and the shadower ghosted in the darkness.

Blazes. Pulse hammering, Ceridwen came to a stuttering halt. Battling one ghosted shadower was suicide, let alone three. She was outmatched. She had no choice but to flee until the clouds parted or morning broke if she would survive to continue the fight. So she spun off at an angle, swept between her foes, and raced toward the Gauroth range.

But in the dark where she had no control, where she relied on Mindar's eyesight instead of her own, where there was nothing but the wind rushing past her ears and the synchronized pulse of heartbeat and hoofbeat and horse and rider moving as one, she simply hoped she survived.

FIFTY-FIVE: JAKIM & RAFI

Aodh bears the wounds of the world.

The look he had seen in Ceridwen's eyes haunted Jakim. He tried not to think of it. He breathed deeply as he walked, filling his sore lungs with air that smelled of hope and freedom . . . and the reek of horse sweat clinging to his clothes. Who would have thought the legendary steeds of Soldonia would smell so strongly? Siba would never believe he had ridden one, but he couldn't wait to tell her. Sack swinging over his shoulder, grass swishing against his legs, he set a jaunty pace, path lit before his feet by the enormous moon hanging low in the night sky.

It was almost the color of an overripe mango—not the skin but the flesh—and it shone so fiercely the stars paled in comparison. But at least they did not weep, and Jakim could still see the constellation Ceridwen had identified as an anchor westward toward the coast, toward his family and his home. Until now, he had not let himself think beyond the immediate needs of transportation and survival, or the constant slow and steady work of forgiveness. Now he let himself imagine the moment of his return.

How Siba would weep and crush him in her arms, how his father would blink blearily and wonder where he had been—as if he'd been gone for minutes instead of years—how his brothers would redden and shuffle their feet and refuse to meet his eyes, and how he would stammer and stutter and choke over the words he'd traveled so many leagues to say.

Jakim sighed and hefted the sack higher on his back. Still, he would do it.

But as he plodded resolutely forward, an invisible string tugged inside his chest. It plucked a chord that resonated within his entire being and reverberated in the distance behind him. Something that was not quite a voice and not quite words whispered a humming of intention and purpose and a call to . . . turn back?

He slowed, looking over his shoulder, and in the moon's craggy surface, so low and close to earth it seemed within reach, he saw Ceridwen's eyes reflected. Shadowed, haunted craters of despair. When they had spoken, she'd had the look of one longing for death, a look he'd seen many times as a slave, and still he had walked away, for he had found no wisdom to offer in comfort.

He, a Scroll of Aodh.

Giving his head a shake, he continued on, and though he could not hear Siba's promise, he repeated it to himself—*"You will save your people"*—and increased his pace. His people and his vows awaited him beyond the coast. The Nadaari occupied the ports, but maybe he could barter passage . . . or steal a boat . . .

Surely that would be excusable under these circumstances.

The churning of his stomach dragged him to a halt. So, he would be a thief now as well as a liar? Or at least willing to become one, and ignore the guiding hand of Aodh too. Siba's image seemed to fade from his mind more with each passing day, but he could imagine her disappointment if he admitted that. "Aodh have mercy." He scrubbed at his stinging eyes and tilted his head back toward the stars.

A pale light winked out, and his breath caught. Were the stars weeping again?

Scrollmaster Gedron had warned that Aodh's purposes were rarely clear. Perhaps his purpose here was not yet done. Perhaps his path remained intertwined with Ceridwen and her warriors. Perhaps the way home was not yet open to him.

He flung up his hands and turned around. "Fine, I will stay!"

Only Aodh grant that wherever his path led it required walking instead of riding.

Rafi limped through the grasping dark of the jungle, slapping tendrils of mollusk moss away from his face, hoping he didn't stumble across a python—or worse—distracted as he was by the story Sev had relayed. The facts had unraveled with brutal simplicity: Sahak had stormed into the village, thirsty for Rafi's blood, and some coward had identified Sev as his friend. Rather than hunt Rafi himself, Sahak had dragged away Kaya and half the village in chains. How Sahak had found him during that disastrous raid with Nef remained a mystery, since Sev had failed to track him down for weeks before returning to the beach in hopes that Rafi would eventually do the same. When he had come without Iakki, Sev had seized the chance to retrieve his brother and summon Sahak to complete the capture.

Thus, Rafi Tetrani had nearly been eaten alive.

With Sev's voice still raw in his ears, Rafi had abandoned the fire, desperate for space to think, to breathe, to escape. *Do you remember, Rafi*, the jungle seemed to say to him, and he remembered fleeing again and again and again.

Stirred by the thought, the ghost whispered to him too. *Run, Rafi.*

So he ran, limping, teeth clenched against pain. He didn't make it far before collapsing in a patch of rubbery grass lit by orange-tinged moonlight that streamed through a gap in the canopy. Something heavy rattled the bushes to his left.

He forced his aching head up. "Moc? What happened to blundering quietly?"

But instead of the big Alonque, it was a long solemn face crowned with wispy, white hair and inquisitive ears that parted the bushes, nickered, and shuffled clumsily toward him. Rafi found himself smiling, pleased that the colt had escaped too and had located him again. "Ah, it's you." He didn't bother rising as it nuzzled his head, snorted in his face, and only weakly shoved its nose away from his wounded hand when it tried to eat his leafy bandage.

"You're going nowhere." Iakki flopped unexpectedly beside him.

Rafi eyed him sidelong. "Where did you come from? How did you find me?"

"You were running in circles."

Around. Around. And around again.

Rafi shook off his disorientation. "I thought you were sleeping."

"Too much talking."

"You could sleep through a hurricane."

"Yeah." Iakki grinned. He gestured at the colt. "What's its name?"

Rafi shrugged. "I didn't think it needed one. Just days ago, I was returning it to the sea so it could be free." Since he could not be. That thought still rang with nauseating truth. Run in circles all he wished, he could not escape it. He was Rafi Tetrani. It was the one identity he could not shed, and now the villagers of Zorrad had become entangled in it with him, and Sahak would make sure they suffered for it.

"So . . ." Iakki scuffed his heels. "You going to help Kaya?"

Part of Rafi wished he had kept running that night two years ago when Torva had invited him—ragged, rain-soaked, and reeling with exhaustion—in for a cup of seaweed tea. Part of him wished he could keep running now.

But it was too late.

Time to stand, Rafi, he told himself. *Win or lose, to stand.* And this, he decided, he could do. Only . . . he might need help getting to his feet first. "Um . . . Iakki?"

FIFTY-SIX: CERIDWEN, JAKIM, & RAFI

The breath of a dawnling is life, on this all lore agrees.

Dawn slashed a bloodstained scar across the sky as Ceridwen halted atop a barren hill on the edge of the Gauroth range. Her fireborn trembled, snorting cold white smoke, fires dangerously spent, while she could hardly think through the pain radiating from her shoulder. At least the arrow plugged the wound, limiting blood loss, for although two shadowers were down, two remained, and this fight was far from won.

The bald hill offered a fair vantage and little cover—or shadow—for attackers striking uphill. With his bow, Finnian could have held them off. With her blade, the odds were less sure, yet she had battled such odds all night.

The swordswoman had overtaken her once but attacked too cautiously and had been grounded when flames claimed her saddle. Later, Ceridwen had nicked the swordsman's thigh, but he had battered her wounded arm and ripped a gash across Mindar's chest before retreating. He had known she was nearly finished and so was her steed. Fireborn were resilient to minor wounds since their heated blood cauterized naturally, slowing blood loss. More serious wounds drained blood and flame too quickly for compensation.

She dared not risk Mindar longer in a fight she could not win.

Dismounting beside a boulder, she unsaddled, guzzled water from her flask, and offered the rest to Mindar. She eyed the boulder's rough surface, noting potential handholds, but her wounded shoulder would never support her weight, so she lowered herself to its base and set her sabre across her knees. Wind drifted over the rocky hillside, stinging her face with shards of sand. The sensation threatened to draw her across miles and years to the crater of Koltar.

She lost herself in the memory of coal-dark eyes. "There you are, brother," she murmured. "Soon . . . soon . . . we will go home."

Hours later, the hiss of the wind changed, dispelling the fog of the past and alerting Ceridwen to the shadowrider cresting the hill. It was the swordsman. He halted, eying her warily, and lifted his helm to wipe his brow, revealing a craggy face framed by black hair.

Mustering her strength, Ceridwen stood and refitted her mask. Wounded and exhausted as she was, time fought against her, but she could not reveal her weakness, or he would simply delay until she could no longer stand. Facing a mounted opponent while grounded was hardly ideal but not hopeless. The boulder prevented him from trampling her, and attempting to crush her would place the shadower's chest or gut within reach of her blade. She had chosen not to risk her steed. Perhaps he would do the same.

The swordsman settled his helm. "I will not ask for surrender." He had a deep, quiet voice, like gathering thunderclouds. "You have fought well. You need have no shame in death."

Her sabre's grip creaked beneath her hand. "Tell me your name, son of Ardon, that I might speak it when the horns ring out over your corpse."

"The horns? They call for *you* already." He dismounted heavily and drew his sword. Something about his posture seemed off. Stilted. She had nicked his side early on, hadn't she? His thigh too. "Can you not hear them—"

She sprang, forcing him to turn on his injured leg. His eyes betrayed surprise, but his parry nearly shocked the sabre from her weakened grip. She barely evaded his swing, then threw herself at him with all the reckless fury and speed she could muster.

It was not enough. In five hammering strokes, he had won.

The sabre flew from her numb fingers to clatter on the rocks, out of reach. His boot slammed into her chest, snapping her to the ground. Gasping, she crawled backward. The fight had drawn her away from the boulder, away from her steed. The rock . . . the rock . . . she had to reach it.

There–at her spine.

The swordsman stalked forward, limping, gravel crunching beneath his boots until his blade hovered over her heart. Ceridwen licked her dry lips and whistled. A sharp ascending note. Confusion flashed across the swordsman's face. He spun to his right. Toward Mindar's attentive ears and the wisp of smoke curling from his nostrils. *Black* smoke.

"Bair!"

Suddenly, the air was on fire.

Ceridwen rolled, taking out the swordsman's legs and pinning him in place. She gasped as she inadvertently drove the arrow deeper into her shoulder. Coiling fire rolled harmlessly over the oiled surface of her leathers. She brought her good arm up to shield her eyes, but not even the roaring flames could swallow the swordsman's scream.

The voice filling her ears was suddenly familiar. She jerked her head up, heedless of the heat. Hooves flashed before her eyes. Descending. Tearing. Grinding bone. And the eyes that sought hers through the incandescent waves belonged to Bair.

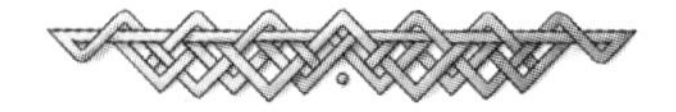

Something tickled Jakim's nose.

He jolted awake, slapping away a fly, and sat up, shaking his head to clear it and rubbing the grit from his eyes. He had walked doggedly all night, hoping he was on the right track, hoping Ceridwen and her riders were where he had left them, hoping he was not insane to turn back and delay his return to his family again, until utterly exhausted, he'd thrown himself down on the hard earth and tossed and turned until sleep finally claimed him.

This country was as rugged and unyielding as its inhabitants. Prickly too.

Eyes closed, he drew in a steadying breath and mentally recited the truths of Aodh to ground him for the day: *Aodh is wise, Aodh is near, Aodh is–*

The sound of a horse snorting startled him to his feet. Solborn surrounded him, all dull grays and mottled earthy browns, ridden by warriors as rangy and weathered as their steeds. Bows creaked, strings strained, and dozens of barbed arrowheads glinted in the afternoon sun, aimed toward his throat.

Tingling shot down his limbs.

A familiar, measured voice ordered the weapons away, and Rhodri te Oengus, traitor and would-be king, emerged on his fiery steed. "So . . ." He seemed amused. "I hunt Ceridwen and find you instead, alone in the wild." His voice hardened. "You risked all I labored for, boy, and for what? What has Soldonia's throne to do with you?"

Jakim shuffled, sick with the knowledge that he was here because Aodh's hand had turned him back, and why would Aodh deliver him into his enemies' hands again? How could this be Aodh's purpose? His eyes darted, searching for an out, but the shadowers were pressed stirrup to stirrup, and when he shifted, the fireborn snorted a flare that could have vaporized his head if it hadn't been aimed a few searing inches from his ear.

One of the archers raised his bow, sighting down the shaft with a snarl. "Shall I put an arrow in his throat, my lord, and cease his tale-telling forever?"

"No." Rhodri drew the word out as if considering, and Jakim squirmed as a prickle ran down his spine. "He may be more useful alive. The engineer has been asking for him." His gloved hand snapped up. "Take him."

Strong hands clamped on Jakim's shoulders, hauling him up and slinging him stomach-first across a horse's back. He struggled, lashing out with his elbows, and got his face mashed against the steed's hide for his pains. Stale dust and dried sweat clogged his nostrils, and he stilled as the steed began to move, carrying him away. But strangely, beneath the fear, beneath the anger, beneath the humiliation too, he felt a settling in his chest, a sense of rightness that exuded hope.

Aodh's hand guiding him still.

Sev, Moc, and Nef were all sitting around the fire when Rafi and Iakki rode the colt back into their makeshift camp. Sleep seemed a rare commodity tonight–or rather, this morning. Rafi's leg gave out when he dismounted, but he managed to avoid falling on his face as he approached Sev. "We're going to save her," he announced, and surprisingly no one laughed.

Sev lifted his bruised face. "You would do that?"

"We're cousins," Rafi said. "Trust me, I'd take you over Sahak any day." He tensed as Sev leaped up and pounded him in an excessively painful hug.

"Touching," Nef grunted, "but do you even know where she is?"

"I might have an idea," Rafi said. "But first, how do you feel about stealing a ship?" That met with blank stares, so he went on to relay the incident with the young soldier's report and his own suspicions. "Sahak is hiding something. It may not be related, but that ship sounded important. Could provide leverage if nothing else. He mentioned a harbor or port. There's several outside Cetmur, but that's a long–"

Moc snapped his fingers. "Yath! That informant we rescued? He talked of a new harbor on the Alon coast. Umut was going to look into it."

"He did," Nef said grudgingly. "Our scout said it was mostly tents, stacked wood, a single dock. Que construction workers. Lots of soldiers. It's not far south from here."

Worth paying a visit, then. Still . . .

"We'll need help," Rafi treaded carefully, half expecting Nef to disagree. After all, Nef did think the revolution capable of destroying the empire, so his concept of the odds seemed questionable. "Sev, how many were left in Zorrad who might be willing to help without trying to kill me on sight?"

Sev's eyes widened then narrowed as he counted. "Uh, maybe . . . ten . . . with old Hanu. Most should be reasonable. Gordu, though . . ."

"Gordu? I thought he was dead."

"Barely scratched and crabby as ever."

Rafi lowered himself painfully to the ground. "So, twelve counting you and me, plus the colt. I'm liking the sound of this." And lying through his teeth, of course.

"Thirteen," Iakki chimed in fiercely. "Don't think I ain't coming."

Moc coughed. "Make that fifteen. You need us." He jabbed an elbow at Nef who caught it and deftly turned it aside before meeting Rafi's questioning gaze.

"Give me another shot at the Emperor's Stone-eye, and I'm in," Nef said.

Rafi slowly gave way to a grin. "Then I can't believe I'm saying this . . . but let's go steal a ship." Moc clapped Sev's shoulder, Nef nodded grimly, and Iakki howled in excitement, and Rafi didn't even need the voice of the ghost in the back of his mind to tell him that they were all of them insane.

"Bair?" Ceridwen broke the suffocating quiet left by the flames. Tears stung her singed cheeks. Wounded arm clenched to her chest, she dragged herself to his side, though she knew what she would see. She had seen it a thousand times in her dreams. Death's savage hand recorded in fire-scorched flesh and hoofmarks upon broken limbs.

Trembling, she touched his shoulder. "Bair?"

But the life had already gone from him. She sought comfort in his coal-dark eyes, but found none in their depths, and the eyes before her . . . were blue. She blinked, struggling to reconcile past and present, here and the crater. Then and now.

A steed nickered softly. She lifted blurry eyes to her fireborn's stooped head. He snorted and backed away from the slain swordsman.

A warrior of Ardon. An enemy.

"*Not Bair.*" She whispered it, anchoring the truth in her mind.

Mindar's shuffling exposed a mud-brown shadower behind him, the grim-faced archer scowling from atop his steed. *Blazes*, the fourth warrior. He must have flanked her during the fight. Doubtless that had been the plan. One to distract from the front. One to close from the side. They had seen her as weak when dismounted and missed the ploy. Even riderless, her fireborn was dangerous. Surely that alone saved her from being trampled now.

His broken bow rested in his saddle-quiver, leaving him armed only with the long knife in his hand, but her sabre still lay beyond reach. Dying without a blade in hand was a sore end indeed, so Ceridwen tried to summon the strength to rise. When she failed, she stared up at him with cheeks wet with tears for the brother who had died, numbness slowly claiming her limbs.

A sweet, brassy horn call filled her ears.

She must already be dying. Only those on death's threshold heard the call. But the archer tilted his head, listening. Did he hear it too?

The shadower suddenly reared back, a brindled gray blur lunging at its throat, and the archer's curse cut off as a bowstring twanged and a copper-fletched arrow sprouted in his neck. He slid from the saddle, dragged by a snarling wolfhound, and landed with a crash.

He did not stir.

There was a soft whistle, and the wolfhound bounded away. Ceridwen struggled to rise, to follow, but the earth betrayed her. It tilted and turned, and she lost her footing. Caught herself on hands and knees and felt a fresh spike of fear when the movement caused no pain. Someone crouched beside her, and she blinked, trying to distinguish the face from the morning sun, but her arms gave out. She fell forward and was caught and lowered gently.

"*Shades*, Ceridwen, not dead yet, I see." The voice cracked with fear and relief.

"No . . . nor you," she whispered.

For at last, at *last*, the endless night was over. The race toward death was finished, and she was still alive. Her vision swam, and the numbness spread from her arms to her chest. With a shuddering breath, she yielded the fight and let the cold take her.

FIFTY-SEVEN: CERIDWEN

But what exactly is granted by this lifebreath of a dawnling–healing, immortality, restoration, regeneration–there, one finds disagreement. The truth has been lost to the haze of time.

Her eyelids fluttered open to a sky of serene blue crisscrossed with spiky green branches clumped with bright yellow berries. A warm breeze skimmed her cheeks and rustled the boughs overhead, disturbing the incessant humming of insects. She took a deep breath and held it in her lungs. It was so . . . peaceful. She could lie here all day and never wish to rise again. Surely this was a dream, for life did not possess such tranquility.

"Of all the sand-blasted, reckless, ill-conceived ideas you have ever had, tal Desmond–and yes, there have been many–this was undoubtedly the worst." Markham's growl jarred her from her peaceful reverie.

She jolted up and fell back with a groan, head spinning. Dull pain flared in her left shoulder, dispelling any notion this might be a dream. Pain was a thing of reality, though how this was reality was beyond her. "Markham?" she gasped, and there were tears in her eyes, though not from pain. "You're not dead, are you?"

His weathered face hovered over her, gaunter than she recalled, marked with deep lines of suffering, and yet very much alive. He studied her and grunted. "This conversation would be considerably stranger if I was."

"Not if I was dead too."

"So . . . this is what you think the land beyond the sun looks like?"

"I don't know *where* this is." Ceridwen struggled up onto her uninjured arm, noting that her cuirass and leathers had been removed, leaving her in a sweat-dampened tunic and leggings. Judging by the hazy light, it was late afternoon–nearly evening. She had been lying on her own bedroll, her saddle beneath her head, amidst a copse of scrubby trees and thorny bushes in the hollow between one rise and the next. Ripples and folds scored the dark rocks in the rounded, flowing patterns unique to the Gauroth range. Nearby, Mindar, Finnian's steed, and an unfamiliar shadower grazed.

"You'll have to ask te Donal." Markham settled against a tree trunk, stretched out his legs, and eased his head back. "Most of the journey out here was a blur. Speaking of that–doesn't he know what a back-rider is meant to do? He should have been at your side, not mine. This is the second time you've ridden into danger without him."

"It wasn't his fault, Markham. I was . . . reckless."

Her gaze dropped to the sling supporting his bandaged arm, and he followed her eyes. "Balances me out, don't you think? One eye, one arm, opposite sides."

Her breath caught. "Markham, I–"

His glare forced her to swallow her apology. She inspected her own sling instead and slid the neck of her tunic aside to reveal clean white bandages. Gently, she prodded the wound. It burned like Koltar's own fire, but after that cold numbness she'd felt before, pain was reassuring.

"You have te Donal to thank for that," Markham observed quietly.

"Aye." She uncomfortably recalled Finnian's parting words and finally dared ask the question that had nagged her for months. "Why did you pair us? You know I ride alone."

"And riding alone has ever worked out for you?"

"You couldn't have foreseen this."

"You'd be surprised." He offered his sardonic grin. "What can I say? You needed each other. You might be reckless and he might be stubborn, and that might be like tossing pitch onto flame sometimes, but your blaze fuels him, and his strength is there when yours turns cold. I thought it might work if you two could just survive the first day out. Turns out I was right." His focus flicked past her. "Isn't that true, te Donal?"

Slowly, Ceridwen turned her head.

Finnian stooped beneath low-hanging branches, arms laden with her battle gear, his wolfhound at his heels. Unkempt hair, stubble darkening his jawline—he looked wearier and more worn than he had in the healer's tent. It had been only days since then, and yet it felt a lifetime had passed. Her lifetime. She had gained a crown and lost it. She had been denounced a traitor and discovered the true traitor in her father's court. She had raced toward death to save her warriors and survived because of Finnian. And now, here he was, and a thousand hooves kicked up a riotous beat in her chest at the sight of him.

"Ceridwen." He smiled a tired, wintry smile.

Cù broke toward her, trampling Markham in his haste to lick her face. Startled, she tried to fend him off, but he was eager and wiggling and ignored Finnian's attempt to whistle him back. Finally, he flopped down, chin on her knee, and she scratched his ears.

"He's the reason you're alive," Finnian said. "We were breaking camp this morning when he started howling and whining and then just took off. I didn't understand until I caught a whiff of Mindar's smoke. When we found you, I thought . . ."

"What fun to patch me up again?" Ceridwen supplied. "You are making a habit of it."

"Only because you're making a habit of almost dying." He laid out her battle gear beside her—freshly patched and oiled—then lowered himself to the ground. "What happened, Ceridwen? Where are the others? Why in blazes were you out here alone?"

She hesitated before answering, but in his face and Markham's, she saw no judgment, only concern. There was healing in the telling of a tale, in the relaying of truths no matter how painful, like excising soured flesh from a wound, and though the lump in her throat only increased, Ceridwen found the weight upon her shoulders easing as she told of Rhodri's naming as heir and hers as traitor, and the realization that now more than ever, she could bring only ruin upon those around her.

"So, you rode off to fight or die alone." Markham snorted. "How noble of you."

"All hail the final ride . . ." Finnian muttered, raking his hair with his fingers, and the words struck a familiar chord. "What I said before I left? I spoke in haste and anger and–"

"And in truth." Ceridwen shook her head. "You are all safer without me."

Markham rolled his eyes and dug for something at his belt, wincing as his injured arm shifted. He drew out his flask and tossed it into her lap. "Salve your self-pity with that, tal Desmond, and let me know when you're through wallowing and feel up to the task again, because we have a kingdom to save and little time to do it. I might remind you there are lives beyond your own at stake."

"I know that–"

His blistering tongue cut her off. "Then maybe you should reconsider before yielding to a traitor who plans to surrender our autonomy as a nation."

"But . . ." She tried to rally against this unexpected attack. "Rhodri already controls the kingdom. I tried to muster the war-chiefs to battle, but they chose him and surrender instead. What can I do?"

"Well," Finnian responded, "you could not go and try to get yourself killed. *Shades*, there are no half measures with you, are there?"

"And you tried?" Markham scoffed. "Please. Tell that to the young warrior I saw dive headlong into the gauntlet on an untrained steed. And you of all should know that a title is not the same as power. Your father bore the title but exercised little control over the kingdom these past years. Rhodri's footing is no more certain than yours. You think the war-chiefs want Nadaar for an overlord? They are afraid. So, bring stability to chaos and quench the blaze of dissent."

Ceridwen ruefully eyed her leathers, now pitted and scarred from many an inferno. "I have ever been better at fanning a blaze than quenching it."

This they surely could not deny. This had ever been her destiny.

Markham worked his jaw thoughtfully, but it was Finnian who spoke, reaching to grip her wrist with the strength of a bowman and a rider. "Bring flame then, Ceridwen. Smoke them into action. Remind them what our enemies have to fear from the Fireborn."

Something in that single word, *our,* warmed her more deeply than flames ever could, and she felt a hint of the peace she had awakened to stealing back over her. She reached for her battered cuirass and fingered the arrow hole. Inches lower or deeper, and she would have found death. That might have been simpler. It would have been over, at least. But perhaps there was yet a task for her to do, whether she was the heir of Soldonia or not.

She nodded and reached for her sabre too. "I will do it."

"Aye," Markham growled, "you will, but you won't do it alone."

"Or before you've slept." Finnian stood, brushing off his leathers, and Cù shot up, tail wagging. "Talk of battle all you will, neither of you is much threat right now." He gestured over his shoulder. "I concealed as much of our trail as I could this morning, but since we're sleeping here, I'll scout around a bit." Ducking under the branches, he whistled a note that sent Cù darting back to Ceridwen. "Fair warning: he'll sit on you if you try to rise."

Ceridwen eyed the panting wolfhound skeptically. "He can try."

She looked over to find Markham regarding her with an all too knowing gaze. "See? You two do need each other. Don't deny it." His voice lowered slyly. "I may have only one eye, but I'm not sand-blasted blind."

A muffled shout intervened before she could muster a reply.

"Down!" Finnian burst back through the branches toward them. "Get down!" He dove into Ceridwen, knocking her into the wolfhound and down as a rattling hail struck the trees and arrows scythed through the boughs, pelting the ground around them. Grit struck her face, and she flinched involuntarily, muscles anticipating each hit.

Blazes, hadn't she been shot at enough for one day?

Without her battle gear, she felt naked, but her outstretched fingers were only inches from her cuirass, so she pulled it over to shelter her head and neck.

"Come out, tal Desmond!" The mocking call rang out over cracking arrows, snapping twigs, and her own stifled breathing. "Come out, if you dare. Your subjects await you!"

Raucous laughter and a hundred hooting voices followed. Spine tingling, Ceridwen tilted her chin up to meet Finnian's narrowed eyes and Markham's ashen face. She knew that thick, rough, brutish voice all too well. It belonged to Ondri te Velyn.

Somehow, the traitors of Ardon had found them.

FIFTY-EIGHT: RAFI

Cast your nets in a dozen places
before you insist there are no fish in the sea.
– Alonque saying

Salt stung Rafi's bandaged wounds as he floated beside the colt, good arm hooked over its neck, legs canted to the side to avoid its powerfully churning hooves. The sun had not yet broken over the sea, so although the sky was rapidly growing lighter, darkness still cloaked the shore and would mask his underwater approach into the bay. Behind him, water slapped against the twin fishing boats they'd borrowed from Zorrad, and Sev's muffled voice briefly berated Iakki for some mischief until the others hissed him into silence.

They were all on edge, with good reason.

Compared to escaping Cetmur's dungeons, attacking a scadtha, and taming a sea-demon, stealing a ship might not have been the most daring thing Rafi had ever done, but it felt like it. Briefly, he wondered if Delmar would be proud of who he had become, but he heard neither dissent nor assurance from the ghost.

Only Sev's murmured, "It's time."

Rafi reached up to collect the knotted rope and hook Sev passed over the side, and an errant wave bumped him into the boat, rocking it against its twin until Moc fended it off with an oar. Disapproving glances shot his way. Half a dozen villagers were divided between the two boats, including Elder Gordu, who despite a few glowering looks, had made no attempt to kill Rafi. Yet. The other four villagers had been dispatched inland with Nef.

Iakki popped up alongside Sev and rested his chin on the side. "You scared?"

Sev spared Rafi from answering by shoving Iakki back into the bottom of the boat where he was supposed to be concealed. Both fishing boats would remain sheltered behind an arm of the bay until Rafi signaled. Less chance of discovery. Less opportunity to fail. Less casualties if they did. "Save her, Nahiki, and we will name our child after . . ." Sev faltered, evidently recalling Rafi's true identity too late.

"Nahiki, eh?" Rafi looped the rope over his neck and shoulder. "Has a nice ring to it." With a wink, he shoved off into the bay, staying side by side with the colt to remain low in the water. He swam slowly out until he had a clear shot at the torchlit shore and the long dock that stretched out across the sandy, sloping shallows into deeper water where a single ship was moored. Target in view, he eased onto the colt's back, filled his lungs and dove.

Settling on a plan over the past three days had been a simple matter of ruling out impossibilities, once scouting confirmed that Sahak was indeed here and that he spent an inordinate amount of time both aboard ship and supervising the mysterious construction on the beach before returning to his tent for the night. Soldiers patrolled both shore and dock constantly, ruling out a land attack and making even a boat approach unlikely to pass unnoticed. But underwater, Rafi could close in unobserved.

In this, Umut had been right. The sea-demon was an advantage.

When the dark shape of the ship's hull blossomed in the water ahead, he eased the colt back, slowing it enough that they broke the surface with barely a splash. He breathed greedily. The swim had taken longer than he had calculated and had nearly forced him to surface early, even with his strangely increased lung capacity. Easing the knotted rope from his shoulder, he let the colt rear up to gain more room to swing.

He let the hook dangle from his uninjured right hand, getting the feel for its weight, then flung it up, thankful that juggling had forced him to practice throwing with both hands. It struck the ship low and bounced back, and his outstretched hand caught it before it landed with a splash. Irritated by his movement, the colt snorted and tossed its head, mane snapping wetly against its neck, and Rafi froze, waiting for the alarm to spread above.

He counted the seconds in the droplets trickling down his neck. Nothing.

Releasing his breath, Rafi tried again. His second throw stuck. Gripping the rope in his uninjured hand, he lifted from the colt's back and painfully hauled himself up until he could get his feet on the knots. He ignored the water seething and foaming pale white below, but when the sea-demon let out a faint squeal, his heart threatened to tear through his chest.

One blink, one shriek, one slip of the foot . . .

He would sink into that place of nightmare, that place that existed beyond time and behind his closed eyes, where Delmar fell forever and his scream did not end.

Run, Rafi, the ghostly whisper began, but he cut it off. He was done running.

Only once he doggedly resumed climbing, however, did he recognize the secondary danger, that the sea-demon's shriek might alert the ship before he completed his mission. If only Iakki could have done this instead. Rafi loathed heights on a good day, much less when he had only one useful hand and leg. His wounded grip couldn't support his weight, so he hugged the rope to his chest with his left arm and pulled himself up with his right hand. Without the knots, he never would have made it. His whole body shook from exertion by the time he reached the deck and collapsed behind a coiled line.

Booted feet clunked along the dock below. Voices drifted on the wind, indistinct enough to have originated onshore. Once his limbs stopped trembling and his pulse stopped throbbing in his throat, he inched to his feet and scanned the deck–single mast, raised fore and aft, no one in sight–before limping gingerly off in search of the crew's quarters. Elder Gordu had sailed on similar vessels in his, apparently, wild and roving youth, and so had been able to deliver an agonizingly long lecture on common layouts. Rafi found the hatch as described, complete with the rumble of snores emanating from within, and eased it shut, then rammed the latch home.

With that thud, his tension eased. Time for the signal.

Overhead, Nadaar's banner ruffled in a stiff breeze. He worked loose the hitch and let the line slide through his fingers, head tilted back to watch the banner fall, fluttering weakly against the misty gray sky until it sprawled at his feet like a dead thing.

Well, if he hadn't counted as a rebel before, this certainly made him one.

He reached for the crumpled cloth, and steel pricked his spine. Someone gripped his shoulder and spun him around, and his hands shot up at the sight of a pair of gleaming blades. "Oh . . . Ches-Shu . . ."

FIFTY-NINE: CERIDWEN

Of all shadowriders, the tale of Sidra the Swift was spun most often into chant praising her silent passage, like a breath of wind in the night, and the accuracy of her quick and ready knife.

Finally, the storm of arrows ended. Ceridwen tentatively lifted her head to see arrows bristling all around, piercing saddles and bedrolls, even her discarded leathers, and yet somehow, other than the blood trickling from a cut on Finnian's cheek, none of them had been struck. Yet. Beside her, Markham's lips moved in a whispered prayer of deliverance to Aodh. Her prayers had ever gone unanswered, but perhaps his would not.

They were still alive, after all.

"I know you're not alone, Ceridwen!" Ondri's voice shattered the quiet. "Surrender, and the others will live." His tone attached an unspoken *maybe* to the promise.

Finnian snatched her arm before she could even twitch. "Move," he whispered sternly, "and I won't make Cù sit on you. I'll do it myself."

She yanked free and stifled a wince. Cradling her arm, she racked her brain for options, but they were already pinned down. Their steeds had scattered from the volley, fleeing deeper into the copse where they were sheltered but out of reach and unsaddled, and if she and the others fled bareback, without her oiled leathers, she lacked shielding against Mindar's flame. The sol-breath offered some protection but did not make her wholly invulnerable to it. Still . . .

"Mounted we have a chance," she mouthed, nodding at the steeds.

"We fire again in three," Ondri called.

But it was the rumble of hooves vibrating through the earth, shivering the dirt pressed beneath Ceridwen and reverberating up through her, that concerned her most. Was Ondri preparing to charge? How many warriors did he have?

She met Finnian's eyes, and he nodded grimly. "All of us together."

"One!"

Setting her teeth, Ceridwen withdrew her arm from its sling as Finnian raced to bridle their steeds, bow slung over his shoulder. She had no time to throw on leather chaps or jerkin, even if they weren't riddled with arrows. Shrugging into her cuirass proved challenging enough, and buckling the straps on her own, impossible.

"Two!"

Catching up her sabre, Ceridwen dragged it from the scabbard and tossed that aside. Markham beckoned her, and together they worked straps and buckles and then stood. Steadying one another, they hurried forward. Too slow.

"Three–"

Her breath caught in her throat.

But instead of arrows hissing for their flesh, hooves thundered, voices shouted, steel clashed, and the Outriders' war cry rose like a song. Finnian lifted his head from bridling, eyes alight with hope that vanished as three shadowriders crashed into the copse behind him, fading visibly as they crossed from sunlight to shadow until only vague shapes remained.

Ceridwen ground to a halt. "Behind you!"

He was already on the move, slinging his bow from his shoulder and fitting an arrow as he whipped around a tree seconds before an arrow lodged in its trunk. "Go! I'll hold them off!" He scowled as she hesitated, longing to join the fray. "You can't see them. I can. Go!"

Bowstrings sang, arrows whistled, and an invisible battle raged. She cast a final glance toward the smoke shrouding her anxiously darting fireborn, but he was unbridled and far from reach, and she might not even be able to mount bareback with only one strong arm. Nor did she dare summon remote flame, lest the blast swallow Finnian too.

Blazes, he was right. She was no use here.

So with Markham, she turned, each half leaning upon, half supporting the other, and staggered free of the copse into a battle she could see. There, wreathed in hazy sunlight that flashed off spears, swords, and the occasional steel breastplate of a searider, Outriders tore through the warriors of Ardon. There, loping on her stormer with the blue-black wings was Iona, and there, behind her on his riveren, Liam.

Stunned, she gasped at the sight.

Markham hauled her back as an arrow splintered at her feet. "We need to move!"

She scanned for shelter and spied a rock outcrop partway up the slope. "There." She set off toward it, weaving around the loose riders and downed warriors that fringed the melee, sabre raised to ward off attack. Markham had left his weapon in the copse, but he scavenged a fallen spear and leaned heavily on it, breath coming in uneven gasps. He was too weak for this, and so was she. Her own vision was spotted and hazy before they neared the outcrop.

"Go on," Markham rasped. "Don't wait for me."

She teetered as she slowed to his uneven pace. "*Flames,* Markham, I won't–"

Something enormous slammed into them. It tore Markham away and flung Ceridwen across the rough earth, scraping over rocks and spiked plants. Pain ripped anew through her shoulder and lodged like embers in every bone. She rolled onto her back and gasped in air, each breath flaming in her lungs, as Ondri te Velyn loomed over her, a hulking form on his rangy steed, rough-hewn face twisted in triumph.

She closed her fist, expecting to grip her hilt, but grasped only a handful of gravel. Beyond Ondri, Markham sprawled, barely moving.

No aid. No blade. No steed. No flame. But she *would* stand.

She staggered to her feet, praying Markham would not attempt to rise. It was her blood Ondri sought, not his. What need had he to die?

"You know," Ondri said, hefting his spear. "Rhodri wanted to slay you himself, but he'll have to settle for receiving your head on a spike." His grin turned brutal. "Kilmark beheaded a king. It's fitting I fell an erstwhile queen."

"You're welcome to try," Liam growled.

Ceridwen's heart stuttered as the boy jogged up on his riveren, long-spear couched under one arm. He had lost his helm–again–and a cut above his eyebrow bled down his cheek. But he would try to save her, and Ondri would revel in his death, and what could she do to stop it, unarmed as she was? "Liam, please–"

He ignored her. "You got one thing wrong though. She *is* queen."

Wings throbbed overhead, stirring up dust, as a stormer swooped in low. Iona leaned in the saddle to aim her bow, drew, and loosed. Ondri looked up in time to be struck in the neck. He coughed out blood, eyes bulging, and then toppled from the saddle to crash at Markham's feet who had been limping up behind, spear held in a one-handed grip.

Ondri te Velyn was dead.

"That she is," Markham gasped, letting his spear fall and sinking beside it. He bowed over his wounded arm, chest heaving. "That . . . she . . . is."

Yet never had Ceridwen felt less deserving of the title.

She dropped to her knees, breathing raggedly, only dimly aware when Iona landed and her warriors closed in around her. Iona hugged her so tightly she winced. Liam clapped a hand unwittingly on her wounded shoulder. Then Nold was there too, kneeling to offer her sabre. She looked at them, overcome. "Why are you here? You'll be branded traitors now. Couldn't you see I sought to save you?"

Iona laughed and removed her fur-lined hood, hair drifting loose across her face where it had worked free of her crowning braid. "I will earn a traitor's brand if I choose to, Ceridwen tal Desmond, and don't think you can stop me! Besides, Rhodri would be hard-pressed to label half the nation's war-chiefs as traitors, don't you think?"

Half the war-chiefs?

With a wink, Iona offered a hand, and she took it. Her warriors parted as she stood, revealing the battle resolving below. Outriders and warriors of Lochrann herded together the unhorsed traitors while the mounted remnants galloped away, and in pursuit raced a mass of Telweg's silvery seabloods and Eagan's shadower kill-squads. *Blazes*, could it be?

She lifted watering eyes to Iona and was met with a broad smile. "Aye, my queen, Cenyon, Craignorm, and Lochrann have answered the muster. You have your war-host."

SIXTY: RAFI

Hope, like a seedling, is both fragile and resilient.
– Mahque saying

It was not Sahak, or even his soldiers, Rafi realized as his two captors closed in, forcing him against the mast. They wore strange armor and wielded blades with abalone-like inlays on the hilts, and lobbed questions at him in an unfamiliar language. Slowly, he understood. They might have sailed under the empire's banner, but they were not Nadaari.

He tried a breezy laugh. "Did you take a wrong turn crossing the ocean?"

Nothing. Not so much as a twitch or a nod.

"No? Must have been me then. So, if you'll excuse me . . ." He started to brush past, but the blade at his throat made a fairly convincing argument to stay. With his injuries and limited weapons–only a knife tucked in his belt–he disliked his odds in hand-to-hand combat. So, he let his tongue go instead, spilling out a rambling cascade of words to confuse and distract. Their eyes had just about glazed over, when the jungle exploded with wild, screeching cries.

Hoots of graybeard monkeys. Warbling calls of asha birds. Shrieks of sea-demons. Natural sounds ringing out in the most unnatural way, and blending with it all into a furious cacophony, the deep, guttural war cry of the Tetrani. That had been included just to unnerve Sahak, but it made Rafi's skin crawl too.

His captors' eyes shifted toward the shore where flames would now be springing up along whatever stacks of building materials Nef and his screeching band had found nearest the jungle. Rafi reacted immediately, pitching low to kick out the closest knee, propelling the man forward, blade stabbing into the mast.

Another kick–to the gut–dropped the man.

Rafi dove behind the mast to avoid the other warrior's strike. He circled the mast, wounded leg screaming, reached for the lodged blade, and yanked his hands back in time to avoid losing them to a wicked slice from a second blade. Horrified, he backed away. Into the first man's hands. One seized his throat. One gripped the roots of his hair. Wheezing breaths rasped in his ear. He was shoved, struggling, to his knees to watch the blade slicing for his throat.

It missed as the warrior toppled, revealing Sev standing behind.

Rafi's captor grunted and slumped against him, and he collapsed under the crushing weight. It took both Sev and another to wrestle him free and haul him up. He stood face-to-face with Elder Gordu's glowering form and managed to gasp out a "thanks" before Sev cut in. "Is she here? Have you seen her?"

"Ship first," Gordu urged. "We've a fair wind to carry us out. Best not waste it."

Sev grudgingly assented and tossed lines to the villagers waiting in the fishing boats, which would tow the ship's nose around and away from the dock while Gordu readied sails for a swift departure. Rafi scrambled to the mooring line, fumbling the knife from his belt with his left hand before grimacing and switching it to his right. Sawing at the taut rope, he scanned the shore where tents were emptying of laborers and soldiers who raced to extinguish the flames engulfing a circular wooden enclosure. Some created lines for buckets of water and sand. Some shouted and shoved and called out commands. Some drew weapons and advanced toward the rustling, hooting, howling tree line.

There, encircled by calm amidst the chaos, stood Sahak.

In a breath, the mooring line parted with a twang; the ship shuddered, sails snapping into the wind, and began to drift around; and Sahak turned to look back over sand and sea as the sun breached the horizon, bathing the beach in golden light. His gaze landed on Rafi.

Rafi pushed back from the rail. "We need to go!"

"Working on it," Gordu snapped. "But it will take time."

Rafi glanced back. Sahak was sprinting across the beach, royal guard falling in behind, but instead of tearing across the dock, they veered toward a longboat beached in the sand. With so many hands at the oars, if they could catch the ship before the wind did, they could reclaim it.

"Nahiki, some help!" Sev hauled on lines as Gordu directed.

Rafi turned to join him, ignoring his weak hand and leg, but a keening shriek reminded him of the colt waiting below.

"Nahiki?"

He hesitated, heart racing.

Then climbed up onto the rail and dove headfirst.

He plunged into water that fizzed as he shook away the sting of the impact. When his vision cleared, the colt was nuzzling at his hair, hooves striking up a whirlpool around them. He settled onto its back, and down they dove.

On the sandy floor of the bay, they waited until the shadow of the longboat neared, then Rafi urged the colt to climb, neck straining and muscles rippling with each stride. It wasn't exactly swimming, at least not in the way Rafi swam. The colt moved far too naturally for that, and the water itself seemed to ebb and shift eerily around it, reducing drag and resistance, and propelling them toward the longboat with increasing speed. Rafi veered at the last instant and felt the colt lash out with its hindquarters, jostling the boat with its wake. Down, they swooped and around to strike from the opposite side.

The boat heaved as if caught on a wave and smacked down again.

Muffled voices cried out above and faded as the rush of water filled Rafi's ears. His lungs were burning for lack of air, so he spun around for one final pass. Upward, they surged, and breached the water in a flying leap.

No, lifted upon a wave.

Over the longboat, they soared, raining droplets that spattered off helmets, armor, and Sahak's gilded breastplate as he crouched, gripping the sides for balance. Rafi flung his arms wide, roaring the war cry of his ancestors, as the sea rushed up toward him, and the wave crashed over the longboat behind.

The impact swept Rafi from the colt's back.

He was tossed and dashed breathless before coming to a dizzying stop, wounded leg spasming with a cramp. He clawed his way to the surface and blinked the water from his eyes to find the colt calmly munching on a string of seaweed while the stolen ship winged round the curve of the bay, and the swamped longboat rolled drunkenly as the royal guard used their plumed helmets to bail. Sahak stood dripping in the prow, gripping a pair of blades as he watched the receding ship.

Rafi crawled onto the sea-demon's back, suddenly bone weary.

"It won't work, you know." Sahak eyed him over the water with a hatred so intense he could almost feel it. "You can tell your friend he won't find his wife or his friends, but he can rest knowing his actions have doomed them all."

So, the villagers weren't aboard the ship.

Rafi hadn't really expected them to be, but Sahak's actions proved the ship itself was valuable. He rested an elbow on the sea-demon's neck and wiped the spray from his face. "I don't think so, cousin. I have your ship. Harm one of them, and I will burn it and its cargo. If you want it back, you must release them. I'll meet you in one week on the shore outside Zorrad."

Sahak's hand flicked, and Rafi dove to avoid the knife. It skipped under the waves, and he surfaced again with it in hand. "One week, cousin!" Then he surged after the ship, leaving Sahak spluttering with rage behind him.

SIXTY-ONE: CERIDWEN & RAFI

Of all seariders, the name of Anor the Keen echoes forth through the ages for her wisdom, insight, and skill to plumb the depths of a heart and of the raging sea.

Ceridwen slowly wended her way across a battleground strewn with the slain, and she did not let herself shrink from the sight of wounds that no longer bled or eyes that no longer saw anything the living could comprehend. This was battle in all its horror, and she must face it as unflinchingly as its glory. Occasionally, her breath caught at a familiar face, but everywhere there were more dead bearing Ardon's sun than not. Something within her urged that their deaths should grieve her too, since they were her countrymen. But she could no more muster feeling for them than for the Nadaari.

Iona trailed behind her, encouraging the wounded, taking reports, and arguing incessantly with Liam. "Told you that helmet was too big, lad. You should find another."

"I'm not a child, Aunt. I'm a stone-eye killer and a warrior."

"Oh, are you? Give the lad a spear and suddenly he's a man, is that it? Be glad your mother can't hear you. Now sit and let me tend that cut before the rot sets in!" Iona demanded, and Liam dropped with a huff. It was dangerous to interrupt Iona when she was intent on mothering, so Ceridwen hovered until Iona turned with a wink. "Finnian was near the trees last I saw, in case you were looking for him–his report, I mean."

His report. Of course.

Until then, Ceridwen had not known whom she searched for, and she did not breathe freely until she spied him sitting on a rock with his shadower and Mindar behind him, Cù sprawled at his feet, and a clump of bandages pressed to his head. He smiled wearily and lowered his hand, revealing a jagged cut oozing dark blood through his hair. "Are you all right?"

"Am I all right?" She managed to keep her voice steady. "Are you?"

"Fine, fine, just not going to try to stand until my ears stop ringing." He pressed the bandages to the gash again and squinted up at her. "*Shades*, that hurts! How is Markham?"

"He's fine too. Really fine, not like you. What hit you?"

"Not really sure, to be honest. It might have been a sword hilt."

"Don't strain yourself trying to remember," Telweg said, striding past Ceridwen and depositing the reins to her seablood in her hands without so much as a nod. She imperiously waved Finnian's bloody clump of bandages aside and scrutinized the gash. "Fortunately, you seem to have a thick skull."

Her voice was blunt and her hands no less so, judging by Finnian's wincing as she cleaned his wound. He looked relieved when Iona arrived to take over the bandaging.

Telweg stood back, wiping her hands distastefully on her cloak. "It would seem, tal Desmond, that our interests are still aligned. When I rode forth from Rysinger, I planned to continue this doomed war alone if need be, until I discovered that Eagan felt the same. When we met your lieutenant"—she gestured at Iona who looked amused at the title—"she relayed the information from the war-slave, and my resolve solidified."

"You believed her?" Ceridwen asked.

"Unfortunately, the facts also align." Telweg's lips tightened. "I would not see our kingdom surrendered by traitors, especially one of my blood."

So coldly she spoke of her own daughter.

So Ceridwen's father had spoken at her branding.

Ceridwen drew the ring from beneath her tunic and clenched it in her fist. "Would you see it surrendered to one bearing the *kasar*?"

Telweg broke her gaze to survey the battleground, and when she spoke, her words came slowly, thoughtfully. "Your warriors are willing to lose all for you. Loyalty like that cannot be bought. It can only be given. And what, I ask, can cancel a blood debt if not such sacrifice?" She glanced back to Ceridwen, and some of the eternal frost in her expression seemed to melt. "In the end, tal Desmond, they are your atonement. In my eyes, at least."

Ceridwen had no voice to reply. There were tears in her eyes as she turned to meet Finnian's warm smile. If they were her atonement, it was one she had not earned and could not deserve. But she would cling to it with all the hope that still beat inside her chest.

She pried open her fist to stare at her father's ring and finally slid it on.

Telweg cleared her throat. "We have little time and fewer allies, but we must act soon if we are to forestall disaster. Our enemy has reached Rysinger and–"

"What? How? The main column should still be crawling across Lochrann, weeks away."

"Ah, but this isn't the main column," Eagan said, coming up silently on his shadower and dismounting. "'Tis a rapid strike force that pierced Ardon an' approached Rysinger from the south–doubtless with the aid of our would-be king. Large enough t' threaten the fortress if not t' claim it until the main column arrives."

The breath left her lungs in a rush. It must be the third column the priest had mentioned so long ago, before the Voice spoke, shattering thought and sight and sound. Rhodri was supposed to have dealt with it, but then Rhodri was not supposed to have been a traitor. She had been too short sighted, too narrowly focused, to see the full scope of the attack.

"Aye, and enough to convince the war-chiefs to consider surrender," Telweg added. "The final negotiations will occur five days hence."

"Not that there will be much negotiation involved," Eagan muttered, "since the terms have doubtless been long established."

Five days . . . *blazes.*

Ceridwen ran a hand through her matted hair and retreated to Mindar's side. He snorted softly as she scratched his neck. Telweg's resolve might have been solidified, but she felt her strength unraveling. Five days to do what? Defeat their enemy? Impossible. Depose their newly acknowledged and traitorous king? Also impossible, unless . . . "Could you speak with the other war-chiefs? Convince them to join us?"

They would never heed her, but they might listen to someone else.

Eagan shook his head. "'Tis too late for speech, tal Desmond. If we are t' halt the destruction of our nation, we need action t' force their hands."

Not just action, but the shock of a firestorm.

Suddenly, the world shifted into place, and she knew what must be done. She turned to Iona who had finished her bandaging and rocked back on her heels to clean her hands. "Do any of your stormriders still have strength to fly?"

"For their Fireborn, always. Where to?"

"To summon all the fireriders from the Outrider *ayeds.* We have negotiations to halt." She looked from Iona to the war-chiefs, then across the field of death toward Markham limping up, supported by Nold and trailed by Liam, who was once more chattering about wild battlefield exploits. Finnian's eyes she met last, and he smiled curiously at her with a tilt to his bandaged head, as though she were a riddle he had only just begun to solve.

"*Bring flames,*" he had said, and together, they would.

Together, they would ride once more. Out of ash, into hope, and onward to victory.

Rafi boarded the ship to cheers from the villagers, a hug from

Iakki, and something that was not quite a smile but definitely not a scowl from Elder Gordu at the helm. Shaking off Moc's enthusiastic congratulations, he wrung the water from his clothes and drew in a bracing breath of salt-tinged air before sagging, wearily to the deck. Every bone in his body ached, every cut–and courtesy of his cousin, there were many–stung, and he was so exhausted, he could pass out right there though all the sea-demons in the deeps were screaming in his ear.

He let out a relieved laugh. "I can't believe it actually worked."

"It shouldn't have," Gordu grumbled morosely. "It was only the barest bones of a plan. I thought you were dead three times over."

Rafi couldn't tell whether it was his near death or survival that concerned the elder.

Muffled shouting and thudding rang out behind the locked hatch, and Moc stamped a foot on the deck. "Quiet in there!" He met Rafi's curious look with a shrug. "Seems the crew objects to their accommodations."

"Oh, we can't have that."

"Could drop them off for a short swim to shore?"

"Doesn't have to be short," Gordu muttered, and Moc laughed.

"We don't want them knowing where we hide the ship," Rafi acknowledged, then paused. "Speaking of . . . where are we going to hide the ship?"

Gordu scratched his chin. "I know a place. Smuggler's cove. Might could work."

"And the ship is the least of our worries," Moc added, clapping Rafi on the shoulder. "Just wait until you see what is below."

That sounded ominous.

Rafi glanced from one to the other. "What is below?"

Iakki insisted on showing him, which meant it took about ten times longer than if Moc had done it because he darted from side to side to watch the sea-demon circling the ship, paused to hang upside down from the rigging, and tried to balance atop the rail with his eyes closed. "Say, you thought up a name for that colt yet?"

Rafi steadied him. "I have a few ideas."

"Good, 'cause you're going to need them." Iakki dropped over the ship's side. Rafi bolted to catch him and found him dangling from a trailing line. "What about Seabolt?"

"What?"

"The colt's name! Seabolt . . . or . . . Blue-Eyes?"

Rafi rubbed his aching skull. "Iakki."

"Yeah?"

"Get up here."

Iakki scampered back up and over the rail. "You got a better idea?"

"Actually . . . yes." One he had been harboring secretly, hesitant to speak out loud, however fitting it felt for the creature with eyes like Delmar's and a shriek that would not let him forget. "Ghost," he said, mostly to himself, then liking the sound of it, repeated it louder. "Ghost."

"Ghost." Iakki smiled broadly. "I like it." He bolted off toward Sev, who was closing an enormous hatch in the center of the deck.

When he saw them, Sev's shoulders slumped. "She's not here, Nah–"

He broke off, and Rafi swallowed a twinge of guilt at the realization that matters between them were far from resolved. "I know, but we will rescue her."

"And then?" Sev's tone was sharp.

Rafi understood his despair. There was no going back to the way things had been. They were all rebels now, willingly or no, and the empire would not stop hunting them. The Que Revolution might be doomed, but short of fleeing to the wastes of Broken-Eliam, it was their only option. Beyond that though, something within him had shifted, and he knew this was right. Now that he had seen, now that he had been made to know, now that he had witnessed the suffering firsthand, he could not deny it.

He could not stand idly by and watch.

He could not keep silent.

"Then," Rafi declared, "we will fight."

Sev shook his head in disbelief. "How? The empire's reach expands by the day, and we are but fisherfolk and soil tenders. We are not equipped for *this*." He threw open the hatch, letting daylight flood the hold, and Rafi sank to his knees in awe. There below stood an enormous gray steed with massive hooves and a hide like splintered rock, and farther in, one with coal-black wings netted to its back was tethered beside a waterlogged creature with white smoke puffing from its nostrils. Dozens of steeds had been crammed into the narrow stalls that partitioned the hold, and the reek of damp straw, sweaty beast, and fresh manure was overpowering.

Stone-demons. Sky-demons. Fire-demons. More.

His mouth had gone dry as sand. These beasts might not look it at the moment, but they were legends. None of these had ever been seen before in the empire of Nadaar, and if Rafi had managed to confuse and overwhelm Sahak and his royal guard with only a single sea-demon, what sort of damage could be wrought with all of these?

Either against the Que Revolution . . . or maybe for it.

Rafi met Sev's eyes and grinned.

EPILOGUE: RHODRI

Rhodri te Oengus rode forth as a conqueror on the day he would trade a kingdom for a throne. All the war-chiefs flanked him, their chieftains filled out his train, and hosts of solborn followed in vast array like the stars in the sky. Brightest of all, his sun, Astra tor Telweg rode at his side, and if he was a conqueror, she was victory incarnate, and he basked in her light as he surveyed the Nadaari forming up in rigid lines on the opposite end of the plain, several leagues distant from Rysinger.

He had been hesitant about this final stage in the plan, allowing them to close in around the fortress, and yet it had done its work in convincing the war-chiefs to support him. Now, banners snapped in the wind, solborn stamped restlessly, and Rhodri thrilled with the intoxicating knowledge that all the world hung upon this moment.

This moment he had readied, like a steed tacked and awaiting its rider.

"*Sky's blood,* I feel a traitor today." Craddock scowled atop his rose-gray earthhewn and flicked a dismissive hand toward the Nadaari. "Look at them. You can feel them gloating."

"No, they do not gloat." Telweg's voice was like ice. "That is scorn you sense, Craddock, that we, the strength of Soldonia, the strength of the solborn, should be brought to our knees so soon. It is not to be borne."

"Better scorned but alive than venerated but dead," Ormond said.

"I expect such sentiments from you, Ormond, but not, Rhodri, from you."

He could feel Telweg's stare like a blade pressed to his neck. Astra offered him a wry glance. The Cenyon war-chief, apparently, would make for a formidable mother-in-law.

"It is because we are strong, Telweg, that we must negotiate now," Glyndwr said, voice quavering like a reed in the wind, and Rhodri smiled faintly at how readily the old man now leaped to his defense. Earning his trust had not been simple, but once won, it seemed he could do no wrong. "Thus, we will retain our strength and our pride."

Eagan snorted. "Ye have a strange notion o' pride."

Rhodri held his tongue. They could quarrel as they willed. The kingdom was his to do with as he willed. After all, it was not the Nadaari who had conquered Soldonia, but him.

Gongs crashed among the Nadaari, and twenty chariot and tiger teams advanced, followed by a company of soldiers carrying long spears. This was it. Rhodri signaled the horns, summoning the war-chiefs to follow as he rode onto the plain as conqueror and king.

Vakhar pranced beneath him, streaming ribbons of flame. Heat danced across Rhodri's skin, riffled through his hair, and swept his cheek like Astra's gentle touch. His senses were gloriously alive. He was gloriously alive. Equally aware of the triumphant presence of the golden circlet on his forehead and the painful absence of the signet ring on his finger.

Inviting Ceridwen to the war-meet had been a gamble that had nearly paid off. Soon, Ondri would return with Ceridwen in chains. Soon, his blade would sever her spine. Soon, her head would ornament his father's silent halls beside that of Desmond, her father. His gloved hand tightened on the reins, and Vakhar tossed his head.

Soon. Soon.

Astra's hand brushed his fist. "One step at a time, my love."

But Rhodri had not been born to step but to run, ever striving, never satisfied, and never able to satisfy the father who drove him ever to rise. "*Rise*!" How often had Oengus gripped him by the shoulders, eyes glinting with the shards of shattered dreams, and uttered that word? In exhortation, in reprimand, and finally in bitter disappointment as a broken man on the sickbed he would never leave. When you soared high, only to plummet, it made for a long fall. Rhodri halted in the center of the plain and swore that would not be his end.

Astra danced closer on her seablood, studying the approaching chariots, eyes glinting steel beneath calm aquamarine. "Do you trust him?" she asked softly, nodding toward the tsemarc who rode in the lead chariot beside the priest, Nahrog. Though the tsemarc's column still plodded across Lochrann, Rhodri had ensured Izhar and his entourage received safe passage to the negotiations. Only the tsemarc could deliver what had been promised.

Still . . . "I trust no one, dearest. Only you."

And the value of an effective bartering tool, like the manuscripts Astra had stolen or the two prisoners he kept in reserve. The tsemarc had sought to alter their agreement once with his demands for solborn. Rhodri fully expected him to try again.

He straightened as the stone-eye tigers prowled to a halt before him. All wore blindfolds, but their handlers could no doubt drop them in an instant just as he could summon flame with a touch of his spurs. Still, it was exhilarating to stand only paces away from something nearly as deadly as he. Perhaps that was why he had bonded a fireborn, sought out Desmond as a mentor, and loved Astra tor Telweg with every aching beat of his heart.

In the central chariot, Izhar removed his plumed helm.

Rhodri opened his mouth to speak, to utter words he had known must come since rumors first spread of the Nadaarian intent to further the Dominion of Murloch, and he had known that invasion was inevitable, defeat was unavoidable, and survival could only be assured by one with the wits to think the unthinkable and the fortitude to see it done.

But before those words were formed on his tongue, the earth trembled. For one brief, thoughtless, distracted moment, it seemed just the final shifting of the world into stride with the course he had set, like a high-spirited steed settling beneath saddle and bridle.

Then his elation faded and his mind caught up, and he recognized the rumble of hooves. Many, many hooves. He turned instinctively toward his war-hosts, but that roar did not come from behind but from the east, and it was followed by a crackling, snapping sound that sent a shiver through his bones.

Astra's eyes were suddenly more steel than blue. "Look."

He twisted in the saddle, dread pooling in his gut.

Smoke boiled over the long low hill that bordered the eastern side of the plain. Thick, black smoke. The smoke of flames racing before a brisk wind. Or before fireborn. Scarcely had the thought crossed his mind than thousands of solborn crested the hill and swept across the plain toward him. Fireborn broke off in a blazing mass that melted into a single-file column and tore like a comet between the negotiators and the opposing lines, lighting the dry grasses ablaze while stormers descended in a cloud and hovered, straining, wings beating up a wind to fuel the wall of fire and impel it toward the Nadaari.

Rhodri found himself surrounded by the rest of the solborn who formed a ring around war-chiefs and chariots alike, leaving them stranded amidst a sea of teeming steeds and warriors wearing the badge of the Outriders.

"It is her, is it not?" Nahrog demanded, eyes alight. "She that rides the fireborn?"

"She that *is* the Fireborn," Eagan corrected in a voice thick with pride.

"*Floods*!" Astra said beneath her breath, and Rhodri silently echoed it.

His mouth had gone dry, but he forced himself to swallow, to breathe, to regain control. His was the art of subtle manipulation rather than outright force, like tiny flames creeping along root systems underground, unseen, unknown, until they burst forth unexpectedly miles away. Ceridwen's was the firestorm, the charred earth, the radiant blast, and the blistering power of a heatwave. Still, whatever thousand warriors she had, he had thousands more, and the Nadaari had thousands more than both of them combined.

The reins could yet be wrestled back into his grasp before this day ended in violence and bloodshed and the loss of his crown.

He lifted his horn and turned to summon his war-hosts but found them blocked by a mass of Cenyon and Craignorm riders who had broken formation to flood the gap, facing his warriors with weapons bared. He could not restrain his curse this time. Telweg met his wrath with an imperiously arched eyebrow that invited his gaze forward, toward a coppery streak that parted from the column of fireborn and raced toward him, followed by specks of duller gray, brown, black, and white that resolved as they neared into steeds.

Smoke seeped before them, dust coiled in their wake, and the Outriders parted to let Ceridwen tal Desmond and her motley band of warriors through. She swept back her mask and hood and her smile was a sabre twisting in Rhodri's chest as she glanced from the war-chiefs to the Nadaari, and lastly, to him. "Someone, I hear, was about to surrender. We are here to accept."

THE STORY CONTINUES IN

THE FIREBORN EPIC BOOK 2: OF SEA AND SMOKE

ACKNOWLEDGMENTS

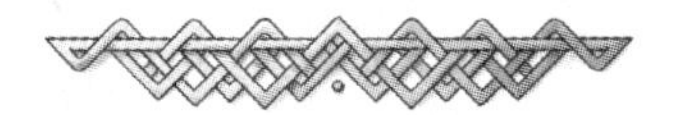

I set out to write an epic, and write an epic I did. This story has existed in my head, in scribbled notes on scraps, in marked-up drafts, and in cuttings left scattered on the floor for nearly ten years, and now, at last, it is in your hands. Writing this story has been an *epic* undertaking, so it should come as no surprise that I couldn't have done it alone. But if I thought capturing this wild, untamable beast of a tale in an entire novel was hard, trying to squeeze my gratitude into a page or two at the end feels impossible. Still, I shall try!

Mom and Dad, thank you for believing in me and always encouraging me to dream. Brynne, thank you for answering a hundred design questions and lending your skills where mine are lacking. Maris, you always inspire me to work harder, reach farther, and dream bigger. Ryan, one of these days, I *will* write a book you will read—and no, I have not forgotten about that character namesake I promised you. Lydia, you constantly lift my spirits whenever life gets me down. I pictured you laughing while I wrote all of Iakki's lines. I hope he makes you smile.

Mollie Reeder, I owe you a million thanks for all the hours you spent brainstorming with me, cheering me on, and believing in this book before you'd even read it! It's incredible to realize how many of these chapters were drafted sitting across a coffee shop table from you, and it's safe to say I would never have conquered my monster self-edit without you cheering me on!

Jill Williamson, thank you for reading those first few chapters way back when and telling me to let Finnian make the shot! You were right. He needed that win.

Inkwell crew, I'm thankful for all the late-night writing sprints—even if all of you can write five sentences to my one. You guys spur me on and are such a joy!

Outrider Street Team, you all are incredible! Thank you for supporting this story.

Darko Tomic, thank you for another incredible cover image and for capturing the vague hopes I offered—vivid, breathtaking, fire and smoke—and making it real! And Jamie Foley, thank you for lending your amazing design skills and artistic imagination to every detail on the back cover, spine, and the interior of the book too.

Gerralt Landman, this map is breathtaking! Thank you for giving your creativity and skill to bring the nation of Soldonia to life in such gorgeous detail and for also crafting such beautiful artwork for the chapter headings!

Steve Laube, a thousand thanks for believing in this massive beast of a story, and for not crushing my soul with an immediate "No" when you saw the word count for the first time after I stayed up all night to turn it in. Thank you, Lisa Laube, for reading the manuscript four times—*four!*—and for caring so well for the heart of the story as you worked to make it shine. Lindsay Franklin, thank you for wielding your copyediting magic on this book. And Trissina Kear, Jamie Foley, and the entire Enclave crew—you all labor so tirelessly to help share beautiful stories with the world. I'm so thankful for you and for all that you do!

To the One who bears all scars, thank you for bearing mine.

Finally, to all of you readers whose eyes lit up at the words "magical horses," thank you for reading and journeying alongside me, Ceridwen, Rafi, and Jakim. The adventure has only barely begun. Onward together, my friends, onward!

ABOUT THE AUTHOR

Gillian Bronte Adams is a sword-wielding, horse-riding, wander-loving fantasy author, rarely found without a coffee in hand and rumored to pack books before clothes when she hits the road. Working in youth ministry left her with a passion for journeying alongside children and teens. (It also enhanced her love of coffee.) Now, she writes novels that follow outcast characters down broken roads, through epic battles, and onward to adventure. And at the end of a long day of typing, she can be found saddling her wild thing and riding off into the sunset, seeking adventures of her own (and more coffee). She loves to connect with readers online at www.gillianbronteadams.com.